$\mathcal{S}$he could se[...] [...]ass as he leaned indol[...] [...]her. He was silent [...] [...]air, not speaking until [...] the pins and combed her finger [...] [...]gh the thick mass.

"You always had the loveliest hair. Like Russian sable. Rich and silken and luminous."

Julienne kept her lips pressed together, refusing to respond.

"And you have the face and body of a temptress."

"I'm no temptress," she retorted. "And I am no longer a green girl, susceptible to your flattery."

"No, not a girl at all. You've flourished into a ravishing woman."

She felt Dare move behind her. Julienne froze as he took up the hairbrush and began drawing it slowly through her long hair.

"I always relished doing this. Remember?"

The warmth in his voice touched a chord in her that left her trembling. *Remember? How could I possibly forget?* She closed her eyes at the drugging shock of recognition and familiarity: the feel of Dare at her back, the vibrant heat of his body, the sweet sensation of his touch, his erotic tenderness. It had been so long. . . .

Heaven help her, she wanted him. . . .

By Nicole Jordan

The PRINCE of PLEASURE

A NOVEL

NICOLE JORDAN

BALLANTINE BOOKS • NEW YORK

2005 Ivy Books Mass Market Edition

Copyright © 2003 by Anne Bushyhead
Excerpt from *Master of Temptation* by Nicole Jordan copyright © 2003 by Anne Bushyhead.

Published in the United States by Ivy Books, an imprint of The Random House Publishing Group, a division of Random House, Inc., New York.

IVY BOOKS and colophon are trademarks of Random House, Inc.

This book contains an excerpt from *Master of Temptation* by Nicole Jordan. This excerpt has been set for this edition only and may not reflect the final content of the novel.

ISBN 0-345-48642-0

Printed in the United States of America

www.ballantinebooks.com

OPM 9 8 7 6 5 4 3 2 1

To my wonderful readers,
whose enjoyment of my stories
keeps me going

With special thanks to
the lovely ladies of the Beau Monde,
particularly that fount of Regency wisdom,
Nancy Mayer

Prologue

Kent, England, August 1807

The scent of roses filled the summer afternoon, but Julienne Laurent scarcely noticed the sweet fragrance as she waited anxiously for her lover to arrive. What could be keeping him?

Her nerves on edge, she began pacing the cottage floor, her disquietude increasing with each passing moment. Today, Dare had intended to inform his grandfather of their betrothal, and she feared the elderly nobleman's objections had been fierce.

Finally hearing hoofbeats, Julienne went to the open window to look out. The diminutive cottage where they held their lovers' trysts lay nestled in a cherry orchard, hidden from direct view of the lane. When she spied the sleek horse and elegant rider, she momentarily forgot her anxiety.

Dare. Her heart thrilled at the sight of him, while her thighs clenched in anticipation. She could almost feel him moving inside her—

Flushing, Julienne tried to quell her shameful hunger. She was a wanton where Dare was concerned. She had surrendered her innocence to his expert seduction

1

with a scandalous eagerness. But what mortal woman could possibly have resisted him?

She watched as he sprang lithely down from his horse and strode purposefully along the path through the overgrown rose garden. He moved with a combination of polished elegance and raw virility that stirred all her feminine instincts, while his handsomeness stole her very breath. Possessing lean, aristocratic features and fair hair that glimmered flaxen and gold in the sunlight, he was endowed with a physical beauty that startled at first glance.

But it was his outrageous charm and penetrating wit rather than his striking looks or exalted title that had ensnared her heart. His magnetism, too, was exhilarating. There was a hint of wildness about him, an unpredictability that made him dangerously exciting. Even his name, Dare, a shortened version of his middle name, Adair, fit him to perfection. He was called so by his friends because he was willing to dare almost any challenge.

Including her. He had worn her down with relentless persistence.

Despite all her scruples and misgivings, she had risked her heart and found love in the arms of a wicked rake she had once vowed to resist.

The door swung open, and Jeremy Adair North, the Earl of Clune, stood there, his vivid green eyes searching the small cottage impatiently. When his gaze fixed intently on her, the flare of heat in the emerald depths was unmistakable.

"Did you miss me?" he demanded, his low voice stroking her like velvet.

"Dreadfully."

"Good."

In three strides he was across the room, reaching for her. Only then did Julienne recognize the tension smoldering in him. She could see the fire of anger in his eyes, feel it in his touch.

"Dare, what is it—?" she began, but he cut her off.

"I don't wish to talk."

She was in his arms instantly, gathered hard against him. His hands twisted in her hair as his lips crushed down on hers.

His fierceness caught her off guard. Ordinarily he was an amazingly tender lover who made her feel cherished and adored. Yet his urgent hunger now aroused a matching response in her. Her senses reeling, Julienne forgot her questions and surrendered to his ardent embrace.

Moments later his scalding kiss ended and his attention shifted to her body. She wore no corset, and he easily freed her breasts from the confining muslin bodice. His hot mouth suckled her nipples forcefully as he backed her against the door.

Julienne gasped at the delicious sensations that flooded her. With no other preliminaries, he pulled up her skirts and thrust his seeking fingers between her thighs. She was already wet for him.

She heard his groan of approval, then his harsh whisper: "God, how I want you."

He yanked at the front placket of his breeches as if he was desperate to have her. His penetration was hard and deep; her body trembled under the impact of it. He had never acted with such primal urgency, yet she made no protest. Instead Julienne moaned with incredible satisfaction as he filled her, excited beyond bearing.

He took her against the door, thrusting heavily into her with the sheer, overpowering need to mate. His sexual hunger was almost frantic, his rough fervor overwhelming. She wrapped herself around him, attempting to ease the violence of his desire, the raw intensity of his need—but then she too was caught up in the rush of heat, the burning fever. She clung to him, gasping, her hips writhing as she strained to take him even deeper into her body.

His release came swiftly. She felt the shudders that rocketed through him before the same frenzied explosion swept her. A hoarse cry burst from her as she succumbed to him with abandonment.

When the searing aftershocks faded, she realized Dare had sagged against her, pinning her to the door with his lean hardness. He was still panting for breath as he buried his face in the curve of her throat.

"My lovely Jewel," he rasped finally. "Did I hurt you?"

"No," she lied, ignoring the protest of twinging feminine tissues, content to savor the aftermath of his exquisite ravishment.

Eventually, however, he drew away. Lifting her in his arms, he bore her soft and willing to the bed in the adjacent room, where he undressed her with his usual attentive care.

When he was naked as well, he lay beside her and gathered her against him, then closed his eyes.

Silence reigned for a time.

Julienne yearned to know what had kindled his dark mood, yet she was afraid to ask if he had spoken to his grandfather. Finally, though, she could bear the uncertainty no longer.

"What did he say?"

At Dare's continued silence, her heart sank. The Marquess of Wolverton would not want his only grandson and heir to wed a French émigré, even if her pedigree was nearly as distinguished as their own. She was still considered a foreigner by many, for all that she had lived in England since she was four years old.

Julienne raised herself on one elbow so that she might search Dare's face. The frown between his eyes told her more than any words ever could. "Your grandfather refuses to accept me as your bride, is that so?"

"He has no say in the matter," Dare answered grimly.

She tried to steel herself against the hollowness in her chest. She was of noble birth, the daughter of the late Compte de Folmont, who had been guillotined during the Terror in France. But she owned a hat shop, and the stench of trade clung to her, tainting any claim to aristocracy she might have made. Yet she had never regretted her lost birthright as much as at this moment.

"He will not sanction our marriage," she said, her tone dismal.

Dare's lean jaw clenched. "My grandfather's wishes mean nothing to me." Reaching up, he clasped her face gently while his searing green gaze searched her face. "I want us to elope, Julienne."

"Elope?" she repeated doubtfully.

"Yes, elope . . . leap over the anvil . . . flee to Gretna.

It is but three days to the Scottish border, and we could be married next week."

"Dare . . ."

"If you love me, you will come with me. Do you love me, my precious Jewel?"

She loved him so much, it was an ache inside her. Yet it distressed her to think she would come between Dare and his grandfather, who was practically his only family. "Of course I love you. My heart is yours. But elopement . . . It is such an irrevocable step. Your grandfather will be even more enraged by such rashness, won't he?"

"I trust he will be," Dare replied darkly.

"Perhaps we would do better to let him grow accustomed to the prospect of our marriage."

His bark of humorless laughter told her how improbable her suggestion was, but then he shook his head. "Stop worrying so much about my damned grandfather."

"It is not your grandfather who worries me," Julienne said, carefully choosing her words. "It is you, Dare. If we rush into an elopement, you might someday regret it. You might even come to despise me."

His gaze speared hers, holding her riveted. "That could never happen." Rolling over with her, he pinned her naked body beneath his own. "I know what I want, Julienne, and it is you, as my wife. Forever. Nothing could change what I feel for you."

Despite the heat in his passionate declaration, a sudden chill swept Julienne with enough force to make her shudder. She couldn't shake the fear that their happiness would never last.

Yet she shut her eyes and gave herself up to Dare's embrace, hoping with all her heart that he would never have cause to rescind his fervent vow.

Chapter
One

London, March 1814

Flickering firelight cast a golden glow over Dare's nude body as he stood before the bedchamber hearth, yet no flame could warm the chill in his heart. His mind flooded by thoughts of a beautiful, deceptive enchantress, he stared down at the playbill advertising her latest performance at the Drury Lane Theater.

Julienne Laurent.

He didn't need the artist's sketch to prod his recollection, for everything about her was burned into his memory. Images of her assaulted him: her exquisite body arched in passion. Her sleek limbs wrapped around him. Her luxurious hair like a mantle of sable fire about her shoulders. Her skin so flawlessly white, it looked like fine porcelain. Her laughter and her smile. Her keen wit. Her dark, luminous eyes with their incredible sensuality . . .

It was all branded upon his memory with a sharpness and clarity that still seared.

"What a bloody fool you were," he murmured, the accusation hoarse in the quiet of the bedchamber.

Dare locked his jaw, distressed that Julienne's sudden

appearance in London had awakened emotions he'd presumed long dead. He'd thought himself over her years ago. Free of the tormenting memories, free of the regrets and loneliness that plagued him.

Yet given the savage pain that lanced through him now, he knew he still hadn't fully recovered from his shattering encounter with Julienne. Apparently the adage was true—that a man never forgot his first love.

He hadn't intended to lose his heart to her. He'd been young and hot and full of himself, eminently secure in his powers of seduction. But the girl he set out to conquer had become the woman who taught him about love. About betrayal.

The first time he'd laid eyes on the beautiful French émigré, Dare knew he had to have her. He'd come to Kent in June for a cousin's wedding, putting up at his grandfather's estate of Wolverton Hall near the small seaport of Whitstable, where Julienne's millinery was located. He'd wound up staying for the entire summer, intent on wooing her.

His intense attraction had surprised him. He'd had dozens of women as alluring, in countless affairs that had never touched his heart. Love for him had never been fiery and urgent, as it was with Julienne.

He'd wanted her far beyond the usual dalliance or casual taking. He wanted to possess her, to give her everything in return. His heart, his body, his very soul.

He hadn't known she lied as easily as she breathed.

Bitter memories of her rushed through him, centering on their final shocking encounter. . . . Julienne's look of dismay to have been discovered in the arms of another lover; his own anguish when he comprehended the depth of her deception. He hadn't believed it until he saw it with his own eyes, heard Julienne's admission from her own lips.

Against his will, Dare traced her sketch with his fingertips. His grandfather had claimed the Earl of Ivers was her lover, but he'd scoffed in the old man's face. After stalking away from another violent argument with the marquess, Dare had sought Julienne out at her millinery, where he'd caught her with Ivers.

Only the slightest hint of remorse had shown on her patrician features when Ivers revealed they were long-standing lovers, and no remorse at all when Julienne had curtly ended their betrothal.

With her simple declaration, Dare felt as if his heart had been ripped from his chest. Her pretense of virginal innocence had been a sham from the very beginning, he realized. Her professed love for him merely a charade.

Only afterward had he put the pieces together and understood how completely he had been played for a fool: Julienne had wanted greater riches than he could give her if his grandfather disowned him. It was even possible she had plotted to wed him from the first but reconsidered when his grandfather's wrath rendered his inheritance uncertain. Perhaps she'd even planned to share the spoils with her lover—

Dare's throat tightened on the razor-sharp edge of memory.

Admittedly, though, he was glad to have discovered the truth about her before he threw his entire future away.

"A scheming French jade," his grandfather had called her, but Dare hadn't listened. He'd been remarkably stupid to fall for her display of virtue, or to believe she could be faithful. He should have known better. His own mother had enjoyed too many lovers to count, making a mockery of the word *fidelity*. He had thought Julienne cut from a different cloth, but she had deceived him so thoroughly, he'd never suspected her treachery until he felt the knife sliding between his ribs.

Dare cursed again beneath his breath. Julienne had vowed to love and cherish him, yet she had shattered those promises with lies and deceit.

He wondered if she regretted her choice now. He finally had come into the title of Marquess of Wolverton, along with the vast Wolverton fortune, for his hated grandfather had died the previous year.

But more than half a decade would have been a long time for a scheming fortune hunter to wait. She apparently had been busy meanwhile developing a successful acting career.

And no doubt cultivating other lovers. Dare had seen her in the park today for the first time, holding court for her love-struck swains.

The sight had rocked him to his core, for until two days ago, he hadn't even known she was in London. He'd been away for weeks, first on an assignment in the north, then on an unrelated mission to Ireland. He'd returned to discover Julienne Laurent the toast of the town, being pursued by a multitude of bucks and dandies. *London's brightest new Jewel* was how she was being termed. Reportedly every man wanted the dazzling actress for his mistress.

Hiding the unexpected pain knotting his chest at the sight of her, Dare had shifted his attention back to his companion, Lady Dunleith. Moments before, the lovely widow had beckoned to him from her carriage as he rode through the throng gathered in Hyde Park for the social hour.

When he questioned Lady Dunleith about the ton's latest novelty, she was cheerfully forthcoming.

"Miss Laurent? She hails from York, I believe. She is all the rage, but deservedly so. She sings like an angel, and she is quite an accomplished actress. Not in the class of Mrs. Siddons, perhaps. But Edmund Kean himself praised her last dramatic performance when she played Desdemona to his Othello."

Dare's mouth tightened. He would have to agree that Miss Laurent was an accomplished actress, although he had yet to see her upon the stage. During their enchanted summer together, he had never once suspected that the same sweet lips that promised him love would betray him so completely.

Lady Dunleith gave him a speculative look. "If you are thinking about pursuing her yourself, darling, you should reconsider. I've heard she is rather cold-blooded as a lover."

Whether the beautiful widow spoke out of jealousy or spite or the charitable desire to spare him a futile effort, Dare wasn't certain. But he could attest that she was mistaken; Julienne Laurent was as cold-blooded as flaming coals.

"And in any case," Lady Dunleith added in an amused tone, "Miss Laurent has announced that she will not make her choice of protectors until the end of the season. Wagers are already flying about who will win her."

Her choice would no doubt have deep pockets, Dare reflected resentfully. Actresses often augmented their meager incomes by finding rich patrons, but he knew from painful experience that the mercenary Mademoiselle Laurent wouldn't settle for any but the wealthiest protector.

What interested him most, however, was the particular gentleman who claimed the Jewel's attention just now. Viscount Riddingham evidently had garnered the privilege of driving Miss Laurent in his curricle. They had stopped in the Row and were surrounded by a half-dozen eager admirers on horseback—

"Darling . . . ?"

The sleepy voice jolted Dare back to the present. Behind him Lady Dunleith called again. "Why do you not return to bed?"

Wincing at the intrusion, he suddenly noticed the cold that roughened his flesh. The chill of the bedchamber reminded him that he was naked, that he'd left a warm bed in order to study the handbill that bore his former lover's image, like a tongue probing an aching tooth.

That same ache had driven him to accompany the Widow Dunleith home and spend the evening indulging her carnal needs. Yet he'd executed the task purely as a mindless exercise, his performance habitual from practice. His lust tonight had been determinedly manufactured—an attempt to exorcise his restless passion and the painful memories of another woman.

He'd attempted a great deal of exorcising in the years since Julienne Laurent had savaged his heart. In the wake of his broken betrothal, he had returned to London and embarked on a rampage of debauchery, including assuming leadership of the Hellfire League, a notorious club of England's premier rakes.

His outrageous exploits and determined pursuit of sexual gratification had added a new luster of glamour and notoriety to his reputation, earning him the nickname the Prince of Pleasure.

Dare disliked admitting even to himself that his profligacy had been his way of drowning his pain, of masking the emptiness of his life. Night after night he sought to lose himself in a warm, female body, to drive away memories of Julienne in an excess of sensual indulgence.

Yet even when he was buried deep inside a woman, bound in the most intimate way possible, he felt alone. Worse, he couldn't stop himself from yearning for the taste of another beauty's flesh. Julienne still tempted him, still tormented him.

Damn her to hell.

Seeing her again this afternoon had made him realize the wound she'd inflicted had never truly healed. He still wasn't completely over her. Even after all this time, his heart had stubbornly refused to abandon its obsession.

"Dare?" the widow implored, this time with a note of impatience.

"Forgive me, my sweet," he forced himself to reply.

He crumpled the playbill in his fist, resisting the urge to hurl it into the fire. A new performance was to begin tomorrow night, starring the celebrated new actress Julienne Laurent. But he had yet to decide if he would attend.

He would do better to keep as far away from her as possible, Dare cautioned himself. He knew how lethal she could be. He would never willingly make himself vulnerable to her again. He'd worked too hard never to feel so afflicted again. Still, a plan had begun to take shape in his mind. . . .

Suddenly impatient for action, he said over his shoulder, "I'm afraid I must go, Louisa."

"Now? But it is so late."

"It is not yet midnight."

Momentarily· ignoring the pouting of the lush, naked lady in the bed, he dressed silently. Then, going to her side, Dare employed his most charming manner to beg her forgiveness, kissing her breathless but evading her pleas to return soon.

All her servants had retired for the night, he realized when he went below. And the mount he'd ridden in Hyde Park this afternoon was snugly stabled in the mews behind Lady Dunleith's mansion. Rather than rouse the household, Dare let himself out and walked the short distance along Mayfair's dark streets to Lucian's home.

Lucian Tremayne, the Earl of Wycliff, was one of his closest friends, as well as one of England's chief spymasters. Lucian preferred not to advertise that he'd employed Dare in the hunt for a deadly traitor, so they had agreed to limit the frequency of their meetings. Yet they needed to confer about the latest developments.

Bending against the frigid night air, Dare drew his greatcoat around him. This was the coldest winter in memory, and only now was the country thawing out. In London even the Thames River had frozen. And in Yorkshire, where he'd recently visited for several interminable weeks, the snowdrifts had piled higher than a man's head, shutting down roads and bringing commerce and travel to a complete halt.

Tonight would be his first opportunity to update

Lucian regarding his clandestine endeavors. He'd sent a message this morning, arranging to make his report.

There were several lights burning in the windows of the regal Wycliff residence. Dare was admitted without question and shown into Lucian's study, where the earl was at work at his desk.

The two men greeted each other with the fondness of long acquaintance.

"And how is your beautiful wife?" Dare asked as Lucian poured them both a brandy.

"Flourishing. Brynn is as round as a melon, even though the babe isn't due for nearly two months."

"I regret I missed seeing her," Dare said, settling in a comfortable chair. "I understand she was in London this past week?"

"Yes, but I escorted her home again. She's safer in the country."

For her confinement, Brynn had retired to Lucian's family seat in Devonshire, where she could more easily be protected. Last fall she and her brother had been menaced by a criminal mastermind who called himself Lord Caliban, after the character in Shakespeare's play. Lucian had destroyed the gold-smuggling operation Caliban used to fund Napoleon's armies, silencing their leader for a time, but the traitor was still at large. Which was why Dare had become involved.

Lucian handed his guest a brandy and then settled in an adjacent chair. "So tell me what you learned in Yorkshire."

"Not much, I'm afraid. I stayed at a friend's estate barely six miles from Riddingham's, but all the damned snow made getting there difficult. Even so, I managed twice to enjoy dinner and cards with Riddingham and his houseguests. Perfectly insipid. He wore the ring the entire time. When I remarked on the uniqueness of the design, Riddingham claimed he won it playing piquet, but he couldn't remember from whom. And he could be lying."

Pausing, Dare took a sip of brandy, absently noting the quality. "Yet he's still wearing the ring now. Even if he has no notion that we suspect him of being Caliban, it seems foolish to flaunt such a distinctive ornament. To be truthful, the more I see of Riddingham, the more I wonder if he's bright enough to be a deadly traitor."

"Perhaps not, but we have to be certain." Lucian's mouth hardened. "It can be a fatal mistake to underestimate Caliban's cunning. Riddingham could be duping us all with his pretense of affability. And he was here in London in January when our man was killed."

A diplomat in the Foreign Office had been found murdered two months ago—the work of Caliban, it was suspected, although there was no proof. But he would strike again, Dare and Lucian had no doubt. They could only hope to unmask the traitor before he could do even further damage.

Cursing under his breath, Lucian brought his fist down hard on his chair arm.

"My sentiments exactly," Dare agreed darkly.

He well understood his friend's frustration at hunting a killer who was little more than a whisper and a shadow. They had only two clues thus far to Caliban's identity, both from a witness who'd had a momentary glimpse of him last year: Caliban was thought to be an

English nobleman. And he possessed an unusual ring embellished with a ruby-eyed dragon's head.

Dare had first spied the ring several months ago on Lord Riddingham's hand. Since then he'd covertly followed the viscount's trail, trying to determine if he could possibly be Caliban. It was that possibility that had led Dare to spend a tedious interlude in Yorkshire, where he could better investigate the theory.

His lack of success galled him. But he could hardly be expected to accomplish overnight what had eluded the nation's best agents. His licentious past, Lucian was wont to remind him, had not exactly prepared him for a career in government espionage.

In fact, Lucian had recruited him last fall primarily because of his well-known predilection for sin—he made such an unlikely candidate as a spy. Caliban would never suspect the Prince of Pleasure of leading the hunt for his capture.

Dare had agreed to help, not only because he was familiar with most of society, both high and low, but because he'd become restless and bored with his life. He was more than a little intrigued by the challenge of pitting wits against a cunning killer. He'd only half laughed at Lucian's assertion that having a serious goal could be the making of him.

He was not laughing now.

Dare took another swallow of brandy, hesitating while he debated telling Lucian of the new twist in the game.

"What do you know of the new actress at Drury Lane?" he finally said. "The Jewel who has the entire ton abuzz."

Lucian sent him a penetrating glance. "Am I to presume you have a new love interest?"

"Hardly. Riddingham is one of her suitors."

"Ah." Lucian leaned back in his chair, looking thoughtful. "I took Brynn to see Miss Laurent perform last week. We both found her surprisingly good. You're suggesting that her association with Riddingham is more than simply amorous?"

"Possibly. She bears investigating, at least. She is French, after all. It wouldn't be impossible for her to be in Napoleon's employ. Given their sparse incomes and dubious moral values, actresses are highly susceptible to bribery."

When Lucian raised an eyebrow, Dare realized how ironic it was for *him* to be decrying dubious moral values.

Yet this was not the first time Julienne Laurent's allegiance to England had been questioned. Seven years ago his grandfather had called her a traitor, claiming she was conspiring with Bonapartists and threatening to have her arrested for treason.

At the time Dare had been certain the accusations were fabricated—merely the old bastard's attempt to force him to end his betrothal. His chief concern had been protecting Julienne from his grandfather's wrathful machinations. But he was more willing now to believe there had been substance to the charges after all.

"I may be leaping to conclusions," he admitted, "but she could be in league with Riddingham."

"Why do you say so?" Lucian asked curiously. "Didn't Riddingham return to London only last week? They would scarcely have had time to meet."

"But they may claim a prior association. Riddingham's family seat is in Yorkshire. And Miss Laurent reportedly has spent the past half-dozen years treading the boards in York."

"Perhaps she was once his mistress."

"Perhaps. When I saw them driving in the park today, they seemed closer than mere acquaintances." Dare forced a smile. "If he isn't already sharing her bed, he certainly appeared eager to. He was hanging on her every word, along with half the male population of London." He hoped his sardonic tone hid the note of jealously he found difficult to repress. "But either way, she could be his accomplice."

"Or," Lucian countered, "he may solely be pursuing her with a carnal relationship in mind. Rumor has it that she is looking for a protector."

"I've heard the same rumor. Apparently La Belle Laurent made a public declaration that her choice will be made at the end of the season. A clever ploy," Dare said cynically. "The better to keep her admirers vying for her favors. Regardless, she merits watching. And you could perhaps use her to get closer to Riddingham."

"I? Don't you mean *you?*"

"I might not be the best man for the task. I had a . . . brief acquaintance with Miss Laurent a number of years ago."

Lucian studied him for a long moment, while Dare struggled to remain unruffled by those perceptive eyes. He was not about to disclose his wretched history with Julienne. How he'd discovered his betrothed in the arms of another lover. How his heart and his pride had been ravaged by her betrayal. Or how the memory still left him aching.

At length, Dare shrugged. "The affair ended unhappily."

"So you think the lady will want nothing to do with you?"

"Yes, I seriously doubt she will."

Lucian flashed him a wry grin. "You, my friend, have never been at a loss with any female. Surely you have only to wield your vast charm to persuade her to change her opinion of you."

Dare stared down at the amber liquid in his glass, wanting to refute the statement. It was true; when he chose to be persuasive, some of the haughtiest and most reluctant females had come into his arms willingly. But in this instance, he would be starting with a possibly insurmountable disadvantage.

Lucian broke into his dark thoughts. "I understand your reluctance to become involved with her, Dare, but clearly you should be the one to investigate her connection with Riddingham."

He grimaced wryly. "I feared you might say that."

Lucian's expression grew intent as he leaned forward. "I'm certain I don't need to remind you that England's future could be at stake."

"No, I need no reminding."

"This bloody war may at last be coming to an end—nearly every day there are fresh reports from the battlefield about Allied victories. But even if Napoleon is vanquished, I don't expect Caliban to retire. A man like that does not simply disappear."

"I'm well aware of the danger Caliban represents."

"Then you will do it?"

Dare took a long swallow of brandy, feeling the burn sear a trail down his throat to mingle with the fire already churning in his gut. "Yes," he said finally, exhaling a reluctant sigh. "I expect the best approach would be for me to join the supplicants for the Jewel's favors. Pretend to be one of Riddingham's rivals. That would give me a legitimate excuse for getting close to him. Stir the pot, as it were. Perhaps he will show his hand if I can manage to burrow deeply enough under his skin."

"Good. And if you find your reservations interfering with your mission, you have only to recall how many innocents have died as the result of Caliban's treachery. Meanwhile, you can use the opportunity to ascertain Miss Laurent's loyalties. You may be right. She could very well be working for the French."

Dare smiled to himself. It would be poetic justice if he could not only unmask Caliban, but discover that the temptress who'd broken his heart was abetting England's most dangerous traitor.

The tension that had gripped him since seeing Julienne this afternoon eased with the sense of having reached a decision.

He would use the dazzling actress to help him get closer to Riddingham, Dare vowed. And if she was indeed a French spy, he would make her pay dearly.

Chapter
Two

The cloying scents of orange peels and tallow from the footlights and torchères seemed almost overpowering tonight, yet Julienne knew the normal stage accoutrements were not to blame for her feeling of faintness. An entirely different cause had set her senses spinning.

He was in the audience, watching her performance.

She found her knees shaking. Even the ogling bucks in the pit couldn't distract her from his relentless regard. He sat in one of the luxury boxes, his fair hair shimmering in the glow of the theater's massive chandelier.

Dare North. The legendary lover who had stolen her heart and left her reeling in the aftermath.

Under his intent scrutiny, Julienne had executed her leading role in the John Webster tragedy in a daze, barely able to remember her lines. Once she had even missed her cue, which had earned her a disapproving scowl from the theater's august manager, Samuel Arnold.

I will not *think of him,* Julienne vowed futilely for the hundredth time as she waited in the wings for her final entrance.

The Theater Royal at Drury Lane was one of two premier theaters in London, and tonight's house was completely full. Filled to overflowing, in fact, a distinction normally reserved for London's reigning thespian, the remarkable Edmund Kean. Yet Kean had reportedly "taken ill," a public fiction to conceal the truth that he was still recovering from a fierce bout of drunken brawling.

Julienne had been given top billing this evening—a splendid coup for a hitherto unknown actress from the provinces. She could not afford to squander this opportunity, or have her wits battered by memories she'd fought so hard to vanquish.

It had taken years to cleanse the ache of Dare from her soul, to conquer her yearning for him. She'd risked coming to London, even knowing of his presence here, yet hoping to avoid him.

A foolish notion, she realized now. The Marquess of Wolverton—his present illustrious title—was one of the chief leaders of the Beau Monde, despite his scandalous reputation, or perhaps because of it. He moved in London's most elite circles, as well as the more disreputable ones. She could no more have avoided him than she could quell the painful memories that seeing him resurrected.

Another foolish notion, believing she could forget someone so unforgettable, or a passion so wondrous. She had loved Dare with a reckless hunger she'd never felt with any other man, before or since. But her love had proved her downfall.

Her eyes blurred as she remembered the last time she had seen Dare, when she'd had no choice but to betray him. In a fleeting moment his regard had transformed from shock to desolation, from disillusionment to chilled contempt.

Unable to explain her reasons, she had watched

through a haze of scalding tears as he walked out of her life. Losing him had left her devastated. Alone. Facing disaster—

A low hiss from the manager made Julienne realize she had missed another cue. Steeling herself, she swept out onto the stage to enact the final gory scenes of *The White Devil*.

It was a coveted role for any actress, playing a scheming Venetian courtesan, and she managed to make it through the dark tale of murder and vengeance with no more serious lapses. But she was grateful when her character's demise came at the end and the company could finally take their bows to shouts and whistles and sincere applause.

That the majority of the accolades were showered upon her surprised Julienne, considering her wretched performance. Pasting an alluring smile on her lips, however, she gracefully accepted the acclaim, executing a deep curtsy for the cheering crowd in the galleries, then the wilder throng in the pit, and finally the nobles and gentry in the boxes.

She was just rising when she made the mistake of glancing at the particular nobleman she'd tried so desperately all evening to ignore. Dare had moved to the front of his box to stand at the railing.

Julienne froze, caught in the hypnotizing power of his gaze; even at this distance, she could feel the searing impact. Her lips parted in a sharp inhalation, while his curved in a faint smile, slow and lazy and provocatively rakish.

She saw his sensual mouth move then, but with the rush of blood in her head making her senses swim, it took her a moment to realize he had spoken to her.

Without volition, she raised a hand, absently signaling for quiet. Slowly a hush went over the crowd, while countless heads swiveled in the direction of her fixed gaze.

Dare called her name again, this time loudly enough to be heard throughout the theater.

"Mademoiselle Laurent," he drawled, conversing as if they were completely alone. "Allow me to commend you on a most excellent performance."

Uncertain of what he planned, Julienne felt an unmistakable ripple of tension course through her, drawing her nerves taut.

"Thank you, my lord," she replied, striving to keep her voice steady.

"Is it true?" he asked.

"Is what true?"

Casually he lifted a hip onto the railing and lounged there, surveying her indolently. "That you intend to make your choice of protectors at the end of the season?"

Bewildered, Julienne thought back frantically to the declaration she'd made last week, half in jest. She had been in the green room after a performance, surrounded by eager swains, all vying for her attention and urging her to accept their unwanted invitations. When one persistent coxcomb crudely pronounced his determination to have her in keeping, she hid her dismay and feigned a laugh, protesting that she couldn't possibly decide from among such delightful gentlemen just yet.

Her indecision was purely a defensive strategy. She had no intention of accepting any man's protection, but neither could she risk spurning her devotees or alienating any of these wealthy theater patrons. She would have to tread a careful line, holding her courtiers enthralled while putting them off, maintaining their admiration without committing herself.

When pressed, she pledged to make her choice at the end of her acting engagement. Her unattainability had an added benefit, she shortly discovered. Being fought over by rich, titled admirers actually increased her value to the theater because it brought in more business.

That Lord Wolverton had learned of the episode, however, was a testament to the efficiency of London gossips, Julienne surmised.

Trying to regain her splintered composure, she uttered a polite response. "I fail to see how my intentions would concern you, my lord."

"I should like to declare myself as a candidate in the competition."

An audible ripple of surprise and interest emanated from the crowd.

To her shock, Dare hoisted himself up to stand on the balcony railing. Julienne wasn't certain if the gasps she heard came from the audience or from her own throat. Both, she suspected. In all her days in the theater, she had never been more at a loss; her mind went blank, and she felt the particular panic that came from forgetting a crucial line.

Except that this time there were no scripted lines to learn. This was no play at all.

The crowd, however, was behaving as though the scene was merely a continuation of the earlier performance, maintaining an expectant hush. Julienne held her own silence, unable to guess what machinations Dare had planned.

Looking totally at ease in his precarious position, he leaned a shoulder against the column supporting one side of the box.

"I have made a wager regarding your choice, mademoiselle," he announced, enunciating clearly. "I've wagered that you will choose me."

The rowdy throng in the pit reacted with a chorus of titters and guffaws, while the rest waited with bated breath for her response.

"Have you indeed?" Julienne managed, stalling for time. "You have a very high opinion of yourself, it seems."

"An opinion that is warranted." His gaze slewed over the crowd. "Does anyone here doubt I can win the heart of this lovely Jewel?"

There were whoops and shouts from the riffraff in the pit and a spurt of clapping from the upper tiers. Dare sketched a debonair bow, acknowledging their approbation.

It was a dangerous maneuver, Julienne thought with alarm. If he were to fall from that height, he could severely injure himself. But he had always been the most reckless man of her acquaintance. Reckless, daring, outrageous. He appeared totally unconcerned that he was making a spectacle of them both in front a multitude of gawking spectators.

And the audience obviously relished his bold tactics, responding with titillation and delight.

Gritting her teeth, Julienne moved along the stage, closer to his box, while trying to recruit her wits. Dare had cleverly trapped her with his public declaration. She had no intention of taking a lover, most certainly not the notorious rake who so forcefully reminded her of the tormenting past, one who still had the power to bring her pain. But she didn't dare refuse him outright, not without jeopardizing all she had worked for. Her livelihood depended on pleasing her audience.

Fortunately, she had performed for years, and she had a great deal of practice dealing with rogues and obstinate pursuers.

Making a belated recovery, Julienne placed her hands on her hips and eyed Dare up and down, looking him over critically as she might a horse at Tattersalls.

"Perhaps your inflated opinion is warranted after all," she agreed thoughtfully. "Your reputation certainly precedes you. The notorious Lord Wolverton—a thoroughly wicked rake, famed for his charm and address and his fondness for debauchery. The Prince of Pleasure—is that not the name I heard? Also known as the scourge of feminine hearts."

"Yet you have fast become the scourge of male hearts, *ma belle*."

"That was not my intention," she said, offering an alluring smile that contradicted her words. "But since you remark on it . . . I might venture to make a wager of my own." She faced her audience, playing to the crowd. "I stand accused of willfully breaking gentlemen's hearts. Well, in this instance, I shall endeavor to live up to the accusation. I wager that I can bring the Prince of Pleasure to his knees."

The roar of approval was almost deafening, punctuated by the thunder of stomping feet and howls of glee. It was several minutes before the theater quieted enough to allow the spectacle to continue.

Dare's own smile was devilish. "So you think you can break my heart?"

"I am certain of it."

"You are welcome to try." He gave another bow, holding her gaze riveted. "I look forward to the first engagement, my beautiful Jewel."

Anticipating a delicious battle, the crowd burst into a wild round of applause. By the time Julienne swept a low curtsy and made her escape, bets had already started flying over who would win.

The manager, Samuel Arnold, lay in wait for her. She could barely make out his words over the pounding of her pulse and the still-deafening clamor behind her, but she realized he was expressing his approval. Forcing a smile, she fled backstage.

There were two green rooms at the theater, one designated for the general members of the company, another more elegantly appointed one for the principal performers. Here the actors met their adoring public and held court for their admirers.

Weakly Julienne sank onto a chaise longue to wait for the expected throng and buried her face in her hands, oblivious to her stage makeup. The rise of emotion churning inside her threatened to suffocate her.

She had thought herself prepared to face Dare, but never under such unsettling circumstances—matching wits with him in so open a forum, on such a shocking subject as what lover she intended to choose as her protector. She couldn't even begin to guess his motivation for issuing his public challenge, unless it was retribution for her past sins.

She could understand his desire for retribution. Seven years ago she had ended their betrothal in such a way that Dare would no longer want her for his bride. She'd purposely driven him away, for his own sake. Yet that

hadn't made relinquishing him any less devastating—
nor, in the end, had it saved her from ruin.

It had been the most terrifying, heartbreaking experience of her life. Not only had she lost Dare, but
subsequently she'd found herself utterly defenseless,
at the mercy of a grasping libertine and the machinations of a venomous old nobleman. Between the two
of them, the Earl of Ivers and the Marquess of Wolverton had destroyed her good name, nearly destroyed *her*.

They had left her broken, her dreams shattered in
fragments, herself shunned, her shop utterly devoid of
customers and income, her beloved *Maman* sharing in
her shame.

She regretted that the most, for the scandal had only
weakened the comptess's rapidly deteriorating health.
To spare her mother further anguish, Julienne had resolved to abandon her familiar life and numbly had
begun the search for another home and occupation.

It was sheer coincidence that a traveling troupe of
actors from York had returned to the district during
her darkest moments. She could claim a slight acquaintance with them, for she had helped with costumes in
past years. When they learned of her desperation, they
offered her a means to escape the scandal, as well as
shelter and solace and friendship.

With little chance of finding any sort of respectable
employment, Julienne had joined their troupe and
wound up settling in York. She spent years honing the
skills of her new profession, her sole focus on survival—
for both herself and her mother.

Most of her small earnings she sent home. And the
millinery, which continued under the supervision of her

sales clerk, initially earned enough to pay the doctors' bills. But the situation grew dire when her mother's wasting disease worsened, forcing Julienne to make some harsh choices so that her mother's final days might be less excruciating.

Even so, she had not stopped loving Dare. Not at first. For years he had haunted her, figuring in her fondest dreams and her darkest nightmares. The memories of his lovemaking had remained intense, desperate, wild. She had ached for his caresses, for the piercing pleasure he had given her.

Yet eventually she had taken control of her life and carved out a new future for herself. Since *Maman*'s death nearly four years ago, Julienne had worked to achieve a kind of peace—and even found contentment of sorts.

When recently she was offered a plum engagement at the Drury Lane Theater in London for a substantial salary, she had accepted, refusing to let Dare's presence here destroy her hard-won opportunity for financial independence. Fame didn't interest her; fortune did. If she was successful enough, if she could command the income of a preeminent actress, then she would be free to make her own choices, to determine her own future. Never again would she be vulnerable and defenseless or dependent on any man's whims.

With trepidation, she had reentered Dare's world, wanting urgently to prove to herself that she was entirely over him. Wanting to close that door to their past irrevocably so that she could move on with her life.

Seeing Dare again, however, had reopened a dormant wound, roused an ache inside her that made it hard even to breathe.

Determinedly Julienne inhaled several slow, deep breaths, practicing the calming techniques she had learned at the beginning of her acting career.

The worst was over. Despite whatever game Dare was playing, she could manage to shield her emotions.

I can keep him distant, she vowed, although the weak trembling in her limbs belied her resolve.

She was grateful when the other lead actors in the company joined her. They were followed shortly by a throng of admirers, and in moments the green room was filled to overflowing, abuzz with talk of a certain scandalous nobleman.

Pretending that the spectacle had not affected her in the least, Julienne summoned a dazzling smile for the gentlemen clustered around her.

They had one intention, she well knew: to bribe their way into her bed. Any female in her profession was expected to be available for the right price. But though she was determined to keep her bed solitary, she had an image to maintain. And tonight she had an additional task—assuring her cavaliers that despite Wolverton's bold declaration, he would prove no rival for her affections.

One of the most vocal of her courtiers was Hugh Bramley, Viscount Riddingham. Tall and slightly gangly, he possessed unremarkable brown hair and nondescript features, but he was affable and amusing and extremely well-mannered, and Julienne found herself fonder of him than any of the others.

Riddingham was clearly unhappy with the turn of events, however, and showed an unmistakable jealousy.

"The nerve of the rogue, making such an exhibition of himself. Miss Laurent, I trust you don't intend to permit that insufferable fellow to make you the target of his depraved amusements. His perversions are legend."

"He will be no danger to me if you are at hand to protect me," she returned lightly, trying to soothe Riddingham's ruffled feathers while keeping a nervous eye on the door, expecting Dare to make an appearance at any moment.

It was all she could do to hide her tension and feign interest in their witticisms. When she was offered a dozen invitations for a late-night supper, she declined prettily, claiming fatigue.

Three-quarters of an hour later, her less persistent swains had retired from the lists and the crowd had thinned somewhat. Having regained a small measure of her composure, Julienne began to hope that she needn't deal with the notorious marquess any further this evening and she could retire to her dressing room and then to her lodgings alone.

She was laughing over one of Riddingham's sallies when she suddenly saw the viscount stiffen. A noted hush fell over the company, and when the sea of gentleman parted, Dare North stood before her.

Julienne's heart somersaulted violently in her chest.

At first glance he seemed to possess the same refined elegance she remembered, the same lithe grace, the same lean hardness. Yet his shoulders were broader beneath his exquisitely tailored blue coat, she noted; his thighs more powerfully muscled, sheathed in formal satin breeches.

His elaborate cravat set off the fine, aristocratic features she found just as striking as they had been seven years ago. His face, with its high cheekbones and noble brow, had always had the devil's own beauty.

It was all Julienne could do to keep from staring.

Dare had no such reservations, apparently. His slow appraisal seemed to penetrate her garments, brushing over her bosom significantly revealed by the low, square neckline of her elaborate costume, moving to her narrow waist, then resting on her hips encased in flaring panniers. It was the measuring scrutiny of a man who knew women intimately.

She took a steadying breath, trying to calm the rapid beat of her heart.

"At last I understand why all London is raving," he said. "From a distance, your stage presence is stunning. But in close proximity . . . your beauty renders me inarticulate."

Julienne eyed him coolly. "I take leave to doubt that, my lord. I would imagine you are rarely at a loss for words."

"Rarely." His mouth quirked with his heart-melting smile, rife with the sensual charm she remembered so well.

She tried frantically to think of something sophisticated and witty to say. Before anything occurred, however, Dare reached out and brought her fingers to his lips to kiss their tips slowly.

Her stomach tightened with a jolt of pure, feminine desire.

His faint smile was knowing and experienced.

Only with great effort did Julienne refrain from snatching her hand away, extricating her fingers slowly instead. Yet she deplored her response to that simple contact, deplored how the memory lingered too long.

"I wonder that you deign to grace us with your presence, my lord. The play has been over for some time."

"I wanted to allow your other courtiers their fair share of your company, since I intend to take you to supper."

There were several immediate objections from the gentlemen surrounding her, Riddingham's being the most adamant. "Miss Laurent will not be accompanying you anywhere, Wolverton."

Dare raised an eyebrow at the viscount. "I regret, old friend, to be poaching on your territory, but I have a wager to win, after all. Surely you understand."

Julienne intervened with a chilly smile, addressing Dare. "Thank you for your consideration, but Lord Riddingham is correct. I must decline. I fear that after tonight's performance, I have a headache."

"All that murder and mayhem, no doubt," he murmured. "But I trust you will allow me to register a protest. You accepted my challenge, mademoiselle. In all fairness, you must give me the chance to woo you. How can I win your surrender otherwise?"

"I fancy that is your problem, not mine."

"What of your vow to bring me to my knees?"

"Some other time, perhaps. Now, if you will forgive me, I must change my costume."

Rising from the chaise regally, she flashed an apologetic smile that encompassed everyone but Wolverton. "I hope very much to see all you gentlemen tomorrow."

Leaving the green room behind, Julienne negotiated the narrow corridor to her dressing room. She was about to close the door when, to her utter dismay, Dare entered behind her.

Whirling, she stared at him indignantly as he locked the door, shutting them in together.

"Your manners always were supremely deficient," she observed. "I thought I made myself clear. I wish to be alone."

"No, you said you wished to change your costume."

His green eyes bright, he surveyed her with interest. Julienne fought the defensive urge to cross her arms over her chest. It unnerved her to be alone with Dare for the first time since their rift. Yet she was not entirely surprised by his presumptuous invasion; Dare North was a man who knew the rules of polite behavior and blatantly ignored them.

She was spared a reply, however, when an urgent pounding sounded on the door, followed by Riddingham's concerned query. "Miss Laurent, did Wolverton follow you here? Do you need assistance?" He pounded again.

"You had best reassure him," Dare murmured, "before he smashes the door down."

She felt a strong desire to box Dare's ears as she watched him slip behind the large ornate dressing screen. He always did have the most incredible nerve. . . .

She unlocked the door instead, opening it partway to find a scowling Lord Riddingham.

"Shall I summon the manager?" he growled.

Julienne had no desire to compound the recent spectacle or rouse the viscount's jealousy further by revealing that Dare was alone with her in her private dressing room. Feigning bewilderment, she gave Riddingham a puzzled frown. "Why would you wish to summon the manager?"

"I thought to find Wolverton here."

"You must have been mistaken." Holding her breath, she opened the door wide, showing him the small dressing room jammed with a wide variety of costumes and props, leaving just enough space for a dressing table and screen.

"See, my lord. I don't require assistance, although I thank you. It was kind of you. Were Wolverton here making a nuisance of himself, I would have been exceedingly glad for you to come to my rescue."

When Riddingham cleared his throat and apologized for disturbing her, Julienne reassured him once more. After he took his leave, she closed the door and counted to ten before saying in a wry tone, "I believe it is safe for you to come out now."

When Dare showed himself, she added with a tart edge, "You disappeared with such ease, I can only assume you have long practice evading outraged husbands and lovers."

"You suppose correctly," he agreed blandly.

"Well, I will thank you to take yourself off now and allow me some privacy."

The grin he flashed was brilliant enough to make her heart falter. "I cannot leave until I'm certain Riddingham is gone. Surely you prefer that I spare you embarrassment. You wouldn't wish me to expose you for a liar, would you?"

"Very well," Julienne snapped. "You may stay for a few moments more. But if it is not too inconvenient, would you mind coming out from behind the screen and allowing me use of it?"

"I hoped you might need help changing," Dare replied lightly, even as he complied with her request.

"No, I do *not* need help."

"How tiresome. But truthfully, I am only here to persuade you to dine with me. One supper. What can it hurt? You can use the opportunity to ensnare my heart."

She gave him a hard stare. "What do you really want of me, Lord Wolverton?"

"I told you. I made a wager that I can win you."

"How much?" When he raised an eyebrow, Julienne crossed her arms with impatience. "What sum did you wager?"

"What does it matter?"

"If it is not too excessive, I will pay it myself, so I won't be compelled to endure this ridiculous charade." She had little doubt the amount of the bet would be well beyond her means, but she wished Dare to know how preposterous she found his game.

"This is not about money," he replied, feigning hurt. "My pride is at stake."

"Your *pride*?" She made a moue of disgust. "You are not truly serious about this public contest of yours, are you?"

"Ah, how little you know me."

It was true, Julienne thought with a sudden sadness. The man she'd once loved had become a stranger to her, one who cared nothing about holding her up to public ridicule.

And yet she couldn't truly blame him. She could only try to defend herself against whatever punishment he had in store for her.

With that distressing thought, she moved behind the screen. To her relief, Dare stepped away, acting enough of the gentleman to allow her a measure of privacy.

But it still unsettled her to have him in such close proximity.

"You agreed to my challenge," he said after a moment. "I should think you would want to make good. That was a swift recovery, by the way. In one brilliant stroke you turned the tables on me."

"I shall take that as a compliment," she said dryly as she removed her costume and began struggling with layers of panniers and petticoats.

"The reports of your talent are not exaggerated. You are extremely good."

"Sometimes I am. I was not at my best for tonight's performance."

"Found yourself distracted, did you?"

"As it happens, I did. I feared you might do something vindictive, and I was right."

He didn't respond to her accusation but returned to the familiar subject instead. "Come to supper with me, *chérie*. We can reminisce about old times."

"I find nothing I wish to remember."

"Not even the carnal delights we once shared?"

"Most *especially* that."

She drew on a modest, long-sleeved gown of dark blue merino, one that she often wore going to and from the theater.

Slipping from behind the screen, Julienne sat at her dressing table to scrub away her makeup. She made every effort to disregard Dare's presence, yet ignoring him was like pretending she wasn't trapped in a cage with a hungry tiger.

She could see him in the small looking glass as he leaned indolently against the door, watching her. He was silent as she took down her hair, not speaking till she had removed the pins and combed her fingers through the thick mass.

"You always had the loveliest hair. Like Russian sable. Rich and silken and luminous."

Julienne kept her lips pressed together, refusing to respond. *He* had always had a silver tongue, she reminded herself. Dare delighted in overstepping polite bounds with his cajolery and too-intimate innuendos.

"And you have the face and body of a temptress."

"I am no temptress," she retorted. "And I am no longer a green girl, susceptible to your flattery."

"No, not a girl at all. You've flourished into a ravishing woman."

Unexpectedly, she felt an ache of sorrow. Once, he hadn't needed to flatter her with words. He had made her feel beautiful with merely a glance. Beautiful and cherished. *Stop dwelling on the past, you fool.*

She felt Dare move behind her. Julienne froze as he took up the hairbrush and began drawing it slowly through her long hair.

"I always relished doing this. Remember?"

The warmth of his voice touched a chord in her that left her trembling. *Remember? How could I possibly forget?* She closed her eyes at the drugging shock of recognition and familiarity: the feel of Dare at her back, the vibrant heat of his body, the sweet sensation of his touch, his erotic tenderness. It had been so long. . . .

Heaven help her, she wanted him. She knew if she merely pressed back against him, he would carry it further . . . reach down to caress her, stroke her, arouse her. The thought of his lean, elegant hands fondling the swell of her breasts made her nipples peak with longing.

Dismayed, Julienne locked her jaw, resenting her body's betrayal, cursing herself again for a fool. She was mad to have allowed herself to be alone with Dare. She'd thought herself strong enough to meet him again after all this time, but she was mistaken. She was too weak. And he was too dangerous.

Unable to bear his nearness any longer, she rose abruptly to her feet, leaving her hair unpinned. In agitation she went to the wall hook and fumbled for her cloak, then flung it around her shoulders.

"If you won't leave, then I will, Lord Wolverton. I bid you good evening."

"No, I think not."

He advanced with slow, determined strides across the small room until he stood directly before her. Warily Julienne took a step backward, but there was nowhere to go.

For a moment he simply stared down at her, his gaze dropping to her mouth. In a daze, she waited as he leaned toward her slightly, lowering his head until his warm breath touched her cheek . . . her lips. He intended to kiss her, she was certain. A ripple of panic flooded her, and she tried to brace herself for the impact—

Yet astonishingly, his kiss never came. Instead he gave her his notorious, bone-melting smile. Bending, he slipped a hand behind her knees and lifted her up in his arms, turning her panic to startlement.

"What the devil are you *doing*?" she demanded, gasping at his unexpected action.

"Taking you to supper; what else?" Dare answered blandly. "My carriage awaits, darling."

Chapter
Three

Dare shifted uneasily in the carriage seat, cursing the hot blood that stirred in his loins. His fierce arousal had taken him by surprise. He'd intended to exercise more control.

And he would have, if not for Julienne's instinctive feminine response to his nearness. He'd seen the blank daze of desire in her eyes, sensed the subtle changes in her body as she parted her lips in expectation of his kiss.

He'd had to veil the shock of raw need that ran through him. In sheer self-defense, he'd taken the first action that came to mind—swung her up in his arms and carried her out to his waiting carriage.

But being alone with her in the seclusion of the town coach had an even more profound effect on his body, rousing his cravings to a painful ache.

Involuntarily Dare cast a glance at Julienne as she sat staring silently out the window, her patrician countenance in profile. She was everything he remembered and more. In the muted light from the outer carriage lamps, her dark hair shone richly, flowing in heavy, silken waves over her shoulders. His gaze wandered to her bosom, where several curls lay in teasing disarray. Even now he had to fight the urge to move closer and bury his face in the luxurious mass, to slide his arms around her, to stroke those luscious breasts. . . .

Dare swore again silently, feeling a surge of resentment that she had remained so alluring . . . that she still had the power to make him feel so much.

He'd been wholly determined to resist her, yet at her sensual response, memory had come rushing back to overwhelm him—every taste, every touch, every sensation, every yearning he'd thought forcibly buried deep in his heart, out of reach.

Perhaps his pursuit of her was a mistake. He had launched the first salvo in his game, declaring his intention to win her, but Julienne had proved just as enterprising, catching him off guard with her daring vow to bring him to his knees.

She had already done so once before, Dare reminded himself, setting his jaw. He would have to proceed with caution if he hoped to emerge from this contest with his heart intact.

His only satisfaction was that Julienne appeared to be as agitated as he was. She viewed him with wariness and mistrust, obviously, as if she feared his retribution. But he knew very well that her apprehension hadn't prevented her from remembering the passion that had once burned between them, or kept her from wanting him.

Beside him, Julienne was having similar thoughts. It dismayed her, how helpless she had been against Dare's brazen tactics. After setting her aquiver with longing, purposely kindling her desire with his nearness, he had suddenly doused the flame he'd created and roused her indignation at the same stroke; he had literally swept her off her feet and carried her from the theater to the delight of numerous gawking bystanders.

The nerve of the rogue, causing such a spectacle! He was exasperating, maddening, unsettling—although she had to admire his ingenious determination. Dare was singleminded when it came to getting what he wanted.

And he had won their first skirmish, Julienne had to admit. If he hadn't trapped her by his wager in front of a gleeful London audience, if he hadn't virtually abducted her, she would not be here with him now.

It was one thing to engage in a public battle of wits with Dare; it was another entirely to be secluded with him for the intimacy of a late-night supper. But she could manage to abide his company for an evening, Julienne silently promised herself. They were merely partaking of a meal. She was experienced enough now to keep Dare emotionally distant. And this was her chance to prove to herself that she was over him.

More critically, she could prove to Dare that she had the ability to resist him. The sooner he realized she would never surrender, the sooner he would give up his attempt at revenge.

I won't succumb to him. I won't.

By repeating that mantra over and over again, Julienne was able to restore some measure of her shaken confidence. Yet she couldn't help her heart beating in anticipation as the carriage slowed to a halt.

Her fierce awareness of Dare only increased when he helped her down. And when he pressed a hand to the small of her back, guiding her toward the entrance stairs, she gave a start at the instant warmth that sprang up inside her, deploring how she was affected by the casual contact.

She would have to do better if she hoped to win this encounter.

It was a private gentlemen's club, Julienne noted, not certain whether she should be relieved. She had half expected Dare to take her to one of his notorious dens of iniquity where, according to the scandal sheets that chronicled his wicked deeds, he conducted his orgies and other debauched entertainments.

They were greeted by a majordomo and led upstairs to an even more private chamber, lavishly but tastefully decorated. Candles glittered in gold sconces on the walls, reflecting the sparkle of china and crystal on the small, damask-covered dining table, while a cozy fire burned in the hearth, casting an intimate glow over the entire room.

As she expected, the scene was set for seduction. One wall was partially concealed by a crimson brocade curtain, but Julienne could see an alcove in the shadows, with a bed large enough for two.

Heat spread through her at the thought of sharing that bed with Dare.

The majordomo seated her at the table and then withdrew, to her regret. To her further discomfort, Dare took the chair beside her rather than opposite her.

"I must warn you," Julienne remarked lightly as he inspected the variety of wines on the table. "You are laboring under a misapprehension. Despite whatever machinations you have planned for tonight, you will not succeed."

His smile came easily. "I never anticipate failure before I have even begun."

Julienne felt a spark of dismay flare inside her at his smooth response. The facile charm was automatic, effortless, and highly potent. Dare still had the power to affect her without the least effort. She wondered how she would endure an entire evening in his company, with him so near and so clearly set on prevailing.

His tone remained teasing as he poured a glass of wine. "I think it poor-spirited of you, *chérie,* not to give me a fighting chance. Or perhaps merely faint-hearted. You are afraid I will win."

"Hardly." Julienne managed a laugh. "I am more afraid I will do you an injury when you continue to persecute me."

"Try this vintage," he suggested. "It comes from Languedoc."

Where her late father's estates had been before his execution, she thought, wincing. Julienne did as she was bid, however, and found the wine delicious.

"The food here is excellent," Dare said, observing her approving expression. "You will appreciate it. The chef is Parisian." At her surprised glance, he added, "Did you think I would forget your fondness for French cuisine?"

She returned a smile that was faintly taunting. "Truthfully, I don't think of you at all."

"I cannot say the same of you," he replied lazily.

He leaned back in his chair, exhibiting his usual elegant grace, but Julienne found it difficult to show the same casual ease. She was too conscious of Dare. His gilded hair glimmered in the candlelight, its soft, thick waves threaded riotously with gold and flaxen. Worse, she kept seeing images of her fingers gliding through it, and images of his fingers reciprocating.

Involuntarily she glanced down at his hands, which held a wine goblet, almost caressing the stem, and an inexplicable yearning filled her. She could almost feel those warm, deft hands on her skin. . . .

"It has been a long time," he murmured, startling her with his perceptiveness.

"Not long enough for my tastes," she rejoined, feigning nonchalance yet glad that the dimness of the room concealed her flush.

She was even more relieved when a discreet knock on the door heralded the entrance of supper, served by two footmen. There were several courses: clear partridge soup with truffles, braised ham, trout in tomato and garlic sauce, peas, creamed artichoke hearts, sweetbreads, prawns, fricassee of veal with Madeira sauce, and finally preserved cherries and plum pudding.

Every dish was delectable, but Julienne barely tasted any of them. Her attention kept straying to her companion . . . those arresting green eyes, the well-shaped, sensual mouth. . . .

Don't think about his mouth, she ordered herself. *Don't think about those firm, warm lips that made you shiver with passion.* The seductive lips that had given and had taken so much pleasure. That wicked, heart-stopping smile that could lure a woman's soul from her body.

That smile had always been Dare's greatest asset. Or perhaps it was his remarkable way of looking at a woman. He focused such thrilling intensity on his target that she felt incredibly desirable.

As he was doing now, Julienne realized. He was watching her as if engrossed, despite the presence of the two footmen. She managed to bear his scrutiny until he dismissed the servers at the conclusion of the meal, leaving her alone with him.

"Did no one ever tell you it is ill-mannered to stare?" she asked, invoking a cool smile.

He grinned, his bearing relaxed. "Can I help but be fascinated by someone of your dazzling beauty? You intoxicate me."

"No doubt because the wine has gone to your head."

He measured her in a slow, exacting way, obviously determined to tear holes in the thin façade of her composure. "So what you have been doing with yourself all these years, mademoiselle?"

Her smile slipped, and she took a sip of wine, reluctant to answer. "I would rather you address me as Miss Laurent. I prefer not to call attention to the fact that I am French."

"Very well . . . darling." Amusement laced the edge of his voice, but his tone remained curious. "Your trace of an accent is no longer noticeable. Is that by design?"

"Yes," Julienne admitted. "It wasn't healthy for my acting career. The English consider themselves far superior to anyone of French origin and dislike any reminders of our differences."

"Our dislike of the French might have something to do with their despot who is bent on world domination," Dare said blandly.

She could have pointed out that many of her compatriots detested Napoleon Bonaparte far more than the British did, but she didn't intend to debate the issue with Dare.

Steepling his long fingers, he continued to watch her

with that disconcerting gaze, although he changed the subject. "Tell me . . . are you sharing your bed with any of those puppies who were panting at your skirts tonight?"

Julienne drew a sharp breath at the boldness of the question. "That, I believe, is none of your concern."

"I simply want to know who my competition is. It is hard to tell whom you prefer most from among all the fops and swells surrounding you. From what I've observed, I would guess Riddingham. Is he my chief rival?"

Julienne allowed her lips to curve drolly and refused to reply.

"I should think you would prefer a real man to warm your bed," Dare remarked. "But if I recall correctly, you are not overly particular about your bed partners." The sudden caustic note in his voice suggested censure.

Calling on all her willpower, Julienne affected an expression of detachment and arched an eyebrow. "I find it incredible that the most profligate libertine in London would presume to judge *my* choices. From all reports, you have never been discriminating about the lovers you amuse yourself with. Or how many you have, for that matter."

"Oh, no, I am exceedingly discriminating. At least I am now. There was a time after you. . . ." His gaze remained fixed on her, slowly shredding her nerves. "After you, Jewel, I didn't much care who I bedded. I was only intent in burying my pain in pleasures of the flesh."

She didn't respond to that admission, either, Dare noted. "It took me a long while to get over your cruelty, *chérie.*"

Some emotion flickered in her eyes, something vulnerable and too fleeting for him to identify. Then she lowered her gaze, her lashes dark against her ivory skin.

"In fact, I could say that you were the one who set me on my path to wickedness."

Julienne lifted her chin at that, her expression skeptical. "You can hardly blame me for your licentiousness. You were a rake long before we met."

"But you were not so chaste yourself, I'll warrant. And I expect you've indulged in a liaison or two since then."

"One or two," she said evenly. "But I know precisely how many lovers I have had. I'm certain you cannot make the same claim, Lord Wolverton."

"Once you called me Dare."

"Once I called you a great many things." That siren's smile flickered on her lips. "I can think of a few choice appellations just now. Reprobate, hedonist, libertine."

Dare affected a grimace. "One thing definitely has changed. Your claws have grown sharper."

"Perhaps. But I will need sharp claws if I hope to defend myself against you."

He frowned slightly. "I suspect I'm the one who will have to defend himself. If memory serves, the last time I encountered you, you were welcoming the caresses of another man. Behind my back, I might add. While leading me to believe that I was your heart's desire." His mouth curled. "Oh, but I *was* your desire, as long as I was heir to a fortune."

Hearing his bitterness, Julienne stared down into her wineglass. Dare believed she was an accomplished liar. That she could make love to him so passionately one moment and then betray him the next with his rival.

A tightness constricted her throat. She'd had a compelling reason to lie all those years ago. She had thought she had no choice. But she didn't deserve Dare's hatred. She had suffered more than he knew. Perhaps if he understood what she had endured, he wouldn't be so eager for revenge. . . .

She lifted her gaze to Dare's, and their eyes locked, the dark past vibrating between them. Pain lashed through her at the cold expression on his face, and Julienne realized the futility of pleading with him for forgiveness.

Perhaps if he had simply asked her for the truth, if two hours ago he hadn't publicly demonstrated his utter desire to humiliate her, she might have risked reopening those savage wounds.

But there was no point now in trying to justify her long-ago actions. It no longer mattered what Dare thought of her. She couldn't undo the devastation, the loss—for either of them. And the truth could have unwanted consequences. No doubt Dare would feel pity for her. And guilt. He might even feel obliged to make amends.

She couldn't allow herself to become tangled up with Dare again, certainly not on those terms. That kind of pain would destroy her. It had taken her years to get beyond the past, and now she only wanted to forget.

No, Julienne concluded, it would be better if Dare continued to believe she had betrayed him. That she had never loved him. She wouldn't protest her innocence, despite his barbs about her being cruel and mercenary.

Instead she would play his game, assume the role he had assigned her. She would keep her responses light and pretend that he no longer had the power to hurt her.

It was an effort to smile, but Julienne managed it with careless elegance, all the while thinking that she had never appreciated her abilities as an actress so much.

"You may think what you choose," she said, "but I have long since forgotten that unpleasant episode. I have no intention of discussing it."

Dare felt a stab of annoyance at her dismissal, but he decided that harping on the subject would only make him seem a spoiled child. "How did you happen to become an actress?" he asked instead.

"Some of us are required to work for a living, my lord."

"You couldn't persuade Ivers to keep you?"

A fleeting look of desolation entered her eyes, but that momentary fragility faded as quickly as it had come. "He offered," she responded without inflection, "but I chose not to accept."

Dare wondered if Julienne was telling the truth— if she had refused the earl's offer because his pockets weren't overly full—or if Ivers had abandoned her because their scheme for gaining the Wolverton fortune had failed. "He couldn't provide you enough compensation?"

Her faint laugh held little mirth. "Indeed, he couldn't. His gaming debts had severly depleted his purse. And I needed a reliable income to support my mother. Her illness grew worse as summer ended."

"What of your shop? Didn't that produce an adequate enough income?" Dare asked, remembering their familiar arguments that summer.

Julienne had claimed that the millinery was her sole means of income and that until their marriage was settled, she couldn't afford to neglect it. Dare had offered to purchase the shop and turn it over to her clerk so she wouldn't be obliged to earn her living, but Julienne had refused, saying she wouldn't take his charity or become his kept mistress—which was why they had gone to such lengths to keep their trysts private. Later, he'd realized she had simply been holding out until she could secure his entire fortune.

When her reply came, however, it surprised him.

"The business did not fare well after . . ." Julienne lifted her gaze almost defiantly. "Your grandfather made several unfounded allegations against me. I left Kent to avoid the scandal and turned the shop over to our clerk."

Dare's frown deepened as he thought back to those wretched weeks after Julienne's betrayal. He hadn't known what happened to her. He hadn't wanted to know. He'd left Kent immediately and had never again returned to Whitstable. Nor had he ever set foot in Wolverton Hall until his grandfather was dead and buried.

But he shouldn't be feeling this sharp prick of guilt now. Julienne had brought her troubles on herself with her duplicity and lies.

"And your mother?" he asked at length.

"She died several years ago." Julienne's eyes shadowed in sad remembrance. "I wanted her to live with me in York, but *Maman* wouldn't hear of moving elsewhere. She disliked leaving all her friends."

Dare nodded, remembering the close-knit community of French émigrés in Whitstable. When the Laurents had fled the terror of the guillotine, they'd settled on the northeastern shore of Kent, near the bustling resort towns of Marsgate and Ramsgate, where they could enjoy the company of other exiled French nobles.

"She refused," Julienne added softly, "to be driven from her home once again."

As she had been during the Revolution, Dare completed the thought. An unexpected wave of tenderness took him by surprise, but he drew back from it abruptly, wary of leaving himself too vulnerable.

"I am sorry," he said with cursory politeness.

Julienne's gaze searched his face, holding an edge of doubt. "Thank you."

He reached for his wineglass and drained the last swallows. "I wasn't sorry when my grandfather died, though. The old bastard held on until just last year."

Julienne looked abruptly away, but not before Dare saw the hot glitter in her eyes. It was raw, naked hatred, he realized.

He hadn't expected her to share his venomous sentiments toward the late marquess. But perhaps she blamed his grandfather for ruining her life. It was certainly true that if not for the old man's threat to disinherit him, Julienne's future might have turned out very differently. His own as well, Dare reflected. He would have wed her, never suspecting her true nature until it was too late.

"You have evidently done well for yourself since then," he said finally. "But there are easier ways to earn a living than acting. I presume you are not planning to tread the boards forever?"

"No, not forever."

"Is that why you intend to take a protector? To raise your income?"

Her smile seemed forced, although her tone remained light. "You may have compelled me to have supper with you, my lord, but I don't believe I agreed to submit to an interrogation."

"When you make your choice, I very much want it to be me."

"Unfortunately," she said sweetly, "you cannot always have everything you want. You have had everyone bowing and scraping before you since the day you were born, and it has obviously given you an exaggerated estimation of your self-worth."

"I know my financial worth, at least. And I am prepared to be extremely generous. I'll triple your usual remuneration. What is it you want? House, carriage, jewelry, allowance?"

Her eyes kindled with amusement. "I am not for sale, Lord Wolverton. I will be no man's plaything, most especially not yours. If I take a protector, I assure you, it will *not* be you."

"I wonder what it will take for you to change your mind?"

"I wonder why you are so set on having me, after our distasteful past? Revenge is a petty motive, after all. I should think you would consider it beneath you."

"I'm not interested in revenge," he replied with less than total honesty. "I'm merely intrigued by the thrill of the chase."

"You mean to say that you are utterly bored with

your indolent life and you require me to provide your entertainment?"

"Perhaps. I admit, I have never known a moment's boredom with you, Jewel."

"Only because I am able to resist you."

"But for how long?" He gave her his most charming smile. "I will contrive to forgive you for your stubbornness, love, but you are only postponing the inevitable. Sooner or later I'll have you again." Intentionally he glanced at the curtained alcove. "It might as well be tonight. Why waste this ideal setting?"

Humor tugged at the corners of her mouth. "I will not go to bed with you, Dare."

"Who needs a bed? Before the fireplace there will do quite nicely. You would look luscious spread out on a sable fur, completely nude."

He heard her sharp intake of breath at his deliberate provocation. Reaching out, he lifted a curling tress from her breast. Her hair was glorious, rich and vibrant in color, thick and silky to the touch. The softness and fragrant scent teased him as he brought it to his lips.

Stiffening, Julienne drew back and raised an eyebrow.

Assuming a look of pure innocence, Dare surveyed her. "Rumor has it that you are cold-blooded as a lover, but I know differently. I know what a pretense that icy façade is, Jewel. I know how hot you can get. . . . How hot I can make you. How a single stroke of my fingers across your stomach makes you quiver. One touch of your delicious sex and you grow wet."

With a graceful shrug, she returned an arch smile. "I told you, I am not the same green girl I was. It takes a great deal more to arouse me now."

Heat coursed through Dare at her words, at the implied challenge. He couldn't say the same; it had taken very little to arouse him tonight.

He hadn't expected to make love to her this evening. Merely to stake his claim. But he should have known the effect Julienne would have on him. How inflamed he would become by their duel of wills. The exhilaration of matching wits with her again was a stronger aphrodisiac than any drug. And the temptation to do more than provoke her was overwhelming. In truth, he had visions of throwing her down on the table, tearing her clothes off, and tasting that body he'd yearned for so much, so long ago.

His jaw clenched against the hot flood of arousal that the image induced. He couldn't remember ever hurting this much for a woman, or wanting one more. And he doubted Julienne was as indifferent as she pretended. He recognized her sexual response with a connoisseur's eye.

"Shall we put your resistance to the test?" he asked softly.

With effort Julienne met his gaze, her feelings a confusion of wanting and not wanting. It unsettled her deeply, Dare's arrogant presumption of victory. Unsettled and vexed her.

But he would not win, she promised silently. She would not make his revenge easy, letting him ride roughshod over her. She would do everything in her power to protect herself from his calculating schemes. If forced to, she would call upon a few seductive skills of her own to defend herself.

Measuring Dare, she took a sip of wine, wondering if she could hope for any better outcome. It would be supremely satisfying to beat the Prince of Pleasure at his own game—to make him fall in love with her and break his heart, as she'd publicly vowed. Regrettably, though, she didn't hold any faith in her ability to carry out her part of the wager. Dare North had long been immune to female schemes to ensnare his heart.

But if he meant to torment her, she would show him that she was his match. She was an actress. She could play the role of a femme fatale.

She wouldn't let it get out of hand, of course. She would merely arouse Dare's lust and leave him panting for more. And when she walked away dispassionately, he would begin to understand that she would never be his conquest.

Relieved to have made a decision that would allow her to take the offensive, Julienne let a tempting smile wreathe her lips. "Why not?"

She saw the instant flare of heat in his eyes and hoped that she wasn't making an irrevocable mistake.

For a long moment their eyes held. Then, taking her hand, Dare slowly turned it over and placed a kiss on the inner side of her wrist. His light caress made her tremble. Next, his lips moved over her palm, his tongue flicking the sensitive skin, and it was all she could do not to pull away.

His breath scorched her fingers as his lips moved to the tips. When he suckled the middle one, a heavy ache flowered low in her abdomen.

"I should warn you," he murmured, his voice husky. "I've learned a few things since I last knew you."

"I can imagine," she said, her own voice dismayingly breathless.

His eyes would not free her from their intensity. To

her surprise, though, he released her hand and stood. Going to the door, he locked it, then returned to her side and set the key on the table, along with the wineglass he took from her.

Time, dangerous with the undercurrents of passion, seemed to hang motionless as he stared down at her.

Her heart thudding, Julienne rose unsteadily to face Dare, unwilling to allow him the advantage. Her legs were weaker than she thought, and she leaned one hip against the table for support.

"Well?" he asked, the lazy drawl filled with challenge.

Holding his stare with bold, cool poise, she reached to unfasten the hooks at her back, slipping down first the bodice of her merino gown, then her chemise. Her breasts spilled out above the white cambric. Offering him a smile, she turned and rested her hands behind her on the table, an elegant courtesan's gesture.

His mouth twisted crookedly. "So you mean to tempt me with your luscious body?"

"Let us see who can summon the greater resistance."

"As you wish," he said, his eyes alive with delighted interest.

With one foot he shoved her chair out of his way and stepped closer, his regard moving with leisurely thoroughness over her. A pulsing began deep inside Julienne in response to his heated gaze.

She managed to conceal her quivering excitement when he slowly drew a finger along the line of her collarbone, then traced a path between her breasts. But when he reached out to cup one curving swell, Julienne felt her heart leap.

With a knowing look, Dare splayed both hands over the ripe fullness of her breasts. Her nipples tightened shamefully, responding to his wicked teasing. His thumbs caressed the rosy peaks until they were distended and hard, and Julienne had to bite her lip to keep from pleading with him to stop the torment. She didn't want him to stop. She wanted to press herself against him, wanted Dare to soothe the delicious ache he was creating.

As if he could read her mind, he took her by the arms and drew her against his chest. The full shock of his hard, supple body went through her. He was all honed muscle and lean strength—and he was wholly aroused. She could feel his rigid erection even through their layers of clothing.

She drew a steadying breath, trembling with need. She felt feverishly hot where her body was held tight against his, excruciatingly sensitive where her bare breasts rubbed the brocade fabric of his waistcoat. Yet every instinct she possessed told her Dare was fighting the same urgent need.

His own breath was rapid as he dipped his head. His lips moved against her throat, then skimmed upward over her jaw, her cheekbone. "Kiss me, Julienne," he whispered, the words like velvet on her skin.

He gave her no chance to refuse. Instead he claimed her mouth, his lips soft and rough in turn.

His kiss was shatteringly familiar. She opened for him, shuddering beneath the raw force of his passion, but he didn't seem satisfied. He slanted his mouth to deepen the kiss further, his tongue sliding in heated, sinuous rhythm within her mouth, awakening her mind and body from their coldly held reserve.

She felt as though he were drinking the breath from her. Julienne shivered uncontrollably. The bold press of his heated loins was making her weak; her soft, secret flesh melted with sleek moisture, even as a warning voice clamored in her mind, telling her to beware.

It was a struggle to remember the femme fatale role she had intended to play. Her breath was coming in soft pants when she finally pushed him away.

At least she was having the effect she wanted, she saw. A dark flush of desire stained Dare's high cheekbones, while his eyes were hot and glittering. Frowning, he raised an eyebrow, as if to demand an explanation for her delay.

Deliberately Julienne glanced down at the swelling bulge at his groin. His breeches stretched taut, concealing his straining manhood. With a siren's smile, she reached out to brush her fingers over the placket, letting her hand fondle his hardness beneath the white satin.

She heard Dare stifle a groan, saw his jaw clench. "Keep that up and we might not reach the bed."

"As you said, who needs a bed?"

Requiring no further invitation, Dare reached down to unbutton his breeches and drawers. Desire burned in his eyes as he released his swollen male flesh. Instantly his arousal jerked upward against his belly, pulsing and erect.

Julienne caught her breath at the sight of him, huge and urgent, her gaze riveted. She badly wanted to touch him, to caress the thick, satiny length, the velvety pouch of his heavy testicles. . . .

Evidently Dare wanted her just as badly. With visible impatience he leaned around her and pushed the dishes and crystal back to give them room. Then he lifted her up and set her on the edge of the table.

Julienne tried desperately to conceal her own treacherous excitement as he pulled up her skirts slowly, baring her to his gaze. It had been so long. . . .

A streaking heat shuddered through her as he stared at the dark curls crowning the apex of her thighs, at the plump folds of female flesh already moist with her own need. His own gaze remained riveted as he reached down to caress her.

All her muscles clenched at the lazy stroke of his hand along her inner thigh. She felt her breath coming short and shallow as his fingers searched out the womanly softness of her—and it faltered sharply as he slid them against her honeyed crease.

"I would say you are thoroughly aroused now," he murmured.

She could feel her will weakening, but when his fingers brushed more boldly, Julienne caught his wrist, staying his hand.

Dare's gaze narrowed on hers. His hand was still between her legs, cupping possessively. "Do you still insist on denying you want me?"

She couldn't bring herself to lie. "No," she whispered.

"Part your legs wider." It was a low, throaty command, one she wanted to obey. She shut her eyes briefly at the wild excitement coursing through her, steeling herself against the burning warmth that flowed from the palm of his hand. When his fingers gently probed her slick cleft and slid inside, she arched against him. Then his caresses became more rhythmic, and she imagined that it was Dare's magnificent arousal thrusting deep inside her. . . .

She tried to stifle a whimper, but it escaped her. In

answer, Dare stepped between her spread thighs, his intent clear.

You should stop him, a desperate warning voice urged. But the blood was pounding in her veins, stirring a fiery heat within her. She couldn't form a protest when he gripped his swollen member and eased the silken head into her quivering flesh.

Julienne gasped at the enormous, pulsing size of him. He was shockingly hard, filling her to bursting.

When he swelled upward into her clinging heat, she tried to writhe away from him, but his hands prevented her, holding her hips still. A faint smile curving his sensual mouth, he withdrew his long shaft almost completely, until she moaned aloud with the loss.

Then he surged into her again, making her softly cry out his name.

It took only one more slow plunge to set her aflame. When he delved even deeper, burying himself inside her in another demanding stroke, Julienne gave in to the ravening hunger. Softening helplessly against him, she began to answer his thrusting hips, matching his pace and his sweet, relentless rhythm.

A sob welled in her throat at the primal force building inside her. It was elemental, primitive, and Dare was using all his skill to drive her even higher. She glimpsed him as her head fell back in surrender; his teeth were clenched, his handsome features contorted with pain and pleasure as he rocked her against him.

Then rapture engulfed her. She gripped his arms fiercely as an incoherent sound of panic sounded from her throat, but his mouth captured her scream. Wildly she dug her nails into his muscles as she erupted in a fiery, shimmering explosion, but Dare responded ruthlessly, his straining thighs forcing hers even wider to prolong her ecstasy.

The powerful convulsions left her so dazed, she could only cling to Dare as he drove himself to his own convulsive climax. When his throes of passion finally diminished, she sagged against him, exhausted.

The tremors faded slowly. She could still feel him pulsing within her own sated flesh, could hear his heart hammering beneath her cheek.

When finally he pulled away, leaving her tender and aching, she could have wept.

He was silent for a moment as he fastened his breeches.

"I think we should call this a draw," he observed impassively, his voice husky yet without inflection of any kind.

Julienne stiffened, suddenly realizing what she had just allowed to happen. Her mind spinning, she glanced down at her wanton dishevelment and drew a sharp breath, aghast. Sweet heaven.

Flushing with shame, she pushed down her skirts and fumbled to straighten her chemise and bodice. She could feel Dare's gaze on her, yet she looked anywhere but at him. She felt stripped bare of all defenses, her emotions naked and exposed.

Dear God, what had she done? She hadn't expected their lovemaking to go all the way, hadn't meant for their passion to flare out of control. She had only intended to tease Dare, to torment him as he was set on doing to her. She hadn't wanted him to win so effortlessly.

Her stomach wrenched. Dare had called this battle a

draw, but he had gotten precisely what he wanted—her panting and moaning with desire for him. Damn him.

And damn her.

Despising herself, Julienne stole a glance at him. Was he feeling the same profound regret that she was?

He didn't seem happy about their carnal lapse. His face was expressionless, with no indication of the dismay that was swamping her, but at least there was no sign of triumph, either.

Then he spoke.

"Come, darling, I will take you home," he drawled, a cynical glint in his eye that mocked them both.

Julienne flinched, unable to protect herself against the pain that sliced through her at his casual dismissal. All she could do was curse herself for acting the fool.

The same witless, love-hungry fool she had been seven years ago.

Chapter
Four

Julienne felt a measure of relief four days later when she was admitted to the salon of Madame Solange Brogard. She had feared she might be the chief topic of conversation at the afternoon gathering of French émigrés. All London knew of Lord Wolverton's vow to win her and was watching for further developments with avid interest.

But the excited chatter that filled the elegant room now was punctuated with words like "Chaumont" and "Castlereagh" and predictions that "the Monster will soon fall." Thankfully, world events had overshadowed her own predicament and provided greater fodder for gossip than the scandal Dare seemed set on causing her.

Lord Castlereagh, Britain's foreign secretary, had persuaded her reluctant allies, Russia, Prussia, and Austria, to commit irrevocably to the defeat of Napoleon. After decades of war, Europe finally stood united to crush revolutionary France. The Treaty of Chaumont that had just been signed was a triumph of policy for Castlereagh, but no one was more pleased than the French nobles in exile, many of whom were in this room.

"It is only a matter of weeks now," an elderly chevalier prophesied. "And then we will see our beloved King Louis reclaim his birthright."

Several heads nodded sagely, but another gentleman contradicted him, suggesting that the Corsican's overthrow would take years longer—which began a fierce argument.

Across the crowded salon, Julienne caught the eye of the hostess, Madame Brogard. The Frenchwoman was one of her few London acquaintances whom she knew well enough to call friend, but Solange was closer to her late mother's age than her own.

Adele and Solange had been neighbors in their youth and had escaped the Terror at nearly the same time, but Solange had come to London fortified by the Brogard jewels and had soon established a salon where émigrés and bluestockings and poets gathered for clever conversation and exquisite food, both more satisfying to French palates than the stodgy prattle and bland fare most of the English thrived upon. Often the conversation was literary in nature, but today it was all political talk of the war and the new treaty and the chances for Napoleon's defeat.

Julienne accepted a glass of sherry from a footman and slowly moved through the crowd, smiling and conversing and flirting effortlessly. She was expected to be gay and dazzling and witty, even if her spirits had plunged so low they were more suited to a walking corpse.

At least forcing herself into company served to keep her emotional tumult and heartache at bay. She had been a fool to let Dare make love to her again, for it brought back such painful memories of what she had lost. Worse, she had taken no precautions against pregnancy. Seven years ago, she hadn't known how, but she couldn't claim that excuse now. It had been criminal to risk conceiving Dare's child. What a disaster that would be!

Over the past four days, she'd had abundant time to reflect on his motives for pursuing her. She could draw only one conclusion: Dare North hated her and was bent on exacting his pound of flesh.

The knowledge set a hollow pain churning inside her. It wasn't hate that Dare woke in her but hunger. Being with him again had left her shaken with the realization of her own need and stirred to life the fervent yearnings she had thought long-buried.

She had meant merely to defend herself that night, and perhaps give him a taste of his own medicine—to torment him a little as he was set on doing to her. But her plan had gone drastically awry the moment he touched her. Her reserve had melted under the heat of his passion, along with any notions of resisting him.

What an utter fool you are, Julienne swore at herself for the thousandth time. She should have been so much stronger.

Since that evening, she had made certain all their encounters were public. She had to concede, however, that Dare had won the first points in the game he had initiated.

He had appeared at the theater nightly to watch her, and once he'd distracted her so badly that she forgot a crucial line. When Dare called down to her on-stage, prompting her, much to the titillation of the audience and the ire of Edmund Kean, Julienne inwardly gritted

her teeth while giving him a deep curtsy to acknowledge the hit. Later, upon taking her bows, she had
commended Dare on his thespian talents.

"If you will permit me, my lord," she had suggested
sweetly, "I shall arrange an audition for you with the
theater manager, Mr. Arnold. No doubt you could
enjoy a splendid career treading the boards."

Her offer had made both him and the spectators
laugh.

She was forced to maintain the spirit of the game,
for the crowds were coming to watch the byplay between them as much as the theatrical drama. But Julienne determinedly avoided any more private meetings
with Dare. When she went out, she deliberately surrounded herself with her beaux. The rest of her time
she focused on her grueling schedule of work—her
nightly performances and rehearsing the lines of the
next play.

Still, that left too many hours to think of Dare as
she tossed and turned in her solitary bed each night.
She couldn't let his planned vengeance go any further. She had spent years trying to mend her shattered
heart, and he could so easily break it again.

She was startled out of her dark reverie by her
friend's greeting.

"Julienne, *mon amie, bonjour,*" Solange said in her
heavy accent. "I am so pleased you have come. I feared
you might have too many other matters demanding
your time."

"You know I try never to miss your Tuesday salons," Julienne returned as they pressed cheeks.

Solange held her away, appraising her with a keen
eye. "You look ravishing as always."

She didn't protest the lie, but returned the compliment. Madame Brogard was not considered a great beauty; her allure owed more to artifice and the skilled application of cosmetics. But with her tall, elegant figure and silvery blond hair, she possessed undeniable charisma that would always catch the eye.

"I daresay I am not the only one who will be pleased to see you," Solange added lightly. She glanced toward a far corner where a tall, fair-haired nobleman stood conversing with several ladies. "Lord Wolverton has been asking for you."

Julienne's smile froze on her lips. Good God, *Dare*.

She felt her heartbeat suddenly race in panic, even before his eyes connected with hers.

He sketched her a brief bow in acknowledgement. Then his gaze made a slow, intimate sweep of her body, traveling the length of her bronze silk gown and up again to linger on her breasts.

Flustered by his brazen scrutiny, Julienne cast him a quelling look. His lazy smile leapt back across the room.

Vexed, she turned a cool shoulder to him, but it was far more difficult to dismiss Dare from her awareness, or to deny the effect his unexpected presence had on her. Why did she have this sudden feeling that her life had begun again?

"What the devil is he doing here?" she demanded of her hostess before she considered the wisdom of curbing her tongue.

"He persuaded me to invite him. He had been told that you often attended my functions and wished for a chance to speak to you alone. He claims that you have been avoiding him, *mon amie*."

Julienne pressed her lips together without responding.

"I heard of the wager he made to win you. Are you not flattered?"

"Hardly. I find it distasteful to be made the public target of his lust and the object of his amusement. Lord Wolverton is the consummate pleasure seeker, a bored nobleman in search of diversion. He deliberately created a sensation with his antics in the theater the other evening for his own sport."

"Pooh, that was nothing. His pranks are legend, *vraiment*. Did you know that he once got Lord Lambton abysmally cup shot and stole his clothes, then had him transported to Hyde Park during the night, bed and all? Lambton caught a chill walking home with only a bedsheet to cover himself."

"No, I hadn't heard that *on-dit*," Julienne said dryly.

"And I have it on good authority that he abducted his good friend's *chère amie* to coerce Baron Sinclair into declaring his love. Lord Sin happily wed his lady afterward, but not before he called Wolverton out for the insult."

She couldn't deny that Dare would stoop to nearly any maneuver to get his own way. Seven years ago he had bought her entire shop's stock of hats simply so she would have the time to accompany him on a carriage ride and allow him to command her complete attention, she remembered. But she didn't intend to tell Solange of her past history with Dare.

Few people knew of their former betrothal, or even of their affair. During his courtship, Dare had respected her desire to keep their relationship as private as possible and had gone to great lengths to shield her from gossip. And his grandfather hadn't wanted to advertise

Dare's intentions to wed a foreign shopkeeper who was so far beneath him.

Fortunately, her friend was too busy singing Dare's praises to ask any probing questions. "I find him delightful and audaciously charming, even if he is an *anglais* and thoroughly wicked," the Frenchwoman confessed.

"Oh, yes, he is universally adored," Julienne remarked sardonically. "But I'm certain he practices to perfection that devastating charm. And his exploits are too shocking for my tastes, even if they seem to be met with approval by the rest of society."

"Not approval, precisely, but a rich marquess is permitted to do shocking things other mortals cannot. A man such as Wolverton is considered above scandal and will be forgiven nearly any sin. It is the way of the world, *n'est-ce pas?*"

Julienne nodded in agreement, but not without a trace of bitterness. If one was impoverished and untitled and a woman, she bore the brunt of society's scorn. A wealthy nobleman, on the other hand, could get away with anything short of murder—and even murder at times was not always condemned, if it came in the form of a duel. Dare had the reputation of being a law unto himself, but only the highest sticklers would censure him for it.

"He is still a conniving rogue," Julienne muttered.

"*Tiens,* but one who makes feminine hearts beat faster. Come, admit it. You cannot possibly overlook a man like him. And you cannot underestimate the irresistible lure of a rake."

No indeed, Julienne reflected with reluctance. What

woman could resist Dare's tantalizing smile, the boldness of his glance, his blatant sexual magnetism? He was striking and dangerously exciting, even more so now than when she had first known him. "He cannot be overlooked, certainly," she conceded.

"And I have heard he has other talents to recommend him in addition to his wealth and looks, such as exceptional skill and endurance in bed."

Absurdly, Julienne felt a pang of jealousy. Everyone knew of Dare's celebrated sexual experience. He'd slept with nearly every highborn woman in London, no doubt. And every woman he'd ever slept with probably fell in love with him. Dalliance for him was more than habitual; it was a compulsion.

"I confess," Solange added wistfully, "I should be very glad to be in your slippers, *mon amie*. If I were ten years younger, I would set my cap at him myself."

"You may have him with my blessing, Solange."

Her friend gave her a curious glance. "What, you do not mean to accept his protection? What would be so wrong with that? An attachment based purely on sensual pleasure . . . And the financial advantages would be enormous. Wolverton is said to be excessively generous with his mistresses."

Julienne was unsurprised by Solange's practical outlook. The French took a much more liberal view of lovemaking and carnal arrangements than the English did. But she didn't share her friend's sentiments.

"I don't intend to allow him to win our wager by becoming another of his sexual conquests."

Solange shrugged, affecting the common Gallic gesture. "Then I wish you *bon chance*. You will have your task cut out for you, I don't doubt."

At her change in tone, Julienne glanced over her shoulder to see Dare moving her way. She felt her heart leap. "Promise you will not leave me alone with him," she said quickly.

Her friend frowned. "If you seriously mean that, then *naturellement*, I will not abandon you, but Wolverton is nothing if not persistent. Perhaps you should hear what he has to say and get it over with."

After a moment, Julienne let out her breath in a sigh. "I suppose you are right." She didn't want Dare to think she was cowering from him, or that their passionate encounter four nights ago had affected her in any but the most superficial way.

Squaring her shoulders, she slipped into her role of popular actress and swept across the room to meet him.

An expectant buzz suddenly flowed around the room when she reached Dare. Julienne knew they were the object of all eyes, so she refrained from snatching her hand away when he bent to kiss it.

His tongue flickered over her fingertips, so fleetingly she might have imagined it—except that awareness flashed in those wicked green eyes, reminding her of the last time he had kissed her fingers.

She quivered at the memory. She could still feel the heavy pressure of his loins against her own, still feel his deep penetration—

Exorcising the provocative image, Julienne shook herself. Dare was deliberately trying to unsettle her composure, as usual.

Withdrawing her hand, she managed an effusive greeting for the benefit of their audience. "Ah, Lord Wolverton . . . the brightest new talent of Drury Lane.

I did not expect to see you here. I was certain you would be practicing your lines for our next encounter."

Dare's eyes sparked with amusement. "I wished to speak with you, Miss Laurent. I have been unable to get close to you with the impenetrable throng of swains around you."

"As it happens, I have been desirous of speaking to you myself." She smiled brightly. "I know much of London waits with bated breath each night to discover what new farce you will enact, but perhaps you might contain your exhibitions until *after* the scheduled performance. Edmund Kean is rather vexed with you for upstaging him, I fear."

"If it will please you, Miss Laurent, I shall certainly attempt to do better."

"It would please me very much indeed."

He placed a hand over his heart and offered her another gallant bow. "I live to make you happy."

With a glance at her nearly empty wineglass, Dare asked if she would like more sherry. When she nodded distractedly, he steered her toward the refreshment table and then to one side of the crowded room so they could have a measure of privacy.

"At last," Dare murmured.

"Why are you here, my lord?" Julienne asked without ceremony, although she lowered her voice to avoid being overheard by the nearest bystanders and preserved a pleasant expression on her face in keeping with their declared rivalry.

"As I said, I wished to speak to you. I was told I might find you holding court here, and I thought it would be easier to separate you from your gallants."

"Well, you have found me, but I would appreciate it

if in future, you would refrain from undressing me with your eyes in public."

A slow grin spread across his lips. "But admiring you is a favorite pastime of mine, *ma belle*. And you must give me some credit. I've been totally discreet. I haven't told a soul that a few nights ago you were crying with passion in my arms."

Julienne nearly choked on her sherry. Cursing herself as she tried to regain her breath, she sent him an accusing frown. She was forever being caught off guard by his audacious remarks.

He raised an eyebrow. "Are you all right, my love?"

"I would be far better if Solange never had admitted you."

"I noticed her glancing at me. Can I flatter myself that you were discussing me?"

"I don't know that you could call it flattery. She was telling me of some of your more outrageous pranks."

"And warning you to beware the dangers of the infamous scoundrel, Dare North?"

"Actually, no. Solange counts herself among the ranks of your admirers." Julienne gave him a thoughtful look. "Perhaps you might consider her as a candidate in your search for a mistress. She is available at the moment."

"I want no other mistress than you, love."

"I am *not* your love. You already have more than enough of those."

"Jealous?" he drawled with a genial smile.

"You know, my lord, you suffer from a vastly inflated belief in your own fascination. Have you nothing better to do than bedevil me?"

"To be truthful, I would far rather make love to

you. Shall I whisk you away from here? We have yet to find a real bed."

His eyes danced with laughter, and Julienne found herself torn between unwilling amusement and the urge to box his ears.

"Do you never think of anything but carnal gratification?" she asked in exasperation.

"Occasionally. On Wednesday mornings, during my regular fencing match at Angelo's Salle. Sex can prove a grievous distraction then."

She rolled her eyes. "One would think your lust had never been satisfied."

"Only when I was with you," he replied, his tone abruptly turning serious.

She felt a distinct shock at his admission.

"You managed to do what no other woman has ever done before, Jewel," he said as she stared at him.

"And what is that?"

"Bring me to the point of obsession. Despite my every instinct for self-preservation, I cannot stop wanting you."

Julienne arched an eyebrow and took another sip of sherry, managing an attitude of cool disdain.

To her relief, Dare's tone lightened. "Do you know, love, you play the role of ice maiden well, but it has the opposite effect of the one you intend. Your coolness makes a man burn for you all the more. Dares him to try melting you."

When she merely pressed her lips together, refusing to respond, he glanced around the crowded salon. "I confess surprise to find you among this den of Royalists. Most of the émigrés here are eager to see Louis XVIII on the throne. Do you share their political leanings?"

That particular question she didn't mind answering. She had neither the time nor the inclination to be drawn into the intrigues and rivalries of the French exiles. "I try to avoid politics as much as possible. I come here primarily for the literary discussions."

His glance returned to her, holding both doubt and amusement. "I never would have taken you for a bluestocking."

Julienne's gaze narrowed in real annoyance at the hint of mockery in his tone. "What is wrong with being a bluestocking? If a woman has a brain in her head, if she is well-read or interested in the world, she deserves to be scorned? A female can only be lauded if she is idle, beautiful, and feather-headed?"

"Not at all. I have immense respect for intelligent females. I consider them one of life's greatest pleasures. Why do you think I am so keen on gaining your companionship?"

He was trying to provoke her, of course, but still it stung to be jeered at for her interests. "You always did consider your intellect superior to anyone else's."

"No," he said emphatically. "Never to yours. Your scintillating wit was one of the qualities I most admired about you. I took as much pleasure in your brain as your beauty."

Discomfited again by the turn of conversation, Julienne stared down at her wineglass, but Dare apparently wasn't finished.

"I have numerous faults, *chérie,* but you may absolve me of judging a woman solely for her appearance. If I mistakenly gave you the impression that I'm averse to bluestockings, it is merely because they are usually trying to convert me to more serious pursuits. Forgive me?"

Julienne hesitated, knowing she had overreacted. In all fairness, she couldn't deny that Dare had always admired intelligence and wit in any of his acquaintances—women included—despite his complete irreverence for anything studious or sacred.

"Very well, I will absolve you of that fault, among your many. It is just that you are so proficient at provoking me, I constantly feel compelled to defend myself. You are continually thinking of new and clever ways to get under my skin." She raised her glass in salute. "I suppose I should commend you on your inventiveness."

"I think you just paid me a compliment."

"I will endeavor not to let it happen again," Julienne said dryly.

His grin flashed with charming brilliance, and she had to catch her breath at the beauty of it.

"To be truthful," she said swiftly, trying to change the subject, "I am not considered a bluestocking in this crowd. Rather I am something of a traitor."

She caught his start of surprise and wondered at it. "A traitor?" Dare repeated slowly.

"I am disdained because I am in trade. Most of these good *aristos* would rather starve than work for a living." She forced a smile. "I am only allowed into their hallowed presence because of Solange. She championed me because of her childhood friendship with my mother, but I am merely clinging to the pretense of genteel respectability."

She paused, eyeing Dare with all seriousness. "Your pursuit of me will only make their acceptance more difficult, do you realize?"

"Do you care so much for their acceptance?"

Julienne shrugged. "London can be lonely."

His gaze lingered upon her face, examining her intently. "Even with all your courtiers vying for your favors?"

Her smile this time was even more fleeting. "How would you like to be considered nothing more than a trophy, desired only for your body?"

"You want an honest answer?"

Surprised that she did, she nodded.

"I might consider it a step up from being desired only for my wealth and title."

At his suddenly grim tone, Julienne winced, remembering that Dare counted her among the ranks of greedy, title-hungry fortune hunters. She could well understand his anger at her, since she'd led him to believe she was no better than the countless other schemers who had pursued him.

After a moment, however, his dark expression faded and he shook his head. "I didn't come here to fight with you, Jewel. Instead I came to issue you an invitation. I am arranging a house party at my country house near Brighton, and I would like you to be my honored guest."

"You cannot be serious?"

"Utterly."

"And here I was just remarking on your cleverness." Julienne smiled. "You must be particularly dullwitted, my lord, if you think I will agree to be your willing victim at one of your infamous orgies."

He shook his head. "It won't be an orgy, I assure you. Don't refuse before you consider the advantages. I should imagine you would enjoy the respite. And the climate is definitely warmer than London's. Come now, I am only asking for a week of your time, ten days at the most. I thought we could depart at the end of next week. It will give you time to prepare—"

"This is one of your tricks, Dare, isn't it?"

"Not at all."

"Then why would you devise a house party?"

"Because I can think of no better way to ensure I spend any significant amount time in your company. Frankly, I don't relish chasing after you, begging for the crumbs of your attention."

"But you mean to try to win our wager."

"Of course," Dare said blandly. "But it will provide you an equal opportunity to do the same. It could put you well on your way to winning. And to show what a good sport I am, I've already invited Riddingham, and I'm prepared to include any other swains you choose. Madame Brogard, as well, if you will feel more comfortable. She can serve as your protection. We can make up several carriages for the journey south next week."

"It would comfort me greatly to have Solange there, but that is beside the point. I couldn't possibly attend. My performance schedule at the theater will prevent me from being free except for a day or two—"

"I've spoken to Arnold, and he is willing to give you the time off. For a significant remuneration, of course."

"You mean to tell me that you *bribed* him?"

"I merely offered to reimburse him for your services. He didn't want to lose the income that your absence would entail. More important, he's eager to placate his leading man. You were right about Kean being piqued by my upstaging him. Arnold is willing to let you go for a time if it means being rid of me.

"Come now, love, if it makes you feel better, you can consider it strictly a business proposition. You are an actress whom I will hire for a private performance. You can't object to earning the fee I'm willing to pay."

"How much?" Julienne asked curiously.

"How does a thousand pounds strike you?"

She couldn't stifle a gasp. That sum was more than twice the salary she would command for the entire theater season, and that was after Arnold had renegotiated her contract to reflect her higher demand.

"I don't intend to take no for an answer," Dare assured her as she deliberated. "I will simply beleaguer you until you agree to come."

She didn't doubt his statement in the least, or his determination. If he continued to infuriate Edmund Kean, Dare could destroy the career she had worked so hard to build. Arnold would fire her long before he risked losing one of the most gifted actors England had ever known.

A sudden wave of bitterness swept Julienne at her powerlessness, and she had to strive to keep her voice from trembling. "You certainly have the resources to play God with my life, Lord Wolverton, but I have worked for *years* for the opportunity to perform at Drury Lane. If you ruin this for me, I *swear* I will make you regret it."

He dipped his head slightly at her warning, but his gaze remained cool. "Then I have your agreement?"

"It seems you leave me no choice."

He bowed in polite acknowledgement of her capitulation. "Then I will leave you to your literary discussions. I suspect I've caused you enough gossip for one afternoon."

As she watched him stride away, Julienne fought the ache of tears. She was immensely glad Dare had left, yet she still had to deal with the turmoil he roused in her each time they met.

How could she possibly spend an entire week with him, even surrounded by numerous other houseguests? She felt suffocated by the prospect. To be with Dare was like sailing in the midst a storm, being plunged in and out of a sea of emotions. It was already a violent ride, and the waters would only grow more treacherous.

She knew very well what he intended. A dangerous game of temptation and conquest. He planned to seduce her and abandon her—after he had broken her pride.

Her gaze blurred. What would be left of her, she wondered, when he was done?

Suddenly realizing how morbid her thoughts had become, Julienne steeled her shoulders. She would not surrender so easily. No, devil take him! Instead she would try to beat him at his own game. If Dare insisted on forcing her hand, she would prove herself equal to his challenge.

He had admitted to having an obsession for her. Well, she would do her utmost to increase that obsession. She would make him totally besotted with her, would make him look the fool when she publicly spurned him.

She would not allow his revenge to succeed. The past seven years had toughened her, had hardened the shell around her heart. She had only to keep that shell intact against Dare—

"Is everything all right, *mon amie?*" Solange asked, appearing at her side. "Are you well?"

Julienne set her teeth and fixed a smile on her lips. "Quite well. Tell me, Solange, how would you enjoy a house party at a country estate of the audaciously charming Lord Wolverton?"

Chapter
Five

Dare left the salon, tasting victory yet strangely dissatisfied. Inexplicably he felt like a villain for forcing Julienne to accept his invitation for a week in the country.

He was unable to dismiss her from his mind as he made his way to Brooks's Club on St. James Street. He kept remembering how Julienne had looked when he first spied her across the salon this afternoon: the exquisite oval of her face, her long, slender neck, her elegant shoulders, how that bronzed-hued gown set off her skin to perfection. . . .

Her sudden appearance had tightened his loins and set his pulse leaping in midbeat.

He had expected his body to be affected, of course, but his natural physical reaction couldn't explain the fierce quickening of his heart.

He couldn't comprehend why he still wanted Julienne so desperately after all this time. Why should he crave a woman who had betrayed him without remorse? What was it about her that obsessed him so?

True, Julienne was beautiful, passionate, intelligent—the embodiment of everything he had ever desired in a woman. Of all the lovers he had ever enjoyed, none had ever measured up to her.

But she had almost destroyed him. Why was it so difficult for him to remember that?

Even now he couldn't deny the excitement she stirred in him with a single glance. Couldn't dispute that her siren's voice could still seduce him with a mere whisper. And her kiss . . . He couldn't possibly forget the incredible softness of her lips.

Julienne was an unforgettable woman who made him burn.

Dare swore in frustration, willing himself to shed the taste of her mouth and the memory of her body as she writhed beneath him.

Hell and damnation, his desire for her was nothing more than lust. Pure, raw, primal lust. Julienne had the face of a goddess, the body of a whore. The heart of a marble statue. If four nights ago he had felt a glimmer of any deeper emotion in her lovemaking, he knew he must have imagined it.

The damnable thing was, he wanted that luscious body beneath him again. He wanted to be riding between her white thighs, tangling his fingers in her glorious hair, tasting the warmth and passion he knew her capable of.

He'd thought of little else the past few days. He had slept restlessly, haunted by dreams of making love to her. He'd awakened each morning hard and aching, still dreaming of her, still touching her, smelling her, feeling her. Still yearning for her.

And for one foolish moment this afternoon he had almost let his yearning overwhelm his common sense.

It had surprised him to hear Julienne speak of her

position in society, of being caught in the netherworld between the aristocracy and demimonde, between her exiled former countrymen and those of her adopted country. Her admission had sounded so much like the truth. And to his dismay, it had touched a responsive chord within him. He had recognized her feelings of isolation, had realized that she must be lonely, as he was, although for vastly different reasons. In response he had only wanted to comfort her, to take her in his arms and soothe the hurt.

Now, however, Dare forced himself to crush the urge. Julienne Laurent was a superb actress. She knew well how to employ her arts to her own advantage. How to garner sympathy from unsuspecting fools like himself. She had that air of sensual allure perfected, along with that fragile, feminine hint of vulnerability that made him question his own urge for revenge.

But he wasn't about to be taken in by her this time, Dare promised himself. His pursuit of Julienne was merely a cover, a means to get close to Riddingham. He would never let himself become so damned susceptible again.

Dare had been surprised to receive Lucian's message this morning, for he'd thought his friend was in Devonshire. Lately Lucian was spending more of his time at his country seat with his wife as Brynn's time grew near. He couldn't retire altogether from the Foreign Office, though; his country needed him too much.

They were to meet at the library at Brooks's, when few members would be present, since the hour was much too early for dinner or gaming.

When Dare arrived at the club, however, he discovered that the meeting place had changed. He was intercepted on the street by one of Lucian's grooms, who led him to the carriage that Lucian had sent for him.

More curious than alarmed, Dare willingly made the short drive to a less elegant part of the city and was set down before a coffin maker's shop. Puzzled, he entered what appeared to be a workroom, where he was met by the smells of fresh-cut pine and the sounds of hammering and sawing. Several apprentices looked to be hard at work, although the din stopped momentarily when the solemn-face proprietor welcomed Dare as if his arrival was expected.

Immediately he was shown into a small sitting room, where Lucian awaited him.

"Weren't you supposed to be in Devonshire?" Dare said, disturbed by the grim set of his friend's features.

"I was called back to deal with a crisis." Lucian kept his voice low, no doubt so he couldn't be overheard. "It's possible that Caliban has struck again."

"Oh?"

"Lady Castlereagh's companion was found floating in the Thames yesterday morning. Come and see."

He led Dare through a door and dismissed the guard who stood watch. Corpses usually rested in rooms such as this until a coffin could be fashioned, Dare knew, to prevent body snatchers from stealing the cadavers and selling them for medical studies.

In the windowless, airless room, the stench of death struck Dare like a blow.

On a wooden table lay a shrouded body. Lucian drew down the covering to reveal a woman who had perhaps been in her early twenties. She wore a dark gown, and her bloodless, bloated face and hands contrasted starkly with the drab fabric.

"This is Alice Watson," Lucian said tersely. "Her burial was delayed until I could examine her body. And then I decided you should see what dire manner of problem we are dealing with."

Dare felt his stomach churning. He hadn't seen much death in his hedonistic past—he'd even refused to attend his grandfather's funeral—so it came as something of a shock to see Alice Watson's body lying there so brutally lifeless. A shock that Lucian no doubt had intended, Dare suspected.

"She was murdered?"

Lucian pressed his lips together. "I believe so, even though on the surface her death appears to be a suicide. She left a note expressing remorse and asking forgiveness for her sins. But the handwriting was not hers. And there are bruises on her throat that shouldn't be there if she had simply thrown herself into the river."

"What sins?"

"That wasn't clear, but for some months she apparently had been sneaking out of the house, presumedly to meet a lover. You cannot tell it now, but Miss Watson was said to be pretty. She was a poor relation who came to London to keep her ladyship company after Lord Castlereagh left for France last December."

"Could her lover have killed her?" Dare mused.

"Possibly. Miss Watson suddenly started wearing a rose-shaped pearl broach that was thought to be a gift from him. But the broach is missing from her possessions. And see, the collar of her gown is torn. She could have been wearing the broach the night she was killed. And why would she have ripped it off if she committed suicide?"

"It could have been taken from her body by whoever fished her out of the river—mudlarks, rookery thieves. . . ."

"Perhaps," Lucian conceded. "But there is another coincidence that seems highly suspicious—and the reason I was called. Several of Lord Castlereagh's letters to his wife are missing. The girl could easily have taken them. Admittedly the odds are long, but Caliban could have seduced her in an attempt to gain state secrets and learn of Castlereagh's plans."

Dare frowned thoughtfully. Since the end of last year, England's foreign secretary had been in France, negotiating with the Allied Powers not only to ensure Napoleon's defeat but to begin discussions on how to settle Europe afterward—the most pressing issue being whether to put a Bourbon king back on the French throne.

"Caliban could not have been pleased by the recent treaty Castlereagh orchestrated at Chaumont," Dare observed.

"No. And doubtless he would like nothing better than to scuttle any future negotiations. England holds the purse strings, but Castlereagh controls those strings, which makes him nearly as powerful as Napoleon himself."

"You think Lord Castlereagh might be in danger?"

"I confess that worries me. I've sent a report to him at Chaumont, warning him to be on his guard. And I've put an agent of my own both in his London household and on his staff in France. But that might be inadequate." With a final glance at the poor girl's body, Lucian covered her again. "Come. I expect you've seen enough."

He led Dare from the room and nodded brusquely to the coffin maker, who scurried off to ready the body for burial.

Out on the street, Dare dragged in a deep breath. The London air was ripe with the usual odors of soot and refuse, but it seemed like perfume after the fetid stench of decaying flesh behind him.

Yet he thought he understood his friend's reason for bringing him: Lucian intended to drive home the seriousness of their mission—finding Caliban and putting an end to the death and destruction he orchestrated.

Dare waited until they had settled into Lucian's carriage and were on their way back to Brooks's Club before he asked the question that had struck him almost from his first moment of seeing Lady Castlereagh's companion's corpse. "Was Riddingham involved in any way with the Watson girl?"

"We have no proof he knew her, but he did attend a rout at Lady Castlereagh's last week. He could have seduced the girl over the past few months, before his visit to Yorkshire." Lucian met Dare's gaze gravely. "This is even more reason to hope your investigation of Riddingham bears fruit soon. I am having him watched, but my agents cannot be too obvious for fear of giving away our suspicions."

It was time to tell Lucian of his own scheme, Dare knew. "I'm planning to hold a house party at the end of next week and have invited Riddingham and some of his cronies. It might generate some new leads. I pressed Riddingham further about the dragon ring he wears—told him I wanted one like it and asked again about how he won it at piquet. He claimed he couldn't remember specifically who lost the ring to him, but he recalled some of his friends who were in the game."

"Indeed?" Lucian said thoughtfully.

"So I arranged to get them together. Riddingham intends to come, if only to keep me from worming my way into Miss Laurent's affections."

"Then your campaign to woo her is succeeding?"

Dare's mouth twisted wryly. "I wouldn't phrase it quite so optimistically. She is to be my houseguest at least. I made certain she will be there to give Riddingham an inducement to come. I mean to observe both of them more closely . . . perhaps search his possessions. When I was at Riddingham's estate last month, I never found myself alone long enough to examine the place or try to discover a vault."

"You should look for ciphers, names, anything that might lead us to determine if Riddingham has an alternate identity. Scrutinize his friends as well."

Dare nodded in understanding.

"As for your Miss Laurent . . ." Lucian added after a moment. "I've investigated her background, Dare. There's not even a whisper that she might be working for the French or have Bonapartist leanings."

"She claims to have no interest in politics, but I don't know that I can believe her or trust her avowals of patriotism. Caliban could have found some means to extort her cooperation. You've warned me often enough that blackmail is his specialty. Faith, your own wife and brother-in-law were caught in his clutches."

He felt Lucian studying him. "Miss Laurent's aristocratic heritage came as a surprise to me. Did you know she is a count's daughter?"

"Even more reason to be wary of her. Émigrés make prime targets for bribery—forced into a life of exile with little or no income, dependent on the generosity of others. If Riddingham is Caliban, it's not beyond possibility that he corrupted her. She is certainly greedy enough to sell to the highest bidder."

Too late Dare recognized the bitterness in his tone and saw how his friend's penetrating regard sharpened.

"You once said you had offered marriage to a woman," Lucian observed slowly. "Is she the one?"

"Regrettably . . . yes." Glancing away, Dare stared out the carriage window to avoid his friend's scrutiny. "But our betrothal lasted less than a month."

"I'm surprised I never heard any rumors of it in the scandal sheets. I should have thought the prosect of your marriage would be considered an earthshaking event."

"We kept it private." He hadn't flaunted Julienne as he might have other women. In fact, his desire to protect her was one reason Dare had realized he was serious about her. He hadn't wanted her reputation to be tarnished by her associating with a man of his rakish notoriety.

How laughable his concern seemed now.

"You must have loved her a great deal to come the point of proposing."

Oh, yes, Dare thought darkly. He'd been young and in love for the first time in his life, as starry-eyed as any infatuated adolescent. According to the poets, first love was always wild, intense, fervent, but that magical summer with Julienne had blazed like a flame. Each small moment was burned deep into his heart . . . the pleasure, the torment. . . .

"I believed I loved her at the time," Dare admitted tersely. "Certainly I would have wed her but for my grandfather's interference." *And if I hadn't found her with her other lover.*

"The 'old bastard'?"

"Yes." His mouth curled as he glanced back at Lucian. "You're aware my father was killed in a duel? Well, Grandfather always feared I would become a wastrel just like my father—follow the same path to destruction. And wedding a 'scheming Frenchy' would not only have lead to my ruin, it would have tainted our illustrious line. When the old bastard learned of my betrothal to Miss Laurent, he threatened to disinherit me. And the lady wanted greater wealth than I could give her without the Wolverton fortune."

Lucian was silent for a moment as he digested that information. "And the experience was enough to make you shun the married state for good."

"Quite."

He had escaped countless marriage traps in the years since Julienne. But never again had he allowed any other woman to wield that kind of power over him. And he had always been coolly indifferent to any feelings of devotion he might have aroused in his lovers.

"I've noted your partiality for brunettes," Lucian remarked. "Does Miss Laurent have any bearing on your preference?"

A ripple of shock went through Dare. He had never realized it before, but he did indeed tend to choose women who resembled Julienne.

"A rather astute observation, my friend," he drawled, hiding his dismay beneath an amused smile.

"I trust you won't be offended if I make another astute observation, then. I think you might be more than a little prejudiced against Miss Laurent because of your past history with her."

"I won't dispute you. But what the devil does it matter?"

"Because your feelings can't be allowed to interfere with your mission. I want you to recruit her to work for us, Dare."

He narrowed his eyes in surprise as he returned Lucian's gaze. "You want Julienne Laurent to spy for the Foreign Office?"

"Why not? She has entrée into the French émigré community and could pass on any information about traitorous activity. And it's possible she could help you prove whether or not Riddingham is Caliban."

"I just told you I don't trust her."

"And I suggested that your judgment may be clouded. Are you certain you aren't acting out of revenge for whatever wrongs she may have done you?"

He did indeed want revenge—Dare couldn't deny it. But he wasn't willing to acquit Julienne of complicity so easily.

"What if she actually is in league with Riddingham?" he asked. "And even if not, were I to request her help, she could warn him of our suspicions merely to spite me."

"It would be a risk, yes. But I have complete faith in your legendary charm. You'll be able to handle her. And with her own charms and skills as an actress, she can doubtless get closer to Riddingham than you will be able to. My advice is to find a way to test her loyalties without compromising your position. Devise a plan to determine if she is trustworthy."

Dare's jaw tightened. He would never be certain if Julienne was trustworthy, even when he had her writhing beneath him with both legs wrapped around his waist. Especially not then.

But his friend would not give up. "You need only use your instincts, Dare."

That was the trouble. He couldn't trust his instincts, for they had betrayed him once before. He was terrified they would do so again. Lucian was certainly right; his judgment of Julienne was clouded by the past. And his fierce urgency to claim her again only compounded the problem.

Lucian was right on another point, Dare knew. Whatever his feelings for her, he couldn't let them interfere with his task. Too much was at stake. And if he expected his doubts regarding Julienne to be believed, he would need to show proof of her guilt. More critically, he needed to prove it to himself. One way or another, he needed to *know*.

Whether or not she was a traitor, however, his mind was made up. Had been the second he had laid eyes on her again.

He wanted Julienne back in his bed. And he intended to have her.

Chapter
Six

It was a large party that left London the following Friday. Julienne found herself surprised at the assortment of guests Dare had chosen. There were some two dozen of them, of varying ages and classes.

Of the females, she suspected at least three were demireps, including a noted actress who regularly performed at Covent Garden. But there were also some older ladies in addition to Madame Brogard, one of whom was a dowager countess. Most surprising were the two genteel wedded couples he had invited—to add respectability to the party, Julienne concluded.

As for the gentlemen, they were mostly members of the Quality. Several were high-ranking noblemen who seemed to be close acquaintances of Dare's—doubtless some of his Hellfire colleagues—while Viscount Riddingham had brought two of his friends. Bringing up the rear of the parade of vehicles were three coaches full of servants.

Julienne had no maid of her own. Normally she shared an arrangement with several other actresses at Drury Lane, dividing the services of a woman who functioned as dresser, seamstress, laundress, and wardrobe mistress. But Solange had offered the use of her own lady's maid during the house party.

The March day was crisp and clear and quite pleasant. Many of the gentlemen, including Dare, rode beside the carriages for the trip south, but Julienne was very glad not to be forced to endure his company in the intimate confines of a post chaise.

Instead she found herself enjoying the camaraderie of several of the ladies. Amazingly they seemed to accept her with little reservation, perhaps because of Solange's distinguished reputation. Or perhaps because anyone who was on familiar terms with the scandalous Dare North wouldn't recoil at knowing a mere actress.

They made the trip in easy stages, stopping frequently to change horses and partake of refreshments, and arrived in the late afternoon.

For the past ten miles, Julienne had admired the picturesque view of the rolling South Downs, but now they turned between iron entrance gates onto a rhododendron-lined drive and drove through an artfully landscaped park.

"*C'est magnifique,*" Solange murmured, and Julienne had to agree: across a sweeping expanse of lawns stood a majestic mansion of mellow red brick, gleaming in the sunlight.

Seeing the splendor of Dare's estate gave her a stark reminder of the vast difference in their stations—a rich nobleman who had inherited his family fortune and a barely respectable actress who'd always had to struggle for her living.

As the passengers disembarked, she was told by one

of the ladies that beyond these cultivated grounds lay beautiful gardens. And one of the gentlemen spoke up, remarking on Dare's superb racing stables.

"Racing stables?" Julienne asked Viscount Riddingham, who had appeared at her side to offer his arm.

"Wolverton breeds and raises racehorses," he replied rather stiffly.

Dare's friend Lord Peter Fulbrook added affably, "Not just any racehorses. Dare has some of the best horseflesh in the country."

"I confess I am eager to inspect his stables," Riddingham admitted. "Reportedly he has two Derby prospects."

Julienne smiled. "Is that why you accepted his invitation, my lord? To view his horses? And to think I flattered myself that you wished to be with me."

The viscount returned a sheepish grin. "But of course, Miss Laurent. The stables were merely an added inducement."

Julienne caught the narrow glance Dare gave her and was inwardly heartened. Part of her plan was to encourage Lord Riddingham as much as possible this week. If this house party was to be a competition for her favors, then she intended to see that Dare had a satisfactory rival.

She was glad, however, that he didn't single her out in particular when he turned the guests over to his staff to be settled in their rooms. It was agreed that they would enjoy a short rest before dinner and then meet in the drawing room at eight o'clock.

The interior of the house was just as magnificent as the exterior, Julienne saw as she was led upstairs to an elegant bedchamber. She took the opportunity to admire the splendid gardens below her window before she bathed and changed with the help of Solange's maid.

By the time she made her way to the drawing room on the lower floor, she was a few minutes late and most of the company had already gathered.

At her entrance, Dare felt his pulse leap. Julienne wore an apricot silk gown of stunning elegance, and the low-cut bodice caressed her figure as lovingly as he longed to do.

He muttered a silent oath, deploring not only his body's reaction but the unbidden eagerness that filled his chest.

All the gentlemen who were seated came quickly to their feet in appreciation of her dazzling beauty. When she apologized for her tardiness, Riddingham answered for them all. "No apologies necessary, Miss Laurent. You are worth waiting for. You make a most fetching sight."

She looked far better than simply fetching, devil take her, Dare thought. Despite his every intention, his gaze fastened hungrily on her. That dress was worse than being naked. Julienne looked utterly female, lush and fragile at the same time.

Her dark hair was piled high on her head with a casual artistry that made him yearn to destroy it. He clenched his jaw as he had an unbidden vision of her glorious hair spilled in splendid disarray across silken pillows. He wanted nothing more than to strip her naked, exposing her entire body to his gaze . . . to his hands and mouth. The mere thought of having her bare breasts in his hands, then sucking them till she moaned, made him instantly hard.

But first he would have to chase away the damned wolves surrounding her. Riddingham led the pack, Dare saw with disapproval. The bloody cur was eyeing her chest, pausing brazenly on the soft, swelling fullness of her bosom.

Just then Julienne laughed at something the viscount said, and Dare felt himself tense with jealousy.

A moment later, though, she turned and caught his own gaze. When she met his deliberate stare, his brow lifted mockingly. Yet he wasn't able to discompose her. Instead the look Julienne returned was cool, self-possessed, and full of challenge.

They were the eyes of a woman who knew her power, Dare realized.

A stab of desire shot through him so raw, so hot that all he could do was wait for the savage ache to ease.

Turning away then, Julienne gave him the elegant line of her back. Her obvious dismissal filled him with frustration. They were playing at seduction, but he was no longer confident of winning the game at which he was so expert. He'd spent countless sleepless nights since having her, lying in bed alone, aching for her. Nor was his body all that ached. The painful tightness in his chest was the throbbing of an old reopened wound.

Dare ground his teeth together. For nearly seven years he had ruthlessly sealed away the part of him that Julienne had left savagely lacerated and bleeding. He would do so again if it took his last ounce of strength.

Julienne had difficulty enjoying the next few hours, even though she wasn't required to endure Dare's close proximity. He accompanied the ranking female guest—the dowager countess—in to dinner and sat at the head of the table, while Julienne was seated much farther down.

The repast was sumptuous, with five courses and dozens of removes, and even the highly discriminating Solange praised the fare. Reportedly Dare had sent his London chef ahead days earlier to prepare for his guests' arrival. But Julienne was too conscious of the awkwardness of her position here at his home to do justice to the feast. Everyone present, she knew, had heard of the wager. And whether or not she was to provide the entertainment for the week, her relationship with Dare was sure to be the focus of all eyes.

She did her best, however, to give her attention to her dinner partners. The one on her right was one of Riddingham's friends, a soft-spoken gentleman named Martin Perrine. His pleasant, self-deprecating manner contrasted sharply with that of Riddingham's other friend, Sir Stephen Ormsby.

When the talk turned to horse racing, Julienne politely asked Mr. Perrine if he was involved in the Turf.

Sir Stephen laughed and answered for him. "Martin is a younger son with no prospects to speak of. He can scarcely afford the cost of a hired hack, much less a string of racehorses."

Mr. Perrine's pained expression was one of acute embarrassment, and Julienne hastened to reply. "I understand that only the wealthiest nabobs can afford the expense of racing. To my mind, it seems a shocking waste. I suppose that is why it is called the sport of kings."

Perrine's forced smile held a hint of gratitude, and Julienne soon changed the subject. Yet she couldn't help glancing at the nobleman at the head of the table. Dare could easily have been mistaken for royalty with his aristocratic countenance. That high brow and classic bone structure belonged to the prince in a fairy tale. And he was reputed to be one of the wealthiest men in the kingdom. He could well afford a lengthy battle between them, bribing her associates and purchasing her time for outrageous sums.

Julienne felt a sharp twinge of dismay as she wondered yet again how she could possibly defend herself against Dare with her own meager resources.

She was glad when the ladies repaired to the drawing room, leaving the gentlemen to their port, but her respite was short-lived since the gentlemen soon joined them.

When someone suggested they have some music, Julienne found herself approached by Lord Riddingham. "You sing like an angel, Miss Laurent. Will you do us the honor?"

She glanced up at Dare, who had moved to stand near her chair. He had offered her a huge sum to attend his house party, but they hadn't actually discussed the terms of her employment.

Resuming her assigned role, she gave him a provocative smile. "So, Lord Wolverton, am I to sing for my supper?" she asked, a challenging edge to her voice.

"Not unless you wish to."

"I believe I shall decline then. I prefer to devote my energies to winning our wager."

Dare's mouth curved in his notorious, wicked grin.

"I look forward to your performance with great anticipation."

Riddingham looked from her to Dare, evidently feeling the sudden sexual tension that crackled between the two of them, and hastened to intervene. "It is just as well, I expect. None of the ladies wish to be outshone by you, Miss Laurent."

Several of the ladies did indeed look relieved when Julienne chose to play cards. They took turns performing on the pianoforte and singing, while the rest of the company made up several tables of whist and one of piquet.

That dinner set the tone for the house party's evening entertainments, but during the next few days, numerous other amusements were offered for their pleasure: riding, playing pall-mall and battledore on the lawns, strolling through the magnificent gardens, and an historical excursion to the local ancient hill forts and shafts where flint arrowheads were once mined.

The gentlemen in particular were anxious to view Dare's prime horseflesh and rose early each morning to watch his racers at their training gallops. They were preparing for the 2000 Guineas to be run at Newmarket in May and the Derby at Epsom Downs in early June.

The first half of the week, Julienne did her best to maintain her public battle with Dare but tried never to be alone with him, determined to avoid repeating the regrettable sexual intimacy of their last private encounter.

Yet evading him proved surprisingly easy. He performed his duties as host with impeccable grace and charm. And to the delight of his guests, he flirted with her outrageously, his rakish wit keeping Julienne constantly on her toes. But he made no effort to seduce her or lure her into seclusion as she expected.

His strategy bewildered her a little. She didn't believe for one moment that he had given up the chase. Dare was a master of subtle manipulation. She suspected he meant to lull her into a false sense of security—but if so, it wasn't working. His delay merely heightened her tension.

She felt on edge in Dare's presence and far too aware of the heat that shimmered in her veins at his merest glance. And when he was absent, she found her heart beating in anticipation of seeing him again. Worse were the charged emotions that kept surfacing between them at the least instigation.

When the party partook of an alfresco picnic on Monday, Julienne couldn't help contrasting the formality of it with the simple picnics she had once enjoyed with Dare. Nor could she forget the scorching memories of the last time they had dined out-of-doors together, when Dare had been far more interested in devouring her skin than the fare.

Now a long table had been set up by servants beneath a beech tree and covered with a pristine white cloth, while footmen served numerous delicacies on china plates and wine from crystal goblets. The blankets upon which the guests lounged seemed the only remnants of those days.

Except perhaps Dare himself. His hair shone with the same flaxen brilliance in the sunshine, his smile was just as wicked when he laughed, his gaze just as compelling.

She found that gaze fixed on her when Solange complimented him on the magnificence of his estate.

"I confess," he replied with a bow of acknowledgement, "I am rather fond of it myself. I purchased the property some years ago when I was looking to set up my racing stables. I much prefer this residence to the family seat I inherited from my grandfather. Wolverton Hall holds several unpleasant memories for me . . . particularly of the last summer I was there."

His gaze locked with Julienne's for a moment, and she felt herself wince at his unspoken accusation.

Her first defensive thought was that Dare would never have inherited his grandfather's estate if she had eloped with him as he'd asked her to. But it hurt too much to remember that magical summer that had ended in such devastation for her.

Pasting a smile on her face, Julienne rose abruptly. "I can certainly understand the appeal of this lovely setting." She gestured toward the stream that meandered nearby. "I wonder if there are any fish to be seen. Lord Riddingham, would you be so kind as to escort me there?"

She took the viscount's proffered arm, yet she couldn't dismiss Dare so easily. She was much too conscious of his magnetism and his studied neglect of her. For the remainder of the afternoon, he gave his undivided attention to his other guests.

And the ladies at least responded with delight. Julienne watched his performance with growing frustration.

It irked her, the way he tantalized all the females in the party with his careless, seductive charm. And the way they all fawned over him in return. Yet she couldn't fault them. Dare North was the most seductive, fascinating man she had ever known, and she found herself wishing she could be the focus of his devout attention instead of all the others—

When she suddenly realized the direction of her thoughts, Julienne scolded herself furiously. She would not be jealous of his lovers or she would go mad.

It was the following day when she intentionally violated her own plan to avoid him in private. The company went riding that afternoon, and during their return, her horse threw a shoe and came up lame. Julienne dismounted at once, as did Dare. Upon inspecting the animal's leg and hoof, he pronounced the injury merely a bruised sole and told the party to ride on ahead while he led the mare home.

When Julienne hesitated, Riddingham offered to let her ride double with him, but Dare intervened quickly, offering his mount.

She allowed Dare to lift her up on his horse but then changed her mind, saying that she disliked abandoning Lord Wolverton.

When Riddingham started to argue, she shook her head gently. "No, please, Hugh, go on ahead. I will come to no harm. I trust Lord Wolverton can act the gentleman for a brief while. And I have something I wish to say to him, in any case."

When the party obliged, leaving them alone, she felt Dare's gaze settle on her.

"Hugh, is it? So you're on a first-name basis with Riddingham?"

Julienne shrugged, feigning nonchalance. "We have

had an excellent opportunity to become better acquainted over the past few days."

"I can't fathom why you spend so much of your
time with him when you would enjoy yourself far
more with me."

"That is certainly a matter for debate."

Dare didn't reply to her jibe at first but instead
coaxed the injured horse forward with a flow of sooth-
ing words. Julienne brought her mount alongside,
matching the mare's slow, painful steps, but listened
with dismay. Dare might have been speaking to a lover
with his velvet-edged voice. In fact, she could remember him using precisely that tone with her during a
soul-wrenching bout of passion as he cooled the flames
and then urged her on to even greater heights.

When after a moment he turned his attention from
the injured mare and glanced up at her, she was certain
he saw the flush on her cheeks.

"At last," he said in a casual tone. "I am gratified finally to have you to myself. If I'd known all it would
take was a lame horse, I might have sacrificed one of
my beasts sooner. I've had the very devil of a time trying to steal you away from your devotees." His gaze
slid down her body. Her petticoats were hiked up, exposing a good deal of leg, since she was riding astride
instead of sidesaddle. "I can't fault them. Every man
wants to bask in your beauty."

"I don't care to hear your empty flattery, my lord,"
Julienne replied as she stirred uneasily in the saddle.

Dare apparently noticed her discomfort. "Would
you prefer to walk?"

"Actually, I would. I have never been much of a
horsewoman."

"I remember. But you are safer up there, out of reach." He let his remark sink in before adding, "So what did you wish to say to me that isn't fit for the ears of my guests?"

"I should like to know what you are up to."

"What do you mean?"

Julienne looked down at him in appraisal. "You went to a great deal of trouble and expense to coerce me here, and yet you have made no attempts at seduction since my arrival. I feel like a mouse under the cat's paw, waiting to be devoured."

"And here I thought I deserved some credit for showing restraint and not making a nuisance of myself." He raised an eyebrow. "What? Did you expect I would bring you here and assault you? That I would have my wicked way with you in front of all my guests?"

"I certainly would not put it past you."

Dare smiled that celebrated smile, devastating and suggestive. "My deepest apologies if you are feeling neglected, *chérie*. If you will climb down from that horse, I will be most happy to apply my best efforts at seduction."

She wanted to deny that she was feeling neglected, but absurdly it was true. She would tread over hot coals, however, before she allowed Dare to know it. "I don't wish you to seduce me. It is simply that I don't trust you. I think you are planning something, and I would like to know what it is."

At her remark about trust, his mouth tightened momentarily, making Julienne regret her choice of words.

Taking a steadying breath, she tempered her complaint. "You have comported yourself as such a gentleman recently that I scarcely recognize you. I keep waiting for you to show your true colors. I thought you intended to win our wager."

"Oh, I do," he said with infuriating smugness. "But allow me to point out that you've made no significant effort to win our wager yourself. What has stopped you? It would take little more than a glance to have me drooling at your feet like those other dim-witted saps. You could have me quaking with just a touch."

The image of Dare shuddering in her arms was wholly arousing and infinitely disturbing, and so was his next remark.

"What do you say that I visit your rooms tonight? We could take up where we left off two weeks ago, but this time we would enjoy a comfortable bed. I assure you, it would vastly improve my mood. I'm finding that celibacy doesn't agree with me in the slightest. It not only has a gravely deleterious effect on my spirits but on my body as well. I feel as if I'm on fire all the time."

Strangely, Julienne felt a measure of relief at his offer. *This* was the Dare North she knew—lustful, seductive, and oh so tempting. But no matter how he had just bolstered her flagging self-esteem with his unexpected admissions, she didn't intend to repeat her mistake of two weeks ago by letting him make love to her.

"Do you know, I believe I will ride on ahead after all," she observed, gathering the reins.

"Coward," he murmured, amusement lacing his voice.

"Not at all," Julienne retorted in a dulcet tone. "I am merely weary of listening to your tedious propositions."

As she spurred her mount forward, she heard Dare's soft laughter following her. But whatever guilt she might have felt for abandoning him dissipated when shortly she passed a groom leading a fresh horse for him.

When she arrived at his residence, she was told by the august butler that the other guests had gathered in the drawing room for tea. Julienne went upstairs to her bedchamber to change her riding habit, but once she had done so, she suddenly found herself reluctant to face the company.

Flinging herself on her bed, she lay staring up at the canopy overhead, feeling restless and dissatisfied and more melancholy than she had any right to feel. It dismayed her how Dare could hold such power over her, no matter what he said or did.

After another quarter hour, however, she finally rose and left her bedchamber, intending to go below to join the company.

She froze when she spied Dare farther down the corridor. He was still in his riding clothes, and he had just emerged from a bedchamber that was not his own.

Dare froze as well. He had expected Julienne to be with the others. He'd paid the Covent Garden actress Fanny Upcott to keep Riddingham occupied while he searched the viscount's room, looking for any incriminating evidence. It was unfortunate that Julienne had discovered him in the act.

Dare set his jaw, knowing he could either try to bluff his way out or risk telling her the truth.

Still weighing the decision, he moved toward her.

"I suppose you have a good reason for being in Lord Riddingham's bedchamber?" she remarked when he reached her.

Meeting her puzzled gaze, he raised an eyebrow.

"How do you know which bedchamber belongs to Riddingham?"

"Because I've seen him entering it before. And pray don't think to avoid my question by changing the subject. What were you doing in there? You are far too wealthy to steal his possessions." When Dare hesitated, Julienne added tartly, "I doubt you want me to tell him that you have been rifling through his belongings."

It was clearly a threat, one that rankled Dare. Thinking to intimidate her, he stepped closer and braced one hand on the wall behind Julienne, deliberately crowding her. He could feel her soft bosom against his chest, her thighs pressed hard against his, and the sudden ache in his loins grew and spread to the rest of his body. Even more deliberately he reached up to splay his hand between her breasts and felt her heart jump against his palm.

Julienne did indeed feel intimidated. The neckline of her afternoon gown was not immodestly low, but she deplored the intensely wicked sensation of Dare's warm hand through the fabric, of his fingers brushing her skin above the bodice.

Taken aback, she stared at the sleek gold column of his throat and the pulse that beat there. Absurdly she wanted to bury her face in the curve in his neck and taste him.

Then he bent his head to nibble her lower lip. Every inch of their bodies touched, scorching her. Without volition, she parted her lips.

"Kiss me, Julienne," he murmured in his husky lover's voice. "Kiss like you mean it. Mold your lips to mine . . . plunge your tongue into my mouth. . . ."

A moan welled up in her throat as he proceeded

to show her what he wanted. Her lips burned beneath his deep, penetrating kiss, while her body turned molten. Yet even then, her mind was protesting violently, trying to comprehend the reason for his sudden sensual assault.

He was merely attempting to distract her. . . . That was it, she thought, suddenly furious at his underhanded tactics.

Her heart hammered as she tore her mouth away. "How dare you—" she began, struggling to elude his grasp, but his mouth clamped down on hers, smothering her angry words.

Flames fanned out over her body, burning her, inciting her as his arms came around her. Somehow, though, she found the strength of will to resist his seduction. Her head reeling, she forced her hands between them and shoved at Dare's chest, finally making him break his hold and his kiss.

"Stop it! Just stop!" Her breath ragged, she glared up at him. "I want to know what the devil you were doing in those rooms."

His lips were still moist from kissing her, and she saw them press together in a tight line. "I'll tell you, but not here in the hall."

Opening her bedchamber door, he pushed her through and followed, shutting them in together.

Suddenly feeling skittish about being here alone with Dare, Julienne moved halfway across the room, out of reach.

"Well?" she demanded, still breathless.

"Riddingham could be a traitor," he said simply.

She stared at him. "What are you talking about?"

"Last year a nobleman calling himself Caliban

wreaked havoc on our war efforts, smuggling stolen gold to Napoleon. . . ."

Julienne listened in astonishment as Dare told her a shocking tale of murder and blackmail, and about the hunt for Caliban and a ruby-eyed dragon ring. That Dare himself might be involved in trying to rid the country of a traitor had been the furthest conceivable thing from her mind.

"And you think Riddingham might be Caliban?" she said slowly at the conclusion of his story.

Where his gaze had been guarded before, Dare's eyes were now narrowed, watching her reaction. "He has the ring . . . although he claims to have won it at piquet. It's possible Caliban decided that keeping so unique an ornament in his possession was dangerous. He might have deliberately palmed it off on Riddingham to divert attention from himself, to throw us off the scent."

She frowned, hesitating to believe such accusations without proof. Seven years ago she herself had been unjustly accused of treason by Dare's grandfather, and she would never leap to condemn anyone else, no matter how strong the suspicions.

"Somehow I find it hard to believe that Riddingham could be a mastermind of espionage. He is quite genial and possesses exquisite manners, but I don't consider him particularly clever. I should think a traitor of the caliber you're suggesting would have sharper wits than I've seen of his."

"I've had similar thoughts," Dare replied. "But he's our only link to Caliban, and I have to follow his trail, no matter how far-fetched."

"Why you? I am frankly astounded that you would be involved in playing spy."

"Worthless fribble that I am?"

Julienne felt her cheeks flush. "I didn't say that. But you *are* known as the Prince of Pleasure. Your part in this seems just as far-fetched as Riddingham's."

"All the more reason for me to be the one to investigate him—because he is unlikely to suspect me. In fact, I invited him here so I could keep a close eye on him."

A startling thought struck Julienne like a blow; it took her breath away. "Is *that* why you decided to pursue me? So you could watch Riddingham?"

Dare's expression was shuttered. "Initially, perhaps. But he's no longer the sole reason. Once we made our wager, I realized how badly I wanted to win it."

Her thoughts whirling, Julienne raised a hand to her temple.

"Actually this house party allowed me to observe some of Riddingham's friends as well," Dare added. "He professes that both Ormsby and Perrine were in game when he won the ring. But nothing in their behavior thus far supports the possibility of either of them being Caliban. And I've searched their rooms and found nothing questionable."

Julienne still didn't respond as she tried to take in his extraordinary revelation: Dare had used her to get closer to his real target. Their entire wager had been a ploy from the beginning.

"So do you intend to warn Riddingham of my suspicions?" Dare asked when she was silent.

"Of course not," she said absently.

He raised a skeptical eyebrow. "You will have to forget this conversation ever took place. If you begin treating Riddingham any differently, you could give the game away."

Julienne's chin came up at that. "You don't need to instruct me how to play a role. I am an excellent actress."

"I know," he drawled mockingly, yet she couldn't help hearing the edge of bitterness in his tone.

When she gave him a sharp glance, he returned a dark stare, his gaze hot, piercing, accusatory. Suddenly Julienne was unbearably aware of the intimacy of being here alone with him.

"You needn't worry that I will give you away," she assured Dare as she brushed past him. "I plan to maintain the ridiculous charade of our wager."

She was about to open the door when his strong arms reached out to draw her back.

Julienne held herself rigid, not daring to breathe. "Let me go, please."

But Dare didn't release her. Instead his arms came around her shoulders. Her pulse leaping, Julienne bit her lip, deploring the way his physical presence engulfed her senses.

"It isn't a charade," he murmured. "I still want you, Jewel."

His breath stirred her hair and sent chills all over her. Even as she shivered, his warm hands slipped inside her bodice and began to play tantalizingly with her nipples.

Julienne squeezed her eyes shut, fighting the instinctive desire to flee for her life—and the deeper desire to surrender to his caresses. She wanted to melt against his warmth. . . .

"My beautiful Jewel," he whispered in that erotic, masculine voice that never failed to bring her senses alive.

Oh, God, she thought, aching as his tongue traced the shell of her ear. His fingers tightened on her stiffened nipples, and she caught her lip between her teeth as a fiery spasm of pleasure shot down to her lower abdomen.

She shook her head, struggling desperately against her long-stemmed hunger. She hungered for physical warmth, for Dare.

"I want you," he repeated. "I want you hot and wild and burning with desire for me." His whisper filled her mind, his words a rich promise, husky, lavish with sensuality. "Say you want me, too, Julienne."

She did want him. She had been alone so long. She craved the intimacy of Dare's touch, needed it. . . .

Whimpering softly, she arched against his arousing fingers. His seductive caresses were scorching her, shaking her resolve, shredding her will . . . reminding her of all he could make her feel, of all the pleasure he could give her, all the devastating hurt—

Her throat constricted at the stab of remembered pain.

"No," Julienne protested, her whisper wild and low. "I don't want this, Dare. I don't want you."

Drawing a shaky breath, she wrenched herself away, then pulled open the door and fled.

Alone, his arms empty, Dare shut his eyes and cursed. His senses still swam with the elusive essence that was unmistakably Julienne's; his body still ached for her. He was hard and hotter than hell.

He could almost feel the wet heat of her surrounding him, feel her gliding tightly around his throbbing shaft. . . .

Yet despite his body's discomfort, the fierce ache in his chest had somehow eased. Julienne had seemed completely taken aback by his revelations about Caliban and his reasons for searching Riddingham's rooms. She didn't appear to be in league with either one of them.

Dare ran a hand roughly though his hair. If she was indeed a confederate of Caliban's, then he had just put himself in grave danger. And if she went running to Riddingham, she would prove her guilt. But at least it would end his uncertainty about her.

He felt a muscle flex in his jaw. Julienne was a consummate actress, true, but his instincts told him she wasn't lying. Which meant she was likely innocent of duplicity.

A pity, Dare thought darkly, feeling an unexpected stab of regret. Her guilt might have freed him of his obsession with her, helped him to break the chains that still held him enraptured.

And if she was innocent? Even before now it had occurred to him that if he dragged her into his investigations, Julienne herself could be in danger from Caliban.

For an instant, the sickening image flashed through his mind of the dead companion's body. . . .

Dare shook his head adamantly. Julienne Laurent could take care of herself. He was the one who was in peril—of succumbing to her insidious allure.

Sardonically, he glanced down at his breeches. His guests would be expecting him, but he couldn't very well face them in this condition. He needed a change of clothing at a minimum. And as he let himself from Julienne's bedchamber, Dare wondered if he had time to take a cold bath as well.

Chapter
Seven

"So?" Solange prodded Julienne the next day as they stood watching Dare dance with the moonstruck daughter of a neighboring squire. He had hired musicians from Brighton for the evening and opened his ballroom to the local gentry. "Are you not worried that you might have competition?"

"No," Julienne answered easily. "Lord Wolverton prefers his partners a trifle less tongue-tied."

Dare was far too experienced a rake to be attracted to a shy young miss barely out of the schoolroom, Julienne knew. More critically, he was unlikely to be diverted from his current goal of making *her* his conquest.

Dare had resumed his full-fledged pursuit of her—much to the gratification of the majority of his houseguests.

Truthfully, though, Julienne felt relieved now that she understood Dare's game. Why he would have swallowed his anger and injured male pride to publicly pursue her now made sense: he intended to have his revenge and attempt to expose a cunning traitor at the same time.

This house party was primarily for Riddingham's

benefit, not hers, she saw now. And perhaps Dare's effort at spying wasn't as far-fetched as she had first supposed. Now that she knew what to look for, she realized that he paid close attention to Riddingham's slightest action or comment, although without appearing to. Dare missed nothing.

And even if she smarted a little from her own wounded pride, knowing that Dare didn't really want *her*, the fact that he was playing cat and mouse with someone else was somehow comforting, for she could better defend herself against his seductive assault. Her heart desperately needed any armor she could find. She would never survive falling in love with him again.

The ball proved a crush, since all his neighbors had accepted his invitation with alacrity. They had all heard of the wager, it seemed. And Julienne was determined to give them what they had come for. On the few occasions this evening when she'd encountered Dare, she had kept up her end of their verbal jousting for the benefit of the onlookers.

"He is a marvelous dancer," Solange commented now, watching with admiration.

He was indeed, Julienne agreed silently—fluid and graceful and highly attentive, focusing intently on his partner, even if she was a timorous young innocent.

"And he is said to be just as marvelous a lover. I hear he is fiendishly inventive in bed."

"His sexual prowess means little to me," Julienne prevaricated.

Just then the cotillion ended, and Julienne felt the bold touch of Dare's hungry gaze as his eyes sought her out from across the room.

"*Mon Dieu,*" Solange breathed. "He looks as if he wishes to devour you."

Julienne managed a shrug. "It is all pretense. Merely a game we are playing."

"*Bien,*" her friend retorted. "But you know what they say about playing with fire, *mon amie*. You should take care you do not get burned."

"I will keep that in mind. Will you excuse me? I think that is my cue."

Julienne could tell by the buzz of anticipation that she was the center of attention as she made her way through the crowd and demanded a waltz from Dare.

"For shame, my lord," she said with a flirtatious smile. "You promised to dance with me, but you have been unforgivably neglectful. Or perhaps it is that you fear giving me the opportunity to win our wager."

"I have been trembling in my boots all evening," Dare responded mildly.

"Quite a feat, since you are wearing pumps."

He grinned and took her in his arms.

Julienne allowed him to sweep her away, waiting until they had settled into the rhythm of the waltz before gazing up at Dare. "Truthfully, I thought perhaps I should rescue that poor girl. She looked rather like she might faint from fright."

Shaking his head, Dare gave a mock shudder. "I'm the one who needed rescuing. I owe you my gratitude, love."

"Think nothing of it, my lord. My gesture was not so selfless. I am eager to have you on your knees."

He chuckled. "Ah, my lovely Jewel, you know very well that you had me on my knees the first moment we met."

"I scarcely think so. The first time we met, I was too busy fending off your cousin's claws."

Dare's eyes kindled with what appeared to be fond memory. "Do you remember the blistering set down you gave her?"

She did indeed. Dare had come to Kent in June for his beautiful young cousin's wedding and, in a moment of ennui, had escorted the haughty Miss Emerson into the millinery. Julienne had waited on them patiently while the spoiled young lady disparaged both the quality and quantity of the merchandise.

"I believe I was entirely justified," Julienne replied wryly. "I held my tongue until she scorned my accent and derided my origins, and then I finally lost my temper."

Her response had enraged the arrogant Miss Emerson but set amusement dancing in the earl's eyes. He had returned alone the next day, bent on seducing her.

"I thought you were magnificent," Dare said, his voice a heated murmur. "I *still* think you magnificent. Why don't we slip away from here and find a bed upstairs?"

Bending to place his lips near her ear, he breathed in a husky, intimate tone exactly what he would like to do to her if he had her alone.

Julienne found herself shivering in response. Even though she now understood the purpose of Dare's public game of seduction, it was more difficult than she expected to keep up the charade, for she couldn't deny the fevered undercurrents of passion that still simmered between them.

But she refused to give Dare the satisfaction of thinking her affected.

Julienne returned a coy smile and whispered sweetly in his own ear. "Do, by all means, go upstairs and undress and wait for me."

"And will you follow me, my lovely Jewel?"

"Indeed, as soon as I can assemble enough of your guests to accompany me. I want witnesses to observe the spectacle of you dancing to my tune."

Her offer earned a bark of laughter from the Marquess of Wolverton and had countless heads turning in their direction.

She should have known, however, that Dare would not allow her the last word. That night after the ball ended, Julienne had just prepared for bed and settled beneath the covers when she heard strains of a violin coming from outside her bedchamber window.

Quickly drawing on a dressing gown over her nightdress, she went to the window and opened it—and found herself staring at the sight below. Multicolored lanterns cast a romantic glow over the gardens, while the musicians played softly to one side.

Directly beneath her window, Dare stood posed on the flagstones, dressed in Elizabethan costume, a rose clenched between this teeth. Romeo, if she wasn't mistaken.

When he spied her overhead, he offered her the rose with a gallant flourish and bowed deeply.

"Ah, fair Juliet," he expounded in a passionate stage voice, "come away with me and be my love."

Julienne was hard-pressed to stifle a laugh at his charming absurdity, but she schooled her features to haughtiness. "I regret, my lord, that I have a great disdain for presumptuous noblemen who mangle Shakespeare. If this is your best effort, I am not impressed."

His smile was part wolfish and part enticing. "You have yet to see my best efforts. Come down here, my darling, and I will proceed to show you."

Several of his other houseguests were leaning out their widows, gaping, Julienne noted, including Solange.

"You are either dreadfully foxed," she declared tartly, "or you've taken leave of your senses."

"Both, I should imagine. You intoxicate me and drive me to madness. You are temptation incarnate. . . ."

He turned his face up to Solange at the next window. "Will you not help me, Madame Brogard? The cruel, fair Juliet is determined to spurn my advances."

"Wicked man," Solange admonished, her tone laced with delighted amusement. "I should say you are doing well enough on your own. A woman cannot resist roses and moonlight and a handsome chevalier."

"Alas, it seems Miss Laurent is able to resist me too well." He clasped his hand over his breast. "I vow my heart is breaking."

Julienne answered this time. "Then I suggest you summon the doctor to patch it up, my lord, and allow me to get some sleep."

When Dare staggered back as if he'd received a lethal blow, Solange laughed out loud.

Quelling her own laughter, Julienne shut the window and returned to bed, but she lay there, finding it impossible to sleep.

The music played on for another half hour at least, and Julienne determinedly resisted the urge to return to the window to see if her Romeo had remained as well. But even as she punched her pillow in frustration, some wistful, foolish part of her wished that Dare's pretense of being her suitor were real.

The weather turned stormy the next day, and the company was forced to remain indoors. When out of boredom someone suggested they stage an amateur theatrical, Dare scotched the idea, saying there wasn't enough time remaining in the week to do justice to a play and that it wouldn't be fair to the actresses present, since for them, a theatrical resembled work.

And furthermore, he added laughingly, Miss Laurent disliked the notion of amateurs mangling the words of her beloved playwrights.

They settled for pantomimes and charades and recitations of poetry. Privately Julienne was grateful to be spared, although being employed might have helped distract her from Dare's proximity.

Fortunately the storms passed quickly, and by the following morning, the sun ended the guests' enforced confinement. That afternoon, most of them elected to play pall-mall—a game where a ball was driven through a ring on a swivel—on the side lawn, but Julienne chose to explore the gardens instead.

There were formal paths delineated by stately flower beds and neatly trimmed boxwood hedges, as well as meandering walks that led through more natural foliage toward a birch wood in the distance.

To her delight, Julienne stumbled upon a small copse—a boxwood thicket really—that secreted a rose garden. Here the foliage had been left artfully wild.

The charming disarray reminded her of the over-grown rose garden where she and Dare had once held their lovers' trysts. It was too early for roses to bloom, but she could almost smell the sweet scent. In one corner sat a stone bench, while the center held a marble statue of entwined lovers.

Julienne sank down on the bench and turned her face up to the sun. For a moment she was nineteen again and painfully, wildly in love . . . foolishly dreaming of becoming Dare's wife.

She had never expected to be his wife *or* his lover. When he first arrived in Kent, she had wanted nothing to do with him, for she had no desire to become the prey of the notorious rake. She knew Dare saw her merely as a diversion and a challenge—because she was unimpressed by his title and could hold her own with both him and his haughty cousin.

Certainly she never dreamed he would ask her to become his countess. Under ordinary circumstances there was only one kind of future for a rakish no-bleman and a young female shopkeeper—and it did *not* entail marriage.

She did her utmost to resist Dare, but gradually his outrageous charm and persistence wore her down, and she fell head over slippers in love with him. In retrospect, Julienne could see that her heart hadn't stood a chance once Dare set his sights on her. It was his pro-posal of marriage, however, that had finally compelled her to believe his professions of love, and to give him her virginity along with her promise to wed him.

Yet all too soon the romantic dreams she had cher-ished lay splintered and broken at her feet, along with her heart.

From the moment she'd first learned of his grandfather's threat to disown him, she realized she couldn't wed him. She couldn't allow Dare to sacrifice his future for her sake, knowing that he might someday come to rue his rashness, fearing he might hold her to blame. . . .

She shuddered at the agonizing memory and bowed her head, suddenly swept by a wave of loneliness that seemed to flood her very soul.

It was some moments before she regained control of her emotions. She should return to the house, Julienne scolded herself, where she wouldn't be assaulted by bitter memories best left in the past.

When she rose to go, however, she found Dare standing at the entrance of the secluded garden, leaning indolently against the hedge. For an instant, her heart leapt with joy, but she strove to quell it.

His own expression was enigmatic as he nodded toward the wild tangle of rosebushes that covered much of the copse. "I grew rather fond of roses that summer, so I had this planted when I took up residence here."

Her heart wrenched at the thought of Dare wanting some keepsake of their wondrous time together, so she was glad to have her attention diverted by distant exclamations of glee as one of the guests scored.

"I should join the others," she said, glancing toward the garden entrance.

"Fleeing so soon?" Dare drawled as he pushed away from the hedge and sauntered toward her.

"There is no point in our being together. Riddingham isn't here to see."

"But he will know that we're both missing, and his

jealousy will be aroused. The more his emotions are engaged, the greater likelihood that he will make a slip and show his hand. Stay a while."

Reluctantly Julienne nodded, but she moved away from Dare, a little farther along the path. Her whole being throbbed with an awareness of him.

Dare took the seat she had vacated. "Is there a reason I find you here alone? You don't care for the entertainment I've provided?"

Julienne shrugged. "I suppose I'm not accustomed to a life of leisure. All your guests do is play."

"That is the general idea of a house party. And I should think you need a holiday, as hard as you work."

"But I enjoy my work."

"What do you find so enjoyable about it? I would have judged you too pragmatic to play make-believe."

The seriousness of his question caught her off guard, but she pursed her lips thoughtfully, willing to give him an honest answer. "It's interesting to delve into a role. To become someone else for a change."

He studied her intently for a long moment. "Escaping into another person's skin?"

"Yes," Julienne answered, surprised by Dare's perceptiveness. Pretending to be someone else banished her demons for a time.

When she didn't expound further, his sober look faded, to be replaced by a deceptively mild one. "If you feel such a need for escape, darling, then I am obviously being remiss as your host. I can see I will have to provide better entertainment for you."

Rising, he begin moving toward her.

"I am not interested in the kind of entertainment

you apparently have in mind, Lord Wolverton," Julienne replied, taking a step backward.

His retort held amusement. "Can I help it if this setting makes me crave wicked sex?"

"I suppose not," she said tartly. "*Any* setting makes you crave sex."

With a charming, predatory smile, Dare kept advancing. Her heart thudding in her breast, Julienne retreated toward the statue. His very nearness stirred a dangerous spark that flickered along the ends of her nerves, as did his next provocative declaration.

"I would like nothing more than to undress you and lie with you here, Jewel."

"I have told you before, you cannot have everything you want."

His gaze was warm, carnal. "I don't want *everything*. I only want you."

Julienne halted, her back against the cool marble, yet it was Dare's look that held her immobile; he had trapped her in his heated gaze.

"You won't take pity on me?" he murmured. "I am in dire pain, and only you can offer me respite."

"Dare . . ." She shivered at the desire that swept over her body at his deliberately alluring gaze.

When he stepped even closer, though, and lowered his mouth to hers, she quickly averted her face. She refused to kiss him. His kisses were far too dangerous, for they seared her, left her panting and breathless.

His lips found her cheek instead, nuzzling.

"Dare, stop this!"

"I think you resist yourself more than me." He slid the tips of his fingers along her nape, while his teeth scraped lightly along the line of her throat, arousing her against her will. His sensuous touch spoke of pleasure beyond imagining, but Julienne fought desperately to resist.

"I won't make love to you again!" she protested, her voice already breathless.

His reply was immediate and husky. "You don't have to do a thing. I can manage on my own. I'll arouse you with just my hands and mouth, my lovely Julienne." His voice was now maddeningly sexual. "I want to see how many times I can make you come."

Even as he spoke, he drew back a little and began unbuttoning the front placket of his breeches. "Look what you've done to me." The ample swell of his manhood sprang free, making her catch her breath. "You've made me burn for you."

Julienne stared at his flagrant erection, at the flushed head gleaming in the sunlight. "Heavens, Dare . . . are there no limits to your brazenness?"

His smile spread, wicked and lazy. "Scarcely any."

Reaching for her hand, he guided her fingers to his swollen member. She felt his hot desire lick at her senses, but she snatched her hand away. "You must have lost your wits. Someone could come along the path and—"

"You can see far enough above the hedge to have warning. And no one can see me kneeling. . . ."

The hedge *was* rather high, Julienne acknowledged; they could only be seen from the shoulders up.

Before she could reply, though, Dare went down on one knee before her. "You said you wanted me on my knees. I am delighted to oblige for the moment."

When his fingers grasped the hem of her gown, Julienne realized his intent.

Their gazes locked. It was a contest of wills, one she feared she was losing.

She wanted to step away, but she couldn't force herself to move; the lure of him was too strong. All she could think of was the savage ache between her thighs, an ache only Dare could assuage.

When she remained frozen, he pushed the hem of her gown upward in a slow slide of muslin. Parting her legs slightly, he kissed the inner skin of her thigh, his lips playing fire against her skin.

"Dare . . ." she rasped.

"Hush. You'll enjoy this, I promise."

Trembling, Julienne found herself unable to fight him. Dare was a supreme expert at making love, an expert at making her feel sensation. The beguiling stroke of his fingers justified his reputation for finesse and raised a throbbing need inside her that built and grew.

His lips traced a molten path upward, his tongue unhurriedly licking the sleek flesh of her thighs. She drew a shaky breath, helplessly caught in the web of her own desires as he raised her gown to her hips, baring her feminine flesh to his gaze. His own searing breath scorched her, and she reached behind her to clutch at the statue.

Her dampness was explicit and pulsing, a fact that Dare noted at once. "I haven't even put my mouth on you and already you are dripping wet," he murmured with satisfaction.

It was true, Julienne admitted. She had only to look at him and she grew wet.

He gently dug his fingers into her thighs and spread them wider, allowing no escape from the sensation of being at his mercy.

"This is your punishment," Dare said in a husky voice. "To burn as I do."

Dazed, she glanced down at his open breeches. His erection thrust prominently upward, rising markedly as her own excitement grew.

With slow deliberation he touched her with his tongue, just caressing the outer rim of her quivering flesh. Julienne was grateful that the statue supported her, for she didn't think she could stand otherwise. Leaning against it, she let her head fall back. Dare knew exactly how to touch her so that she was defenseless, how to cherish her petal-like folds with his strong tongue, how to find her yearning bud of pleasure. . . .

Julienne whimpered as he tantalized her endlessly. She was aroused, past aroused. Then he pressed his mouth right up against her, sucking in a kiss, and her knees went so weak, she practically fell.

His hands framed her buttocks, supporting her, holding her still for his pleasure.

Her breath grew ragged. His mouth was pure magic, tender and demanding. His tongue stabbed deep into her, making her writhe and arch her hips.

It was too much to endure, yet she prayed for him to go on. Wordlessly he obliged, prolonging the building ecstasy.

Her flesh seemed to burn . . . the heat so fierce she thought she might faint. When her climax ripped through her, he made it last, drawing out the devastating bliss till she sagged limply back against the statue, her eyes shut tightly.

He waited a moment as the pulsing rapture subsided. Then, with one last erotic caress of his lips, he let her gown fall.

Still struggling for breath, Julienne allowed her gaze to drift downward. Dare had wrapped his hand around his erection and was fondling himself, stroking his long, thick phallus as she longed to do.

He glanced up at her, his eyes burning with the passion he made no effort to disguise, his faced flushed with his near-orgasmic state. "If you won't have pity and ease my ache . . ."

He let the sentence go unfinished as his expression turned to pleasure-pain. She could see his knuckles strain as he squeezed his arousal harder.

A moment later a strangled groan sounded from deep in his throat as the fierce jet of his ejaculation spurted across the tangle of rosebushes. With a deep sigh, he sank back on his heels, his eyes closing.

"A poor substitute for the real thing," he murmured finally, "but it will have to do."

Glancing at Julienne without the least sign of remorse or embarrassment, he withdrew a handkerchief to wipe away the evidence of his burning passion and then fastened his breeches.

"*Now* I think we may safely return," he said with a very male smile.

The remainder of the house party was nerve-racking for Julienne, since when Dare was near, she could scarcely think for remembering his erotic caresses.

She deplored the sensual power he held over her, yet the emotional turmoil he caused her was even more dangerous. Her soul had been starved for intimacy for years, and she found herself craving the closeness she'd once known with him. Dare was the only man who had ever looked beyond her face and figure to the person she was beneath. The only one who had ever cared about her true thoughts or feelings, who had made her feel cherished as a woman and valued as a friend.

Now, however, he had no interest in her other than to mete out revenge and to slake his physical need and to use her to better observe Riddingham. She was terrified Dare would take ruthless advantage of her vulnerability, leaving her emotions crushed and bludgeoned like before.

When the blow came, though, she wasn't prepared. The day following their passionate interlude in the rose garden, the company took a sightseeing trip to Brighton to view the Marine Parade and the famous Pavilion that the Prince Regent had commissioned to be built. Afterward they enjoyed a late luncheon on the cliffs overlooking the sea.

When the party took a stroll along the cliff path, Julienne found Dare walking beside her.

"You seem quite taken with Riddingham today," he observed in a cool undertone. "Your flirtation with him has reached epic proportions."

She gave him an arch look. Since yesterday she had devoted nearly all her attention to the viscount, for two reasons. First, flirting with him helped her counter the threat of Dare's determined seduction. And second, she hoped to discover something about Riddingham that could be useful in Dare's investigation. If Dare were to unmask the traitor, she theorized, then he might abandon his pursuit of her, and she could have him out of her life for good.

"I am merely staying in character," she claimed, not

wholly truthfully. "I promised you I would maintain our charade, remember?"

"So you did." His mouth curled, while his tone was mockingly congenial. "I'm gratified at least that you didn't go running to Riddingham to warn him of my suspicions."

She felt herself stiffen. "Did you truly think I would?"

"Let's say I wasn't certain I could trust you, any more than you feel you can trust me. But you are doing an admirable job of rousing his lust."

"You cannot possibly be jealous," Julienne returned with sugary sweetness.

The dark flare that suddenly kindled in Dare's eyes told her she had struck a nerve with her accusation. "A primitive male instinct, jealousy. One I will endeavor to contain for the sake of duty. I want very much for you to encourage Riddingham's infatuation. He is more prone to share his secrets with you if he's enamored of you."

"Presuming he has secrets to share."

"You are in an excellent position to discover that. He's eager to become your cicisbeo, and you could easily oblige him."

Julienne gave Dare a sharp glance. "And just what do you mean by that? You aren't suggesting I take him as my paramour?"

"The thought had occurred to me."

She nearly stumbled as she stared up at Dare. "You want me to *whore* for you?"

"Why not?" His eyebrow rose cynically, although there was an intentness in his probing gaze that was far from sanguine. "It shouldn't offend your sensibilities. After all, you have extensive experience seducing unsuspecting gentlemen."

Struggling to hide her hurt, Julienne regarded Dare without expression. "I believe I've told you before, *I* will choose whom I take to my bed, not you or anyone else."

A wintery smile touched his lips. "I'm prepared to make it financially worth your while. You could be a wealthy woman if you play your cards wisely."

Pain sliced through Julienne like a knife blade, making her breath hiss through her teeth. For a moment she couldn't even speak.

But then she summoned her finest acting skills and offered Dare a reckless smile. "Perhaps I will indeed take Riddingham as my paramour. I have no doubt he will make a considerate lover ... unlike some other gentlemen I could choose."

She saw the sharp glitter of emotion that flickered in Dare's eyes—pain? anger?—and knew she had scored a hit.

Ignoring his searing look, she pursed her lips thoughtfully. "On second thought, I don't believe I will. If I were to take Riddingham for my lover, he would doubtless expect me to abandon my wager with you, and I have no intention of losing to you, Lord Wolverton."

Julienne left Dare then and surged ahead on the path, vehemently determined to conceal her own pain and anger. She managed it temporarily, but by the time she caught up with Solange, she was nearly blind with hurt. She could scarcely believe how violently she was trembling.

She shook her head at her friend's questioning glance

and struggled for the appearance of composure, yet it required all her talent to pretend that Dare's suggestion hadn't wounded her to the core.

He thought her a whore. And the worst part was, she couldn't refute him.

Julienne shivered, feeling a sudden chill that went bone-deep.

She was glad when the afternoon at last ended and she could take refuge in her bedchamber. Collapsing on the bed, she buried her face in a pillow and gave vent to her anguished thoughts.

She *had* been a whore for a time. Shortly after her life had been rocked by scandal and she'd taken up acting to survive, her mother's illness had grown hopelessly severe. To provide for *Maman*'s care, Julienne had had no choice but to augment her meager income by becoming the mistress of a wealthy lord.

The first time she gave her body for money, she'd wept agonizing tears. But afterward, she stoically shut off her emotions, determined to endure. It had helped that her protector was a kind, elderly, gentleman whose compassion and consideration won her respect and genuine affection. Yet there had been times during those difficult years when living hurt so badly she'd wanted to die.

Remembering, Julienne felt an aching rush in her chest, as if her heart were bleeding. She had forced herself to go on because her mother needed her. In sheer self-preservation, though, she had escaped into a role she had created for herself—a worldly, sophisticated actress who bore misfortune by laughing in the teeth of fate. And in so doing, she'd discovered reserves of strength she never knew she possessed.

After her mother died, she was thankfully no longer forced to sell herself to raise desperately needed funds. Yet sometimes she couldn't help feeling bitterness for having been condemned to a harsh life with little chance for a respectable future.

Fighting back scalding tears, Julienne rolled over to stare up at the ceiling overhead. She might likely never have the things many women took for granted— husband, home, children . . . love. Certainly she would never feel for anyone else the same ardor she had felt for Dare. The desire she still felt for him.

She had tried once. Two years after her mother's death she had taken a lover on her own terms—another actor. His sweet passion had satisfied her physically, but he had never aroused in her the kind of hot, intense, overwhelming hunger she'd known with Dare. And the intimacy was missing. She had hungered for the emotional closeness that went beyond sex, the tender fulfillment that transcended the corporeal.

She had eventually broken off the affair, unwilling to settle for less. Carnal love, she had discovered, couldn't relieve true loneliness of the soul or quench the need for real love, and she would no longer attempt to manufacture a substitute.

She had kept her heart and her bed empty ever since, and even found a measure of peace with her decision. Yet she had sworn that never again would she be compelled to endure a protector. *That* was why she was so determined to earn a substantial income from her acting: so she would never have to prostitute herself again. So she could have the independence that only wealth could provide. With enough money she would be free to make her own choices.

But now Dare had offered to pay her to whore for him. Pain lashed at her again at the memory.

Fiercely Julienne dashed away the streaks of wetness on her cheeks, reminding herself that Dare was nothing more than a self-serving, licentious rakehell. And in one respect, she was glad he had made his hurtful suggestion, for it helped her renew her resolve.

She intended to win their damned wager. If it took her last breath, she would have his heart on a platter.

Dare was so certain he would conquer her, but she would show him otherwise. If he wanted a war of wills, she would give him one.

She had to, simply to protect herself. She would summon all her powers of seduction to gain mastery over him. . . . She would wait until he declared his love publicly and handed her the victory. Then she would crush his heart beneath her heel without a qualm.

Only then would their hurtful charade come to an end and she could put Dare out of her life forever.

She would finally be free of him. And that was what she desperately wanted.

Wasn't it?

Chapter
Eight

Dare had never known such frustration. He'd returned to London three days ago, after his house party ended, not only lacking any further clues to Caliban's identity but having come no closer to winning his wager with Julienne. And game or no game, he wanted her in his bed.

Getting her there willingly, though, was proving an exercise in futility. Indeed, he'd clearly suffered a setback by suggesting that Julienne use her charms to ferret out Riddingham's secrets.

He hadn't intended to make such a misstep, but his possessive male instincts had interfered with his rational mind. Julienne had accused him of being jealous, and he was. Intensely so. His blood had boiled that day on the cliffs as he watched Riddingham entice a husky ripple of laughter from her. The tender scene had inflamed him, rousing bitter memories of seven years ago—of discovering Julienne and Ivers together, of learning they were lovers.

Momentarily blinded by rage, Dare found himself lashing out at her, offering her a financial incentive that most actresses would have been pleased to accept. Not

Julienne, however. She had seemed taken aback and even offended by his proposition.

His relief at her refusal was overwhelming. He didn't want Riddingham or any other man touching her. And Dare knew he could never have forgiven himself if his reckless resentment had driven her into his rival's arms.

He couldn't deny, either, his vast feeling of relief that Julienne hadn't warned Riddingham of his investigation. Her forbearance didn't totally prove her innocence, of course, but it was looking less and less likely that she was the accomplice of a traitor.

After he'd proposed the viscount's seduction, the change in her had been noticeable. Since their return to London, Dare had kept up the steady crusade of his public wooing of Julienne—at the theater, during another of Madame Brogard's afternoon salons, as a member of a party that escorted Julienne to the British Museum to view an exhibit. But whereas before Dare had detected a hint of vulnerability, of softness, in her dark eyes whenever she was with him, now she was as cool and calculating as any courtesan.

When he'd handed her a bank draft for one thousand pounds—her earnings for attending his house party—she had tucked it in her bosom with a faintly brittle, beguiling smile that had given him an immediate arousal.

He'd never seen this side of her, never seen her behavior so deliberately, wantonly provocative. Julienne had flirted and teased him unmercifully while holding him at arm's length.

It was driving him wild.

He had only himself to blame, Dare knew. The

Jewel had become the fashion among the fast set, in part because of his pursuit. He found it difficult to infiltrate her usual entourage long enough even to speak to her.

Thus, when he managed to persuade her to take a drive in the park with him the following afternoon, Dare felt as if he had scored a major victory.

He called on Julienne at her lodgings on Montague Street, but she kept him waiting for nearly twenty minutes before finally deigning to appear—another deliberate provocation, he didn't doubt.

His pulse quickened at the sight of her, she looked so fresh and lovely. Her carriage dress of pale yellow muslin and leaf green spencer were reminiscent of spring, though the April day was cool and overcast.

"Miss Laurent, you leave me breathless," he said as he handed her into his curricle.

She gave him an alluring smile. "That is certainly my intent, my lord."

"I thought we were beyond such formal terms of address. My name is Dare."

"I would never presume to be so familiar," she replied, lightly mocking.

Belying her words, however, she let her sensual gaze travel down his chest to his stomach, lingering on his groin. Dare felt as though she'd run her hand over him. All the muscles in his body tightened at the heat aroused by her mere glance.

He wasn't certain, Dare reflected as he took the seat beside her, that he liked this new, seductive Jewel, and not simply because it put him on the defensive. Her amiability somehow struck a false note that set his teeth on edge. He had the distinct feeling that he was dealing with an angry female—and that her anger wouldn't be easily placated.

Julienne would have agreed, had she been privy to Dare's thoughts. She was more determined than ever to make him surrender the heart he claimed she had broken. Yet she wasn't as sanguine as she appeared. Dare's touch, when he'd handed her up, had left her fingers tingling beneath her glove. And when he settled next to her, she could feel his hard thigh press against hers through their layers of clothing.

To her further dismay, when he leaned forward to gather the reins, his arm brushed her breast, making her nipples tighten instantly. And the knowing gleam in his eyes told her clearly that his intimacy was intentional.

She refused, however, to let him win. She refused to be the kind of witless female who melted helplessly in his arms. As Dare set the curricle in motion, Julienne gave him back some of his own; she placed her gloved hand on his thigh as if for balance.

When his breath hissed through his teeth, she had to smother a gratified smile.

"If you don't want me to turn this vehicle around," he observed pleasantly, "and carry you up to your rooms to ravish you for the remainder of the afternoon, I suggest you remove your hand from my leg immediately."

Julienne complied, but she arched an eyebrow. "You think I would permit such an act of barbarism when I have no intention of allowing you even to kiss me again?"

He sent her an amused glance. "My apologies if I don't take your illusions too seriously. There's no doubt in my mind that I will make love to you again. And when I do, you will be more than willing—you'll be begging for it."

His arrogance made Julienne itch to take him down a peg. "I should think you would be aware by now of the danger in becoming my paramour. What if you were to truly fall in love with me?"

Dare had no witty retort for that. Instead he frowned and concentrated on his driving.

It was only midafternoon when they arrived at the park—Julienne had been unable to go later with a theater performance scheduled this evening—but the Row was already crowded with riders and carriages of every kind. Furthermore, Julienne discovered, they were the sole focus of countless pairs of eyes.

All London was watching their mating dance, it seemed.

"It amazes me," Julienne said, pasting a smile on her face to cover her exasperation, "how your ridiculous wager has created such a rabid interest in our affairs. It has grown to the point of absurdity."

"But the ton loves a spectacle," Dare replied. "Particularly a battle between worthy opponents. And we are well matched, I would say—the dazzling actress and the notorious rakehell. Although for now the betting books are giving me the edge."

Fortunately she didn't have to think of a retort, for she was hailed by one of her admirers.

They progressed at a snail's pace, since they both were continually greeted by acquaintances. A short while later, she heard Dare curse under his breath as they came across Riddingham driving a curricle.

The viscount looked just as displeased to see them together as he drew to a halt. After the initial pleasantries, Riddingham ignored Dare and addressed Julienne. "I hope you will permit me to take you for a drive tomorrow, Miss Laurent. We can try out my new pair." He nodded toward his horses, matched bays that looked fresh and impatient to be held standing.

"They are very handsome," Julienne said truthfully.

"They are a handful, but exceedingly fast."

"I don't suppose," Dare interrupted, "you would care to put them to a test?"

"A test? What are you suggesting?"

"Your pair against my grays."

"You are proposing a race?" Riddingham asked.

"You sound surprised."

"Perhaps you aren't aware, Wolverton, that I am a member of the Four-in-Hand Club?"

The club, Julienne knew, was made up of England's premier whips who regularly held races to exhibit their driving skills.

"I'm aware," Dare replied dryly. "And your expertise is doubtless unexcelled. But I think I can manage to provide enough sport to make a race worth your while. To keep it interesting, I propose that we each take a passenger—the lady of our choice. I intend to claim Miss Laurent, so you needn't bother asking her. But I'm certain Miss Upcott will oblige you."

Fanny Upcott was the Covent Garden actress Dare had invited to his house party.

"We can race to Hampstead Heath, if you like," Dare continued. "The posting inn at Primrose Hill would be a good place to start. The distance to the Blue Boar Tavern on the Heath would be . . . what . . . five miles? The winner buys dinner at the Blue Boar. What do you say, Riddingham?" When the viscount hesitated, Dare added with a smile, "Surely I'm not so intimidating as to make you refuse a challenge?"

"Not at all," Riddingham said testily. "Very well, I will race you. Barring rain, we will meet at ten o'clock tomorrow at Primrose Hill."

"Will you speak to Miss Upcott yourself, or do you need me to put in a good word for you?"

"I will do it," Riddingham snapped before turning his attention back to Julienne. "I am eager to see your portrayal of Ophelia in *Hamlet* this evening, Miss Laurent. . . ."

Dare allowed her barely enough time to reply before he made their excuses and drove on, looking more than a little self-satisfied.

"What the devil was that about, challenging him to a curricle race?" Julienne asked in annoyance when they were out of earshot.

"I'm simply trying to shake things up a bit," Dare replied blandly.

"You are taking a great deal for granted by assuming I will accompany you. You're greatly mistaken if you think to have me at your beck and call—"

"I promise I am not taking you for granted, *chérie*."

"It certainly seems that way. You left me in no position to refuse. Your underhanded tactics are deplorable, Dare."

"Haven't you heard the adage that all is fair on the battlefield of love?"

His nonchalance irked her. "You are mangling your quotes again!"

Dare turned an innocent gaze on her. "Do you know, you are sure to get premature wrinkles between your eyes if you keep up that savage scowl?"

"Dare!"

His expression sobered in the face of her genuine anger, and he drew the curricle to a halt, giving her his full attention. "Forgive me, Jewel. I am deadly serious, despite my regrettable teasing. I desperately need your help with Riddingham. I beg you, will you please, please agree to accompany me on the race tomorrow?"

Mollified a slight measure by his seemingly earnest contrition, Julienne raised an eyebrow. "Desperately?"

A gleam of humor lit his eyes. "Yes, desperately."

"Very well. I will agree to help you. But you might consider asking next time before you volunteer me for your infamous games."

"Thank you, my love." Transferring the reins to one hand, he raised her fingers to his lips. The lazy, smoldering look from those eyes made her weak with wanting him.

Highly discomfited, Julienne drew her hand away "Are you trying to charm me out of my ill-humor?" she muttered.

His quick grin had a raffish quality. "But of course. I get my way so much more easily with charm."

Julienne raised her eyes to the sky and counted to ten before responding. "If that is so, then why aren't you using it on Riddingham? Why do I sense that you are deliberately attempting to rile him?"

"I told you, to agitate him into making a misstep." Shifting his attention to his horses, Dare set the vehicle in motion again. "In fact . . . we've had so few leads in the search for Caliban that I've decided to change tactics altogether. Stir the pot, you might say."

"Meaning?"

"I've begun putting out word that I am hunting the traitor."

Julienne frowned at his admission. "Isn't that potentially dangerous? If Caliban is as ruthless as you say, could you not be making yourself his target?"

"It would be worth the risk if I could draw him out." When she remained silent, Dare shot her an arch glance. "Can it be that you are actually concerned for my skin, love?"

She was gravely concerned, although she had no intention of admitting it to him. "But of course," she answered lightly. "If something untoward befell you, then I would have no chance to win our wager."

To her surprise, Dare's expression grew intensely somber. "This is a trifle more serious than our wager. Three weeks ago a young woman was found drowned. She was companion to Lady Castlereagh. . . ."

Julienne listened in shock and dismay as he told her about Alice Watson's death and the reasons for believing she'd been seduced to gain access to Lord Castlereagh's letters and then murdered.

Her brow furrowing, Julienne searched Dare's face. "Do you honestly think Riddingham could be so heinous as to murder an innocent girl?"

"I don't know. It would help to discover whether he even knew Alice Watson, and whether he had the opportunity to woo her. I'd give a monkey to know where he was on March seventh when she was killed. It could prove—or perhaps even disprove—his complicity."

"Is there anything I can do?" Julienne offered. "Perhaps I could discreetly question Riddingham and see what I can learn."

"No," Dare said curtly, "I will handle it."

He felt Julienne studying him. "A few days ago you suggested I take him for my lover so I could try to ferret out his secrets."

"A few days ago I was behaving like a jealous ass."

"And you are not now?"

His mouth curved in a reluctant grin. "I admit I harbor a measure of possessiveness where you're concerned. And jealousy isn't my only reason for declining your offer to investigate. If Riddingham is a killer, I don't want you anywhere near him. You should dress warmly tomorrow," Dare warned, changing the subject. "The wind will be wicked with the pace I intend to set."

She sighed. "What time should I be ready?"

"I'll call for you in the morning at half past nine. . . . Unless you mean to invite me to spend the night with you to save time . . . ?"

"Do you *never* give up?" Julienne said in exasperation.

"Never," Dare retorted with an amused laugh.

The remainder of their drive was accomplished in relative harmony. And when Dare returned her to her lodgings, he merely kissed her fingers again. But he wanted to do more. Much more.

Clearly, however, Julienne was not of the same mind, Dare reflected irritably as he drove away. His powers of seduction had never proved so pitiful.

He was getting nowhere with her, certainly not where he wanted to be, which was in bed with her naked beneath him, her legs wrapped around his waist. He was beginning to be positively haunted by visions of making love to her again.

There was only one advantage to their current stale-mate, Dare acknowledged. Since her betrayal all those years ago, he had felt numb inside, but now he felt eager, alive, all his senses teeming. He woke each morning looking forward to the day, counting the moments till he saw Julienne again—

At the thought, Dare cursed. She had been right on that score: she was a supreme danger to him. He was becoming besotted with her, whether he wished to or not.

He needed to conquer his growing obsession with her, Dare chided himself. Needed to prove that he could satisfy his fierce craving by other means.

Accordingly, that night he visited the Widow Dun-leith again. Her cool reception should not have sur-prised him. Louisa clearly didn't like playing second fiddle to a mere actress, and her jealousy showed in every barbed remark she made during dinner. So he left shortly afterward, without so much as a kiss.

He could have charmed her out of her sulks, Dare knew. Most women allowed him anything he wanted when he put himself out to please.

The trouble was, he didn't want most women. Sex with anyone but Julienne left him feeling alone and empty. Every time he touched a woman, he was grasping for the exquisite, primitive intensity he'd once known with her—and not finding it. No matter how many times he warned himself to forget her, the ache of long-ing remained.

He tried to tell himself the feeling was due to sexual frustration. He wasn't accustomed to abstinence, and he didn't like it. Any more than he liked having to fight his way past the queue of calf-eyed, romantic young fools who were always at Julienne's side.

Yet he was very much afraid that his frustration would lead him to do something reckless, like throttle the next man who leered at her.

He'd wanted to do just that earlier today when he'd caught Riddingham staring at her full, ripe bosom. He'd wanted to drag the viscount from his curricle and pummel him with his fists. . . .

What riled him most, however, was the affection Julienne seemed to bear for the man, while *he* only roused her angry defenses.

Cunning killer or not, Dare thought as he tossed and turned in his solitary bed, Viscount Riddingham had best watch his back.

The next day dawned fair and pleasant for early spring. Despite her reservations, Julienne found herself enjoying the short drive to Primrose Hill just north of the city. She had dressed warmly, as Dare suggested, in a green velvet riding habit. And he had laid a carriage rug across her lap to ward off the remaining morning chill.

Riddingham was already waiting when they turned into the crowded yard of the posting inn, with Miss Upcott at his side. The actress was garbed in crimson and a high poke bonnet, which Julienne suspected would catch a great deal of wind once the race got underway.

Not surprisingly a large number of spectators had gathered to watch, she saw as Dare threaded a path through the crush of vehicles. There were several carriages filled with both ladies and gentlemen and more than a dozen sporting bucks on horseback. The wagers flew fast and furious, with most putting their money on Dare.

"Shall we engage in a small wager ourselves?" Dare asked Riddingham as he drew his curricle even. "Say, a thousand pounds?"

"Double that," the viscount snapped, evidently in an ill mood. "Two thousand will make it worth my while."

Julienne heard Miss Upcott gasp at the size of the wager, and she herself shook her head at the exorbitant sums these moneyed noblemen recklessly tossed around.

"As you wish," Dare replied easily. "The first one to reach the Blue Boar Tavern wins."

Shortly all the bets were placed and the congested yard cleared of spectators wanting to be present at the finish line. Willing to give them a headstart, Dare ordered refreshments from the innkeeper, and he and Julienne sipped hot mulled cider while his rival grew visibly more impatient.

They had just handed back their mugs when Riddingham's curricle lurched and he clenched the reins, clearly having difficulty controlling his bays' fidgets. With a polite sweep of his arm, Dare invited the viscount to proceed him out of the yard.

The two men turned on to the road, with Riddingham in the lead.

"Are you set?" Dare asked Julienne as he urged his pair into an easy gallop, as Riddingham was doing up ahead.

"Yes."

"Good. This should be a pleasure."

Julienne kept silent so that Dare could give his attention to his horses. He was an excellent whip, she thought, observing him match his speed to the curricle in front.

He needed to concentrate on the road before him, but she could watch the surrounding countryside. The vast area of heathland spread over sandy hills and secluded vales, and Julienne saw the green landscape rush by in a blur as they bowled along. With the wind in her face, she was glad she had worn a small shako hat rather than the broad-brimmed bonnet the other actress had chosen. Ahead, Miss Upcott strove to keep her bonnet in place with one hand while clinging to the rail of the curricle with the other.

They skirted the village of Hampstead before coming to the Heath itself, with its broad stretches of gorse and grass and numerous stands of trees. Dare leaned forward slightly, his eyes intent on the road and his opponent, and let his horses have their heads.

Julienne felt a rush of exhilaration as they surged forward. There was a risk of danger in racing, with curves and potholes and the possibility of an approaching carriage to challenge them. But as she watched Dare's gloved hands masterfully controlling his grays, urging them to greater speed, she felt complete confidence in his skill.

Ahead, Riddingham was driving with evident skill himself. Julienne doubted either pair could keep up the brutal pace, but for now they were running strongly and showing no sign of fatigue. And Dare's grays were slowly gaining ground.

The road was narrow here, with ditches running on

either side providing barely enough room for two vehicles. But when Dare grinned at her, she realized he would to try to pass. He was thoroughly enjoying himself, Julienne knew.

"Hold on," he shouted over the sounds of whistling wind and pounding hoofbeats.

She obeyed, even as she murmured a silent prayer.

Riddingham blocked their attempts, however, by swinging into the center of the road. Julienne winced and ducked her head to avoid the clods of dirt and mud thrown up by the bays' churning hooves.

Patiently accepting his opponent's tactics, Dare bided his time until a blind curve loomed ahead. Then he feathered the turn expertly while Riddingham's curricle went wide. With a calculating glance, Dare dropped his hands and asked his horses for another burst of speed. The gallant grays shot forward, their lengthened strides eating ground.

They had nearly drawn even when a wheel on Dare's curricle hit a rut. The vehicle tilted crazily, and Julienne gasped, gripping her seat in desperation. The grays took exception to the jarring weight behind, but Dare held them steady, calming them until they responded to his iron control.

At his command they slowly drew forward again, and soon the two pairs were racing neck and neck.

What happened next Julienne wasn't quite certain, but she heard the scrape of metal as the curricles clanged wheels. Both vehicles lurched at the contact, and she was thrown against Dare.

She heard his muffled oath and managed to right herself. But when it happened again, she realized Riddingham had deliberately swung over in an effort to run Dare's curricle off the road.

It was an insanely dangerous maneuver, Julienne knew, and when they clashed a third time, the wheels nearly locked and both drivers and their passengers were almost flung from their seats. Miss Upcott screamed and clung to Riddingham, while Dare cursed vividly.

His mouth had narrowed in a grim line, Julienne saw, giving him a frantic glance. He would have again tried to pass, she felt sure, but just then they rounded another curve and an approaching farm cart suddenly loomed ahead, directly in their path.

To her surprise, Dare drew back on the reins and eased the pace.

"What are you doing?" she asked breathlessly as they slowed to a trot.

"I like to win, but not at the risk of your life. I would rather not injure my horses either."

Julienne suspected that in a simple battle of nerves with Riddingham, Dare would have won hands down, but he had her safety to consider as well as his own—and she was frankly glad for his prudence, even if it cost them the race.

But Dare apparently had no intention of conceding.

"Hold tight," he ordered, guiding the curricle from the road on to a narrow track.

Julienne saw Riddingham's look of startlement as he glanced back at them, and quelled her own dismay when she realized Dare intended to drive cross-country.

It was a jolting ride, despite the slower pace, and Julienne feared they would snap an axle or one of the traces as they bounced over the uneven ground. But she clung determinedly to the lurching seat, and Dare's gambit cut off nearly half a mile from the planned route, allowing them to reach the tavern yard a full minute ahead of Riddingham, to a chorus of shouts and cheers from the crowd gathered there.

Dare brought his horses to a plunging halt and waited until an ostler ran to their heads before dragging Julienne into his arms, catching her completely off guard.

"Are you all right?" he demanded. Before she could react, he had covered her mouth with his own and claimed a fierce kiss.

The shock of it momentarily held her immobile, while heat streaked through her.

"God," Dare murmured, drawing back only slightly. "That bloody fool could have killed you."

Emotion churned in his darkened eyes, but Julienne couldn't determine the cause: relief at their surviving the danger, exhilaration at winning the race, or pleasure from kissing her. Perhaps all three.

To the glee of the spectators, Dare gathered her even closer and bent his head once more. Julienne wanted to protest his reckless passion, but her breath fled at the deep thrust of his tongue. Her lips parted of their own accord, and she sighed, surrendering to his mounting ardor.

She was still kissing him as Riddingham drove into the yard. Recalling her surroundings with sudden consternation, Julienne broke free from Dare's embrace.

At the hint of triumph in his smoldering eyes, she began to wonder if he'd purposely claimed a victory kiss in front of the crowd to suggest that he was winning their wager, or even to taunt his opponent. The possibility vexed her to no end.

The blazing look Dare threw at Riddingham, however, made her fear for the viscount's safety.

Riddingham appeared furious as well, whether at being bested in the race or because of the kiss, Julienne wasn't certain.

Miss Upcott, on the other hand, was white-faced. Clearly shaken, she climbed down from the other curricle without assistance and stood trembling in the yard.

With scarcely a glance at his passenger, Riddingham scowled at Dare. "You managed to win, Wolverton, but by foul means. Leaving the road was cheating."

Beside her, Dare went very still. "I believe our wager was who would reach the tavern first. But as long as we are discussing foul means, what did you intend by nearly forcing us off the road? You could have killed us all with that senseless stunt you pulled."

Riddingham's face turned even darker. "You will regret this, Wolverton," he ground out, obviously reluctant to admit his own unscrupulous actions had cost him the race and the two-thousand-pound wager.

To Julienne's astonishment, the viscount suddenly whipped up his horses and drove off.

Dare's ire seemed slightly dimmed by his rival's rage. "At least we still have dinner to look forward to," he murmured dryly.

He cast a solicitous glance at Riddingham's deserted passenger. "Are you all right, Miss Upcott?"

She held a hand to her mouth and shook her head. "I think I may be ill. . . ."

Turning, she stumbled toward the inn.

Uttering a mild oath, Dare leapt down from his curricle. When he reached up for Julienne to assist her, however, she drew back with a look of fierce exasperation.

"I am not at all impressed by your ham-handed tactics," she declared in a clipped whisper. "Did you never stop to think that savaging Riddingham's pride is no way to persuade him to divulge secrets?"

Dare narrowed his eyes in surprise. "I savaged his pride?"

"Yes. You resemble foolish boys, fighting over a prize. But you could have found a more intelligent way to deal with him."

"I hardly consider—"

"Please, spare your breath and go offer your apologies to Miss Upcott."

Snatching up the reins then, Julienne ordered the ostler to stand back. When he complied, she sent the grays forward at a brisk trot.

She could almost sense Dare's stupefaction as she drove out of the yard. When he shouted after her, she permitted herself a brief smile. After surrendering so witlessly to his passionate kiss, she needed to show their observers that she was still a match for him.

What she had done—appropriating his curricle and stranding him at a tavern—was no more outrageous than Dare's usual antics. He would eventually be able to hire some sort of equipage to take poor Fanny Upcott back to London. And *someone* had to follow Riddingham and try to soothe his ruffled feathers. Perhaps, Julienne reflected, she could use the opportunity to discover what the viscount knew about the murdered companion.

It was likely that Dare feared for his horses, but she wouldn't let them come to any harm. She could tool a curricle more expertly than most women, since one of her beaux in York had taught her. And the grays needed to be cooled down in any case, for their coats were well lathered after their courageous exertions.

But let Dare fret, Julienne thought with more than a hint of defiance. It was time she taught him a lesson.

The arrogant Dare North would learn that he might best most of his opponents, but he wouldn't win the battle with her.

Chapter
Nine

When Julienne returned Dare's curricle that afternoon to his home at Cavendish Square, his august butler gave her a severe glance of disapproval before summoning his lordship.

Dare appeared almost immediately. She could sense his simmering anger as he swiftly descended the front steps to the street in order to inspect the condition of his horses.

Julienne watched as he carefully ran his hands over their legs and backs to assure himself the grays were unharmed.

"I promise I didn't ruin them," she said blandly. "Indeed, I took the liberty of having them unharnessed and groomed while I was having dinner at the Primrose Inn with a certain mutual acquaintance of ours."

With a sharp glance at her, Dare ordered a footman to have the horses driven around to the stables. Then he grasped Julienne lightly but firmly by the arm.

"Before I have someone see you home, Miss Laurent, I hope you will do me the honor of taking a glass of sherry with me," he said, his silken tone brooking no refusal.

"But of course, my lord," Julienne agreed, keeping her smile to herself.

His mansion, what little she could see of it, was magnificent. She scarcely had time to glance around the vast entryway, which was tastefully adorned with statuary and tapestries and paintings in oils, before Dare ushered her into a spacious salon.

"I trust you have an explanation for stealing my horses," he said tersely as soon as he shut the door.

"I am so relieved you managed to find your way safely home," Julienne answered, deliberately taunting him.

She saw a muscle flex in his jaw, but he apparently thought better of giving vent to his anger and playing into her hands. Instead his mouth curved in a reluctant half smile. "I presume you will divulge your reasons in your own good time, my lovely Jewel?"

"You promised me a glass of wine, did you not? I declare I am parched. This spy business is arduous work."

His gaze narrowed at her cryptic words, but he went to the sideboard and poured her some sherry. When he returned to hand her the glass, Julienne stepped back out of range, on the chance that Dare might try to kiss her again. Turning, she settled on a brocade sofa.

"I was endeavoring to seduce Riddingham's secrets from him," she said finally.

She saw some hot emotion flare in Dare's eyes, but he merely moved to stand before the cold hearth and clasped his hands behind his back, as if striving to control himself.

"Happily I had no need to lure him to my bed," Julienne added in a pleasant tone.

"Did you never stop to think," Dare snapped, "that if Riddingham truly is a killer, you could have been in grave danger?"

"Perhaps, but I seriously doubt he is a killer. In fact, I think it can be proved that he isn't. At least in the case of that poor girl, Alice Watson."

His expression remained enigmatic. "Do tell."

"My initial intent, when I followed Riddingham this afternoon, was to reduce his rancor toward you. But then I realized I had the perfect opportunity to question him by asking him to dine with me. He was very angry with you, naturally, Dare. I pretended to sympathize with him."

"To what end?"

"To discover his whereabouts when Alice Watson was killed."

Dare's eyebrow rose, but he remained silent.

"Truthfully, I recalled that Riddingham missed some of my performances several weeks ago, around the time in question, and that afterward, he apologized profusely for being away. So today I asked him where he went. And he seems to have an alibi. He spent the entire weekend with his mother at Lady Smallcombe's estate in Richmond."

"He is claiming his mother as his alibi?"

At Dare's skepticism, Julienne returned a wry smile. "Indeed. And the tale gets better. He was merely supposed to squire Lady Riddingham to a Saturday afternoon garden party there. But when they arrived, her lapdog apparently was terrorized by a stable cat, and she refused to travel until the poor animal was calmer. They even had to summon the local physician to give it a sleeping potion. So Riddingham and his mama spent two nights in Richmond and didn't return to London until late Monday."

"While the companion disappeared Sunday evening," Dare murmured. "Her body was found early the next day."

"I think that makes it unlikely Riddingham killed her, don't you? And his tale is so extravagant. . . . Surely a man of Caliban's cunning wouldn't be foolish enough to make up a story that could so easily be disproved. It would be short work to confirm Riddingham's presence in Richmond that weekend. You could ask Lady Smallcombe . . . or the physician, for that matter."

"I intend to. Did you question him about Alice Watson?"

"I was afraid to press too closely for fear of rousing his suspicion. But I did mention how shocked I was by the death of Lady Castlereagh's companion, that I feared London wasn't safe for womankind. Riddingham said that he barely knew her, that he only heard about her death from Lady Castlereagh recently."

"And you believed him?"

"If he is acting, then his performance is good enough to rival Kean's. I could detect no sign of artifice from him. And I should think by now I know most all the tricks of my profession."

For a long moment Dare's eyes delved into hers. Then, giving his back to her, he propped one booted foot up on the fender and stared grimly down at the empty hearth. "If Riddingham is not our traitor, then I've been chasing shadows all this time."

His tone was so dark, Julienne wanted to console him. "What of his friends, Sir Stephen Ormsby and

Mr. Perrine? You said one of them may have lost the ring to Riddingham. Apparently they both were in London that weekend, for Riddingham had to cancel a planned engagement with them for Saturday night."

"He told you that?"

"Yes—when he was complaining about how his mother had spoiled his plans. Isn't it possible that one of them was acquainted with Alice Watson? Sir Stephen certainly seems enough of a rake to seduce an innocent girl for his own devious purposes. Perhaps Lady Castlereagh could tell you what connection those gentlemen had to her companion."

"Rest assured, questioning her will be my next step. And I will endeavor to find out from Riddingham what his friends knew of the girl."

"How?"

Dare exhaled in a reluctant sigh. "As much as it pains me, I suppose I will have to worm my way back into Riddingham's good graces."

"You might do best to soothe his wounded pride and let him think he is winning me."

Raising his head, Dare glanced back at Julienne. "Better yet, I will find him another love interest."

Julienne didn't particularly like the sudden gleam that entered his eyes. "It will have to be someone other than Miss Upcott. I imagine she is exceedingly unhappy with him at the moment."

"There are better candidates," he answered obscurely. "I think I will invite him to be my guest at a private club I know of."

"A sin club, you mean." When Dare didn't answer, Julienne pursed her lips. "I've heard tales of your Hellfire League entertainments. And I confess, I should like to attend myself. I am curious about what goes on at events like that."

Pushing away from the hearth, Dare moved toward her. "Are you trying to inveigle an invitation out of me, darling Jewel?"

"Would you take me?"

"Not on your life. I would be more than delighted to further your education privately, but I'll be damned before I willingly subject you to the debauchery of one of our Hellfire gatherings."

"Your jealousy is showing again," Julienne said lightly.

"How remiss of me," Dare drawled. "But I think I will do better alone with Riddingham, without your presence to complicate matters. You would only prove a distraction—to both of us. And it's imperative that I succeed this time."

Julienne stared at him thoughtfully. "You seem to have changed from the wastrel I once knew. I understand why you would be ideal for the task of pursuing Caliban, since few people can move among the ton as you can. But I still find it surprising that you have devoted so much effort to the search."

Julienne realized the truth of her words even as she spoke. It was sobering to think Dare wasn't the same reckless rogue she once had known. He had matured a great deal since their love affair. Yet a leopard didn't wholly change his spots, Julienne reflected as he crossed the room to her.

He was looking down at her intently. When his gaze traced the outline of her lips, she could feel its caress . . . the softness, the warmth. The thought of his mouth moving over hers sent an urgent desire burning through her senses—

Julienne froze. She couldn't allow herself to be swept away by his consuming passion again. It was deplorable enough, her need to be near him, to touch him. . . .

"I should go," she murmured. "I'm risking scandal as it is, calling alone at the residence of a notorious rake."

"Are you that concerned for your reputation?"

"Not really. An actress has little reputation to defend, as you well know. But my calling here might give our audience the wrong idea that I had succumbed to your seduction."

For a moment Dare looked as if he might object, but then he cleared his throat and stepped back a pace. "I will have someone see you home."

She set down her untasted glass of sherry and stood. "Will you let me know what you discover?"

"Are you truly interested?"

"Yes. And I went to a great deal of trouble for you today, Dare, so I think I deserve to hear the outcome."

"Perhaps you do. I could kiss you for this, you know."

Julienne gave him a provocative smile. "I would prefer that for once you refrained."

"Very well, love. Whatever you say." He belied his words, though, by bending and giving her nose a chaste peck. "But I could almost forgive you for stealing my grays."

Several nights later, Dare lounged on a couch at one side of the drawing room, watching in satisfaction as three nubile beauties assaulted Riddingham with their sensual arts. In short order they had divested the viscount of his clothing and aroused him till he was near bursting.

Then one of the beauties mounted him while the other two continued to attend him with their hands and mouths and bare breasts.

His face flushed with passion, Riddingham writhed and bucked beneath their erotic ministrations. Moments later his lanky body spasmed, and he gave a hoarse cry of ecstasy as he spent himself. Eventually he fell back, limp with exhaustion.

Dare sighed with ennui.

He had invited Riddingham for an evening of pleasure at Madame Fouchet's salon, so he shouldn't be disappointed that his invitation had been accepted. He'd been forced to arrange this means of interrogating Riddingham, since Lady Castlereagh had recalled nothing further about who might have been pursuing her companion.

It had taken some doing to persuade the viscount to unruffle his angry feathers. But Dare was nothing if not persuasive, and his change of tactics seemed to do the trick. Dare had complained that Miss Laurent refused to forgive him until he'd made peace with his rival, and griped that he was losing the battle for the Jewel's affections.

Letting Riddingham believe he was winning her put the viscount in a more generous mood. Thus, three nights following their curricle race found them at Madame Fouchet's elegant sin club.

"You will take good care of my friend?" Dare had asked the Frenchwoman.

"Mais oui, absolutement," she replied in her husky, welcoming voice as she discreetly nodded to three of her Venuses.

Dare gladly gave Riddingham into the madame's care, knowing she would skillfully ply him with port and sex and make him feel like a king—or at least an Eastern potentate with a luscious harem.

Then Dare settled back in one corner of the room, prepared for a long night.

In his wilder days, he had been a frequent visitor here, and he still knew some of these straw damsels by name. Glancing around the room, he saw that Riddingham wasn't the only gentleman partaking in the debauchery. A half-dozen other acquaintances were enjoying the erotic pleasures Madame Fouchet offered.

But he had no desire to follow suit.

Rising abruptly, Dare poured himself a brandy and went to stand at the French window, looking out at the dark night. Despite his years, he felt suddenly old, raw with weariness, burned to the core.

His brutal discontent had caught him by surprise. For the most part he'd succeeded in denying its existence until recently.

It was no wonder, of course, that he suffered from boredom and loneliness. All his closest friends had married, abandoning their wicked ways in favor of home and hearth with their chosen mates.

Sin had been the first to go. Damien Sinclair was once as notorious a rakehell as Dare himself, until he embarked on a calculated seduction and found the one woman he couldn't live without.

Lucian Tremayne had been content to play his spymaster games until he lost his heart to the flame-haired siren he'd only wed in order to gain an heir.

Lucian's distant cousin, American privateer Nicholas Sabine, had developed a unquenchable passion for the beautiful daughter of a duke and persuaded her to return home with him. And Nick's ward, Raven Kendrick, had wed a stranger to avoid scandal but found her heart's desire in her infamous husband, a half-Irish gaming hall owner named Kell Lasseter.

It was their troubled marriage that had recently caused Dare to cut short his stay in Yorkshire and make a mad dash to Ireland.

Lucian had been amused when he heard the story, Dare remembered.

"Do I assume correctly, Dare, that you've been playing Cupid?"

Dare had smiled faintly at the irony of a jaded rake like himself assuming the role of matchmaker. "I thought someone needed to intervene. Raven planned to leave England without even informing Kell."

"So you went to Ireland to fetch him?"

"Yes. And we arrived at the London docks barely in time to prevent her departure."

The Lasseters had sailed for the Caribbean two days later. It was much too soon to have received any word from them yet, Dare knew, but he had no doubt they would be extremely happy together.

He would miss Raven greatly, even though his feelings toward her were merely those of a protective older brother. The unconventional minx had been a good influence on him. Indeed, his abrupt journey to Ireland on Raven's behalf was one of the few good deeds he could claim in his admittedly dissolute past.

Dare found himself frowning as he took a long swallow of brandy. Julienne's earlier remark about him being a wastrel had stung, probably because it was so close to the truth. For most of his thirty-three years, he'd been nothing more than a consummate pleasure seeker. Except during his former lamentable obsession with Julienne, he had never cared enough about anything in his life to warrant seriously exerting himself. Not until Caliban had appeared, in any event.

If he was to change the pattern of his decadent life, Dare reflected, Caliban was as good a place to start as any. Better, perhaps, because the stakes were so high.

And he found to his surprise that he wanted to change.

For now, however, he was required to spend the rest of the interminable evening at Madame Fouchet's, lulling Riddingham into a state of loquaciousness.

To that end, he endeavored to get the viscount thoroughly sotted, so that by the time Riddingham stumbled happily into the Wolverton town coach, he was three sheets to the wind.

Dare slurred his own words, pretending to be just as drunk when he asked if the viscount had enjoyed himself.

"By Jove, 'twas bloody splendid!" Riddingham exclaimed. "Mush say, Wolverton, you have excellent taste in fancy pieces. Those ladybirds of Fouchet's left me all wrung out. . . ."

"I'm certain they would be glad for you to return any time. The blonde told me she hadn't had a great buck like you in months."

"Did she now?" Sprawled on the seat, his disheveled

clothing reeking of sex and wine, Riddingham flashed a silly grin.

"Saw her admiring your ring," Dare commented. "Wonder if it has some special power over females?"

Riddingham's grin broadened as he held up his hand to peer at the ring. The dragon's ruby eyes winked in the dim light of a passing streetlamp. "P'raps so."

"I really would like to have one of those for myself. You're certain Stephen Ormsby didn't lose it to you?"

Riddingham's brow furrowed. "Doan remember."

"Well, at least your taste in women is better than Stephen's. Heard he was sniffing around that young companion of Lady Castlereagh's a few weeks ago. The girl who wound up floating in the Thames."

"Pity about her."

"Yes, a pity. You and Stephen were both at Castlereagh's rout a few weeks ago, weren't you?"

The viscount gave a woozy nod.

"Did you see him make a play for the girl?"

"Happen I did. But there was another chap . . . tall, dark-haired fellow. . . ." Riddingham gave a drunken snicker. "She was making sheep's eyes at him and scarcely noticed ole Stephen."

"Indeed? She preferred this other chap? Who was it?"

"Can't recall his name but . . . think his title was higher than a baronet. Remember because it miffed Stephen when she snubbed him. Fancies himself quite the charmer, Stephen does."

Riddingham gave a snort of laughter before he laid his head back against the squabs and promptly passed out.

Over his snores, Dare forced himself to consider his next steps. He very much doubted that Riddingham had killed the girl or even hired someone to kill her. And the likelihood that he was Caliban now seemed so far-fetched, it was almost laughable.

Dare frowned. It also seemed laughable that he'd ever suspected Julienne of being Caliban's accomplice. She wasn't in league with a cunning killer. Nor was she a traitor.

The thought brought Dare less comfort than it should have, for now he no longer had any legitimate pretext for pursuing her. At least no pretext that would make Julienne take him seriously.

She thought his public courtship a juvenile act of revenge—and perhaps it had begun that way. But he was fooling himself to pretend that his goal hadn't changed.

Desire tormented him like hot coals, yet his need for Julienne had gone beyond the physical. He wanted more than simply to win their wager; he wanted her earnest surrender.

His loins hardened when he remembered claiming his victory kiss after the race. His fear that she could have been thrown from the curricle. Her soft lips parting warm and moist beneath his. Her heart beating wildly as her soft breasts pressed against his chest. The exhilaration that filled him at her willing response . . .

He could have gone on kissing her forever for the sheer joy of it. Even that simple intimacy touched some part of him he'd kept inviolate for years. For all his sensual expertise, he'd remained emotionally detached from his lovers, holding himself apart even as he sought release from the emptiness that gnawed at him.

He would have to find the strength to hold himself

apart from Julienne, Dare knew. She would only savage his heart once more if he allowed her to.

To care for her again was impossible, unthinkable. Still, he couldn't lose her. Not yet.

And he couldn't prevent himself from contemplating what it would take to truly win their wager.

He found Lucian the following morning, sparring at Gentleman Jackson's Rooms on Bond Street. Dare wanted to catch his friend before he left town for his Devonshire seat and his pregnant wife, Brynn.

Dare winced as he watched the punishing round of fisticuffs, but Lucian appeared to enjoy the physical barbarity, delivering his own share of powerful blows with relish. When the bout was over, Lucian and Dare moved to one corner of the vast room and spoke over the din of another boxing match.

While Lucian toweled himself dry, Dare related what he had learned about Riddingham's alibi for the time in question.

"And you're convinced that Riddingham is not Caliban?" Lucian said at the conclusion.

"I am. We've been looking at the wrong man. Although it's still possible his cohorts were involved."

"Who?" Lucian asked, his interest sharpening.

"Sir Stephen Ormsby and Martin Perrine. Do you know them?"

"Sir Stephen, I do. Perrine only vaguely."

"Sir Stephen is a fashionable fribble, Perrine a dull sort who scarcely says a word in mixed company," Dare said. "They were both at Riddingham's estate in York last month, which is how they wound up as guests at my recent house party. I invited them because

Riddingham could have won the ring from either of them. Moreover, Sir Stephen was seen trifling with the companion in recent weeks."

He recounted Riddingham's delight that Sir Stephen had been spurned by the girl in favor of a tall, dark-haired nobleman.

"That could prove to be a significant lead," Lucian declared, visibly pleased by the information. "I'll look into it at once."

"Martin Perrine shouldn't be disregarded entirely, though," Dare remarked. "It's common knowledge that his pockets are terminally to let. As a younger son, his prospects must not be too promising. He could have turned traitor for financial gain."

Lucian's brow creased in contemplation as he donned his shirt. "I will have him investigated, but I doubt Caliban is in the game solely for wealth. He's a brilliant strategist who revels in outwitting his opponents."

"Perrine certainly doesn't strike me as brilliant. And he isn't of noble blood."

"Still, his quiet manner might simply be a cultivated disguise. And it's possible he calls himself Lord Caliban to increase his importance to his victims. I'll see what my agents can find out about him, along with Sir Stephen and this unnamed nobleman."

Dare started to reply, but just then Gentleman Jackson, one of England's former champions and the owner of the boxing salon, came over to commend Lucian on his bout.

When they were alone again, Lucian began tying his cravat as he said to Dare in a low voice, "I'll have to ask you to keep up your hunt, since unmasking Caliban has become even more urgent. This morning I received a communiqué from France. A few days ago there was a failed attempt to poison Lord Castlereagh."

"And you think it is Caliban's hand at work?"

"Our foreign secretary has enemies here at home, certainly," Lucian admitted. "And since he isn't here to defend his policies, several members of Parliament have become more vocal in denouncing him. Even the Cabinet is seriously divided. But I can think of no one who would resort to murder to be rid of him."

"But how would his death benefit Caliban?" Dare asked.

"It might simply be revenge. If Napoleon abdicates as expected, his successor must be determined. Castlereagh is finally convinced it would be better to have a Bourbon monarch on the throne rather than Boney's young son, and his lordship is leaving Chaumont for Paris soon to settle the issue with our Allies and the French Senate. That could be Caliban's motive: retaliation against Bonaparte's biggest rival. He could be planning to assassinate Castlereagh."

"So we should assume that he is Caliban's next target," Dare said thoughtfully.

"I think we must. And Caliban will doubtless have accomplices. He's a master at developing conspirators—finding their weaknesses and exploiting them. Brynn's brother Grayson is the only person I know to have escaped Caliban's web, and he only managed it by fabricating his own death. Which reminds me . . . have you come to any conclusion about Miss Laurent's involvement with Caliban?"

Dare grimaced involuntarily. "Yes."

"And?" Lucian prompted.

"And I think she's innocent. I was mistaken about

her, I realize now. She was the one who discovered the evidence that exonerates Riddingham. If not for her, I might still be chasing a dead end."

"So I was right after all?" Lucian's question held an edge of amusement.

"Yes, damn you," Dare replied good-naturedly. "I admit I allowed my past with her to influence my judgment, just as you accused me of doing. I've since revised my opinion of her. I believe she would make you a good spy after all."

"Oh? Then you'll approach her about working for us?"

"If you are still interested."

"I am. I would ask her myself but I am leaving for Devonshire later today." Lucian paused. "You know my assistant, Philip Barton? If you discover anything at all of importance, contact Philip. He'll know what to do."

Dare nodded. "Give my love to Brynn," he said absently, his mind already debating how he would broach the subject with Julienne. "By the time you return, I should have something to report."

Chapter
Ten

Dare allowed nearly a week to pass, however, before approaching Julienne. He forced himself to keep away for several reasons.

The first and most practical was to let Riddingham think he was winning the beautiful Jewel. Too swift an about-face might raise questions in the viscount's mind and call unwanted attention to his drunken divulgences about his friends and the dead companion.

The second, Dare calculated, was to increase Julienne's eagerness for their next encounter. She had asked to hear the outcome of his interrogation, and delaying his disclosure would only whet her curiosity.

And the last, most critical reason was to give himself time to try to control his obsession with her. The effort, however, had been futile, Dare realized as he sat in his box at the Drury Lane Theater watching the current play, *Richard III*.

It was a brilliant performance. From the first lines, Edmund Kean's genius shone through as he portrayed the evil Richard, who had murdered his way to a throne and then to his own destruction. But Julienne as Lady Anne was a perfect foil for him as she attempted to avoid Richard's deadly spider's web.

The wooing scene during the mourning procession for the late king was a public match between two wily opponents, a twisted mating dance rife with almost erotic undercurrents.

Dare, like the rest of the audience, sat riveted. The scene took on added meaning because of his own public mating dance with Julienne. He frequently felt himself the focus of probing glances from the bejeweled lords and ladies in the adjoining boxes.

He knew the ending of Shakespeare's play, of course. Lady Anne lost the battle with Richard and her life, poisoned after she had served her turn. But it became stunningly clear to Dare as he watched Julienne's dazzling performance that he was fighting a losing battle himself.

Your beauty was the cause. . . . Your beauty that did haunt me in my sleep.

He'd tried to convince himself that in time he would get over her. But she had crawled under his skin again, damn her.

Nothing could stop him from wanting her constantly, endlessly. Nothing would stop him from pursuing her.

Not even knowing the pain he might suffer in the end.

Dare left the theater immediately after the performance, intending to wait for Julienne at her lodgings. A chill wind whipped around his greatcoat as he stood on the street while his town coach was summoned from the long queue of carriages.

When a footman opened the coach door for him, Dare started to enter. But then he caught sight of a small object resting on the velvet seat, gleaming in the light of the carriage lamps.

A piece of jewelry. A pin, perhaps. Picking it up, he inspected the design. A flower . . . with stem and leaves of gold and petals made of pearls. A rose?

A dark suspicion struck Dare suddenly. What was it Lucian had said as they'd stood over Alice Watson's bloated body? *She wore a rose-shaped pearl broach that was thought to be gift from her lover.* Was this the broach that had been torn from the dead girl's collar? And how in hell had it come to be on his carriage seat?

Was it the work of her killer?

Dare's head whipped around, and he searched the crowds milling in the street in front of the theater. A fortnight ago he'd deliberately announced he was hunting a deadly traitor named Caliban. Was this the response?

Was Caliban taunting him by leaving clues? Watching him even now? Was Caliban the girl's killer?

Dare's mouth tightened grimly. It was difficult to believe the two were unrelated.

He intended to question his coachman and footmen, but he doubted he would find any leads as to who had placed the broach here. Caliban was too clever.

This time, however, the treacherous mastermind had overplayed his hand. Caliban might delight in showing his superiority by mocking his opponents and stirring fear in their hearts, Dare thought stonily. But this apparent attempt to intimidate him only strengthened his resolve to find the traitor and bring him to justice.

It was after midnight when a hackney carriage deposited Julienne in front of her lodgings and then rattled off down the mist-shrouded street.

When a dark figure stepped out of the shadows, she gasped and fumbled in her reticule for the small but deadly blade she carried for protection.

"Late night?" Dare asked casually as moonlight illuminated his handsome features.

Julienne put a hand to her heart. "Dare!" Her tone held both relief and vexation. "You frightened ten years off my life!"

"The play has been over for hours."

Frowning, she studied him in the dim light, trying to read his enigmatic expression. "I accepted Riddingham's invitation for supper." When he made no reply, she lowered her voice. "You can hardly object when you yourself asked me to be with him. Moreover, I haven't even seen you in days."

"Did you miss me?"

"No," Julienne lied. "But I expected you to contact me sooner—although not at this hour of the night."

"Will you invite me in?"

Julienne hesitated. "This is a respectable rooming house. The landlady won't look kindly on my entertaining a gentleman caller, especially one of your notoriety."

"She doesn't need to know."

"She is extremely watchful."

"I came to report on my investigation of Riddingham," Dare said when she still wavered, "but if you prefer I left . . ."

"No," Julienne replied in a rough whisper. "Just please keep your voice down."

"I watched your performance tonight," Dare murmured as he followed her to the front door.

"I know. I saw you." She didn't add that she had scanned the audience each and every night since that first one, searching for Dare's shining gilt hair. Nor did she confess the leap of gladness that had surged through her when she'd spied him tonight, or her disappointment when he never came backstage to the green room.

After using her key to unlock the door, Julienne lit a taper in the entrance hall. Quietly she led him up the dark stairway and down a corridor to the rooms she had rented for the season.

The parlor was chilly, for she preferred to avoid the expense of lighting a fire when she would only be going to bed in a short while. The bedchamber would have coals burning in the grate, though, since she paid the landlady to see to it before her expected return from the theater each night.

Leaving on her cloak, Julienne offered Dare a seat, but he remained standing. As she lit a lamp, his glance took in the sparse furnishings, and he frowned.

"So what happened with Riddingham?" Julienne asked, not wanting to defend her modest dwelling or her decision not to spend her salary on greater luxuries. "Did you discover if his friends knew the companion?"

"Sir Stephen was seen speaking with her at Lady Castlereagh's rout. But there was also a stranger who appeared to claim her interest. I've passed on the information for investigation. With any luck it could put us a step closer to finding Caliban."

"So what now?"

"We continue the hunt."

She gave him a look of exasperation. "Is that all you intend to tell me?"

"That depends on you, Julienne."

"What do you mean?"

"I've been commissioned to offer you a job."

"A job?"

"As a spy for the British government."

Taken aback by his unexpected answer, she stared at him.

"The gentleman," Dare explained, "who heads intelligence in the Foreign Office believes you could be an asset to the country, since you have entrée to the émigré community. If you worked for us, you would be required to glean any information you can on the intrigues of the Royalists and pass it on. The government will pay you, of course."

His glance took in the shabby parlor, and she could tell what he was thinking: that she could obviously use the income. She remembered as well that Dare thought her greedy and grasping. No doubt he believed there was little she wouldn't do for money.

Julienne pressed her lips together. "I wonder that your offer comes now," she said coolly. "Is it because I proved my usefulness by helping you with Riddingham?"

"That, and the fact that your actions seem to absolve you of guilt."

"Guilt?"

Dare's green gaze bored into her. "I couldn't be certain of your complicity when I first saw your close association with Riddingham. For all I knew, he was Caliban, and you were in league with him."

Her breath caught at his implication. "You thought I was in league with . . . You suspected me of *treason*?"

"The possibility did cross my mind." Dare smiled with a hint of mockery. "This isn't the first time your name has been linked with the Bonapartists."

Julienne felt herself tremble. "Are you speaking of the charges your grandfather laid against me?"

When he remained silent, a raw upwelling of grief and fury coursed through her. Seven years ago she had been the victim of his grandfather's evil machinations, when she had been completely innocent.

She heard her own tone turn icy. "Your grandfather accused me of treason. Did you believe him?"

Dare shrugged, an elegant gesture that told her nothing. "I wasn't sure what to believe then. Given your other lies, I think I would have been justified in assuming the worst about you. And I certainly couldn't trust your loyalties when you might have been Caliban's accomplice."

His response wounded her to the quick, and Julienne lowered her gaze to hide her bitter hurt. She had betrayed Dare, true. And he had a right to despise her for that. But it was one thing to hate her for playing him false with a lover; quite another to consider her guilty of betraying her country.

How could he believe something so despicable of her?

For a moment she stood there shaking, remembering that terrible time seven years ago—the vile rumors that had placed her under suspicion of treason, her defenselessness, her utter inability to refute the charges. Those scurrilous accusations had destroyed her life when she had never done anything to deserve it. When her only crime had been to love Dare.

He had no right to think her guilty! Dare's admission just now was a betrayal in itself. He should have known the allegations were all lies.

Julienne raised her head to glare her anger. "Your

grandfather falsified those charges in order to intimidate me. I'm surprised you were taken in by him."

A flash of pain flickered in Dare's eyes before his
gaze turned as cool as her own had been. "I was taken
in by *your* wiles, wasn't I? Perhaps I was merely gullible in my youth. Then again, my grandfather could
have been right about you."

His retort set rage unfurling inside Julienne. She
looked at Dare through a red mist, wanting to strike
back at him, yearning to punish him for his lack of
faith. "If you think me such a femme fatale, I wonder
that you even risk being here alone with me."

"I am better armed than I was seven years ago."

"Are you?" Julienne said, her tone dangerously
silken. She would show Dare that he wasn't nearly as
well-armed as he thought. "Would you care to put
your armor to the test?"

His gaze made a slow sweep of her body. "What did
you have in mind?"

In answer, she spun on her heel and opened the door
to her bedchamber. Pausing, she glanced back at him,
her look filled with challenge. "Are you coming?"

For once, Julienne saw with satisfaction, she had
rendered Dare speechless. But he hesitated only a moment before following her.

It was warmer here, she noted. She stirred the coals
in the grate to a cheery blaze and then lit a lamp and
set it on the mantel. Dare had shut the door behind
him and was surveying the drab room's meager furnishings: a narrow bed, a washstand, a wardrobe and
dressing table, and a single wooden chair placed near
the hearth.

"Take off your clothes," Julienne ordered as she

shed her cloak and hung it on a wall peg. When she turned, she found Dare watching her with half-lidded eyes, heat and wariness glittering in their depths.

"Just like that? You expect me to undress with no preliminaries?"

Her smile was at once seductive and scornful. "Are you afraid, Lord Wolverton?"

"With you in this mood?" His mouth curled. "I think perhaps I should be."

"Indeed you should," she taunted with a coy toss of her head.

Her mind told her she was playing with fire, but she refused to back down from her challenge. The anger driving her was too fierce to ignore. She felt like a powder keg on the verge of explosion. She wanted to punish Dare, to hurt him as he had hurt her. She wanted to conquer him.

Thus far she had claimed few victories in their battle, but that would change tonight, Julienne vowed. And she would use her body as her weapon.

"Well?" she asked impatiently, placing her hands on her hips.

He did undress then, albeit more slowly than she would have liked. While she watched, he removed his coat and cravat and draped them over the back of the chair, then drew off his linen shirt. His bare torso gleamed golden in the firelight, rippling with corded muscle.

He sat to remove his pumps and stockings and reached for the front placket of his breeches. Hesitating, he glanced up at her, as though to see if she was watching.

Julienne curved her lips in a half smile and met the

dark challenge in his eyes. Unfastening his breeches, Dare stood and slowly peeled them down, revealing the hard, flat contours of his belly . . . the tantalizing pelt of dark gold hair that swept down to his groin. . . . He eased the satin fabric lower. Freed from constraint, his rampant member jerked upward toward his belly, already flushed and engorged in anticipation.

Julienne's mouth went dry. Despite her determination to remain unmoved, she felt her body respond. But she refused to let Dare know of her weakness.

"I would say you are rather eager for me," she mocked.

"I am always eager for you, *chérie*," Dare retorted wryly. "That is nothing new."

He drew the garment down farther, exposing the velvety pouch of his heavy testicles, his sinewy thighs and calves. Then he stepped out of his breeches, leaving his lean, powerful body naked.

He was beautiful, Julienne thought in reluctant awe. Lithe and strong and sensual, the focus of all her fantasies. Desire clawed at her, insistent and sharp, as she moved to stand before him, but she tried to hide it with a mocking smile.

Deliberately she ran the tip of her finger along his hard-muscled ribs, over his flat belly to his swollen phallus that seemed to beg her for attention.

Dare's eyes narrowed, but she ignored the danger in his green gaze as she curled her fingers over the silken-steel shaft.

"Shall we see how long you can resist me?" she asked.

"Do your worst," he said with maddening nonchalance.

Oh, I will, Julienne thought darkly. She would break him. She would make him plead with her for mercy. . . .

She stood on tiptoe to kiss him, but there was nothing tender about her gesture. Instead she bit at his lips, raking her teeth against his flesh.

She heard his low grunt of surprise as he recognized the primal, dangerous edge to her lovemaking, but other than the tensing of his body, he made no protest.

Still holding his arousal in her hand, Julienne nipped at his jaw, the strong column of his throat, the sleek skin of his shoulder, then moved to his chest, to the flat male nipples. When she bit lightly, he drew a sharp breath. With a faint smile of triumph, she spent a long moment on his nipples, licking and suckling and grazing with her teeth, before gliding on.

When her fiery mouth trailed downward toward his stomach, though, Dare realized her intent and grasped her arms, halting her. "I want you naked first. Unless *you're* afraid?" he added when she looked up at him.

Her eyes flashed, but she turned silently to present her back for him to unfasten the buttons of her gown. When she faced him again, their gazes locked, two passionate people determined not to give way.

Her mouth curved in a half smile then, and she stripped off her garments slowly, one by one, her movements deliberately provocative.

Her erotic performance held Dare's gaze riveted. He didn't understand the brittle anger that gripped her, the icy disdain, but he fully fathomed the effect her meagerly clad body had on him. Heat burned through him, making his blood pulse with need.

When her tongue slowly licked her lips in carnal invitation, excitement flared through his senses. It was all he could do to feign indifference when Julienne drew her chemise over her head and stood garbed in nothing more than silk stockings held up by strips of ribbon.

Bending, she untied the knots of her garters and rolled the silk down her long slender legs, the ripe, full globes of her breasts dangling like luscious fruit.

Dare felt sweat break out over his skin. God, but he wanted to taste those sweet breasts, to suck on those taut nipples until she was as feverish and aching with need as she had made him.

She stood again, and the sultry, glittering light in her eyes told him clearly she knew how much her nude body captivated him.

Against his will, his gaze traveled the length of her . . . her flawless bosom, her narrow waist, her rounded hips, the dark curls shielding her feminine mound. . . . Julienne ravished his senses, even as jaded as they were. It was a struggle to keep from reaching out and hauling her into his arms and putting a swift end to her teasing.

But she wasn't done making him suffer, apparently. He watched as she went to her dressing table and withdrew a small coffer, recognizing the contents instantly: sponges and vials of liquid—no doubt vinegar or brandy—to guard against pregnancy. Absurdly he felt a twinge of regret at her making certain she would not conceive his child.

Julienne wet a sponge and made a great show of inserting it between her legs, deep within her feminine passage. Then she let down her hair, shaking her head so that the shining sable mass spilled over her bare shoulders to curl around her naked breasts.

For Dare it was a siren's call. He nearly groaned out loud as all the muscles of his body clenched in torment. Julienne damn well knew what her silken hair did to him, how fiercely it aroused him. Knew that one of his greatest pleasures was the feel of her dragging the soft skeins over his body. He could lie for hours with her torturing him that way.

Dare knew he was vanquished. He might have been strong enough to fight himself, but he couldn't fight Julienne when she was like this, a temptress bent on seduction.

He locked his jaw as he strove for control, but there was no resisting her. Not when she sauntered toward him and reached down to cup the sac of his testicles. Already his cock was lifting and jerking helplessly in response to her skilled caresses.

Her stroking fingertips sent fire racing through him. Dare shut his eyes, but the scent of her heat filled his nostrils.

Leaning closer, she pressed her loins against his cramping erection while rubbing her stiffened nipples against the wall of his chest.

Dare did groan then. He wanted to throw her down on the bed and sink himself into her, but she was in command, a wild creature of fire and moonlight. And he was in thrall to her.

His breath fled as she parted her legs to straddle his thigh and slid her already slick cleft against his leg, grinding down hungrily. His senses reeled, rawly frenzied. His hands tightened on her waist, but she pulled away.

"No," Julienne warned with a taunting glance before she bent to him again.

Her mouth pressed hot, open kisses against his chest, and lower, trailing fire over his muscles. It was almost more than he could bear.

Talons of passion clutched at him, raking him with need. When she knelt before him, he shuddered, anticipating her erotic intentions.

He wasn't mistaken. Delirious sensation ripped through him as she attended him, running her tongue around the head of his shaft . . . wetting the sensitive tip . . . blowing a tender, hot breath that aroused him wildly.

His entire body clenched.

And that was before she fastened her lush mouth around him.

"Sweet Christ," Dare ground out harshly.

She showed him no mercy, though. His engorged shaft jutted out blatantly now, throbbing with a relentless ache. Every inch of his skin burned with fever for her. But her tongue and lips and teeth continued their sensual assault, forcing his surrender to the exquisite torment.

Dare gritted his teeth at the incredible onslaught of pleasure. He felt his sanity slipping away as she suckled him, drawing him into a vortex of fire. It was only moments before his rigid control broke.

Grating out her name, he dug his fingers into her shoulders and pulled her upright. Her beguiling mouth was moist and triumphant, but he felt the coiled tension in her body, saw the smoldering flames of desire in her eyes, and knew she was trapped in her need, as he was.

His hands clasping under her buttocks, he lifted her

off her feet and spread her thighs, prepared to take
her. A charge of bright lightning arced between them
as their eyes met.

Dare held her stormy gaze as he slid upward into her
molten, silky sweetness with a violent, thrusting need.

The stunning heat of her nearly made him explode.
And Julienne's gasping moan told him she was at the
point of climax, as did the way she sank her fingers
into his hair and arched against him.

Unable to speak, barely able to breathe, he carried
her to the bed and fell with her. For a moment they
rolled and tussled on the narrow mattress in a duel of
desire, the turbulence of their clashing wills only adding to their passion. Julienne had wrapped her legs
tightly around his hips and now was bucking and
writhing beneath him. Dare felt his own arousal spurred and heightened by her tempestuous hunger.

Fearing he would burst, he covered her mouth in a
deep, violent kiss of longing, and she responded just as
fiercely, digging her nails into his shoulder blades, her
fervor singeing, scalding, searing.

An instant later he felt the violence of her release.
Julienne convulsed beneath him in a white-hot erup-
tion, her scream captured by his mouth as he held her
surging body down. The feel of her sleek, tight chan-
nel clutching around his shaft sent him over the edge.
He sheathed himself to the hilt, his own hips jerking in
a spasm of completion as savage, unrestrained pleasure washed over him in endless caresses of fire.

For a dozen heartbeats he lay sprawled on top of her,
too exhausted to move. Finally, though, he eased his
weight off her and gathered her limp body against him.

In the aftermath, Julienne lay wrapped in his arms,

enveloped by his sinewy strength, her body boneless but her thoughts in turmoil. Her plan to punish Dare had gone awry; her lonely, yearning flesh had betrayed her, her resolve melting as anger turned to fervent hunger.

It was foolish to have succumbed to her passions, and yet she felt almost cleansed by the release of pent-up fury and hurt after so many years. Their lovemaking had been explosive, but she hadn't wanted careful tenderness from Dare. She'd been wild and wanton—burning for him.

She had relished the fiery tempest. And she cherished more the peace that came afterward. She had missed this desperately, the intimacy of lying with Dare, their bodies entwined. His lips felt so right, his arms felt so right, *he* felt so right. She could feel his heartbeat like an echo of her own.

And yet he thought her a traitor.

A long moment passed before she could control her resentment, her wrath.

"Despite what you believe of me," she said at last, her voice low and raw, "I would *never* aid the current regime in France. I hated the Revolutionists for murdering my father and destroying our future, but it was because of Napoleon that we remained destitute. If we had been able to recover even a part of the Folmont lands and fortune, I never would have—" She fell silent, gritting her teeth, knowing it was useless to ponder what-ifs.

"Never what?" Dare prodded, his warm breath brushing her temple.

"I never would have been compelled to prostitute myself."

She felt him go very still. She had shocked him, as she intended.

"What do you mean?" The question held a sharp edge that surprised her.

Can you possibly care? she thought defiantly.

"Your grandfather's allegations caused such a scandal for me that I could no longer show my face in public without creating a scene. I was branded a treacherous whore even by my friends." Anger drove her to continue. "I might have borne it, perhaps, but *Maman* was devastated. I left town, hoping to spare her. But the income from the shop wouldn't fully support her. . . . And then her disease grew worse. She needed constant care and relief from the pain. So I took a protector to pay her bills."

"A protector?" Dare's voice was a low rasp.

Remembering, Julienne swallowed hard, fighting a sudden rush of ancient grief. "I had no choice. I was all *Maman* had."

His expression unreadable, Dare rose up on one elbow to stare down at her.

His image swam before her eyes, shimmering with the firelight and her foolish tears. She dashed them away furiously. She would *not* fall victim to self-pity. And she would not countenance his suspicions.

"I sold my body, Dare, but not my loyalty to this country."

At his intense scrutiny, she looked away, trying to hold fast to her anger; it was her sole defense against him. "I am not for sale! Not inside my soul. And I am not a traitor."

Dare remained silent, recalling when he had first met Julienne, how she had shielded her mother with all the fierceness of a lioness protecting her cub. She had sacrificed far more than most daughters would have, selling her body to sustain her mother's final days. He felt a fierce stab of guilt that she had been brought so low—

Grimly Dare caught himself. He shouldn't feel guilt over what had become of Julienne. If she had never betrayed him with her lover, her mother would have been well cared for. He would have seen to it, even if they hadn't wed. But Julienne never had even given him the chance to make the offer.

"It hurts that you believed your grandfather's lies," she said after a moment.

I hurt, too, he thought. *You cut out my heart.* But he'd known those particular accusations of the old man's were lies. And he knew Julienne was still enraged by it. He could see the fire in her eyes—a long-burning, powerful anger amid the pain.

"I never believed my grandfather's accusations of treason," he said quietly.

"But you do think me capable of it now."

Dare bit back a sigh. "I admit when I first saw you with Riddingham, I wanted you to be guilty. I was still bitter about your betrayal seven years ago."

And he would never shake that bitterness, Dare reflected, feeling an ache in his chest at what they had lost. He lifted a loose curl from her cheek, brushing it against his lips and inhaling the sweet scent.

This was part of his shattered dream, holding Julienne in his arms, feeling her luscious warmth against him, the silkiness of her skin beneath his hands. . . . He had hungered for this closeness, this intimacy he had known only with her. The solace he craved was always her. He still craved her, not only with his body but with his heart—

Dare shut his eyes. Was it possible, he wondered, that he still loved her? God help him. That kind of weakness could destroy him.

But if he'd thought that making love to Julienne would lessen her hold on him, if he'd hoped to take her body and walk away triumphant, he realized now how gravely mistaken he was. A single violent coupling couldn't quench his passion for her. It might never be quenched.

I'll never be free of you, his heart whispered. *You'll haunt me forever.*

He could do his damnedest, however, to haunt Julienne in return. He wanted her as hungry and vulnerable as he was.

Deliberately he rested his palm on her breast—and felt her flinch.

At his arousing touch, Julienne drew a sharp breath, recognizing the instantaneous return of sexual desire. She squeezed her eyes shut, trying not to think, to breathe, to want. Dare made her feel desperate with wanting—

In despair she untangled her limbs from his and sat up abruptly.

Behind her she heard Dare's murmur. "We're on the same side, Jewel. We are not enemies."

"It would be easier if we were," she replied in a hoarse voice.

He hesitated. "I don't know about you, but I would rather call a halt to this miserable style of warfare."

"So would I." She exhaled slowly. "If you are serious about wanting me to spy for you . . . I will do it."

"Willingly?"

Julienne glanced back at him. "That is the only way
I can prove my innocence to you, isn't it?"

His lashes lowered, hooding his gaze. "You needn't
prove your innocence to me."

"Do I not?" Rising from the bed, she went to the
wardrobe and pulled out a wrapper, using it to cover
her bare body.

"As I said," Dare remarked, "you will be well
paid."

Julienne forced a shrug. "The income will be welcome, but I would have agreed in any case. I want
Napoleon defeated as much as you do, perhaps more
so." She tied the sash with a jerk. "What do you want
me to do?"

"Discover whatever you can from the émigré
community. We're especially interested in hints of
anti-Royalists plots or rumors about Napoleon
sympathizers."

"While you continue to hunt for Caliban?"

"Yes. You will report to me for the time being."

"Very well. You should go now."

It was a dismissal, and to her relief, Dare didn't pretend to misunderstand her. He rose silently to dress.

Julienne moved to stand before the hearth, holding
out her hands to ward off her sudden chill.

She would do whatever Dare asked of her, whether
it was spying on scheming émigrés or helping him find
Caliban. She was determined to prove her innocence
to him.

And she was even more determined to make the elusive rake fall in love with her again. She would win

Dare's total surrender in their battle of seduction, Julienne vowed.

But first she would have to conquer her own emotions. If tonight was any example, she was in danger of having her own sensual weapons turned on her.

She would have to do far better at hardening her feelings and bolstering her heart's defenses if she wanted to survive.

Chapter
Eleven

Julienne began her commission as a spy much sooner than expected, for the next day brought news that eclipsed all else: Napoleon Bonaparte had abdicated.

For hours pandemonium reigned in London as crowds took to the streets in celebration. Amid the blaring trumpets and banging pots and pans came ecstatic cheers and triumphant shouts of "the Corsican Monster is vanquished!" All Europe had been ground under Napoleon's boot heel for so long that his defeat seemed almost miraculous.

The émigrés could talk of nothing else, Julienne discovered when she attended the impromptu gatherings at Solange Brogard's salon over the next several days. She shared their jubilation, even though her future wasn't directly dependent on the fate of Napoleon's successor, as theirs was. When the French Senate had declared in favor of King Louis, it meant that many of the exiles would be able to return home. But Julienne had no close family remaining, and the Folmont estates had been confiscated long ago.

At week's end, however, she had little progress to report to Dare. He called at her lodgings to take her for a drive in the country.

Even though it was a beautiful spring day, Julienne felt a definite tension between them. But Dare made no mention of her revelations about her shameful past, and she was determined to keep tight control of her emotions and pretend their angry lovemaking had never occurred.

She waited until they had left London's main streets before summarizing her lack of success as a spy.

"Everyone I observed is elated that Louis will be returning to France, along with the Compte d'Artois, the Prince de Conde, and other members of the exiled court. But I found no one at all who raised my suspicions or seemed to support Bonaparte. I'm sorry."

Dare shook his head. "You needn't apologize. And I sympathize with your frustration. We've had no luck in the search for Caliban."

"You haven't been able to identify the companion's lover?"

He hesitated, making Julienne wonder if he had indeed uncovered a new lead. But all he said was, "No. It's too soon yet to expect any breakthroughs on that front."

Then he surprised her by asking an entirely unrelated question. "That is quite a fetching hat. Did you design it?"

She reached up to touch the wide-brimmed silk bonnet that was adorned with tiny roses. "Not I. *Maman* was the one with the creative talent."

"While you were the one with the business sense."

"I suppose," Julienne said, puzzled by his change of subject.

For years after escaping to Kent, she and her mother had lived on the charity of distant relatives, in genteel shabbiness, struggling to make ends meet—until Julienne had hit upon the idea of selling bonnets and chapeaus that her artistic but frail mother designed. Like many Frenchwomen, the comptess had an astute eye for fashion, and her creations were in great demand. The business prospered well enough to eventually allow them to open a millinery and even to employ a clerk. They were scorned by both the French and English gentry for earning their living in trade, but at least they could afford the comptess's medicines.

Julienne couldn't understand, however, why Dare would make such an oblique observation unless it was to distract her from interrogating him about Caliban.

"You shouldn't underrate your own talents," he added smoothly. "You have an amazing gift for acting."

"Thank you," she said, deciding not to press him.

"I'm looking forward to your performance tomorrow night."

"Even though you've seen the same play a half-dozen times?" The run of *Richard III* had been extended another week by popular demand. "I should think you would be tired of watching me by now."

"I never tire of watching you, my sweet. And I must maintain my effort to win our wager."

"But of course."

At her tart tone, Dare's eyes glimmered with wry amusement. "Speaking of our wager, I have another opportunity to offer you. I plan to attend a race meet at Newmarket the first week in May—I have two colts running in the 2000 Guineas—and I would like you to accompany me."

Julienne frowned. "I cannot leave the theater for so

long. Not after spending so much time at your house party last month."

"Even if your government requires you?"

"You mean if *you* require me."

"You agreed to act as an informant for us."

"There are few émigrés in Newmarket," Julienne retorted. "You are simply manipulating matters for your own benefit."

"True," he admitted, sounding unrepentant. "I will arrange it with Drury Lane so that you will be free for the week."

"You won't ever give up, will you?" Julienne said in exasperation.

Dare flashed his notorious grin. "Certainly not. You should know me better than that by now."

"Regrettably, I do. I have no doubt you will spend the entire week trying to seduce me."

"What else? But Madame Brogard can come along to play chaperone if you feel you need protection."

"She hasn't proven to be adequate protection in the past," Julienne muttered. "What sort of living arrangements did you have in mind?"

"I always hire a lodge at Newmarket each spring. It's not luxurious, but it's comfortable."

"And totally unacceptable. I am not about to live there with you, Dare. It would appear too much like you are winning our wager. Solange and I will stay at an inn instead."

"It will be nearly impossible to find rooms at an inn at this late date. The Guineas is a leading meet, and the entire racing world will be in attendance."

"Well, if you want me there, you will find a way."

Julienne gave him an arch smile of her own. "I'm certain the resourceful Marquess of Wolverton can rise to the occasion and charm a set of rooms from a Newmarket innkeeper."

"You drive a hard bargain, love, but I will do my best to satisfy you."

"Satisfying me will be quite a feat," she reminded him in dulcet tones.

Dare's frustration hadn't lessened as he watched Julienne's performance the following evening. He had sidestepped her questions about the companion's lover because he could see no point in alarming her unnecessarily.

There was no reason to tell her about finding the pearl broach in his carriage or the likelihood that Caliban had planted it there. Lady Castlereagh had confirmed that the bauble was indeed the one Alice Watson had worn, which made Dare almost positive Caliban had been taunting him.

Dare's thoughts were centered on his nemesis rather than Shakespeare's play by the time Lady Anne was supposed to be poisoned. He watched Julienne take a sip from her wineglass and launch into an impassioned speech lamenting King Richard's malevolence. It was perhaps five minutes later when her voice suddenly quavered and she touched her throat. She managed a few more words, but then her delivery faltered altogether, making Dare wonder if she had forgotten her lines.

Suddenly she swayed and slowly sank to the stage floor, as if in a faint.

Her collapse just now was *not* part of the script, Dare was certain.

Her fellow actors seemed bewildered by the digression. One of the "palace guards" knelt at Julienne's side, making up lines as he went. "My queen! Are you ill?"

When Julienne gave no response, fear snaked along Dare's spine. Without conscious thought, he rose from his seat and hurriedly left his box, making his way along the corridors and down to the pit.

By the time he leapt up on stage, a crowd of actors had gathered around Julienne, and there was an audible buzz from the puzzled audience.

He pushed his way through to kneel beside Julienne.

She was barely conscious, he realized. Her breathing was shallow and her pulse so weak it was almost undetectable.

"Summon a doctor!" Dare demanded, his voice rough with dread.

He chafed her wrists to no avail. When someone handed him a vial of smelling salts, he waved it under her nostrils. Her eyelids fluttered and she gave a soft moan, but her body remained limp.

Lifting Julienne in his arms, he carried her backstage to the green room, ignoring the questions directed by the anxious manager, Samuel Arnold.

Dare laid her down on the chaise and loosened the tight bodice of her gown, his gaze riveted on her pale face, her blue lips that were barely moving as she tried futilely to speak. The last time he'd seen such a bloodless visage, it was that of a dead woman.

To his relief, a man claiming to be a physician appeared almost immediately, saying he had been in the audience. Dare paced the floor during the examination of Julienne, scarcely hearing one of Kean's oratories in the distance as the play continued.

In only moments, the doctor frowned. "Perhaps the wine she drank was noxious, but it is possible . . . My lord, I wonder if she might have been poisoned."

"Poisoned?" Dare rasped, his chest clenching, while Arnold echoed the same shocking question.

"Yes. Ingesting wolfsbane will have this particular effect."

"Will she die?" Dare forced himself to ask.

"I doubt she drank enough to kill her, but the poison must be purged from her body, else her heart will slow too much."

Dare stared down at Julienne as she lay there so weak and helpless. His own heart had stopped beating the moment she sank to the floor, but the possibility that she might have been poisoned sent fear and rage pulsing through his veins.

"Someone fetch me some vinegar, if you have it," the doctor urged. "Or some soap and a glass of water, if vinegar cannot be found."

The manager hastened to do his bidding, returning shortly with a half-full bottle of vinegar. While the doctor made preparations, Dare drove all the onlookers but Arnold from the room so as to give the patient privacy.

The doctor forced Julienne to drink, then turned her onto her stomach. With her head hanging over the side of the chaise, he pumped on the small of her back until she emptied the contents of her stomach into a chamber pot.

"I think that should do the trick," the doctor said, his tone grave but satisfied.

After a moment he gave way to Dare, who sat beside Julienne on the chaise and gently sponged her face and lips with a moist cloth.

At length her eyes fluttered open, and she raised a hand weakly to her temple. "What . . . happened?"

He brushed a tendril from her damp forehead. "Something you drank disagreed with you," he said with a warning glance toward the doctor, not wanting to alarm her. "We'll talk later, love. I will have my carriage summoned and take you home to your lodgings. For now just try to rest."

A puzzled frown etched her brow, but Julienne nodded trustingly and shut her eyes.

Dare covered her with a blanket, then ushered the other men from the room, leaving Julienne in peace for the moment.

The doctor could have been mistaken about the poison, Dare knew, but he didn't believe in coincidences. He suspected, rather, that Caliban was worried he was getting too close in his investigation and that this was an attempt to warn him off.

Dare's mouth thinned with determination. He would take the warning to heart, of course. If Julienne were to die because of him . . . It didn't bear thinking on.

He had no intention of abandoning his search, though. But he would have to change tactics if he hoped to win the battle against a determined killer.

Dare took Julienne home and arranged for her landlady to watch over her for the night. To his relief, when he called at her rooms the next morning, she had recovered enough to sit up in bed and question him about what had happened.

Dare told her about the suspected poisoning and how the manager's inquiries after the play had lead nowhere. No one in the theater company had any notion how poison could have come to be in her wineglass. No one had seen anything suspicious.

"Do you honestly think Caliban meant to kill me?" Julienne asked.

"No," Dare answered. "I think he merely meant it as a warning for me. But I'm taking no chances. I've arranged for a footman to escort you to and from the theater and to be with you wherever else you go."

"Surely you are exaggerating the threat," she protested.

"Perhaps, but I don't want your demise on my conscience," Dare replied emphatically.

What worried him, though, was that if Caliban truly wanted Julienne dead, there might be no way to stop him.

He sent a report to Lucian in Devonshire about the attack and conferred with Lucian's assistant, Philip Barton. But they uncovered no clues of any sort during the next two weeks. Once again the treacherous Caliban had eluded any efforts to trace him.

There were no further threatening incidents in the interval, at least. Dare considered canceling the trip to Newmarket, but decided that having Julienne out of town was preferable to letting her remain in London as a target. And by leaving town, he could give the appearance that he'd abandoned the investigation, even if he had no intention of doing anything of the kind.

Caliban's taunts, however, had affected Dare more than he cared to admit. He could go nowhere without looking over his shoulder, searching the shadows for further threats. And he knew he would spend the entire time at the race meet doing the same thing.

It was late afternoon when they arrived in Newmarket. Dare had again urged Julienne and her friend to stay with him at his lodge, but Solange declined, saying that it was one thing to enjoy a house party with dozens of other guests but quite another to be quartered with a notorious bachelor with no one but servants to play chaperone, and that surely whatever madman had poisoned Julienne in London would not follow them here.

Dare reluctantly agreed. He didn't believe Caliban would pursue them here, but he would take the added precaution of arranging with the innkeeper to keep a sharp eye out for the ladies' protection.

All the inns were packed, as Dare had predicted, but for the eminent Lord Wolverton, waters parted. The Harriford Arms managed to provide two very elegant rooms for Miss Laurent and Madame Brogard and maid during the week of the race.

Solange professed to be weary after the fifty-mile drive, even with Dare's well-sprung traveling chaise, so he proposed they remain at the inn to rest before his coach returned for them at seven, when they would dine with him at his lodge.

As the ladies were settling in their rooms and being refreshed with tea, their rotund host became effusively forthcoming about Lord Wolverton and his racers.

"His lordship has winners more often as not, and I've reckoned a good bit of blunt on him this week. He is a member of the Jockey Club, too. When he wanted rooms, I gave him rooms. A canny sort don't refuse a request from him."

"What is this Jockey Club?" Solange asked.

"I believe they are the rulers of the British Turf," Julienne said wryly. "Dare will no doubt be happy to satisfy our curiosity tonight."

As she expected, Dare's hired lodge turned out to be a mansion. And as usual, his chef had prepared an excellent dinner.

The conversation proved just as fulfilling to Julienne. She had resolved to think of this outing as a holiday—to enjoy herself and try to forget the danger lurking over their heads. Since she had never attended a race meet, she found Dare's explanations about the racing of blood horses highly engrossing.

"The race this week will be run over a mile on a straight course," Dare said. "And the winner will receive a purse of two thousand guineas, thus the name."

In past centuries, grueling heats were run over distances as long as four miles, he explained. But nowadays match races were shorter and run for money, while plate and cup races were run for trophies. The 2000 Guineas on Friday was a match race, with a field of twenty-three horses. Huge sums would be wagered on side bets, Dare added, predicting that the amount for this race would reach two hundred thousand pounds.

"So much?" Solange exclaimed.

"Would you care to place a wager?" he asked.

"Not I," Julienne responded first. "I have no intention of depleting my hard-earned purse on an absurd wager like some outrageous noblemen we know."

Dare merely grinned at her jibe. "Well then, if you

ladies are amenable, we will observe the training at the course tomorrow morning and tour the Jockey Club headquarters in the afternoon. And there is an assembly tomorrow night. Newmarket boasts some of the premier studs in the country, but we can save visiting them till the following day."

Solange wrinkled her nose. "*Mais non,* I do not care to suffer a smelly stables, but I should very much like to attend a dance."

The following morning, they rode out on hired hacks to watch the training on Newmarket Heath. The mist was just dissipating, and Julienne could see vast stretches of green sown with copses of splendid beech trees. On the landscape beyond rose the turrets and cupolas of countless stud farms and stables.

The horses looked magnificent, with their coats shining in the sunlight and powerful muscles flexing as they cantered past in warm-up laps.

"Possibly a third of the Thoroughbreds in England train here," Dare informed them.

Several dozen trainers and owners stood beside the course, studying watches and giving instructions to jockeys.

There were no special seats for spectators or booths selling food or any other amenities. As a result, there were few ladies present, for few of the fairer sex would tolerate the spartan discomfort of the Newmarket course. Most of the observers, Dare said, would watch the race from horseback or from the top of coach roofs.

"You cannot expect us to climb upon a coach!" Solange protested—to which Dare flashed an amused grin and assured her that his servants would provide his guests with every comfort.

Despite the current lack of accommodations, however, the excitement was contagious. They saw the two colts Dare had entered in the race and watched their breathtaking performance as they pounded down the heath in a surge of thundering hooves and flying manes. Afterward, Dare introduced his trainer and spoke privately with him while Julienne and Solange waited.

"My apologies," Dare said at the conclusion. "The fellow is as temperamental as any blooded mare and must be handled with care. But he's the best there is at his profession."

That, too, didn't surprise Julienne, for she suspected Dare would hire only the best.

They lunched at a public house in Newmarket and later toured the Jockey Club on High Street, the center of breeding and racing in England, where the Stud Book and Racing Calendar were kept.

That evening they attended an assembly at the home of one of the local noblemen for supper and dancing. Dare, it seemed, knew *everyone*. The moment his party entered the ballroom, he was surrounded by acquaintances wanting to renew old friendships and requesting his opinion on their racers.

Julienne and Solange were given little chance to feel neglected, though, for the company was lively and congenial, and both ladies found themselves much sought after by gentlemen eager to dance.

Eventually Julienne enjoyed a waltz with Dare. And they partook of the buffet supper with him. But then she was drawn away again when her next partner claimed her.

Near the end of the evening, Julienne was returning from the floor to where Solange awaited her when out of the corner of her eye she caught a sight that froze her in her tracks: a tall, dark-haired figure of a man hovering at the edge of the crowd.

Ivers.

He disappeared from view just as suddenly, but a sense of unease washed over Julienne. Her skin felt cold and clammy, and she had difficulty breathing.

"Are you unwell, *mon amie*?" Solange asked solicitously. "You look quite pale."

"No, I am fine," she lied, telling herself she had only imagined him. Ivers was nothing but a remnant of a particularly unpleasant nightmare.

She hadn't seen him for seven years and had hoped never to see him again. Anthony Gale, the Earl of Ivers, had been a neighbor of Dare's grandfather—a wild young buck who'd developed a not-so-friendly rivalry with Dare over the course of that infamous summer.

They were both considered rakes and both stunningly handsome, but Ivers's coloring was as dark as Dare's was fair, while his suave charm had always seemed too calculating for Julienne's taste. Even she, however, hadn't realized just how despicable a cad Ivers was— to her everlasting regret.

With a shudder, she fixed a smile on her lips and greeted Solange's latest dance partner. But she was glad when the assembly ended and they drove back to the Harriford Arms in the quiet of Dare's luxuriously appointed coach.

He escorted them inside the inn, reminded Julienne that he would collect her at ten in the morning for her tour of the local stud farms, and then left them with a bow.

She had started to follow Solange up the stairs when the innkeeper spied her from the taproom and hurried to catch up to her. It puzzled her when he handed her a note.

"Go ahead, Solange," Julienne told the French-woman absently as she tried to peruse the writing in the dim light. "I will meet you for breakfast in the morning."

Unable to make out the message, though, she mounted the stairs after a moment and moved down the corridor toward a wall sconce. It was quieter here away from the noise of the crowded taproom, so quiet she could hear the thudding of her heart as she began to read.

My dear Miss Laurent,
   I believe we have much to discuss. Meet me at dawn tomorrow behind the inn.

It was signed with a bold scrawl: *Ivers.*

Prickles crawled along her spine at the same moment she heard the stealthy fall of footsteps behind her.

Whirling, she stared, her heart in her throat as the Earl of Ivers came sauntering toward her.

He stopped barely a few feet from her. He seemed to have changed little in the past seven years, Julienne thought. Except there were more lines of dissipation etching his noble features, and his eyes were a trifle bloodshot.

"Mademoiselle Laurent."

His knowing smile chilled her. She couldn't breathe,

couldn't speak. Help was only a shout away, but she was too shocked to move.

"How fortuitous that I find you alone. I thought I would have to wait till the morrow."

"What . . . ?" The word came out a croak. Swallowing, Julienne tried again. "What are you doing here?"

"Why, I wish to speak to you."

Knotting her fists, she struggled for a semblance of composure. If he smelled her fear, he would only be more dangerous. "I am listening."

"I believe you can help me. I find myself in rather straitened circumstances at the moment. Debts of honor, you see. The Turf has proved my weakness, alas. I may have to flee the country if I cannot raise the necessary funds."

"What could that possibly have to do with me?"

"I was in London recently, and yours was the name on everyone's lips. You've become renowned as an actress. And you have several rich patrons at your beck and call . . . including Wolverton, I understand. It seems you've come full circle if he is your lover again. It shouldn't be difficult for you to wrest some of his wealth from him."

"You must be mad," Julienne said through gritted teeth, "if you think I would give you so much as a shilling for any reason."

"Not mad. Merely desperate." His eyelids drooped in speculation. "The Jewel of London . . . How long would your fame last if your past nefarious activities were made public? If it was revealed that you committed treason?"

"You know very well those accusations were false!"

"But you should have no doubt that I can unearth any amount of evidence against you if I choose."

Julienne felt her stomach knot. Ivers could doubtless fabricate more lies, but she wouldn't bow to his threats this time. "I have no intention of succumbing to your blackmail again."

"It would be foolish to ignore my request."

"Then I will simply be foolish. My answer is no."

He took another step toward her. "I can see I will have to attempt to persuade you."

Julienne cast a wild glance over her shoulder, finding the corridor deserted. She could scarcely believe Ivers would be brazen enough to accost her at a crowded inn. But he was a villain with few scruples, one who followed his own sinister rules.

When he reached out and grasped her shoulder, she flinched in revulsion; his mere touch filled her with dread.

Yet she was no longer the young innocent he had tormented seven years ago. She knew how to fight back.

Frantically Julienne fumbled in her reticule and gripped the handle of her knife. Drawing the blade from its sheath, she brandished the sharp steel in his face.

"I don't think you will persuade me to anything, Lord Ivers," she said, her voice low and fierce. "I've learned how to defend myself from vermin like you."

His smile turned grim yet taunting. "You won't use that."

"No?"

Schooling her features, she let her contemptuous gaze flicker over his face, noting the faint scars on his jaw just below his left ear. Scars that her nails had made years ago. "You still have the marks I gave you, my lord. But I assure you, they will be nothing to the ones I will carve in you if you dare touch me again."

His amusement faded, his gaze narrowing in doubt.

"Back away," Julienne demanded. "Unless you want me to slit your gullet."

A wild laugh almost escaped her. She had abundant theatrical experience making such melodramatic declarations, but no lines from a play had ever given her as much satisfaction as now. And she wasn't acting. She would kill Ivers before she allowed him to hurt her again.

He seemed to believe her. "You will regret this, Miss Laurent," he warned.

"Not as much as I regret letting you go unscathed all these years. If you threaten me again, I promise I will remedy my error."

He stood in indecision for an endless moment while Julienne's heart drummed in her ears. Finally backed away, then spun on his heel and stalked off, disappearing down the stairs in an irate clatter.

When her knees began to buckle, Julienne leaned weakly against the wall. She was shaking with reaction and the aftershock of confronting her nemesis again.

Dear heaven . . .

A dry sob escaped her, and she curled a fist into her stomach to try to ease the churning nausea. She hated feeling so vulnerable, so helpless.

She forced herself to take deep, steadying breaths, but her hands shook deplorably as she returned her knife to its sheath. She might have to keep it strapped to her wrist for protection from now on, Julienne realized.

The reminder that she wasn't entirely defenseless

gave her comfort. She refused to let Ivers take any more from her than he already had. Then another thought struck her, renewing her alarm. Could he make good his threat to expose her as a traitor?

Her mind whirled. It was possible he could bring more fabricated charges against her. . . . But she was no longer a helpless girl. She had resources now, powerful friends . . . Dare.

A faint sense of relief washed over her. She had Dare. He would believe her, surely. He would protect her from an unscrupulous beast like Ivers.

She needed to find Dare. There was no place where she would feel safe except for his arms. . . .

Blindly she turned to seek him out—and halted abruptly.

Dare stood at the end of the corridor, watching her.

"I thought to return the gloves Madame Brogard left in my carriage," he said finally. "Imagine my surprise to see the Earl of Ivers descending the stairway."

"It isn't what you think. . . ."

"Isn't it?" Dare remained where he was, casually slapping the gloves against his thigh, but the glint in his eyes was as hard as steel. "I was a gullible fool once, never realizing that you were plotting with your lover behind my back. I'm not about to be taken in again, darling."

"No, Dare, it isn't like that."

His cold, penetrating gaze bored into her as he moved toward her. "You aren't lovers?"

The allegation hung between them, a keen reminder of their bitter past.

"No," Julienne repeated in a raw voice as Dare came

to stand before her. "Ivers is not my lover. I haven't even seen him in years."

"So what was he doing here? Trying to get you back in his bed?"

"No."

His beautiful mouth curled in a twisted sneer. "You expect me to believe you?"

"Yes," she insisted. "I would never have him for my lover. I consider him no better than vermin. He makes my skin crawl."

Dare's face showed no signs of softening, though.

Julienne felt her heart sink at the accusation in his blazing eyes. She averted her gaze, knowing it was futile to plead further. Dare would never believe her after her betrayal seven years ago.

A savage ache clawed deep in her chest as desolation swept over her. She couldn't face his condemnation tonight. She wasn't strong enough to bear it.

She turned to go, but he reached out to grasp her wrist. When she recoiled instinctively, he pulled her hard against him, wrapping her in an unyielding embrace.

"Dare, no!"

He paid her no mind. His grip tightened to iron intensity as he bent his head to kiss her. The contact of his hard mouth was jarring, sending heat and lust and despair exploding through her. His kiss ravished without ardor; he was a man bent on punishing, intent on claiming what was his.

Julienne began to struggle as dark memories assaulted her. Panic hovering at the edges of her mind, she struck out at her attacker with her fists. *"Stop!"* Desperately fighting to be free, she tried to push him away. *"Don't touch me!"*

Her cry must have broken through his rage, for Dare suddenly released her.

She almost fell. Backing away, she slumped against the wall.

For a long moment Julienne remained there trembling, staring at his angry, unforgiving features. Then with a sob, she turned and stumbled down the corridor to her room.

Dare watched her flee, heard the slamming door, then the bolt being driven home as she locked herself away from him. He cursed. Vividly. He was still seething with jealousy, yet shaken by the knowledge of his violence.

He had frightened Julienne. He'd felt her cringe in his arms, had seen the flash of fear in her eyes when she fought him off.

God, what had he done?

Never before had he ever touched a woman who was less than eager. It was no excuse that the thought of Julienne betraying him a second time brought out the savage male in him. No excuse that he was terrified Ivers would take her from him again. No defense that he'd reacted with sheer primal instinct, his heart crying out in denial, pounding with the cloying dread that he might lose her once more.

Dare squeezed his eyes shut, remembering seven years of pain. He couldn't bear to endure that torment anew. He *refused* to endure it. He wouldn't let that bastard Ivers near Julienne again if he had his way.

And he bloody damned sure would make certain he had his way, Dare vowed harshly.

* * *

Julienne was eating breakfast in the public room with Solange the next morning when Dare came to fetch her. She eyed him warily, wondering if he meant to ignore last night's angry incident between them, but his enigmatic expression gave no clue as to his mood.

His farewell to Madame Brogard, however, was all charm as he promised to take good care of his charge.

When he escorted Julienne to the inn yard, she found herself glancing over her shoulder, nervously looking for Ivers. She was glad to have Dare beside her, even if he didn't seem to be speaking to her at the moment. Given his silence, she assumed he had no intention of apologizing for his brutal kiss. She would just as soon forget it herself.

When they settled in his traveling chaise, Julienne sank back against the squabs gratefully. She had slept badly, with Ivers figuring prominently in her nightmares. She would be glad for the distraction of visiting Newmarket's prime breeding stables.

It was some little while after the coach got underway before she noticed they were moving at a speed that was hardly in keeping with the usual leisurely pace for touring the countryside.

She sat up to peer out the window, realizing that the road resembled the major thoroughfare they'd taken from London.

"You might as well make yourself comfortable," Dare said in response to her unspoken question. "We have a long drive ahead of us."

Julienne's gaze flew to his. She could read grim determination there, but for a moment she was too surprised to speak.

"Is this an abduction?" she asked finally.

He didn't give her a direct answer. "There are five days left of our week. I don't intend to share any of them with Ivers."

"Nor do I." By willpower alone she fixed a cool smile on her face. "Does Solange know what you've planned?"

"I told her last night. In fact she gave me her blessing. I had your bags packed and loaded while you were breakfasting."

Solange had acted oddly this morning, almost apologetically. Julienne had thought it was because the Frenchwoman hadn't wanted to spend the day touring stables. "She actually agreed to let you carry me off?"

"I convinced her you were in danger from a madman who was stalking you—which, after your poisoning, she had no trouble believing. She thought you would be safer with me."

"Where are you taking me?

"I have a house in Berkshire. A very private house."

"A love nest for your paramours, I presume."

"Precisely."

Julienne pressed her lips together. She should be furious at Dare's high-handedness, but the truth was, she would be glad to leave Newmarket. She couldn't bear the thought of encountering Ivers again. Thus she made no protest other than to say, "You are taking a great deal for granted."

She almost flinched at the jewel-hard clarity of Dare's gaze.

"I want you all to myself. Alone. And I don't want there to be any mistake about who your lover is."

His implication burned her. Defensively she crossed

her arms over her chest, shielding herself against his mockery. "I don't intend to discuss Ivers with you."

"Good. I don't intend for you to. I don't even want you thinking about him. During the next few days I mean to make you forget him entirely."

His tone was dispassionate, Julienne observed, but she knew he was deadly serious.

"And if I refuse to accompany you? Do you mean to hold me prisoner?"

"I don't think you will refuse. You want the same thing I do."

She arched an eyebrow. "And what is that?"

"Pleasure." His faint smile held a predatory edge, even as his voice dropped to a seductive murmur. "Four days and nights of intense, mind-numbing pleasure. Carnal delights so hot, so raw, so wild, it will make you scream."

Against her will Julienne felt the muscles of her inner thighs contract at his sensual promise. Four days of intimacy with Dare. Something they had never had together, even during their tender summer of being lovers.

It would be torment.

It would be ecstasy.

"The decision is yours," he said.

So he wouldn't hold her captive, Julienne reflected. Dare would let her go if she demanded it. He was making the choice hers.

Without answering, she turned her head to stare out the window, unwilling to give him the satisfaction of knowing how much she wanted to accept his proposition.

* * *

It was indeed a long drive. They spoke little for the next several hours, even when they stopped to change horses and eat a light luncheon.

Julienne fell asleep afterward. Dare watched her, feeling a strange mix of regret and tension. It bothered him to see her withdraw so totally after the progress they'd recently seemed to be making in their relationship. But he wasn't about to turn away from his chosen course.

He was determined to force the merest thought of any other man from Julienne's mind. She wouldn't, Dare promised himself, want any other lover but him when he was done.

He was driven by a primitive passion as old as time—the need to possess his woman and make her his alone. For a few days Julienne would be *his*.

A powerful satisfaction filled Dare as he listened to her quiet breathing. He could count on one hand the number of times he'd seen Julienne sleep. She looked so incredibly appealing like this . . . her defenses down, beautiful enough to make his heart ache . . . her dark lashes fanning against her ivory complexion, her rose-tinted lips slightly parted.

Unable to resist, he reached for her and carefully drew her into his arms. She curled against him with a faint sigh.

A fierce feeling of protectiveness surged over him to mingle with his longing. There was an added benefit in bringing her to his secluded pleasure house in the Berkshire hills, Dare reflected as he held her. He would be taking Julienne away from the danger Caliban posed. He could better protect her there, for no one would know where to look for them. Ivers included.

Last night Dare had sent a message to Lucian, asking that Ivers be investigated, believing it simply too strange a coincidence that his old nemesis should appear in Newmarket at just that particular moment.

He wanted Julienne safe, although down deep he knew his prime reason for arranging this trip was more selfish than merely her protection.

Dare shut his eyes, relishing the softness of her body, her fragrant scent. The thought of having Julienne alone for the better part of a week made his loins clench in anticipation, while the feel of her nearly drove him over the edge.

He could arouse her now, he didn't doubt. All he needed was to stroke her lush breasts, to raise her skirts and slide his fingers inside her sleek warmth, and she would come alive in his arms. . . .

Dare muttered a low oath. It was all he could do to steel his body against his raging desires and not take her right here while she slept. But he would force himself to wait. He wasn't going to behave like the brute he'd been last night.

And if Julienne refused his offer of mad, passionate, carnal pleasure?

In that case he would simply have to convince her to change her mind.

It was midafternoon when the coach drew to a halt. Julienne came awake with a start. She felt so warm and cherished—

Flushing, she pushed away from Dare and sat up.

Beyond the window, she could see an immense chateau of honey-colored stone, glowing like a jewel in its secluded setting of a beechwood forest.

To her surprise, Dare made no move to leave the carriage.

"Is this where you hold your Hellfire gatherings?" she asked.

"Some of them."

"A den of debauchery, no doubt."

"Are you willing to brave the experience?" His bright gaze held hers, searing her with heat. "Do we stay, or do I return you to London?"

Julienne looked away. Ivers might be planning to return to London, she reflected. But here she would be safe. Here she would be alone with Dare, experiencing his passion, free from gossips and rumormongers and jealous suitors and deadly traitors.

When she hesitated, he took her hand and drew it to his groin, pressing her palm against the bulge in his pantaloons. "Feel my cock and then tell me you don't want to stay."

Julienne felt a rush of fire spear through her. It really was no choice at all.

Accepting to his challenge, she met his gaze evenly. "I do intend to stay, Lord Wolverton. I want what you promised. Pleasure so raw and wild it makes me scream."

Chapter
Twelve

He gave her a smile of breathtaking charm and helped her to descend from the carriage.

"How many of these pleasure houses do you own?" Julienne asked as they mounted the front steps.

"Several." The lazy gleam in his eyes held a hint of wickedness. "I have my reputation as a rake to maintain, after all."

They were met at the entrance by a butler and several footmen who scurried to see to their bags.

"Which rooms will you be using, my lord?" the butler inquired.

"I shall allow the lady to choose."

She noted Dare hadn't mentioned her name, and he answered her silent question without prompting.

"The staff here is highly discreet," he murmured as he escorted her from the entrance hall, "but there is no need to advertise your identity."

"They seem to have expected us."

"I sent a messenger last night with my orders."

Julienne raised an eyebrow, even as she bit back a wry smile. Dare had certainly been sure of himself—and of her. But she wouldn't allow it to intimidate her.

She intended to use this time together to implement her own plan of ensnaring his heart.

He gave her a tour of the mansion. The furnishings were elegant and tasteful if rather decadent, with erotic statues and paintings of nude orgies adorning the corridors and main rooms.

There were nearly two dozen bedchambers whose purpose seemed blatantly obvious: sheer debauchery. One suite on the first floor was made up to resemble a Turkish harem, while another chamber seemed designed more for pain than pleasure.

Julienne was actually a bit shocked by the accoutrements she saw there—leather whips and steel shackles and ominous contraptions that looked like medieval torture devices.

"Some guests prefer more unique forms of entertainment," Dare explained.

"And you?"

"I've never found pain to be arousing, although bondage can be interesting." A sensual glint warmed his eyes as he looked at her. "For years I fantasized about having you spread-eagle on a bed, at my mercy. Even now the notion is vastly appealing, and not just for the purpose of revenge."

Feeling herself flushing, Julienne turned away.

"Truthfully," Dare added in a provocative whisper as she proceeded him to the next room, "I thought I might have to tie you up to keep you from escaping."

"I have no intention of escaping."

In yet another chamber she was surprised to find mirrors hung from every inch of wall and even on the ceiling.

"I think we will make use of this room tonight," Dare said.

"Why this one?"

"So you can see from every viewpoint who your lover is. Here you won't confuse me with any other man."

The barb stung, but Julienne refrained from comment, not wishing to revisit that argument again.

For her own use, she chose a bedchamber done in lovely peach and ivory and gold shades on the second floor, primarily because its erotic embellishments were the least noticeable.

"I will send a maid to you so you can refresh yourself," Dare said. "Shall we meet in the lower drawing room in, say, an hour?"

"That will suit me perfectly."

"Until then, *chérie*."

He gave her a polite bow and lingeringly kissed the tips of her fingers. Julienne felt her breath catch at the warm feel of his tongue on the sensitive pads, but she promised herself she would get even with Dare later.

She was glad for the time to bathe and change her gown. A quiet, self-effacing maid assisted her, and soon Julienne was making her way to the drawing room. She hadn't bothered to arrange her hair in anything but a simple chignon, for she doubted any coiffure would be safe for long in Dare's company.

In that respect, however, he surprised her. The evening began rather tamely, with sherry and desultory conversation in the drawing room. Dinner was of the usual excellent quality, served by almost invisible servants.

Dare spent much of the evening telling her about

the history of the estate, which had been a minor site of conflict during Cromwell's bloody reign. Julienne listened politely, but all the while a sense of feverish anticipation was welling inside her. If Dare was deliberately prolonging the moment, his tactics were proving effective. By the time he finally pushed back his chair, her nerves were screaming.

"If you are finished," he said, "we can retire upstairs."

When she agreed, he rose and moved around the table to draw out her chair. "Go ahead and make yourself ready," he murmured, planting a light kiss on her bare nape. "I will wait for you in the mirror room. Oh, and Jewel?" he added when she turned to obey. "Don't undress just yet. I want that enjoyment for myself."

Despite her determination to maintain her composure, she felt her excitement rise.

Julienne went to her bedchamber and utilized her coffer of sponges, then went in search of the mirrored room. Dare was waiting for her as promised, lounging against the pillows of the large bed, his lean, elegant body reclining with a lazy grace. He appeared to be nude except for the red silk sheet drawn up to his waist. Several candelabra lit the chamber, the flames reflecting brightly in the myriad mirrors.

When Julienne shut the door behind her, Dare remained in his sprawl and laced his hands behind his head. "Now you may take off your clothing."

"I thought you said you wished to undress me."

"I've changed my mind. I can enjoy the sight as much from here. And turnabout is fair play, after all."

She remembered the last time they'd made love,

when she'd been so angry at him for thinking her a traitor. She had ordered him to undress in front of her while she watched.

But Dare apparently had more in mind now than reprisal. "From the first moment I saw you on stage, I've imagined you giving me my own private performance. Do it slowly, Jewel. I want to see every inch of your beautiful body . . . every lush, tempting curve."

She might have protested his arrogant directive, except that the devilish, even taunting, smile on his face could melt the strongest resistance. And this was one command she wanted to obey.

She began with her gown, unfastening the hooks and letting it fall to the floor. She hadn't worn a corset, only a chemise.

"Are your nipples hard?" Dare asked when she slid the fabric over her shoulders. "Let me see." When she drew the bodice down so that her nipples jutted out, hard as pebbles, he gave her a lazy smile of admiration. "I would say so. Now the rest."

When finally she stood naked before him, his gaze traveled slowly down her bare body and even more slowly upward again. His eyes burned, seeming to brand her where they touched.

"What now?" Julienne murmured, her own tone challenging.

"What do you want?"

"I want to see you."

"Then I am happy to oblige."

Throwing off the sheet, Dare rose gracefully and stood before her fully aroused. Incredibly aroused. His phallus was magnificent, darkly engorged, long and thick and silky smooth. Julienne's mouth went dry. "You are very large."

"The better to pleasure you, my sweet."

He moved toward her till he was almost close enough to touch. "Do you want to feel my cock sliding inside your quivering flesh?"

Her blood surged at the question. Julienne moistened her lips. "Yes . . ."

Grasping her shoulders lightly, Dare guided her backward till her spine was pressed against the mirrored wall. The glass felt cool against her hot skin, making her shiver. But it was Dare's emerald gaze that countered the chill. His indolent scrutiny brushed over her with an intimacy that set her senses on fire.

"I see before me an irresistibly aroused woman," he whispered, drawing a finger down her throat to her collarbone.

Deliberately he rested his hands on the pale, high curves of her breasts as if they were his property. A jolt of sensation burst through Julienne.

"I want to suck on your nipples till you come."

She had no doubt that he could. And she wanted him to.

"Do you want me to make you come?" he queried.

Aching from temptation, she nearly moaned aloud. "Yes."

"My name is Dare. Say it."

"Yes, Dare. . . ."

His hands moved over her breasts, fondling them leisurely as his gaze narrowed. He watched her as he played with her straining nipples. A shameless need grew in her with each caress of those strong, elegant fingers. Eventually he bent his head, planting soft, teasing kisses around the rosy areolas. Julienne thrust her aching breasts helplessly against his lips, longing for release.

Then his mouth took over from his fingers, capturing one taut bud, tugging at the crest, drawing it over the rough, wet surface of his tongue.

The soft sound of his sucking was somehow powerfully erotic, and made Julienne groan. She arched her back, bracing her palms against the mirror behind her. Obligingly, Dare shifted his body so that his knee rode intimately between her thighs, the rigid blade of his manhood prodding against her belly. Julienne felt the quaking between her legs intensify.

"You're very excited, darling, aren't you?" When he let his fingers slide down to the apex of her thighs, her harsh gasp sounded loud in the silence. "Yes, let me hear you. I want you frenzied and breathless."

The caress of his mouth, the heat of his hard, lean body against her, was a delicious torment and roused a burning need in her loins to feel him driving deep into her.

Dare seemed to understand.

"Open your legs." His husky whisper took on a tone of command. When she obeyed, he rewarded her by rubbing the swollen head of his erect member up and down her moist cleft.

Julienne's resistance broke completely. "Dare, please," she pleaded.

"Want me?" The velvet texture of his voice sent flames rippling up her spine.

"Merciful heaven, yes. . . ."

His slow smile set her blood racing as his massive member nudged between her slick flesh. She parted her legs wider to give him full access and bit back a cry of need as he began to enter her.

His fingers cupped her throbbing breasts, squeezing lightly as he swelled upward into her clinging heat, filling her. With a whimper, Julienne softened against him helplessly, dizzy with pleasure, her eyes falling shut. . . .

"No, don't close your eyes. Watch while I'm taking you."

With effort she focused her dazed gaze on the mirror to her right. She could see his long, thick shaft gliding into her. . . .

Julienne groaned again, her inner muscles contracting, clamping around his hardness. Over his shoulder, she saw their reflections in the opposite mirror, saw his buttocks flexing as he slowly pumped between her legs. It was the most erotic sight she had ever seen.

She began to writhe against him, urging him to increase his unhurried rhythm, but he refused to comply. Each time he withdrew, she strained to hold the sweet fullness buried deep inside her, but he wouldn't allow her to.

She wanted to curse him. Dare knew what she needed so desperately, but he deliberately held her on the edge, her body pulsing and craving more. He was skilled in the art of prolonging pleasure, and he used every talent he possessed to bring her to a fever pitch of desire.

She lost count of how many times he drove her to the brink, only to deny her. It was exquisite, agonizing. Her breath was rasping rawly in her throat as she pleaded with him, begging for release.

"I'm going to let you come now," he warned at last.

"Yes!" she cried, nearly sobbing. Her nails dug into the flesh of his back as he thrust fully inside her, building the firestorm.

When she bucked wildly against him, he thrust again harder, impaling her to the hilt. "Scream for me, darling. Scream like I know you want to."

She did scream. The brutal rush of feeling when she climaxed left her shuddering and shattered. She felt Dare plunging inside her as he found his own explosive release, but she could only cling helplessly to his broad shoulders.

His shaft was still throbbing sweetly, deep within her as her last melting spasms ebbed away.

With a groan, Dare sagged against her. Several heartbeats later she felt him smile into her hair.

"You screamed for me," he murmured, his voice a satisfied rasp. "But we've only just begun. I intend to make you hoarse before the night is through."

His fingers slid through her hair, searching for pins. "Next time I take you, I want you sprawled naked on the sheets . . . your incredible hair cascading wantonly across the pillows. . . . I want your smell on my body, your breath on my skin. . . ."

The last words were whispered as he captured her mouth, and this time Julienne surrendered with no resistance at all.

That first night set the stage for their time together. Dare pleasured her ruthlessly, but Julienne proved his match in their erotic battle for supremacy. She was passionate, greedy, hot, reveling in his raw sexuality, and in her own.

The mirrors served the purpose he'd intended. From then on the image of their twisting, nude bodies locked in carnal embrace was branded on her mind. She had only to look at Dare to remember, and the fire between them leapt instantly to life.

By tacit agreement they never spoke of the danger that threatened them, both preferring to see this interlude as a respite from the world. Yet Julienne soon recognized another source of danger: too many opportunities for emotional intimacy and tender remembrances.

The day following their arrival, the weather turned inclement. Rain came down in torrents, bringing back a winter chill to the air and forcing them to remain indoors.

After a lazy breakfast, they strolled in the conservatory, which was regrettably scented with roses. And listening to the rain beat against the panes of glass reminded Julienne too poignantly of a particular afternoon she'd spent with Dare in their cottage during a summer storm.

When she met his eyes briefly, she could tell he was recollecting the same moment.

"So tell me about your years in York," Dare prompted as if to change the subject.

His choice of topics was scarcely any more comforting to Julienne's mind.

One of the things she had appreciated most about Dare in the days of their courtship was that he was always so interested in her thoughts and feelings. Now his interest was simply worrisome. And yet Julienne found herself reminiscing about her life as a fledgling actress. There had been far more good times than bad, possibly because she had quickly become a success.

"So what have you been doing with your life all this time?" she asked in turn. "Has it been all debauchery and pleasure?"

Dare visibly winced. "Much of it, I'm afraid. I was serious when I said that after you, I lost interest in much of anything else."

She drew a measured breath and replied in a low voice. "I am sorry, Dare."

It was the first time she had apologized for breaking his heart, but he shrugged off her reply with a forced smile. "Let's forget about it, shall we? For these next few days we'll pretend the past never happened."

And yet Julienne wasn't able to forget. If anything, her remembrances only grew stronger the more time she spent with Dare.

He devoted every moment of the following days to entertaining her, displaying the consummate artistry of his passion in countless ways. He was a man of smoldering sensuality and insatiable appetites, with a demanding eroticism that ravished her senses. Even so, he was somehow different from the charming, wicked rakehell who had wagered to make her his mistress. In the tender intensity of his wooing, at least, he resembled much more the lover who had once utterly captured her heart.

It was his tenderness that Julienne considered most dangerous. The rivalry between them was more arousing than any aphrodisiac, more primal than any courtship, but Dare's tenderness penetrated every defense she had. And with every caress, every kiss, every sweet new intimacy, she found it harder to shield herself.

She tried to remind herself of their game, that Dare was merely set on winning their wager and repaying her for her past cruelty. But while her rational mind warned her to beware, her heart seemed to whisper something else altogether, something she wanted with a desperate longing.

Dare, too, felt the same longing. Their third night together he chose a different room, this one a study on the lower floor made up like a hunting lodge, walled with stag antlers and stuffed boars' heads.

"Another fantasy of mine," he said when Julienne saw the sable furs spread out before the hearth.

He built a roaring fire, and they toasted bread and cheese and fed each other between languid, heated kisses. Then they undressed each other slowly, taking their time, savoring the moment.

Dare left her hair for last . . . discarding the pins . . . letting the shining cascade tumble to her shoulders. Tangling his fingers in the silk, he tilted her head back so he could taste her warm parted lips, ready for his own. Then gently he lay Julienne down before the fire and ran his hands over her body, stroking the intoxicating softness of her skin.

He found the contrast of her luminous flesh against the luxurious fur riveting. And when her scent filled his nostrils, musky and beguiling in the warm room, every muscle in his body tightened with need.

"You're tempting as sin, lying there."

He was just as tempting, Julienne thought. His eyes glowed in the warm light of the fire, while his hair shimmered like molten gold.

With careless grace he stretched out beside her on the furs, lounging on one elbow. He gazed down at her, studying her with a mesmerizing intensity as palpable as a caress. His eyes took possession of her wherever they touched. Then his warm, naked fingers joined the exploration, finding her most sensitive spots, skimming over her flesh with the same seductiveness as his voice.

Julienne lost her breath long before he rolled her over so that she was lying facedown on the fur. He ran a finger along her spine, making her arch her back. Then, lightly grasping her hips, he lifted her to her knees so that she was bent over, with him kneeling, poised behind her.

Her fingers clenched in the rich fur when she realized his intent. But she craved the thrill of his possession any way he wanted her. She was hot, aching inside, the emptiness between her legs throbbing.

For a moment Dare stroked the smooth bottom cheeks that were brazenly presented for his attention. Julienne tensed as she felt his rigid maleness probe the center of her body, while her heart began a steady hammering.

"Dare?" she murmured.

"Easy," he said, calming her. He gripped his engorged shaft in his hand and slid the swollen crest over the lips of her sex, anointing it with honeyed liquid from her body.

Her breath grew shallow. She felt the press of his

thighs, lean and powerful, urging her legs wider, felt the scoring heat of him as he leaned into her. Sweet shocks ripped through her as he invaded her sleek feminine passage, filling her inch by inch with his massive member.

Desire coiled inside her at his deep penetration, but then his hips began a slow undulation, rousing a devastating buildup of feverish hunger.

A gasp lodged in her throat as his hands reached for her dangling breasts, stroking them, teasing her hardened nipples, inflaming her bare flesh, even as he whispered heated, erotic love words.

The burn sharpened, intensified, when he slid his hand around to her throbbing sex. All the while he was moving inside her, ravishing her with long, slow strokes, sheathing and drawing away till it became exquisite torture.

Her body turned molten. When she surged back against him, impaling herself, his rhythm increased. In time to her whimpers, he drove deeper and deeper, every rocking movement, every possessive claiming forcing a husky cry from her. In only moments she felt delirious ecstasy rush toward her, felt Dare surrender as he was caught up in the same fierce tumult. At his ragged groan, fire exploded through her veins. Julienne threw her head back as shudder after shudder racked her.

The warm, pulsing rapture throbbed through her senses long after she collapsed bonelessly on the fur.

Dare followed her down. Bracing himself to spare her the full force of his weight, he curled his body around hers and reached up above her head, entwining their fingers together. Her ivory skin was moist in a silken sweat, and he pressed his lips against the flesh of her back.

The room was quiet but for the crackling fire and their raw, rasping breaths. He lay inside her half-hard, wholly intoxicated, desperately wanting more of her, desire still sharp and insistent.

He *wanted*.

He wanted to stay with Julienne like this forever, lost in this moment. Wanted to keep her here with him, where he could cherish her to his heart's content. It was a primal, elemental need that was soul deep.

It was love, he no longer had any doubt.

His chest squeezed with a hollow ache. Despite everything, some uncontrollable part of him loved Julienne still, had always loved her.

He shut his eyes, filled with a blind yearning. He had vowed to drive her other lovers from her mind, but by his very act of possessing her, she had managed utterly to possess him.

The victory was hers.

And if she came to realize her power over him? If she chose to wield it? If she betrayed him once again?

Dare felt a blade of fear stab him. The pain this time would be unbearable.

The possibility made him even more keenly aware of the heavy urgency of his task. He needed to make Julienne as obsessed with him as he was with her.

And yet, Dare realized with a sinking heart, his time with her was running out.

The rain finally ended the following day, and the sun at last reappeared. They spent the morning tramping through the beechwood like young lovers, laughing and sharing kisses beneath the bright canopy of spring leaves that had burst out almost overnight.

Dare displayed his chivalry by finding patches of wildflowers for Julienne, and she made a wreath of them, crowning her flowing hair so that she resembled a pagan goddess. Dare found the sight irresistible, even though it reminded him so painfully of their long-ago summer together.

When he commented on her luscious appearance, however, Julienne shook her head with a provocative smile.

"Not a goddess, a fairy queen. I've always enjoyed playing Titania in *A Midsummer Night's Dream*. But I suppose I will never again have the chance if I remain in London."

The laws governing the thespian world were strict, Dare knew. Only two London theaters held royal patents that permitted them to enact tragedies—Drury Lane and Covent Garden. As a result, it had become common practice for actors to perform in tragedies or comedies, but not both. The public's expectations precluded switching roles.

"You can play Queen Titania if you will allow me to be your King Oberon," Dare said, nuzzling aside her sweet-scented tresses to kiss her nape.

Throwing him an alluring glance over her shoulder, Julienne murmured, "If you can catch me." Then, with a laugh, she ran off into the forest. Dare sprinted after her, eager for the chase.

For the rest of the day, he kept the mood in the same light vein and teased her by promising her a surprise later. Julienne thought his promise fulfilled when on the edge of a meadow they found a picnic prepared by invisible servants, but Dare denied it.

When they returned to the house, he led her to a chamber she had never seen, this one on the first floor.

"Is this my surprise?" Julienne asked as he opened the door.

"In part."

Inside the air was warm and moist—caused by steam rising from the surface of a large, rectangular tiled pool, she saw.

"A Turkish bath?" Julienne said with delight as she moved across the floor. "I have heard of these."

"Heated pipes feed the pool and keep the water hot."

It seemed the height of luxury to Julienne, who was accustomed to cold York winters. The height of decadence as well, knowing Dare as she did. "This seems an ideal place for an orgy," she remarked archly.

His eyes glinted wickedly. "Patience, sweet. We will get to that."

To one side of the room, French doors opened onto a private courtyard, letting in the sweet smell of spring and a flood of sunlight that warmed the room further. It spilled over the lush pile of cushions that were spread beside the pool.

When Dare led her over to the cushions, she gave him a skeptical glance. "What do you have planned, Dare? Are we not to try the bath?"

"All in good time. I mean to introduce you to the pleasures of an oil massage first. You won't be disappointed, I assure you."

Beside the cushions sat a glass flagon of what looked like oil, Julienne saw. Eager to begin, she started to undress, but Dare stopped her by kissing each one of her fingertips.

"No, you aren't to help. Just relax and allow me to perform my duty."

"Your duty?"

"You would agree that it is my duty as your host to keep you properly serviced?"

A streak of heat coursed through Julienne at the thought, a heat that had nothing to do with the elevated temperature of the sunlit room.

Deciding to play along with his seduction, she allowed him to undress her. For once he pinned her hair up instead of taking it down.

"The better to reach all your skin," he said in explanation.

When she was naked, Dare arranged her as he wished, so that she lay in beautiful disarray on the cushions, her dark hair coiled high in a glorious mass.

He gazed down at her, his eyes heavy-lidded, sweeping every curve and hollow of her body. He felt his loins harden. "Titania never looked so tempting."

Julienne felt herself flush at the flames in his eyes. She couldn't look away as he sat beside her and reached for the bottle.

The oil was jasmine-scented, and the sweet fragrance filled the air as Dare poured a small amount on his palms and warmed it between his hands. When he cupped her breasts, she gasped softly at the sensation.

"Do you find that enjoyable?"

"You know I do," she said rather breathlessly.

"The enjoyment is mine as well. You're aware by now that I take great delight in your body."

"You take delight in any female body."

"Not any longer. You have spoiled me for anyone else, my lovely Jewel."

He had spoiled *her* long ago for any other man, Julienne reflected.

The thought fled her mind, though, as he dragged the oiled tips of his fingers in slow, circular motions over her entire body, arousing her in a way different from anything she had experienced before. Her skin responded with a tingling urgency, while a hard ache flared between her shivering thighs.

Reflexively Julienne caught her lower lip with her teeth. Dare's gaze moved to her mouth with raking leisure, and he dipped his head to kiss her briefly before returning to his task. His hands wandered with deliberate slowness over every detail of her, fondling all her curves . . . her arms, her shoulders, her nipples, her belly . . . moving down her legs to her calves, gently kneading. Wherever he touched her, she seemed to burn with fierce heat.

Then slowly he ran his oil-slick hands up her inner thighs, caressing, rubbing. The sensation was exquisite. Julienne felt as if she were melting, even before his thumbs found the dark thatch of curls that hid her feminine folds.

Her breath wedged in her throat, but Dare went on stroking the bud of her sex until she arched and whimpered with the searing swell of heat. Then he bent to her, his lips replacing his hands.

A stabbing pleasure flooded Julienne. He licked deeply with his long, clever tongue while his hands continued to stroke and squeeze her throbbing breasts, filling her with sensations so vibrant they hurt her with their brightness.

The orgasm that suddenly claimed her was so intense, she almost fainted.

Her scream of ecstasy echoed throughout the chamber, dying away as the relentless contractions of her body eased. Weak, boneless, she fell back among the cushions, shutting her eyes.

"You don't mean to fall asleep yet?" Dare murmured, the amused question intruding on the sweet glow of repletion.

"Devil," she retorted weakly.

She no longer had the will to move. She felt luxuriantly, lavishly sated by a man who knew exactly what a woman wanted. She was his now, completely in his power; he could do as he wished with her. Yet in some dazed part of her mind, she wanted Dare to share the tantalizing, pleasure-drenched rapture.

Forcibly Julienne opened her eyes. "You are wearing too many clothes."

A half smile of pure devilry tugged at his enticing mouth. "Do you want to undress me?"

"Yes, but I no longer have the energy. You may do the honors."

He complied and, after a moment, stood over her, his splendid erection blatant. "You look like a woman ready for a lover. Perhaps I should oblige you."

Languidly she spread her legs wide, arching for him. "Perhaps you should."

His luminous eyes sparked with wanting her.

"But not yet," Julienne added in a taunting tone as he started to kneel. "I think I should like to know how your oil feels inside me. You may do those honors as well, since you are such the expert. Arouse yourself while I watch."

He chuckled, a low, rich sound of appreciation. "As you command, your highness."

As his oiled hands glided over his hard, swollen shaft, Julienne moistened her dry lips. Watching his fingers curling around the long, smooth, rigid flesh, she wished she could do the same.

"Do you find that enjoyable?" she asked, her voice edged with huskiness.

Dare's face was flushed with his effort at control. "Not as much as if you were attending me."

"Very well," she said at last. "My turn."

"I thought you would never relent."

She rose to her knees and oiled her hands. Then she curled her fingers around his magnificent length.

Heat coursed through Dare at her erotic touch. Instinctively he thrust his hips toward her, even while trying to stem his mounting arousal.

"I will explode all over you if you keep that up," he warned.

"No, you cannot," Julienne said softly. "You have to wait. I believe I would like to try out the bath now." Releasing him, she stood and moved toward the pool.

Dare's muscles went rigid with sexual frustration. Clamping his jaw, he watched her delectable hips swaying as she crossed to the tiled steps and entered the water. The level was almost chest deep, not quite covering the white globes of her breasts. The sight of her taut, rose-hued nipples bobbing so invitingly tormented him.

"What are you waiting for?"

Her taunting voice slid across his senses and brought him even nearer to bursting. Swiftly Dare followed her into the pool, almost groaning as the heated water flowed over his aching cock.

To his relief, Julienne didn't move away but stood waiting, a challenging half smile on her lips.

Her eyes gleamed dark and slumbrously exotic as he reached for her. Feverish excitement surged in him as he clasped her shoulders. Her oiled body was still sleek and supple under his hands, but he spent only a moment playing with her breasts, molding and shaping the high, firm swells before he grasped her hips and lifted her up, pressing between her thighs.

Gritting his teeth, he fondled her buttocks until he felt Julienne glide lusciously around him. His mouth found hers as she locked her legs around his flanks and returned his kiss.

Their tongues entwining like their limbs, they swayed in their erotic dance for a dozen heartbeats, moving and pulsing with pleasure in the rippling water.

Just when Dare thought he could hold back no longer, Julienne contracted the inner muscles of her feminine core, clasping him even more tightly while her hands slipped downward over his hard, flexing buttocks.

Dare groaned raggedly, his face contorted in a grimace of ecstasy as his seed erupted in a white-hot stream. Julienne convulsed around him almost at once, shuddering against him. With her own groan, she buried her face in his neck, raking her teeth over his shoulder.

His breath jagged, his legs weak, Dare sank farther down into the water and leaned back against the pool's edge. An exquisite peace came over him as the heated waves lapped gently around their joined bodies.

"Are you falling asleep?" he heard Julienne whisper hoarsely after a moment.

"Mmmm. I was having dreams. Erotic dreams."

"Of me?"

"Who else?"

She stirred her hips in provocative answer. "What if I am not yet satisfied?"

"I fear you will have to wait, love. I couldn't possibly move. You've depleted all my reserves of strength."

Julienne raked her teeth over his skin again. "You cannot be exhausted just yet. We have one more night together."

Her teasing remark made Dare's exhaustion suddenly fade. He drew back to regard her solemnly. "We can have more than just a single night together."

"I have to return to London by Saturday if I hope to have a career. But I admit," she added softly, echoing his thoughts as she laid her head on his shoulder again, "I almost don't want this to end."

He reached up to fondle a sweetly-rounded breast. "It doesn't have to end, Julienne. You can remain here with me."

"If I did, I would no longer be employed."

"Your employment would be to provide me companionship."

She smiled wryly against his shoulder. "Become your mistress, you mean. But then you would win the wager."

"So?"

Her laughter was muted, shielding the wistful train of her thoughts.

After this magical time with Dare, it would be incredibly difficult to return to her daily life, she knew. During the past few days, as pleasure played upon pleasure, she had found herself pretending that nothing had ever come between them. Worse, she'd found herself thinking of what might have been, dreaming of what the future could hold.

For so long she had refused to dream. But locked in Dare's arms like this, their heartbeats mingling, she could let her imagination wander freely. She could picture herself staying with him, sharing this sweet ecstasy, lovers forever.

For a moment, Julienne closed her eyes, letting that vision fill the emptiness within her. Dare was the only man she had ever wanted, ever loved. The only man to bring her happiness. She had loved him so deeply. . . .

But that happiness had been shattered long ago. And this magical interlude had to end.

It was foolish to think it could go on. Foolish to hope for anything more. They had even less of a future together now than they'd had seven years ago. The obstacles for an exalted nobleman and a simple shopkeeper were now magnified a dozen times over. Dare could never take her for his wife. She was a notorious actress, no longer the virginal innocent she'd been when she first met him. And after all that had happened between them, the bitterness and pain . . .

Dare wanted her for his mistress, she had no doubt, but she would never agree to that role. It would give him too much power over her. Financially and, even more damning, emotionally. In such a dependent relationship, she would be too defenseless; it would be too easy to let herself fall in love with him again.

Julienne silently shook her head. She understood clearly the lunacy of handing her heart to a gazetted rake who was relentlessly set on breaking it.

Even so, she thought wistfully as her lips nuzzled Dare's sleek, wet skin, she still wanted to dream.

Chapter
Thirteen

Returning to London proved to be a dose of cold reality for Julienne. Indeed, if not for her career, she might have remained away a good deal longer. She worried that in his determination to continue the search for Caliban, Dare would make himself a target and put himself in grave danger.

Moreover, it required all of her acting skills to resume her public game of seduction with him and pretend to be unaffected by the passionate interlude they had shared.

The current gossip about them in the scandal sheets was even more pronounced. Their disappearance from Newmarket had been particularly noted, since one of Dare's colts had won the 2000 Guineas race and he was nowhere to be found. The speculation that he had gone into seclusion with London's brightest Jewel was the talk of the town.

Julienne refused to confirm or deny the reports with her sulking admirers, but she was required to satisfy Solange's curiosity when her friend called at her lodgings immediately after her return.

"And so?" the Frenchwoman demanded, settling herself in a chair in the cheerless parlor. "Was the Prince of Pleasure as marvelously wicked as legend holds?"

Absurdly Julienne felt herself flushing. "The tales of his prowess were not exaggerated, I admit."

"*Tiens!* Does that mean you will agree to be his *chère amie*?"

"Not at all. I have no intention of letting him win our wager."

Solange frowned. "Perhaps you are wise. Wolverton is such a prime catch. How do the *anglais* say it . . . if you 'play your cards well'? I begin to wonder if you should hold out for marriage."

Julienne's eyebrows shot up scornfully at the mere suggestion. "A marquess would never in this world wed a mere actress."

"It has been done before. And I should think a nobleman of his scandalous ilk would not be put off by a bride with a trifle notoriety of her own."

But not one he despised for betraying him, Julienne reflected silently.

"If he truly wished to wed you—"

"It is out of the question," Julienne declared, dismissing the subject altogether. She was reluctant to reveal even to her friend her former association with Dare. She would rather forget everything about that devastating summer.

Regrettably, however, Julienne feared that was beyond her ability now, for she had encountered the nightmare from her past at Newmarket.

Ivers. She dreaded the very thought of him. But she suspected she would be forced to deal with him sooner or later. He was in London, she knew, for Lord

Ridingham had spotted him at one of the popular sporting gentlemen's hotels.

Everywhere she went she kept a nervous watch out for Ivers, involuntarily starting at shadows despite her determination to conquer her fear. She kept her knife near to hand, strapped to her wrist. And when she returned home from the theater late at night, she always made certain she had an escort, either the footman Dare had provided for her physical protection or one of her admirers.

She stayed close to Riddingham in particular, for she felt safest with him. And Riddingham wasn't inclined to ask unwanted questions.

Oddly she found herself relieved that Dare had made himself scarce following their return from Berkshire. She couldn't possibly ask him to defend her from Ivers for fear of his explosive jealousy.

It would have surprised her to learn that Dare was keeping his distance because he thought it wiser. After their intense interlude at his pleasure house, he needed to determine how best to deal with Julienne. For weeks now his feelings for her had taken on the dark strains of obsession, and he was struggling with the problem of how to extricate himself—if that was even possible.

In his more rational moments, Dare understood what course he should take: he needed to relinquish this haunting fantasy of love, the intense need simply to have Julienne near.

Loving her defied all reason, he knew. The only way to master his craving for her was to absent himself.

He was considering leaving town when he received an urgent summons from Lucian. Even though it was barely noon, Dare immediately called at the Wycliff residence and found his friend at work in his study.

"Why," Lucian asked at once, "did you send me that cryptic message all the way from Newmarket last week to ask about the Earl of Ivers?"

Dare settled himself on the couch. "Because I hadn't seen him in well over a year, and I thought it odd that he showed up on my heels so soon after I advertised my search for Caliban."

"Well, it seems there is at least a possible connection between Ivers and the companion's murder. The man I installed at the Castlereagh household found a witness who recognized Ivers as the lover Alice Watson had been secretly meeting. And he uncovered further proof that Ivers has recently been spying on Lady Castlereagh's doings—paying the servants to report to him."

The tall, dark-haired stranger. Dare frowned at the implication. "You don't think Ivers could be Caliban, do you? I've known him since I was in short coats— his family seat is barely a dozen miles from Wolverton Hall—and while he might be capable of killing, I wouldn't think him cunning enough to be a criminal mastermind."

Thoughtfully Lucian shook his head. "I tend to concur, although he may be ruthless enough. Last year one of his former mistresses was mysteriously disfigured after she sent Ivers packing in favor of a new, wealthier protector who could afford her extravagances. And it's common knowledge that he has been flirting with penury of late. Not only does he owe half the tradesmen in town, but he's been unable to repay his debts of honor. There are rumors he may be asked to leave his club. It's possible he is in Caliban's employ for the income, or simply because he's being black-mailed, like so many other of Caliban's victims."

"What of Sir Stephen Ormsby and Martin Perrine?" Dare asked. "Did you discover any leads that might suggest either of them are involved?"

"I had them both investigated as you suggested," Lucian replied, "and found nothing more to incriminate Ormsby. Perrine, we're now certain, was in town at the time of the companion's death, and also in January when our diplomat was killed. But there is no direct evidence linking him to either murder. Still, Caliban has always been extremely careful to cover his trail. His pattern is to remain behind the scenes while his victims execute his orders. In any event, this is the first real break we've had in the case—and we have you to thank for it."

Dare remained silent for a moment while he debated how much to reveal about his knowledge of their chief suspect. Finally he decided it would be wisest to tell Lucian everything he knew on the off chance that there was a connection between events. "Ivers has a past relationship with Julienne Laurent," Dare said in a toneless voice.

"Oh?" Lucian responded curiously.

"They were lovers."

Lucian's eyebrow rose. "The reason for your broken betrothal, I gather?"

"Yes. So admittedly I have a vested interest in wanting revenge. I may not be the ideal candidate to pursue Ivers, since my judgment may be impaired, but I've been thinking of returning to Kent for a few days. I haven't visited the ancestral pile since Christmas. If you like, I could see what I can discover about him."

"That's an excellent idea," Lucian commented. "Meanwhile I intend to keep my agents hard on his trail. Ivers is putting up at Limmer's Hotel for now, but if he should be evicted, he could go to ground and be impossible to find."

Dare left London that afternoon and arrived in Kent late at night, startling his household staff. The Wolverton principal seat was a vast estate with a large, elegant brick manor and an attractive park surrounded by numerous tenant farms and orchards. Dare rarely visited, for it held such unpleasant memories for him.

It was too late to begin inquiries tonight, but he intended to question his servants first thing in the morning, starting with his grandfather's elderly secretary. If anyone would know about the neighboring peers, it would be Samuel Butner. Butner had been privy to all the late marquess's business affairs, and while he'd been pensioned off when Dare succeeded to the title, he still lived in the manor as he had for the past thirty-odd years.

Too weary and restless to sleep after his long journey, Dare found himself in the comfortable library, drinking an excessive quantity of his late grandfather's excellent brandy, remembering the last time they had been together in this particular room.

It was the third day of their argument over Dare's marriage plans. Robert North, the sixth Marquess of Wolverton, had been enraged to the point of apoplexy because his grandson and heir refused once again to call off his betrothal to the scheming French jade.

"She has duped you, you damned young fool! She only wants you for your fortune. She will bleed you dry!"

"You are entirely mistaken, Grandfather," Dare responded tightly, barely keeping his own temper in check out of respect for his relative's advanced age and position as host. This was the marquess's house, after all.

"I won't stand for it, do you hear me? I will disown you before I allow one drop of her blood to taint our line!"

"I have told you more than once, your threat of disinheritance holds no weight with me," Dare reminded him.

"Your jade is not as sanguine about you losing your inheritance. I think you will find her opinion of you greatly changed now that she knows she won't get a penny of my fortune."

Dare's eyes narrowed. "You spoke to Julienne?"

His grandfather's craggy brows knitted together in a scowl. "I made certain she understands the consequences of your insupportable marriage."

For an instant Dare thought back to his last tryst with Julienne, remembering her reluctance to elope with him. But she hadn't known then of his grandfather's threat to disown him, for he hadn't told her. Dare shook his head. "She is not interested in your fortune."

"The devil she isn't!" The marquess's voice rose again to the level of a shout. "Hell and damnation, lad, don't you see? You are letting your cock rule you!"

"No, Grandfather. For once I am letting my heart rule."

A dark and furious flush suffused the old man's cheekbones, but he made a visible effort at restraint. "I tell you, you are a blind fool. That Laurent trollop has been cuckolding you for months now with her lover. Ivers shared her bed long before you began sniffing at her skirts."

Dare stiffened with instinctive jealousy. Ivers's attentions to Julienne had always made him grind his teeth. But the idea of her cuckolding him was laughable.

At Dare's scoffing sound, his grandfather waved an accusing finger at the library window, in the direction of the earl's nearby estate. "Ask Ivers if you don't believe me."

Dare returned a wintery smile. "You will have to come up with a better tale than that if you expect to turn me against her."

Giving a growl of pure rage, Lord Wolverton shook his gnarled fist. "How about this tale then? Your jade is guilty of treason. I will see her in prison or worse if you try to wed her."

A sudden chill swept through Dare. His grandfather was powerful and influential enough to make good such a threat if he wished to.

When Dare hesitated, the marquess's rheumy gaze narrowed with malice. "They hanged two English sailors from Whitstable last month for treason. Your whore was their accomplice."

"You know damned well that is a lie."

"I know nothing of the kind! Those bloody émigrés are always short of funds and willing to sell their loyalty for gain. I could easily find proof of your tart's guilt."

Dare's hands momentarily clenched, but he kept his voice under tight control when he issued his own warning. "You would be ill-advised to threaten her with harm, old man."

"Then do not force my hand, boy! I mean what I say. Your betrothal will not stand. *It will not stand*, do you hear me!"

Ignoring the aging nobleman's shout, Dare turned abruptly on his heel and stalked from the room, intent on calming his own seething rage before he rode to meet Julienne at their trysting site.

Until that afternoon, he had been fiercely determined to defy his grandfather's wrath, regarding the possibility of disinheritance as inconsequential to his future happiness.

But this new threat against her was enough to give Dare pause. Certainly enough to make him question the wisdom of an elopement. He wanted Julienne as his wife, but not at the risk of endangering her. His grandfather was powerful enough to cause her a great deal of trouble, perhaps even to give real substance to any fabricated charges of treason.

Dare realized he had a momentous decision to make. He couldn't stand by and allow Julienne to be hurt. And even if he could convince her to elope with him against his grandfather's objections, there was still the problem of her invalid mother. The comptess refused to leave her home, and Julienne would never abandon her mother.

One thing Dare knew for certain. He would end their betrothal before he allowed her to suffer from the old bastard's machinations. Despite his ardent feelings for Julienne—or because of them—he would give her up before allowing her to be hurt.

Now, seven years later, Dare recalled what a bloody fool he had been. His grandfather had been right on that account.

He felt his throat close on the bitter memory. Julienne had agreed to meet him at the cottage that afternoon if she could get away from her shop, but when she didn't come, he rode into Whitstable to find her.

It was then he discovered her betrayal—her lover. Until then, he hadn't believed a word of his grandfather's accusations about her relationship with Ivers.

His chest aching with remembered pain, Dare stared down into his empty brandy snifter. The old man had gotten his way; he'd caused the dissolution of the betrothal. But Dare had left Kent immediately afterward and never again set foot under his grandfather's roof until the marquess was dead and buried.

With a raw, mirthless laugh, Dare threw the crystal snifter at the hearth, watching it shatter in the fire. He hoped the sixth Lord Wolverton was happy in his grave. His bloodline had remained untainted by the jade's French blood, even if he had lost his only grandson in the process.

Dare slept poorly, enduring dreams of being entangled in his grandfather's malevolent spiderweb. The next morning, directly after breakfast, he summoned the marquess's former secretary, Samuel Butner, to the library in the hope of uncovering evidence linking Ivers to Caliban.

"Is it a fair statement," Dare began after a spate of congenial small talk, "that after living in this district for so many years, you are somewhat acquainted with the Earl of Ivers?"

"Yes, my lord," the elderly secretary answered respectfully. "I would say I am acquainted with him as well as most."

"I'm interested in anything you can tell me about Ivers. It seems he has run up a vast number of gaming debts recently, and there are rumors that his loyalties might have been bought by the French." Dare regarded the secretary with a penetrating look. "Perhaps you'll recall the summer I spent here almost seven years ago: Two sailors from Whitstable were hanged as spies for collaborating with French Bonapartists. Could Ivers possibly have been associated with them or anything resembling treason, do you think?"

Butner narrowed his craggy brows. "Lord Ivers was always a rum sort, but to my knowledge, he would not have stooped so low as to consort with the enemy. But . . . "

"Yes?" Dare prompted.

"He was regularly short of funds, even then. And I am aware that he found a way to line his pockets that summer. Lord Wolverton paid his gaming debts."

"How do you know?"

"Because I wrote out the draft, my lord. It was a vast sum . . . six thousand pounds. I presume it bailed him out of the River Tick."

"Why would my grandfather be so generous?"

"I'm not certain, my lord. But I believe it had something to do with your . . . young lady. The one who owned the millinery."

Dare felt his heart rate quicken uneasily. "Go on."

Butner frowned thoughtfully, as if trying to remember. "His lordship summoned Lord Ivers here one afternoon and was closeted with him for the better part of an hour. I always suspected that large payment was for services rendered. That your grandfather employed Lord Ivers for some purpose."

"But you have no idea what that purpose might be?"

The elderly secretary hesitated a moment. "I have my suspicions. If I may speak freely?"

"By all means."

"His lordship was exceedingly pleased that you decided to stay here at Wolverton Hall that summer. I believe he thought he could groom you to assume his place . . . once you had sown your wild oats, that is."

Dare pressed his mouth together to keep from showing his cynicism. "Instead I proved a grave disappointment to my grandfather," he said evenly. "I was never serious enough for his taste. Never had aspirations of settling down and becoming an apple farmer."

"No, my lord. But it wounded him deeply when you became betrothed to the . . . French lass. He was a proud man, you know—"

"He was a manipulating old bastard."

"Just so. But he did not wish to see you wed her."

"Because a Frog would taint his impeccable bloodlines," Dare said sardonically.

"Yes. And because . . . he suspected her of treason. He intimated to me that she was involved with the spies who were hanged."

Dare found himself grinding his teeth. "That was a falsehood he concocted to force me to end my betrothal. Miss Laurent had nothing whatever to do with treason or spying."

"I suspected as much. I admit, it never set well with me that your grandfather would intervene in your affairs so flagrantly. But he was adamant. You were his hope and pride. He did not wish to see you go to . . . Begging your pardon, my lord. My tongue does run away from me at times." Looking uncomfortable, Butner flushed.

"No, please . . . I value your honesty. What were you about to say? Go where?"

"To the devil, the way your father did."

With effort Dare kept his lip from curling. "So Grandfather employed the same high-handedness with me that he'd tried on my father."

"Lord Wolverton hoped to compel you to call off your betrothal."

"By threatening to disown me, I know. For years I thought he had done so."

"He never changed his will. He had no reason to, once your betrothal ended. At the time, however, he was utterly determined. He said that whatever it took, he would gladly pay. He wanted to 'free you from the clutches of a scheming fortune hunter.' Those were his words, if I recall correctly."

Steeling himself against his growing disquietude, Dare managed a calm reply. "I gather he intended to use Ivers to frame Miss Laurent for treason."

"Possibly. After you left here, vowing never to return, Ivers called to collect. And he came two years later to request a loan. His pockets apparently were empty again."

"Did my grandfather comply?"

"No, he refused adamantly. I overheard their argument. Ivers said he would go to you if Lord Wolverton wouldn't pay, that you would want to know the truth."

"The truth about what?"

"Again, I'm not certain, my lord. It had something to do with Miss Laurent, because I heard her name spoken."

"But you're certain Ivers threatened to blackmail my grandfather?"

"It seemed that way. His lordship was so enraged, he had the footmen throw the earl out of the house. Ivers never called again, to my knowledge. I am not surprised that he has fallen under suspicion now, though. I always thought he would come to a bad end."

"Thank you, Mr. Butner. You have been a great deal of help."

Once the elderly secretary had gone, Dare sat unmoving, trying to grapple with the fear hovering in the back of his mind. Had his grandfather actually hired Ivers to spoil his betrothal? And had Ivers held the threat of being hanged for treason over Julienne's head?

Dare felt a knot tighten in his stomach. Had he somehow mistaken the situation regarding her relationship with Ivers that day? If he could set his jealousy aside for a rational moment, he would have to admit that even before the secretary's revelation just now, he'd begun to question their alliance. In Newmarket Julienne had seemed to regard Ivers with an enmity bordering on loathing.

Was that because Ivers had abandoned her all those years ago? They had been lovers then, hadn't they? Dare had seen it with his own eyes, heard the admission from Julienne's own lips.

His gut churning with unease, Dare rose to call for his carriage. He needed to speak to someone who had greater knowledge of Julienne and what might have happened that long-ago summer.

Famous for its oysters, the small seaport of Whitstable boasted several excellent inns, two dozen shops, and a minor shipyard. The town hadn't changed much in the years since his last visit, nor apparently had the hat shop where his life had been turned upside down.

Stepping from the carriage, Dare stood outside the door of the millinery, hesitating. He had hopes of finding the sales clerk who had been in Julienne's employ, but his skin felt suddenly cold and clammy with apprehension at what he might discover. He had to force himself to open the shop door and enter.

Memories rushed in on him all at once, reflections of the last time he'd been here. . . .

He'd thought it odd to find the millinery empty and unlocked, with no sign of Julienne or the girl she employed as a clerk. Hearing voices coming from the floor overhead, he'd climbed the stairs to the large room above the shop that was used for storage and sewing and occasionally as sleeping quarters.

Julienne sat on the cot, her disheveled hair spilling from its pins, while the Earl of Ivers stood beside the bed, hovering over her. When she spied Dare, she clutched a hand to her heart.

She looked dismayed to see him—although no more dismayed than he felt, seeing her with his rival in such an intimate setting.

Ivers's expression remained cool, however, as he rested a hand possessively on her shoulder. "Clune . . .

I am glad you have come. Julienne has something she wishes to tell you."

Unwillingly Dare shifted his attention to the earl. His first impulse was to strangle the man with his bare hands for daring to touch Julienne—

"Tell him, my dear," Ivers urged.

"Tell me what?" Dare demanded, his anger welling to dangerous heights.

"She intends to end your betrothal," Ivers said when Julienne remained silent. He squeezed her shoulder. "Isn't that right, my dear?"

For a moment she shut her eyes. Then with a slow, shuddering breath, she stiffened her shoulders and raised her gaze to Dare's. "Yes. I no longer wish to marry you, Dare."

A sharp hollowness clawed at the pit of his stomach, while his mouth suddenly felt filled with sawdust. "What the devil are you talking about?"

"I . . . You never told me your grandfather would disown you if you wed me."

Dare stood frozen, staring at her as he tried to comprehend the import of her words. Did she care so much about the Wolverton fortune after all?

Watching his face, Julienne reached a trembling hand out to him. "Dare . . . I cannot marry you."

As if to comfort her, Ivers patted her shoulder. "I regret that you had to discover the truth this way, Clune, but it is better that you finally know. Julienne has always been mine. I enjoyed her favors long before you did."

His breath seizing in his lungs, Dare found he couldn't move. Every muscle in his body was paralyzed by shock and disbelief.

"Julienne?" The raw word finally scraped from his throat. "It isn't true."

Fleetingly she glanced up at Ivers, then lowered her gaze to stare at the floor. "I am sorry," she whispered hoarsely.

Ivers smiled in triumph, while turmoil rocked Dare. He staggered backward, recoiling as if struck by a blow. He'd expected her to denounce Ivers's sickening claim, not to uphold it.

His rival's exultant voice pierced the tumult of his thoughts. "It has been difficult for me, keeping quiet all this time while you courted her, Clune. But Julienne insisted that I stay out of her way. Fortunately she decided that if you are to lose your inheritance, she prefers me to you."

Reeling, Dare focused on Ivers, seeing the revolting smirk on his dark face . . . the blood coming from his split lower lip.

With a wry smile, Ivers reached up to gingerly touch his wound. "She does enjoy rough play, as I'm sure you know."

His gut heaving, Dare abruptly backed away and stumbled from the room, too stricken even to think of calling Ivers out. He felt as if his heart had been ripped from his chest. . . .

Feeling his head spin now, Dare pressed a hand to his temple. Had he been too swift to condemn Julienne? She hadn't refuted Ivers's claim, certainly. What words had she used precisely? *I am sorry*. He had taken that for an admission of guilt. . . .

Dear God, could he have been so wrong? Had she been a victim all along? Or was it his memory now that was at fault? It had happened so long ago. And his own devastation might have led his recollections of that cataclysmic event to change over the years—

"My Lord Wolverton?" A grim female voice interrupted his churning thoughts. "May I be of assistance?"

Dare looked up to find a dark-haired woman perhaps in her mid-twenties standing in a corner near the counter, adding a plume to a bonnet. Her rather plump face seemed vaguely familiar.

"Do you know me?" he asked, frowning.

Her expression remained grave. "Yes, my lord. You were once my mistress's suitor. I could never forget you."

For an instant Dare saw a flash of something like antipathy flash in her blue eyes. Puzzled, he advanced farther into the shop. "You were Miss Laurent's sales clerk seven years ago."

"Yes . . . Rachel Grimble. I am now the proprietor."

Her antipathy was clearer now. Her tone held none of the deference a shopkeeper usually showed a nobleman of his consequence. Rather it held contempt.

"You seem to hold me in dislike, Miss Grimble."

"I have good reason, my lord—because of what you did to Miss Laurent. Or perhaps I should say, what you did not do."

"I trust you mean to explain?"

"You allowed the wolves to devour her."

Dare's eyebrows narrowed to a frown. "That tells me little."

"You left her at the mercy of that beast. I found her. . . ." The shopkeeper took a deep breath. "Miss Laurent had sent me to deliver a commission, and when

I returned . . . Lord Ivers had just driven away." The
woman glanced toward the back of the millinery where
the stairs were. "He had violated her, my lord."

Air hissed sharply between Dare's teeth; his gut
clenched as if a knife had been plunged into him.

With sudden brutal clarity he recalled the blood on
Ivers's lip, an injury the earl had claimed was due to
Julienne's preference for rough play.

Oh, God. His heart thundered while a wave of horror crashed through his mind.

"He forced himself upon her," the Grimble woman
repeated, twisting the knife further. "You didn't know?"

"No . . ." Dare whispered, the word a raw rasp. "I
never knew. Perhaps I should have."

"Aye, I think you should have. He was a beast, but
you . . . She loved you, my lord, and you abandoned
her."

Raising a hand to his head, Dare clutched at his
hair. Understanding nearly brought him to his knees;
the violent reality of it was paralyzing.

He had fled Kent that very afternoon, too intent on
his own bleeding wounds to question the fate of the
beautiful deceiver who had savaged his heart. He had
kept away for years, forcibly attempting to shut out
even the slightest thought of Julienne.

The shopkeeper merely stood there, not speaking,
her silence eloquent with condemnation while Dare
grappled with the enormity of his transgression.

"Why in God's name didn't she tell me?" he said
after a time.

"I don't know, my lord. I wanted to go to you. I
thought you would somehow protect her, even after . . .
what Lord Ivers did to her. But she wouldn't let me. I

think she must have been too ashamed." Miss Grimble's tone hardened. "That was not the worst of it, either. Lord Wolverton made certain her reputation was utterly destroyed by rumors of treason. No one would give her business any longer, and the scandal nearly killed her mother. Miss Laurent was forced to leave town. His lordship drove her away. And by then you were long gone."

Dare couldn't speak. There was nothing he could say, no apology he could make to excuse his ignorance or his actions.

Turning, he blindly made his way out to his carriage. Self-contempt stuck in his throat, hot and thick, as he fell back against the squabs of the landau.

Julienne had been assaulted—raped by that vile bastard—and he had walked away.

They were never lovers at all. She had only wanted him to believe it. But in God's name, *why*? Had Ivers threatened to hurt her? Forced her to support his claim? Dare's mind rebelled at the possibility. Surely Julienne knew he would have done everything in his power to keep her safe.

But he hadn't kept her safe. Instead he had failed her in the worst possible way.

He squeezed his eyes shut. Julienne had never betrayed him with Ivers. She had been faithful all along. But his own jealousy had blinded him, caused him to condemn her as deceiver.

Was that why she hadn't told him? Because she'd anticipated what his response would be? Or had she thought he wouldn't want her as his wife after she had been violated? Or was there another, more immediate reason? Had she been afraid he would call Ivers out? That he would kill the man?

Dare's fists clenched. He *would* have killed Ivers if he'd had the slightest inkling of the truth.

Rage gripped him in its power, along with an acrid shame. However unwittingly, he had let Julienne suffer alone the consequences of their passion. Abandoned her to the mercy of his grandfather's wrath and brutal scheming. The marquess apparently had hired Ivers to break up their betrothal by whatever vile means necessary.

What a stupid, blind, *bloody* fool he had been! He had known his grandfather could be a ruthless bastard. He just hadn't known *how* ruthless.

For a long while Dare sat there, rocked to his soul by a tempest of emotions—grief, raw fury, hatred, self-contempt. The truth burned too hot and fierce for anything else to penetrate his dazed stupor.

"My lord?"

The concerned voice finally registering, Dare raised his gaze. His coachman was looking over his shoulder at him, his expression troubled.

"Are you unwell, my lord? Should I drive you to a doctor?"

A doctor could never cure his malady, Dare thought with a bitter, mirthless laugh. "No, no doctor."

"Where do you wish to go then, my lord?"

The coachman was waiting for orders as to his destination, Dare realized. He had to return to London at once. He had to see Julienne.

He gave the command to return to Wolverton Hall so that he could pack and collect his traveling chaise. But as he sank back into the searing turmoil of his thoughts, there was one agonizing question that burned brightest in his mind.

How in this lifetime could Julienne ever forgive him?

Chapter
Fourteen

He waited for Julienne in the shabby parlor of her hired rooms, counting the minutes until she returned from the theater. When finally he heard a carriage out on the street, Dare went to the window and peered down.

Riddingham had escorted her home, he saw, forcibly quelling a spark of jealousy. He had no right to object to her choice of protectors. He had lost that privilege long ago.

His stomach churning, Dare returned to the worn settee before she unlocked and opened the door. Upon seeing the lamplight, Julienne stopped abruptly, her eyes wide with fear and defiance as she searched the room.

She had a knife in her hand, and his conscience smote him once more as he realized the significance of it.

At least her relief seemed sincere when she recognized him.

"How did you get in here?" Julienne asked, shutting the door behind her.

"Your landlady allowed me to wait here for you."

"I don't understand—" she began, but he cut her off.

"I've just returned from Kent . . . from Whitstable."

Julienne said not a word. She merely stared at him.

"I spoke to your former shop clerk about Ivers. You were never lovers."

Her face drained of color. Her fingers trembled as she set the knife down on a table. Then, moving like a sleepwalker, she sank into the chair opposite him.

For a moment Dare lowered his gaze to veil the stark emotion in his eyes. It hurt just to look at her and know what he had done, to comprehend the ugliness that had been thrust upon her. It sickened him to realize how badly he had mistaken appearances, but Julienne had permitted him to believe the lie. What he couldn't fathom was why she hadn't denied the claim outright, then or even later.

"Why, Julienne?" He heard the ache in his voice as he said her name.

She winced but refused to look at him. Instead she stared down at her hands, which were clasped tightly in her lap. "I didn't lie to you," she said in a voice so quiet, it was barely a whisper.

"You let me believe you were lovers. You never refuted him."

"I thought I had no choice. He threatened to harm my mother."

"I would have protected her—did you never consider that?"

When she raised her gaze, there was such pain in her eyes that it almost broke him.

She gave a faint shake of her head. "It would not have mattered. I knew I could never wed you, Dare. I couldn't let you sacrifice yourself for me. Ending our betrothal was the only way to save you from being disowned."

Dare felt his heart twist with agony. "Did you think my grandfather's fortune meant so much to me?"

"Perhaps not then, but you might have come to resent me if I had caused you to lose your inheritance."

I couldn't let you sacrifice yourself for me. The words haunted him. Julienne hadn't wanted him to suffer, so she had made the sacrifice herself.

"The Wolverton estate was entailed," Dare said softly, yet with an edge of irony. "It would have come to me on my grandfather's death, along with the title. And in any case, I had already amassed a considerable fortune of my own by then. I would never have missed his wealth."

Julienne returned his regard solemnly, dismay shimmering in her dark eyes.

"Why didn't you even give me the chance to discuss it?"

She clenched her fingers more tightly in her lap. She felt raw and exposed under the unwavering intensity of Dare's gaze. "It all happened so quickly. Ivers had just made his threats before you arrived. He said that your grandfather was determined to separate us, that Lord Wolverton would never let our betrothal stand. Then you walked in, and Ivers made that claim about being my lover. . . ."

She took a steadying breath. "I *wanted* you to believe we were lovers, that I had been unfaithful. I knew you would never let me end our betrothal otherwise."

She closed her eyes, remembering the pain and betrayal on Dare's face. That tormented look had haunted her for years.

"I didn't want to lie to you," she added, her voice low. "I hated that you could think so badly of me. And in my secret heart . . . I hoped that you would see through his lies and realize that I still loved you. But then Ivers . . . I was such a naive little fool."

She attempted a self-deprecating laugh, but it stuck in her throat; her laughter was too bitter to release. "I didn't realize what a black-souled villain Ivers truly was. I thought that since I'd done as he demanded— called off our betrothal—he would be satisfied. But that wasn't enough for him. He wanted to make certain I was thoroughly compromised. That you would never want me for your wife. Your grandfather had paid him to make certain of it. After you left . . . I tried to fight him. I scratched his face till it was bloody, but he was too strong. . . ."

"*God.*"

She opened her eyes at his tortured whisper. Dare had sunk his head in his hands and was clutching his hair, as if he might tear it out by the roots.

"You could not have known what he would do," she said quietly.

His groan was low and harsh. "Don't try to absolve me, Julienne. I should never have left you there with that devil."

"It wasn't your fault. If anything, it was mine, for being so utterly gullible. Afterward . . . I could scarcely believe it had happened. When he was done, I lay there dazed, stunned. The shock must have dulled my memory, but I remember I swore that I would kill him if he touched me again, if he harmed my mother. He seemed to believe me, for he went away. But I realized that any hope for a future with you had been shattered."

Dare raised his head then, and the pain in his eyes mirrored her own. "You should have told me."

"How could I? If your grandfather was set against our marriage before, what Ivers had done made it a thousand times worse. I was ruined, damaged goods. I had been violated by another man, and I feared you would never want me again. Or worse . . . that you would do something noble like insist on marrying me. That would have exposed you to scandal and ridicule and caused your grandfather to disinherit you after all. I couldn't let that happen."

Scalding tears filled her eyes as she felt the helplessness again, the hopelessness. The sheer misery of having lost Dare. She had wanted so desperately to tell him the truth, to make him understand that she would have died before willingly betraying him. But she couldn't take the risk.

Agony rushed to envelop her as she remembered, and her tears began to fall.

In two strides he was at her side, lifting her up and wrapping her in his arms, hushing her sobs against his chest.

She wanted to resist. She hated for Dare to see her so vulnerable, so weak. But she had no defenses left. She wept against him, clinging to him tightly.

Dare could barely stand the anguish. It seemed so inadequate to hold her, to try to comfort her, when he'd been the one to hurt her so badly. To see her like this was agony. He ached for her, ached with the need to banish those terrible memories.

After a moment her sobs lessened. Finally she drew back, dashing fiercely at her streaming eyes. "I don't want your pity, Dare. I won't stand for it."

He saw wellsprings of pain in those dark depths, but there was infinite courage amid the vulnerability.

"No," he whispered. "Not pity."

It wasn't pity that smote him. Shame seared at the remnants of his soul. Shame and remorse and self-blame for the nightmare she had endured.

He could picture Julienne then—desperate, devastated, alone. He could only imagine the strength it must have taken to bear the rape and the scandal of his grandfather's accusations afterward. To earn her living in such a difficult profession as acting. To sell her body so that her mother's final days could be less agonizing.

His heart hurt, ravaged by a misery greater than any he had ever known, even when he had thought his love betrayed by a scheming enchantress.

He drew Julienne over to the settee and pulled her down with him, holding her tightly against him, his face buried in her hair, until her trembling gradually quieted.

The constriction in his throat made his voice shaky when at last he spoke. "Julienne, I can never deserve your forgiveness. I can only tell you . . . I would have cut out my heart before letting you be hurt."

With a shuddering breath, she shook her head. "You weren't to blame, Dare."

"I *was* to blame. I was young and stupid and hotheaded—determined to defy my grandfather at all costs, damn the consequences. But you paid the price for his wrath."

Tenderly he brushed the dampened tendrils of hair from her cheeks, kissed the tears from her face. Then he drew her close again, so that her head lay on his shoulder.

His voice dropped even lower, his tone grim as he recalled that disastrous afternoon. "I was considering ending our betrothal even before I discovered you with Ivers. My grandfather had threatened to charge you with treason, and I feared he might actually attempt it. I was coming to discuss it with you that afternoon. But then . . . When I saw you with Ivers and he claimed you were lovers, I was insanely jealous. I wanted to kill him merely for touching you."

"You only believed him because I didn't deny it."

Dare's mouth curled sardonically. "And I suppose I was predisposed to think you guilty. My mother had countless lovers during the course of her marriage. She came from a generation that raised infidelity to a fine art, and I grew up believing it the natural way of things. But I should have known you weren't like her."

His tone turned darker, bleaker. "I should have suspected my grandfather's machinations. *I* was the fool—for not realizing the lengths he would go to in order to have his way. And then I left you to deal with the aftermath alone. He destroyed your life, but I let it happen. I should have protected you."

"You would have, had you known, I'm certain of it."

He gave a bitter laugh. "At the time I was only concerned about surviving my own wounds. All I wanted was to get as far away from you as possible. If I had remained . . . at least I could have saved you from the damage my grandfather inflicted on your reputation afterward. Your sales clerk told me he ruined your business and drove you to leave town."

"Yes. I had no resources to fight him, and I had my

mother to support. But I couldn't hope for any respectable employment after he tore my name to shreds."

"So you turned to acting."

"That actually was the one good thing to come of the calamity, Dare." A faint smile curved her mouth. "I found a vocation—something I truly love doing. Acting proved my salvation. It helped me banish my demons."

"But then you were forced to take a protector," Dare said, his voice ragged.

Julienne was glad the lamplight was not overly bright, for the flush of shame on her cheeks would have been even more noticeable. "It wasn't . . . It was simply something I had to do. And after losing you, nothing much could hurt me. The gentleman I chose . . . he was very kind. It made it easier to give my body for money."

Fresh tears scalded her eyes as she remembered. She had thought she might die from a grief-stricken heart, but the struggle to survive had given her a reason to go on.

She had eventually managed to overcome the darkness and shame that had nearly swallowed her. In time she had even healed from the brutal ordeal. Ivers had violated her body, but he hadn't touched the core of her.

He hadn't destroyed her physical need for passion, either. It had helped that her gentle protector had banished the last vestiges of her fear. But Dare had been the one to show her what true ecstasy was. What it was to feel truly alive. Because of him, she knew that lovemaking had nothing to do with the act of violence that had been perpetrated against her.

She reached up to touch his cheek. "There were some things about that summer that I never regretted. You taught me about love, about passion. Without that, I never could have overcome the rest."

He squeezed his eyes shut, as if he couldn't bear to accept her forgiveness. "You can't absolve me of guilt, Julienne."

The look of pain on Dare's face made her heart ache. She wanted to wrap her arms around him and help him find peace. He was holding her so gently, as if she were made of fragile glass, as if he feared to touch her.

Lifting her face, she pressed her lips against his. "Dare . . . make love to me."

He drew back to stare at her. "How can you possibly want me after what I did to you?"

Julienne had to smile just a little. All she could think of was how fervently she wanted Dare, how much she needed him. She needed him to exorcise her dark memories. Needed him to drive away the terrible loneliness of the past years.

In answer, she reached up to caress his cheek, feeling the day's stubble that roughened his jaw. "How can I possibly *not* want you?" she asked, raising her lips to his again.

His mouth descended on hers fervently, his kiss desperate, as if he needed her to save his soul. With their lips still joined, he lifted her in his arms and carried her into the adjacent chamber, where he lay her down on the narrow bed.

In the glow of the fire, he undressed her, but his touch was tentative—nothing like that of the passionate lover who had become a legend. And when she was fully naked, he sat beside her, hesitating.

"Dare . . . I won't break," Julienne murmured restlessly.

Perhaps not, he thought, but he felt as raw and uncertain as a boy with his first love.

As if understanding, she sat up and cupped his face in her hands. "You won't hurt me," she whispered. "You could never hurt me."

Dare nearly groaned as his heart twisted in his chest. She was trying to console *him*.

She kissed him tenderly, letting her warm mouth linger against his as she untied his cravat and let it drop to the floor. He drank in her kiss but then took over from her, removing his jacket himself.

While he unfastened the buttons of his waistcoat, Julienne rose from the bed and went to her bureau, where she made use of the coffer of sponges and unpinned her hair. His gaze remained riveted on her as the silken mass fell down her back.

When she returned, she finished undressing Dare, kneeling beside the bed to remove his boots and then his breeches. He reached for her then, but with her hands on his shoulders, she urged him to lie back. "No, I want to do this . . . please."

He lay back, quiescent, instinctively understanding her need to be in control, to prove she wasn't powerless or helpless or vulnerable.

Easing onto the bed, she knelt over him, pressing her lips against his bare chest. She kissed his entire body slowly, deliberately sweeping her hair over him as she moved lower.

Her caresses felt like silk, so soft on his skin, so

poignant and incredibly erotic at the same time. He was already heavily aroused, but he hardened even further when Julienne swirled her tongue over the sensitive area of his inner thighs. Then she moved back up his body, her lips trailing fire over his flesh . . . his phallus, his belly, his chest. . . .

It required almost herculean effort for Dare to lie totally still while she attended him, licking, stroking, tantalizing. . . . She paused to brush his male nipples with her tongue before returning to his mouth, delivering a featherlight kiss that made his stomach clench in a mixture of tenderness and wrenching desire.

When her kiss deepened, his fingers wrapped helplessly in her hair. He tried to be gentle, but the coiling tension became too much to bear. Drawing her down to cover him, Dare whispered her name with a note of pleading. In response, Julienne lowered herself onto him slowly, taking him fully into her body.

Their joining was heaven. A hoarse sound escaped him at the blinding throb of sensation; his heart ached with a wild rhythm. He could feel the twisting need within her, the desperate longing to become part of him, and he reciprocated, giving wholly of himself.

They claimed each other with fierce tenderness, and in only moments the firestorm overcame them. They moved together in the throes of passion, drinking each other's cries, cresting on shattering swells that seemed to last forever.

When finally the rapture ended, Julienne collapsed limply upon Dare, trembling. She lay against his warm, powerful body, listening to the force of his thundering heart.

A serene peace washed over her. Dare finally knew

the truth, that she hadn't betrayed him. She could lay the last of her demons to rest. Their lovemaking had been as exquisite as usual, but there was a newness about it . . . a heightened sweetness, a caring. They had given solace to each other.

She exhaled softly on a sigh. Dare no longer blamed her for the past, or for what Ivers had done. Nor had he condemned her because she'd been forced by dire circumstances to share her body. She felt cleansed somehow, as if a great burden had been lifted from her.

Her heart felt almost light. She scarcely recognized the feeling. Hope. It was an unfamiliar emotion, something she hadn't allowed herself to feel in years. She was free of the hurtful past at last.

Dare, however, could not forget, it seemed. He lay staring up at the ceiling for a long while.

"How you must have hated me," he said finally.

"No, not you," she replied, her voice soft. "Never you. I hated Ivers. I wanted to kill him."

"I intend to," Dare muttered darkly.

A sharp arrow of anxiety shot through Julienne, and she raised her head from his shoulder. "Dare, you cannot."

"Why not?"

"Because the satisfaction couldn't possibly be worth the possible consequences. If you killed him, you might very well have to flee the country. I couldn't bear it if you sacrificed yourself for my sake."

His green eyes flickered with pain as they searched hers. "Don't you want even the slightest measure of revenge?"

"At one time I did, but now . . . I only want to bury the past and move on with my life."

"Are you so certain Ivers will let the past stay buried? What did he want with you in Newmarket?"

Julienne flinched at the question. "He wanted money to pay his debts. He threatened to renew those old charges of treason against me if I didn't pay him."

Anger darkened Dare's eyes. "And you intend to surrender to his threats?"

"No, of course not. I told him to go to the devil. He can't hurt me any longer."

"And yet you carry a knife."

"For protection, yes."

Dare's expression hardened. "He won't get away with what he did, Julienne. He deserves punishment for his crimes."

Dare was right, she knew. Ivers shouldn't be allowed to go unpunished. But she couldn't bear the thought of Dare suffering as a result.

She gave him a pleading look. "Dare, please, promise me you won't kill him."

He tightened his jaw. "Very well . . . I won't kill him outright."

She stared at him a long moment, as if not quite believing him.

"Trust me," he said quietly. "I won't do anything foolish this time."

He was relieved when Julienne finally laid her head back down on his shoulder and allowed him to wrap his arms around her. But even while relishing the sensual contentment of their embrace, Dare found himself staring at the dancing shadows on the ceiling, hating with a lethal passion the vile bastard who had violated her.

He couldn't let that lie. Ivers would pay for hurting

Julienne, one way or another. He would make damned certain Ivers hanged if he had murdered Alice Watson. And if Ivers was an accomplice of Caliban's, he would prove it and let justice take its course. . . .

He hadn't told Julienne about that probable connection yet, and he wouldn't until he had Ivers in chains. This score was his alone to settle. He didn't want Julienne involved, or for her to feel required to face her attacker.

After a while, Dare heard the even sound of her breathing, and his churning thoughts turned from revenge to his own transgressions. He should be flayed alive for leaving Julienne to the mercy of that devil. He wondered how many years would pass before he could call up the memory without being sick to his soul from it.

Dare shut his eyes to cover the surge of emotion clawing inside him. He had never felt so worthless, so unworthy. Julienne had sacrificed herself for him in an effort to save him from being disinherited. It had been a noble gesture, even if misguided, and because of it, her entire life had been shattered.

He inhaled slowly to draw air into his tight, aching chest. He would have given everything he owned to be able to undo the past.

His fingers rose to her hair, caressing the sable tresses as Julienne lay sleeping. Somehow he had to earn her forgiveness. He could never make up for all the pain, for all the wasted years, but he had to try.

A desperate longing welled up within him, a fierce craving to win her heart again. Perhaps if he was incredibly lucky it might be possible. . . .

Vowing to try, Dare slipped from her side, careful

Chapter
Fifteen

It was some time later when Julienne woke, missing Dare's warmth. Confusion was her first reaction as she wondered what could have driven him to leave her bed at this late hour.

Then a sharp twinge of panic hit her. *Ivers.* Would Dare have gone to confront him?

She knew where Ivers was staying, for Riddingham had discovered it for her when she'd claimed the earl was plaguing her with his unwanted attentions.

Throwing off the covers, she hastened to dress.

Dare stood in the darkness of Ivers's hotel room, watching the bastard sleep.

Limmer's Hotel was dark and grimy but always well-patronized; its public rooms were the choice of London's hard-drinking, sporting bucks. It had been the work of a moment for Dare to bribe his way into the earl's bedchamber.

Ivers hadn't heard a sound above his own snores. He was sprawled facedown on the bed, only partially dressed. He'd removed his boots and breeches but not his shirt, and the linen barely covered his white buttocks.

Rage knotting his gut, Dare struck a flint and lit a candle. The clock on the mantel said it was four in the morning. Withdrawing the blade from his swordstick, Dare poured an ewerful of water over the earl's rumpled head.

Ivers bolted upright, sputtering in startlement, only to find Dare's rapier point pressed into the hollow of his throat.

He froze, his eyes wide with alarm. "W-Wolverton . . . what . . . ? What do you w-want?"

Dare's mouth curled in a wintry smile, a baring of teeth. "I expect you can guess. You were never Julienne Laurent's lover."

"I . . . yes, of course I was. If she said otherwise, she is lying."

Only with effort did Dare keep rigid control of his fury. Using the steel point of the rapier, he traced the scars on Ivers's left cheek, pressing hard enough to draw blood. "Would you care to reconsider your answer?"

Ivers hissed in pain as the blade dug into his skin. "Do you mean to call me out?" He eyed the rapier with fright. "You are an expert swordsman. It would hardly be fair odds."

"What kind of odds did you give Julienne Laurent when you violated her?"

"I . . . I am sorry. . . . It was nothing personal. Your grandfather—"

The rage that flared through Dare burned whitehot. Shifting the tip of the blade down Ivers's shirtfront to his groin, Dare pushed the point into his left testicle.

Ivers screamed and grabbed his loins, while blood trickled from between his fingers.

"I suggest you keep your cries down," Dare admonished in cool drawl, "or my next target will be your heart. You forced yourself upon her, didn't you?"

When Ivers glanced wildly around the room, as if seeking to escape, Dare shook his head.

"No one will come to your rescue. You're completely at my mercy. You defiled her, didn't you?"

"Yes! God, no, please . . ." Ivers whimpered when the blade moved back up to his throat. "Don't hurt me!"

"Why not?" Dare asked, his voice very, very soft. "Tell me why I shouldn't kill you this instant."

Ivers began to sob.

"Perhaps I should cut you into pieces and feed you to the fish in the Thames. You're familiar with the Thames River, aren't you, Ivers? You killed Lady Castlereagh's companion there last month."

"No! I didn't kill her, I swear." When the tip gouged his throat, he fell back on the bed, cringing. "But I can tell you who did."

Dare lowered the rapier. "You begin to interest me."

Struggling against tears, Ivers took a shuddering breath. "I didn't kill the girl, I swear. I wooed her, yes. She was to meet me that night. But when I arrived, she was already dead."

"Who murdered her then?"

"It was Perrine . . . Martin Perrine."

Dare his stomach muscles tighten. "You saw him with her body?"

"No, but I'm certain he was the one."

Dare hesitated. "Is he Caliban?"

"I don't know. I swear. Perrine tells me what Lord Caliban orders are, and he ordered me to court the girl. I had no choice. Perrine bought up most of my vowels and promised he would call them in if I didn't oblige Caliban." ·

"What did he want from Alice Watson?"

"To discover Lord Castlereagh's plans—what he intended to do about Napoleon after the peace, where he intended to be."

"So you persuaded her to steal Castlereagh's letters to his wife. And after the girl died, you bribed his servants for information."

"Yes."

"What were you doing at Newmarket? Following me?"

"Yes. Perrine heard you were putting your nose where it didn't belong—searching for Caliban. He thought it amusing, but he wanted to know why. I was supposed to see what I could discover."

"But you accosted Miss Laurent instead."

Ivers gave another whimper. "I didn't touch her!"

"No, you only tried to extort money from her by threatening to spread your spurious tales. What punishment do you think you deserve for that?"

"Please . . . don't kill me."

"I won't have to. What you did was treason. No doubt you'll hang for it."

"Wh-what . . . what if I have knowledge that could save Castlereagh's life? He is in grave danger."

"I'm listening," Dare said.

"Perrine was angry that I couldn't wring any more information from the servants—"

Just then Dare heard a sound behind him. He turned slightly, raising his rapier against a possible threat as the door opened. His heart jolted in his chest when he recognized the newcomer.

Julienne stood there, her eyes dark with concern.

She stepped into the room, shutting the door softly behind her. She was clutching her knife, Dare noted as she moved closer. He saw her reaction when she spied the cut on Ivers's cheek . . . the blood soaking into the mattress from his injured loins.

Her searching gaze shifted to Dare's face. "I thought you might have killed him," she murmured.

"I promised I wouldn't dispatch him outright," Dare said evenly. "But you can still change your mind."

Julienne eyed the cringing nobleman on the bed. "I confess I would not grieve to see him dead."

Ivers's chest heaved in a sob.

Dare smiled. "I think you should plead with the lady for your life, Ivers. She might be willing to spare you."

"Please," he mewled, "I beg you, spare me." His hoarse entreaties were those of a broken man.

"Don't kill him," Julienne said finally, her voice edged with scorn. "He is too pitiful. And I wouldn't care to have his blood on your hands."

Dare raised an eyebrow as he surveyed the earl. "You are fortunate, Ivers. She is far more magnanimous than I could ever be. And I expect death would be too merciful for you."

At his reprieve, Ivers squeezed his eyes shut.

Dare bent to pick up a discarded pair of trousers from the floor and tossed them at the earl. "Get dressed."

"Where are you taking me?"

He would deliver Ivers to Lucian, Dare had already decided. "There are several gentlemen in the Foreign Office who will be interested in hearing what you have to say about Perrine and Caliban. After that . . . I have no doubt you'll be thrown in prison to await hanging."

"But . . . if you put me in prison, Perrine will know I told you. He'll kill me for certain."

"At least that will save the government the trouble of hanging you."

"Please . . . let me go. I'll go away, I swear. I'll leave the country."

When Julienne gave Dare a quizzical look, he answered her unspoken question. "It seems our enterprising Lord Ivers has been up to his neck in treason and he hopes to save his skin. He claims to have information about our friend Martin Perrine and his dealings with Caliban."

"I do!" Ivers insisted. "I think Caliban means to kill the foreign secretary."

"Who is Caliban?" Julienne asked sharply. "Perrine?"

"I don't know," Ivers said. "It's possible. Perrine said Caliban couldn't trust anyone else but himself for this mission. And Perrine left town yesterday." Ivers turned his pleading gaze back to Dare. "Please, let me go. I don't want to hang."

"I'll leave that decision to the Foreign Office," Dare replied. "Now get up."

With a groan of pain, Ivers rose from the bed and limped over to the hearth to dress. Dare saw Julienne turn her back and move toward the door, possibly because she could no longer bear to look at her assaulter.

"I'm bleeding like a damned butchered pig," Ivers complained.

"And you expect me to cry for you?"

Ivers bent over, seeming to fumble with his trousers. Out of the corner of his eye, Dare saw Ivers raise a fire poker over his head just as Julienne cried out in warning, "Dare!"

Ivers charged, but Dare had time to defend himself. Sidestepping swiftly, he drove the blade through the fleshy part of Ivers's waist.

A stunned look on his face, Ivers clutched at his side and sank to the floor. He curled into a ball, whimpering in pain. "You've killed me. . . ."

"Regrettably, no," Dare drawled.

He found a cravat among the slovenly pile of discarded clothing and knelt beside the injured man, pressing the linen against the seeping wound.

"You'll live, more's the pity. As you said, I'm an accomplished swordsman, and I was very careful not to wound you fatally. But you've put me to the trouble of fetching a surgeon."

The door flew open and a man burst into the room, brandishing a pistol. He was a rough-looking character, despite the fact that he was dressed like a dandy. He took in the scene in a rapid glance: Julienne with her hand to her throat. Ivers wounded and half-naked on the floor, his shirt stained scarlet. And Dare with the blade of his swordstick covered with blood.

"Pardon, your lordship," he said, addressing Dare, "but I heard a cry. I thought murder might be being done."

"Attempted murder, perhaps." Dare rose to his feet. "And you are . . . ?"

"Henry Teal, in the employ of Lord Wycliff, sir. I've been keeping an eye on this scurvy gutter rat"—he shot a glance at Ivers—"so he didn't brush and lope. My partner has summoned Lord Wycliff. He should be here shortly."

"Excellent. Wycliff is just the man to sort out this mess." Dare moved toward the door. "Will you oblige me and keep an eye on our prisoner?"

"Aye, milord."

"And, Teal? We want him alive. If he tries to escape, please direct your bullet to a nonlethal portion of his anatomy."

Teal grinned. "Aye, milord."

Taking Julienne's arm, Dare escorted her from the room and shut the door behind him. Several groggy patrons garbed in nightshirts had gathered in the dimly lit corridor.

"A small mishap," Dare reassured them. "No cause for alarm."

He waited until they had returned to their own rooms before pulling Julienne into his embrace.

"I was afraid he would force your hand and make you kill him," she murmured against his shoulder.

"No. But he will pay for his crimes."

Julienne shuddered.

"It's over, love," Dare said softly. "You won't have to deal with Ivers ever again."

"Thank you. But . . . it isn't entirely over." She drew back to search his face, keeping her voice low and hushed when she asked, "Is Perrine really Caliban?"

"I think it likely. Certainly our mild-mannered house-guest has just become our chief suspect." Dare frowned, suddenly wondering how Julienne had come to be here. "How did you know where to find me?"

"Riddingham. I had asked him to keep a watch out for me, and he told me Ivers was staying at this hotel. I managed to hail a hackney, even at this late hour, but discovering the exact room was more difficult. The proprietor was reluctant to allow me up here." Her mouth curved sardonically. "I persuaded him that you had summoned me here. No doubt he thinks me your doxy."

Dare reached for her arm again. "Come, I will take you home."

Julienne shook her head. "I'm not leaving, Dare. Not when the matter of Caliban is still unresolved."

"You can't mean to involve yourself with hunting for him?"

"I already am involved. I am in the government's employ, remember?"

Dare hesitated.

"You will have to follow Perrine to France, won't you? Well, I am French. I think I can be useful in searching for him."

When his frown deepened, Julienne raised her chin. "You are not just going to send me away," she insisted.

"Well, I don't intend to stay out here in a public corridor debating it with you."

This time Julienne's smile held faint amusement. "Then I suggest you find the proprietor and hire a parlor so we may argue about it in private."

It was perhaps three hours later before Lord Wycliff joined them in the private parlor.

"I am honored to meet you at last, Miss Laurent," Lucian said when Dare had made the introductions. "My wife and I both have enjoyed your performances."

"Thank you, my lord."

"Have some breakfast," Dare suggested, "while you tell us what more you learned from Ivers."

Lucian brought them up to date as he filled a plate

from the sideboard. Ivers had been stitched up by a surgeon, interrogated intensely, and hauled off by two of Lucian's chief agents to the Foreign Office, where he would be questioned yet again before being charged and imprisoned by a magistrate.

"And do you think Caliban and Perrine are one and the same?" Dare asked when Lucian was seated at the table.

"All my instincts tell me so. As an untitled younger son, Perrine may have discovered that manipulating his victims satisfied his hunger for power as well as his desire to fill his pockets. And he has long had political connections. Perrine is a close friend of Lord Aberdeen."

"Wasn't Aberdeen appointed our ambassador to Austria last year?"

"Yes," Lucian said, his tone edged with scorn. "Despite the fact that he was far too young and inexperienced for the role. Aberdeen's incompetence nearly sabotaged our negotiations with the Coalition—which is what forced Castlereagh to take over. As for Perrine's guilt . . . the man I had watching him confirmed that he left London yesterday for Dover and boarded a packet to Calais. It's likely he is bound for Paris, where Castlereagh is."

"I understand," Julienne said, "that the foreign secretary is heading the current conference?"

Lucian nodded. "Napoleon has abdicated, but it remains for the Allied Powers to conclude peace with Bourbon France. We've long suspected that someone is eager to kill Castlereagh. He barely escaped being poisoned last month. But he's been well-guarded since the first attempt on his life. Perrine may be hoping for the chance to get past his guards."

"I suppose you cannot simply arrest him," Dare mused.

"We could, but we have no proof of his guilt other than Ivers's accusations. And if Perrine isn't our culprit, then Caliban will still be at large." Lucian's mouth tightened in a grim line. "We can't risk losing his trail yet again. The trick will be not only to prevent Castlereagh's assassination, but to lure Caliban out and finally make him reveal himself, whether he is Perrine or someone else."

"Do you intend to pursue him to France?" Dare asked.

"It would be unwise of me to try. I want nothing more than to put a period to Caliban's existence after all the carnage he's caused, but I'm not the right man for this mission. I'm too well known to him. I would never be able to get close."

"Besides which you've sacrificed enough for your country. Brynn is expecting your first child any day now. You can't go haring off to France."

"I mean to send my best agent, Philip Barton, in my stead. He's been following Caliban's career from the first. But Barton is known to him as well."

"I want to go," Dare said, "but Perrine knows of my interest in Caliban."

Lucian's brow furrowed in contemplation. "We would have to devise a plan that made use of your acquaintance with him. . . ."

"Perhaps we simply need to bait a trap for him," Julienne said quietly.

Dare regarded her with unease. Julienne's determined

expression heightened the hollow ache in his chest. "There is no reason for you to become involved," he said once again. "You will only be endangering yourself."

She met his gaze evenly. "There is every reason. My name has been under the taint of suspicion for years, and this is my chance to clear it once and for all."

"What did you have in mind, Miss Laurent?" Lucian asked.

Julienne turned to him. "A scheme that will trap Perrine into showing his hand."

"You are offering to be the bait?"

"No, absolutely *not*," Dare said emphatically. "It's out of the question. He already almost killed you once before."

"I should like to help," she insisted.

Dare drew a sharp breath. The thought of Julienne risking her life by trying to lure out a deadly traitor filled him with dread. He loved Julienne; he had never stopped loving her. He didn't want her to be hurt. "I don't want you going," he said again.

"Why not?" Lucian asked.

Dare gave his friend a dark glance. "Would you allow Brynn to risk her life that way?"

Lucian smiled faintly, his eyes softening in reflection. "I don't think I could stop her if she thought she could help end Caliban's reign of terror. Last fall he put a death sentence on her brother's head, and Gray will never be safe until Caliban is dead."

"I want to do this, Dare," Julienne repeated. "And my going could provide you an excuse to be there yourself."

He ground his teeth but, after a moment, responded with reluctance. "What excuse?"

"We could say that I am eager to regain my late father's estates in Languedoc, and that I have demanded that you buy them back for me if you ever expect me to become your mistress."

"So that brings us to France. What of your scheme?"

"Perrine is aware of our wager and knows that I don't want to lose, but he doesn't know the reason for our animosity. If we find him in Paris, I can claim that I want revenge against you for spurning me all those years ago and ask him to help me be rid of you."

"And in exchange," Dare said slowly, "you will offer to aid him in getting rid of Castlereagh?"

"Yes. And if I can gain his confidence, perhaps I can discover something of his plan to kill Lord Castlereagh."

"It has possibilities," Lucian said, deep in thought.

Roughly Dare raked a hand through his hair. He wanted to refute Julienne's plan. He wanted to keep her safe and protected. But his own personal wishes mattered little compared to the present stakes.

"Very well," he said grimly. "We'll go to France together. I presume we should leave as soon as possible," he said to Lucian. "Perrine already has more than a day's head start."

Lucian nodded. "We'll meet with Philip Barton this afternoon and work on the details. Meanwhile you should both read the dossier on Perrine and pack your bags for a journey to Paris."

Chapter
Sixteen

Paris, May 1814

Julienne remembered nothing of Paris, since she had only visited it as a very young child. But Solange Brogard, who accompanied them, knew the city well.

At the moment, Paris was bursting to the seams, not only with the occupying armies, but with Royalists determined to be present for the restoration of the Bourbon monarchy. Louis XVIII had returned several weeks before to lay claim to the throne, and with him had come a multitude of aristocratic émigrés eager for restitution and revenge.

Many of London's elite had flocked to Paris as well, to indulge in long-denied pleasures—chic fashions, delectable food, superb wines, and elegant wickedness. As a consequence, the Marquess of Wolverton's party blended in well.

They took rooms at a luxurious hotel on the Rue de Clichy, near the center of the social whirl. Philip Barton thought it wiser to lodge at a different hotel, but they arranged to meet regularly in hopes of untangling the deadly web of intrigue that Caliban had spun.

They had not confided fully in Solange, merely

sketched some vague suspicions regarding a possible traitor they were investigating. But Julienne had argued for the Frenchwoman's inclusion in their trip to France. It would appear more natural if Solange acted as her chaperone as she had on past trips with Dare. And Julienne knew her friend could be trusted completely.

During the journey to Paris, Julienne had been glad for both Solange's and Philip Barton's company, for their presence provided her a distraction and gave her less time to think about her own future with Dare.

Now that the demons of her past had been exorcised, she would have to consider how to proceed. Her defenses against Dare had grown perilously thin. And actress or no, she was finding it more and more difficult to maintain her façade of indifference. Her longing for him was becoming a torture.

She had no doubt that continuing their current affair was the certain path to heartache. If she allowed herself to love Dare again, the hurt would be even more agonizing when he moved on than before. She would be totally, eternally lost. And he was certain to move on.

The truth was, they *had* no future together. Not one she could bear. There was only one accepted relationship for a notorious actress and a nobleman of Dare's exalted rank, no matter how infamous his reputation.

But she would never agree to become his mistress when such intimacy would only imperil her heart further. Nor would she accept whatever charity he might deign to dispense. His conscience, Julienne suspected, would dictate that he make some sort of amends for the misery his grandfather had inflicted upon her. But

Dare didn't owe her anything, even if he held himself partially to blame.

Admittedly it had surprised her when he'd responded so violently to her assault—that he had been willing to kill Ivers to avenge her. But she couldn't put much stock in Dare's reaction when he could be acting out of wounded pride or male jealousy or simple possessiveness.

No. When their search for Caliban was over, Julienne knew, she would have to extricate herself somehow. It would be better to end their relationship cleanly and swiftly. She had already allowed herself to become far too vulnerable.

Indeed, perhaps it had been foolish to come with Dare to France, despite her eagerness to clear her name. It was possible he didn't need her help to expose Caliban. Dare was no longer the devil-may-care rogue she had once known. There was a hardness to him now. A purpose and determination that boded ill for his enemies. She had no doubt that he was prepared to risk his life in pursuit of a deadly traitor.

They saw no immediate sign of Martin Perrine, however. It was not until their third day in Paris when Philip Barton spied him at the British embassy, where most of the English gentlemen in the city gathered from time to time.

"Perrine is billeting with Lord Aberdeen in a hired town house," Barton informed them.

"We will have to arrange to encounter him," Dare replied. "And we must make it look as natural as possible."

They had no difficulty finding social opportunities. The Prince of Pleasure was much sought after, as was

Solange Brogard. From the moment of their arrival they were showered with invitations for a profusion of dinners, balls, receptions, and salons.

Although Julienne was included in the invitations, she knew she would forever be relegated to the fringes of society. The fashionable English set tolerated her only because she was Dare's guest. And the French aristocracy was only slightly more forgiving. She was the daughter of the late Compte de Folmont, and in France that meant something. Even so, she would always be disdained because of her profession.

Of Lord Castlereagh they saw nothing during the first few days, for he was closeted in conference with the most powerful leaders of Europe—Tzar Alexander of Russia, King Frederick William of Prussia, Chancellor Metternich of Austria, along with French foreign minister Talleyrand—negotiating terms of peace.

"Castlereagh's absence from the public eye," Dare remarked to Julienne, "is actually fortunate, since his habits are well known. Normally he makes daily visits to the baths at the Bain Chinois so he can nap, rumor has it. He's said to be so fatigued by the affairs needing his attention that he can't sleep at night and so spends most of his time there dozing. And his favorite promenade is the gallery of the Palais Royal. If Caliban is targeting him for assassination, the Palais would be a prime location. That may be the most likely place to find Perrine."

The Palais Royal, Julienne learned shortly, was a massive amusement center where every vice and pleasure could be found. The tamer offerings included gardens and galleries of shops—jewelers, milliners, modistes—as well as numerous cafés and restaurants.

Above were apartments to let. But it was the gambling hells and brothels that made the Palais a center of dissipation and depravity. The evening entertainments, Dare said, rivaled London's most scandalous.

It was there during their fifth afternoon in Paris, as Julienne strolled the arcaded pavements with Dare and Solange, that she first spied Lord Castlereagh. The foreign secretary was plainly dressed in a blue coat and hardly looked like a man of such enormous power. His entire posture was solemn and weary, as if he truly did have the weight of the world on his shoulders.

He wasn't alone, Julienne noted. Two British soldiers walked a discreet distance behind him.

"Are those his bodyguards?" she asked Dare.

"I expect so. And it seems we may have guessed correctly. Our friend Martin Perrine is sitting at the next café, with a clear view of the gardens. Shall we see what he is up to?" he asked, steering the two ladies on his arms in Perrine's direction.

Julienne had to look twice to recognize the nondescript fellow sitting at a table at the open-air café. With his brown hair, average build, and modest attire, he would easily disappear into a crowd.

As they passed Perrine's table, Dare pretended not to notice him, but Julienne paused, flashing a brilliant smile. "Why, Mr. Perrine, is that you? How delightful to see you here."

Perrine rose politely and bowed to her, then Dare. "Miss Laurent, Lord Wolverton . . ." He gave Solange a quizzical glance.

"May I present Madame Brogard?" Julienne said easily. When the niceties were observed, she added, "It is so comforting to see a friendly face. May we join you? Darling," she said to Dare, "will you be so good as to order me some wine? I declare I am parched."

Dare looked appropriately reluctant, but he did as she bid, raising a hand to summon a waiter.

"What brings you to Paris, Miss Laurent?" Perrine asked in an idle tone as she settled in the chair next to him.

Julienne held out her arm smugly, flashing the diamond bracelet Dare had just purchased for her. "Lord Wolverton has been extremely generous, but I hope he will be even more so. You may know that my father was a noble. . . ." She told Perrine of her desire to recover the Folmont estates. "I have asked Dare to visit the south of France with me, but he says it is too dangerous just now to travel." Julienne pasted a slight pout on her lips. "I told him we can hire outriders to protect us from bandits—"

Just then Solange was hailed by friends, and Dare's attention became occupied with greeting them.

"I must speak with you in private," Julienne murmured under her breath to Perrine. "Can you meet me?"

His brows drew together sharply, and he studied her for a long moment, his eyes showing a momentary flash of the keen intelligence that was attributed to the cunning Caliban.

Then he gave a shy smile. "I am at your command, Miss Laurent, of course."

"Then come to the Hotel Clichy for tea tomorrow at four," Julienne whispered. "Dare will be gone by then— Do tell me what brings you to Paris, Mr. Perrine," she added when Dare turned back to her.

He launched into a story about Lord Aberdeen, the British ambassador to Austria, who was a close friend and who had invited him to participate in the historic marking of the liberation of Europe.

Solange and Dare joined the conversation then, leaving Julienne little to say. But a half hour later, as they prepared to leave, she gave Martin Perrine a meaningful glance. "It was delightful to see you again, Mr. Perrine. I hope we may meet again very shortly."

"That would please me a great deal," he replied in his usual unprepossessing tone.

Later that night, after a ball given at the British embassy by Sir Charles Stewart, the popular English ambassador to France, they met with Philip Barton to discuss various contingencies of their plan. Dare severely disliked the thought of Julienne meeting alone with Perrine, but she reminded him that she had her knife for protection, adding that she doubted Perrine would do anything to harm her just yet, since he was obviously curious about what she had to say.

In the morning Solange left the hotel to spend the day with friends. Julienne engaged a private parlor for the afternoon and arranged for tea to be served. In the event that Perrine was watching, Dare planned to make a show of leaving the hotel early in the afternoon but return shortly through the back entrance. He and Philip Barton would be in the adjoining room in case of trouble.

Martin Perrine arrived punctually and was shown up to the private parlor where Julienne awaited him.

"You must be wondering why I asked to speak to you," she said as she poured his tea.

Mr. Perrine gave a shy smile. "I confess to a great curiosity, Miss Laurent."

"Actually, I thought to warn you." Pausing to let her remark sink in, Julienne stared thoughtfully at her guest. "Wolverton has been trying to discover the identity of a cunning traitor who goes by the name Lord Caliban."

The puzzled look on Perrine's face would have done justice to the best actors of her acquaintance, Julienne thought. "What does that have to do with me?"

She passed his cup across the table to him. "He thinks you might be this Caliban, or at least that you know his true identity."

"*I*, a traitor? Whatever gave him such a notion?"

"You were once in possession of a ring that was known to belong to Caliban."

"Indeed?" Perrine murmured, lifting an eyebrow.

"The Earl of Ivers was arrested last week," Julienne added evenly. "He implicated you."

Not so much by a blink of an eye did Perrine exhibit any emotion that could be considered distress. "I own myself astonished that Ivers would make up such tales. He owes me a large sum of money. Perhaps he thinks to cause trouble for me so he can avoid having to settle his debts. If he impugns my honor, then my power to collect will be lessened."

Julienne feigned a frown. "Wolverton was extremely suspicious to find you in Paris. He thinks your connection to Caliban may have brought you here."

"I came," Perrine replied easily, "because my good friend Ambassador Aberdeen invited me to partake of the festivities. Not because I am engaged in treason—or because I know of anyone who might be a traitor." His mouth curved in an amused smile. "It does make me wonder, however, why a libertine like Wolverton would be hunting this traitor."

Her own mouth twisting cynically, Julienne nodded. "It does seem absurd, I know, but he is acting for a friend who was badly harmed by Caliban."

Reaching for an almond biscuit, Perrine remarked in a bland tone, "Even if I were this traitor you speak of, I could hardly wish to own it, would I?"

She leaned forward, giving him an earnest look. "It makes no difference to me, one way or the other. England is not my country, and I don't give a fig for politics."

"You seem to be very fond of Wolverton."

Julienne shook her head, injecting scorn into her tone. "That is mere pretense, I assure you. I've had to make a public show of interest because of our wager. But I will never become his mistress."

Perrine chewed thoughtfully for a long moment. "So why did you decide to 'warn' me, Miss Laurent?"

"Because I hoped you knew Caliban." Averting her gaze, she let her lower lip tremble. "It isn't common knowledge but, I have an . . . unsavory history with Wolverton. Seven years ago, his grandfather accused me of treason and ruined my life."

"And were you guilty?"

"No, not at all." Julienne took a deep breath. She had decided to stick close to the truth, in the event that Ivers had revealed her past to Perrine. And because the truth would give her stronger motivation to want to hurt Dare.

"I might have been able to fight those charges, but his grandfather hired Ivers to . . . to violate me." She bit her lip, letting her eyes fill with tears. "Dare not only did nothing to stop him, but he cast me aside afterward . . . because I was soiled goods."

"So you want revenge?"

Julienne looked up sharply, letting hatred show in her shimmering eyes. "*Precisely*. I want Wolverton to pay. I want his heart on a platter . . . literally. I was glad to see Ivers go to prison. I hope he hangs for his crimes. I want him dead for what he did to me. But it won't be enough. I want Wolverton to suffer as well."

Wiping her eyes, she made a visible effort to compose herself. "If you truly know who Caliban is, I thought . . . I hoped to hire him to rid me of Lord Wolverton." Julienne twisted her fingers in her lap. "Our journey to the south of France would be a prime opportunity. If our coach were to be set upon by bandits, Wolverton could be mortally wounded while defending me."

"But why can you not hire your own bandits?" Perrine asked.

"I suppose I could try. But I wouldn't know where to begin. And I want no suspicion to fall on me. I must be particularly careful, since my friend Madame Brogard will be accompanying us."

"I believe you said Wolverton was planning to buy the Folmont estates for you. I should think you would prefer to wait until after the transaction is completed to be rid of him."

"No," Julienne replied adamantly. "I merely used that as an excuse to get Wolverton away from England, where it should be easier to accomplish my goal. Recovering my father's properties isn't as important to me as finally giving Wolverton his just desserts. And to be perfectly frank"—she flashed him a smile that was a trifle flirtatious—"I have faith in my charms, Mr. Perrine. I'm certain I can find another wealthy patron who will purchase the estates for me."

Holding out her hand, she took Perrine's cup from him and refilled it, then passed it back to him. "I suppose the method of Wolverton's demise doesn't really matter. It doesn't have to be bandits. He could meet with an accident on the Paris streets."

Perrine was silent for a moment longer. "I'm sorry, Miss Laurent. I don't know this Caliban you speak of."

Her shoulders slumped in discouragement. "Even so . . . do you think you might help me? As a man, you can make discreet inquiries with much more freedom than I." She gave him a pleading look. "I understand your purse is not as full as you would like, Mr. Perrine. I would be willing to pay you well. Wolverton has given me several costly pieces of jewelry recently. You can have those, or whatever else you ask."

"I am not a murderer, Miss Laurent."

"No, of course not. But I hoped . . ." She looked crestfallen. "Then you won't help me?"

"I didn't say that. I might be able to put you in contact with someone who could meet your needs. I will make some inquiries if you like."

Julienne's smile turned brilliant. "*Thank you*, Mr. Perrine. I would be *very* grateful."

After a few moments more of inconsequential conversation, Perrine rose and took his leave. Julienne watched from the parlor window as he mounted his horse in the yard below. Then she went to the connecting door and admitted Dare and Philip Barton.

"I'm not certain I made any progress," Julienne said after telling them the details of her discussion with

Perrine. "He repeatedly denied even knowing Caliban. Certainly he didn't trust me enough to confide any secrets to me. But I think I convinced him that I want you out of the way. He said he could perhaps find someone to help me and that he would contact me in a few days."

A muscle flexed in Dare's jaw. "Then we will just have to wait," he said, visibly clamping down on his impatience.

It was the following day that the First Peace of Paris was signed between the Allied Powers and France. The terms of the treaty were exceedingly lenient. The boundaries of France were to be returned to those before the Revolution. And France would not be required to pay restitution for the vast sums it had cost the countries of Europe to prosecute all the years of war.

The Bourbon restoration was to begin officially the following week, on June fourth, with a public celebration planned to commemorate the event. Dare and Solange both received invitations to watch Louis XVIII resume the throne.

They heard nothing from Perrine until the day before the celebration. His brief note to Julienne said merely: *I made the inquires you requested of me. Meet me at the Tuileries Palace tomorrow during the festivities if you wish to discuss further.*

"Tomorrow is a likely time for Caliban to strike," Dare observed during their daily consultation with Philip Barton. "Until now, Castlereagh has been carefully guarded, but he will be more vulnerable during a public event."

Philip concurred. "Caliban could be planning to use

the crowds to create a distraction. And if Perrine is the traitor, he is no doubt counting on his friend Lord Aberdeen to help him gain entrée to Castlereagh's inner circle. We will have to make certain the foreign secretary is closely protected tomorrow."

"And yet we want Caliban to show his hand. Our best hope is to catch him in the act while keeping Castlereagh safe."

"I will ensure," Philip said, "that his lordship is surrounded with an additional score of guards in disguise, the better to fool Caliban."

Julienne asked a question that had been bothering her. "Why do you suppose Perrine wants to see me specifically at the festivities? He must know I will accompany you, Dare. If he is planning an assassination, he would not want you present to witness it."

"I don't know," Dare replied. "But I don't like it."

"Perhaps," Philip said, "he truly isn't Caliban, and tomorrow's celebration will simply provide him a convenient place to meet with Miss Laurent."

They all three fell silent, thinking similar thoughts, Julienne suspected. By this time tomorrow, it might all be over. They could have brought a criminal mastermind to justice. Or they could have witnessed the assassination of one of Europe's greatest men. Either way, the situation was fraught with danger.

When Barton had gone, Dare gave Julienne a brooding look. "I will come to you tonight."

She lowered her gaze, and yet she nodded. They had not been intimate since the night Dare had learned the dark truth about her past and taken his revenge on Ivers. But this could be their last chance. Caliban's deadliness was unquestioned, with murder a chief weapon in his cunning arsenal of tricks. It was possible that she or Dare would not survive the morrow.

She didn't want to go to her grave without being with Dare once more, without feeling his touch, the ecstasy of his caresses. After that, however . . .

Regardless of what happened, Julienne was determined that tonight would be their last night together. If they survived, she intended to find a way to say good-bye.

When he came to her that night, she was waiting by the window, gazing out at the moonlit streets of Paris, the heaviness in her chest a tangle of sorrow and fear. She felt Dare move silently behind her, felt his arms slip around her waist.

Julienne leaned back full against him. She didn't want tomorrow to come. Didn't want to face the future. When they parted, she would be left alone, nursing her terrible ache for him. Her breath caught on a surge of yearning so intense it felt like pain.

His hushed whisper brushed her ear: "I want this night to last."

So did she. She needed this final night with him. She would take the memory with her, to sustain her during the long, empty years that she would have to live without him. The thought brought scalding tears to the inside of her eyelids.

She swallowed hard, refusing to surrender to despair. Tonight she would pretend they were young lovers again, that the enchantment of their love had never ended. Their passion would be just like it once was: simple, pure, intense.

As if he shared the same feeling, Dare pressed his lips to the exposed curve of her neck, his touch hot and tender. It wasn't the fiery caress he usually used to seduce and inflame her; this had a poignancy that went directly to her heart. Julienne arched backward in mute appeal. She wanted Dare so desperately. She wanted to fill herself with him.

His long fingers cupped her jaw and slowly turned her face to his. His features were tight with emotion, as she knew hers were.

Julienne drank in the sight of him, committing him to memory. The moonlight illuminated the flaring elegance of his cheekbones, gilded his hair. He was such a beautiful man, she thought, surveying the aristocratic angles of his face.

"Julienne . . ."

He started to speak but she pressed her fingers to his sensual lips. "Just make love to me."

He obliged her at once. His mouth descended to hers with throat-tightening gentleness, dredging a sigh from deep in Julienne. For this moment, there was no past, no future.

They undressed each other without haste, taking their time, their hands searching each other with silent hunger. Her heart beat in a slow, heavy cadence when they both stood naked.

Then Dare kissed her again. He drank from her mouth as if he could absorb her, and the knot of tension in her stomach pressed up into her chest and turned searing. She arched against him, craving for his hands to soothe the aching fullness of her breasts.

His drugging, demanding kiss continued while the

rhythm of his hands became urgent. Julienne felt passion rising powerfully from deep inside her as he roused her.

"Please," she whispered as his mouth left hers to trace a burning path down the side of her throat.

Needing no further invitation, he took her hand and led her to the bed. Laying her down, he followed with his body, his manhood, rigid and needy, settling intimately in the cradle of her femininity.

Julienne met his wantonly ardent gaze as he remained poised above her. Dare had made love to her many times, but never with such graveness.

Reaching up, she drew his head down to her, tasting his breath, feeling his hands cherishing her body as his thighs pressed hers wide.

He entered her with a sureness that kindled a soft cry from her, but she welcomed him eagerly, sliding her legs around his hips. Suddenly fierce, he withdrew only to surge into her again, then again. His relentless claiming threw her breathing into a series of sharp gasps, yet she responded with his same intensity.

Their lips met bruisingly in a fevered urgency as his body enveloped her, covered her. They clung to each other as the burning need built, holding on with a tight, quiet desperation. Their bodies twisted together, entwined, mating savagely, striving to become one with each other, fighting to deny anything but the primal moment.

The explosive conflagration came without warning. Julienne cried into the hollow of his shoulder as shudder after shudder shook her and swept Dare along with her.

When it was over, they lay gasping for breath, the sweat cooling on their overheated bodies. Julienne felt her eyes sting with fresh tears. That had been their deepest bonding, and the power of it made her heart ache. She wondered if Dare had felt the same way.

She squeezed her eyes shut, forcing away the wrenching thought, vowing not to cry.

It was a long moment before Dare eased his weight from her and gazed down at Julienne's passion-flushed face. She lay naked, shimmering with moonlight, her hair spread upon the pillow, flowing like dark silk.

Desire poured through him, filled him. A feeling so strong it was pain. And yet his yearning for her was edged with fear.

He gathered her in his arms, cradling her so she was cupped in his body. There had been something different about her passion tonight. He didn't understand the whisper of sadness in her eyes, but it disturbed him even more than his fear of the danger she might face on the morrow.

He didn't want her risking her life to deal with Caliban. His heart clamored with the need to keep her safe, to hold and cherish her forever. He couldn't bear the thought of losing her. Not when he loved her so fervently.

Love. The emotion he'd denied needing the past seven years abruptly swamped him. What a fool he'd been to think he could ever live without her.

He had been only half a man without her, a hollow shell. Julienne completed him—he knew that now. She filled the emptiness inside him. She had dispelled the barrenness in the dark, hidden recesses of his heart and made him feel whole. Making love to her had been like finding the missing pieces of himself.

He wanted Julienne to be part of him for the rest of his days.

Dare's breath caught in a hard knot in his throat. What he wanted might not matter. He hadn't earned the right to have Julienne love him. He didn't deserve her—he knew that better than anyone. He wasn't worthy of her.

But he could change. He could prove himself worthy.

And he would, Dare vowed solemnly. When this was all over, he would win Julienne's love, even if it took his last breath.

Chapter
Seventeen

The night was poignant and passionate but morning came too soon. Julienne woke with her nerves raw, a feeling that never diminished as she bathed and dressed for the grand festivities that were to begin at noon at the Tuileries Gardens.

When Dare called at her room, she met his eyes, and the dark solemnity she saw there mirrored her own.

"Solange has left," he informed her in a quiet tone.

"I know. I said farewell to her a short while ago."

They had arranged for the Frenchwoman to attend the celebration with friends, so as to keep her out of danger.

"Here," Dare said, handing her a small pistol. "Do you know how to use this?"

"Yes. After . . . the assault, I learned how to defend myself. But I have my knife tucked in my garter."

"Even so, I want you to be well-armed. That's the only way I will allow you to get near Caliban."

Julienne nodded and slipped the pistol into her reticule, which was hanging from her wrist.

Offering his arm, Dare escorted her below to the hotel entrance, where his carriage waited. The glorious June day, Julienne thought absently as they stepped out into the sunshine, presented a sharp contrast to the tension roiling inside her.

Her tension increased sharply when Dare suddenly came to a halt. She followed his gaze to see more than a dozen mounted British soldiers milling around his carriage.

Upon spying her, one of the soldiers broke away and rode up to them. "You are Julienne Laurent?" he asked, his face grim.

When she acknowledged that she was, he dismounted. "I am Captain Pritchard, and you are under arrest."

She felt the muscles of Dare's arm clench, but he held on to his temper and coolly raised an eyebrow. "What the devil are you talking about?"

"I am to arrest the lady, by orders of Lord Aberdeen."

"On what possible charges?"

"Attempted murder, my lord. Miss Laurent has been plotting to have you killed. I have a warrant sworn out against her by one Martin Perrine." He turned and motioned to one of his men, who led forward a riderless mount.

Dare's jaw hardened. "Miss Laurent is not going anywhere with you, Captain."

"Dare, it's all right," Julienne interjected. "I'm certain this is all a simple mistake."

"It is damned well not all right. I don't intend to stand idly by while you're prosecuted with fraudulent charges."

"You may accompany us if you choose, Lord Wolverton," the captain offered. "Lord Aberdeen said you would likely not believe the charges."

"No," Julienne said urgently, "you cannot come,

Dare. You have business to attend to elsewhere. Please," she entreated in an undertone. "This is most likely a ploy to keep you occupied while our devious friend accomplishes his goal. I will go with the captain while you attend the celebration."

In response, Dare glanced around him, as if judging the odds. The carriage was surrounded, Julienne realized, and would be useless as a means of escape.

Offering a grim smile, Dare withdrew a pistol from inside his coat and aimed it at Pritchard. "I fear I don't have time to resolve this misunderstanding just now, Captain. Stand aside."

A look of outrage suffused Pritchard's ruddy face, and Julienne watched with apprehension as he debated what to do. Several of his soldiers had drawn rifles from their scabbards, she saw.

"I also suggest," Dare said pleasantly, "that if you wish to prevent your immediate demise, you will tell your men to put down their weapons."

With a low curse, Pritchard commanded his men to obey.

Then, before the captain's astonished eyes, Dare grasped the reins of the riderless horse and leapt into the saddle. Reaching down, he pulled Julienne up behind him.

The narrow skirts of her gown hampered her mounting, but she managed to wrap her arms around Dare's waist. Her heart pounding, Julienne clung tightly as he spurred the horse past the soldiers and onto the busy boulevard, heading for the Jardins des Tuileries.

Hearing shouts behind her, she glanced over her shoulder to find Captain Pritchard had mounted and was giving chase with his men. Dare must have realized the danger for he bent lower and urged the horse to greater speed as he weaved through the heavy traffic.

"Hold on!" he warned Julienne as they clattered over the cobblestones.

She hoped Pritchard wouldn't risk shooting for fear of hitting the multitude of carriages and riders surrounding them. And Dare seemed to be drawing away. . . .

Julienne's breath was ragged by the time their mad dash ended at the spectacular gardens. Dare had to slow their pace as he plunged into the crowds congregating on the elegant esplanades.

The vast acreage of the Tuileries was formally laid out with wide, paved paths flanked by lush flower beds and neatly trimmed shrubbery. Numerous fountains and statuary and tall shade trees completed the adornment, with an occasional pavilion artistically erected here and there.

The numbers of merrymakers were smaller than Julienne expected, perhaps because the French populace had accepted the return of the Bourbons without enthusiasm. But the mass grew more dense as they neared the parade passing in front of the palace. Evidence of the new regime showed in the uniforms of the cavalry troops and the horses whose bridles sported white Bourbon cockades.

She and Dare received countless stares as they doggedly made their way toward the main entrance, but when they crossed the columns of the parade, they were showered with angry oaths and denunciations.

Reaching the other side, where he quickly halted, Dare swung his right leg forward over the pommel and sprang down, then turned and caught Julienne by the waist and set her on her feet. Taking her hand, he quickly pushed through the crowd and up a curving sweep of marble steps, hoping to gain access to the royal residence.

Julienne's pulse was racing as Dare pulled her behind him, and she barely had time to glimpse the famous palace. The building itself was large and rather cumbersome, with long, narrow wings and high roofs and countless arcaded windows. Here Louis XVI and his queen, Marie Antoinette, had been held under house arrest for nearly three years before a hostile mob stormed the palace and killed more than a thousand guards, taking the royals to the Temple prison, where they would live out the rest of their lives.

The fact that the current guards bristled with muskets and blunderbusses and sabers, however, suggested the new king preferred to take no chances that his subjects might become as unruly as his late brother's.

The king's household troops refused them admittance until Dare showed his invitation. They were permitted inside just in time, Julienne realized, for Captain Pritchard came charging up the steps, hard on their heels.

"Miss Laurent, halt! You are under arrest, I tell you!"

The guards blocked his entrance as Julienne swiftly asked in French where Lord Castlereagh might be found.

They were escorted through the palace to the royal audience chamber. Knowing they could be too late, Julienne felt anxious fear well inside her as she and Dare made their way through the cavernous halls. They passed an endless number of arches and massive stone columns before arriving at a grand room that was three stories high, with lofty, curved ceilings and railed galleries above.

Julienne halted in dismay at seeing the size of the crowd. In this packed chamber, a killer could easily strike and fade away undetected.

"What should we do now?" Julienne asked Dare, raising her voice to be heard over the din of the laughing, chattering guests bent on celebrating.

"Follow our original plan," he replied. "Locate Perrine but try to keep from being seen ourselves. By now he probably thinks he's taken care of us, that you've been arrested and that I'm on a rampage to try to get you released. Do you have the pistol I gave you?"

"Yes," Julienne said after glancing down at her reticule. Surprisingly it was still attached to her wrist.

"We should separate." Dare's gaze surveyed the gallery above. "You'll be safer up there, and you can better watch for Perrine."

"Dare, my safety is not my first concern."

Raising his fingers to her face, he gave her cheek a light caress. "I know, but it is mine. I'll stay near Castlereagh in case Perrine acts."

"Please, be careful," Julienne begged.

"You, as well."

He grasped her face and planted a hard kiss on her mouth, then left her to enter the audience chamber. For a moment she saw him skirt the crowd before he disappeared in the sea of bodies.

Turning, Julienne retraced her steps till she located a wide stairway that led to the upper floors. She chose the west gallery over the others, since it lay in shadows, and moved behind a column so she could covertly view the throng below.

The perspective was far better up here. The king stood out like a peacock in his magnificent costume. Louis XVIII, whom Julienne had heard described as gouty and clumsy as well as courteous and genial, beamed as he mingled among his distinguished guests. She saw numerous dignitaries, as well: Alexander, Metternich, Frederick. And, to one side, Lord Castlereagh.

Her heart beginning to thud, Julienne searched for Martin Perrine. There was no sign of him, but she spied Dare, partly hidden behind a column, his fair hair gleaming as he conversed with several members of the French aristocracy. He had lost his tall beaver hat in the wild ride, she realized for the first time. And he had positioned himself with a clear view of Castlereagh, who stood near the buffet table.

The table groaned with delicacies. Even from a distance she could make out crab patties and sugared grapes and small, frosted cakes among the ice sculptures formed in the shape of busts, including a large centerpiece of King Louis.

A score of footmen moved about the room with difficulty, offering glasses of wine and champagne. And stationed at frequent intervals were both French and British soldiers, all armed.

She saw nothing, however, of the man they feared was a ruthless assassin. When Dare glanced up at her briefly and met her gaze, Julienne gave a slight shake of her head to communicate her lack of success.

Slipping her hand into her reticule, she closed her fingers around the handle of the pistol and settled down to wait.

Nearly an hour later, Julienne had begun to grow weary and her nerves felt raw with strain. She had just shrugged her stiff shoulders to ease the tension when she saw a man push through the crowd below. He had brown hair, but his build was too slight for him to be Perrine.

The unkempt, dark blue coat he wore looked wrinkled, as if it had been slept in, and he was stumbling slightly as though drunk.

Julienne frowned, unable to shake the feeling that his actions had a sinister quality to them. Moreover, he carried something in his hand. A pistol?

Her heart leapt when she realized he was heading directly toward Castlereagh.

She tried shouting in order to warn Dare, but she couldn't make herself heard over the babel of the crowd. She waved her hand frantically, trying to catch Dare's eye, but to no avail. So she did the only thing she could think of: she withdrew her pistol and fired in the air.

The shot echoed around the vast chamber, taking a chunk out of the plaster ceiling and raining down a spray of dust and chips. For an instant, silence prevailed. Then, with startled cries, some of the guests began a mad rush toward the doors, while others fell prostrate on the floor, covering their heads.

But at least she had managed to attract Dare's attention, Julienne realized. And he understood when she gestured wildly at the blue-coated man.

The man had his pistol raised and aimed as he charged toward Castlereagh with the grim determination of a general going into battle.

Dare leapt forward, shoving people out of his way, and rushed the assailant, knocking him to the floor just as the pistol discharged. An ice sculpture exploded two feet from Lord Castlereagh's head, while the blast of the gunshot brought more screams and cries of "Assassin!" and "Murder!" as the guests scattered like frightened sheep.

For a dozen heartbeats, Julienne's gaze was riveted on the chaos below. Yet once she realized the foreign secretary was safe, she forced her gaze to sweep the remaining assembly of stunned onlookers, looking for Martin Perrine.

It was only when she leaned over the railing that she saw him. He was almost directly below her, concealed in the shadows.

His fists clenched as he watched Dare haul the assassin to his feet. Then Perrine's gaze lifted, his narrowed eyes searching the galleries.

When his gaze locked with Julienne's, she saw his fury. His seething reaction left her with no real doubt that he'd employed the assassin and was enraged by his failure.

Dare was shaking the blue-coated man, obviously grilling him intensely. Perrine threw one last fulminating glare at Dare, then spun on his heel and disappeared into the crowd of fleeing guests.

He was leaving, Julienne thought, because he feared the blue-coated man would expose him. But if he escaped, the world would never be safe. . . .

Forcing her sluggish brain to think past the frightening possibilities, she turned and raced for the stairs, knowing she would have to move quickly if she had any hope of keeping Perrine in sight. She had almost reached the bottom steps when a figure suddenly broke from the shadows and came to stand directly below her. Julienne stumbled to an abrupt halt.

She raised her pistol defensively, though she knew it was empty and useless. Her futile gesture earned her a scornful look.

Martin Perrine offered her a deadly smile as he aimed his own pistol at her. "Are you perhaps looking for me, Miss Laurent?"

The assassin, Dare quickly discovered, was a minor French noble, a baron. Dare could scarcely make out his confession, though, for he was sobbing in French and broken English.

"*Ma fille, ma pauvre fille,* forgive me. . . ."

His story spilled out: his daughter had been abducted two days ago, and he had been blackmailed to gain her return. If he hoped to see the girl alive, he was to kill that man—he pointed at Lord Castlereagh. He'd drunk three full carafes of wine before he could summon the nerve to try, but now he had failed and his daughter would likely die.

"*Je suis coupable,*" he moaned, dropping weakly to his knees.

"There may be a chance to save your daughter," Dare said bracingly.

The baron drew a strangled breath and grasped Dare's hands, his pleading look holding desperation. "Monsieur, can you help me? I beg you—"

"Who is the man you say forced you?"

"*Il s'appelle Caliban.*"

"Could you identify him? It is of vital importance."

"*Oui.*"

"Brown hair, brown eyes, average height?"

"*Oui. Il est un monstre.*"

"So I understand," Dare muttered, agreeing that Caliban was a monster.

"I did not want to kill anyone," the baron whimpered. He gazed up at Lord Castlereagh through streaming eyes. "Forgive me, please, forgive me. *Je suis désolé. . . .*" His face suddenly crumpled in agony. "*Je sais . . .* you cannot save my daughter."

He bowed his head and began to weep brokenly, hopelessly, his face in his hands.

Castlereagh drew Dare aside to ask what had happened.

"I suspect," Dare answered, "that Caliban sent this wretch in his place because he knew we were watching him."

"Is it Perrine, do you think?"

"Undoubtedly. But we still must prove it."

Castlereagh frowned down at the sobbing man. "The poor sod. He didn't stand a chance against Caliban. I would imagine his daughter is dead."

Dare nodded grimly, but his mind had already shifted to Julienne. Glancing up, he searched the gallery above, expecting to see her. Perhaps she was making her way down to the lower floor. Then again . . .

A stark foreboding gripped him. Was it possible Perrine had feared discovery and somehow taken her as leverage? Dear God.

He had to find Julienne at once. His interrogation had taken no more than two minutes. . . .

Snapping out a harsh order, he told Castlereagh to deal with the baron's arrest. "And keep him safe. He can identify Caliban."

Not waiting for a reply, Dare snatched a musket

from the hands of the nearest British soldier. "I need to borrow this, if you please."

Spinning on his heel, he practically ran from the room.

To his left was a stairway leading to the gallery. The stairs were empty but for an object lying near the bottom.

Needles of panic drove deep into his chest when he recognized the pistol he had given Julienne. The thought of her in Caliban's clutches made him wild with fear.

Frantically his gaze moved about the hall. He doubted Perrine would still be in the palace, and they might have taken any one of a dozen exits. Making an instant decision, Dare broke into a run, heading for the nearest door, which faced south.

Another object lay on the marble floor nearby. Julienne's reticule. They had passed this way, Dare was now certain. In fact she might have dropped it deliberately to give him a clue to follow.

He burst through the door, wincing at the bright sunlight, and nearly stumbled over two bodies.

The king's troops.

Lying in a pool of blood.

Both their throats slit.

The fear that tore through Dare was tangled up with fury and fierce self-recrimination. Cursing himself for having allowed Caliban to dupe him, for allowing Julienne to become exposed to such lethal danger, he sprinted across the lawns, through the gardens.

The crowds were thinner on this side of the palace. In front of him lay the River Seine and one of its many arched bridges—the Pont Royal. Beyond the stone quay he could see gaily decorated barges plying the river, along with several small sailing vessels.

If he were Perrine, he would have arranged a method of escape, Dare thought; perhaps more than one. He might have crossed the bridge and disappeared in a closed carriage. Or he could have planned to leave by river, thinking no one would suspect that mode of transportation.

Dare ran to his right, along the upper level of the quay, perhaps a hundred yards past the bridge, seeing nothing suspicious in the milling crowds or on the lower level below him. Retracing his steps, he went east another hundred yards beyond the bridge—and saw exactly what he dreaded.

Twenty yards ahead, beside a skiff that was tied up at the quay, a man and woman struggled.

The sight made Dare's heart go ice cold. Perrine held a pistol to Julienne's head as she resisted getting in the small craft, while the boatman looked on uncertainly.

Dare skidded to a halt, gripping his musket, momentarily torn between taking the stone steps he'd just passed or making the ten-foot drop to the lower level. It was too far to shoot accurately without risking hitting Julienne.

The choice was taken from him, however, when Perrine glanced up and spied him. "That is close enough, Wolverton!" he called, dragging Julienne in front of him to use as a shield.

"Let her go, Perrine!" Dare shouted in reply. He heard the desperate edge in his own voice and cursed himself; it was foolish to reveal to his enemy how much he cared.

Aiming the musket, Dare moved closer, till he was

almost directly above them, and repeated his demand more calmly. "I said let her go."

"I don't believe I will. She is my security."

"You must realize that you have lost, Perrine. You failed to kill Lord Castlereagh, and you left alive a witness who can identify you as Caliban."

Perrine shook his head sadly. "Alas, that is regrettable. And my career may be at an end. But I have a fortune to last me a lifetime, and I mean to disappear. I warn you, Wolverton, if you try to follow me, I will kill her. You know what I am capable of."

Dare offered him an icy smile. "But you have no notion what I am capable of. If you hurt her, you won't be safe anywhere, I promise you. I will find you wherever you hide, even if it is the ends of the earth."

"You may try. Meanwhile, I hold the upper hand here. Put down your weapon, or I will blow her brains out."

"Dare, don't listen to him!" Julienne exclaimed.

Gritting his teeth, Dare flexed his finger on the trigger of his musket. And yet he knew he couldn't take the chance that Perrine would make good his threat to kill Julienne. Reluctantly he averted the barrel of his gun, but he took a step closer, hoping to draw Perrine's fire.

The ploy worked. Perrine shifted his aim, pointing his pistol directly at Dare's heart.

In that instant, Julienne whirled and attacked her captor, arms flailing, nails raking, trying to scratch his eyes out, diverting his attention.

Seizing the opportunity, Dare leapt the ten feet to the lower quay, just as Perrine struck her a vicious blow. Dare saw Julienne fall back as he landed with a jarring thud and sank to his knees. From the corner of his eye he watched her draw up her skirts and fumble for her knife. Perrine leveled the pistol at him once more.

Dare sprang from his crouch, moving at a dead run.

Julienne was there before him, though. Her knife held out in front of her, she charged Perrine. They collided with a jolt, knocking him to the quay and her falling with him.

Dare's heart stopped when they both remained unmoving.

Reaching them, he clutched Julienne's shoulder just as she drew a shaky breath. When she tried to push herself up, he hauled Julienne to her feet and dragged her behind him. But Perrine lay completely still.

With a foot, Dare cautiously rolled the prone man over onto his back. Perrine stared up at the sky with lifeless eyes. Julienne's knife protruded from his ribs, but it was the blood seeping from his temple that suggested the cause of his demise: his head had cracked open on the stone pavement when he landed.

Dare bent and pressed his fingers against the side of their nemesis's neck.

"He's dead," Dare said very softly.

Julienne shuddered. When Dare straightened and reached for her, she flung herself into his arms. Biting back a sob, she pressed her face into his shoulder and clung as he enfolded her in his embrace.

She was shaking badly, and so was he. She felt his pounding heartbeat as he scattered light, desperate kisses against her hair.

He drew back long enough to kiss her mouth hard,

before wrapping his arms tightly around her again, as if afraid to let her go. "Are you all right?"

"No," she whispered in a trembling voice. "I was so terrified. I thought he would kill you."

"*You* were terrified?" His tone was incredulous. "That devil held a gun to your head and you were afraid for *me*?"

"Yes."

"You could not have been any more terrified than I was."

For a long moment, they simply held each other, celebrating their deliverance. It was longer still before Julienne began to feel her quakes subside.

She sighed, cherishing the protective circle of Dare's arms. "I'm glad it is finally over."

Dare made a fervent sound of agreement. "I'm glad you didn't need me to rescue you. I don't think I could have reached you in time." He raised his head, meeting her gaze. "I envy you, angel."

"For what?"

"You saved us both, *and* you had the satisfaction of killing that bastard." A strained but teasing smile curved Dare's lips. "Do you realize what a blow that is to my self-esteem? You might have allowed me to play the role of hero."

She gave a shaky laugh at his attempt to lighten the horror she was feeling at having taken a man's life. "I've engaged in enough stage fights during my acting career to know a trick or two."

"Well, I only wish I could have been spared the uncertainty. I lost ten years off my life in the last ten minutes." His gaze suddenly grew solemn as he searched her face. "We've lost too many years, Julienne."

Julienne flinched at the reminder, then felt her heart plummet as she remembered the vow she had made to herself. There would be no more years together. She would have to leave Dare now.

A slashing pain pierced her at the thought.

But she would be spared the devastation for at least a while longer, she realized, glancing up to see a crowd gathered above them on the upper level. "Now is not the time, Dare."

Even as she spoke, she saw Lord Castlereagh descending the stone steps toward them, followed immediately by his bodyguards. Julienne stepped back, relinquishing Dare's embrace.

Castlereagh took in the situation at a glance. "I believe I have you to thank for my life, Wolverton."

Dare shook his head. "No, it is Miss Laurent who deserves your thanks. She not only prevented your assassination, but she managed to dispatch the man responsible."

The foreign secretary looked down at Perrine's body. "So this is Caliban? The villain who murdered and blackmailed his way across half of Europe?"

"I have no doubt," Dare answered.

Raising his gaze, Castlereagh smiled gravely at Julienne. "Our countrymen owe you a tremendous debt, Miss Laurent. And so do I. It will be a great relief to no longer live in fear for my life. I hope you will tell me how I may repay you."

Julienne wanted to respond with a polite demur, but her legs suddenly felt as weak as wet noodles. "I think perhaps I should sit down, my lord."

"But of course. You have been through an ordeal that would drive most ladies into hysterics. Will you allow me to escort you back to the palace?" Castlereagh gave her his arm. "The king of France would like to express his own gratitude, I'm certain. And he will be delighted to hear the tale of how you defeated a deadly villain. . . ."

Watching them walk away, Dare shuddered at the image of Perrine holding a pistol to Julienne's head, knowing it would haunt him for a very long time. He seized a raw breath, realizing how close he'd come to losing her.

He could not have gone on without her, he knew. Julienne held his heart, his soul.

He felt a fierce ache in his chest as he watched her retreating figure. She had set a fire burning deep in his heart—but it remained for him to kindle the same fire in her heart, Dare thought grimly.

It would not be easy. He had felt her withdrawal just now, the same emotional resistance he'd sensed last night when he held her in his arms: hunger edged with despair.

Dare felt his hands curl into fists. He had no intention of losing Julienne now. He had initially pursued her for the wager, in order to ferret out her secrets, but he would do it earnestly this time.

He would find a way to truly earn her love and bind her to him for all time.

Chapter
Eighteen

London, June 1814

If Julienne had been the subject of gossip before, upon her return to London she became a genuine celebrity.

In his dispatches Lord Castlereagh had lavishly praised her role in defeating a criminal mastermind, and the newspapers embellished the tale to make her into a heroine. According to the latest rumors, she and Dare had single-handedly brought down one of Napoleon's chief disciples.

Julienne discovered herself wildly popular with the commoners of London and even many members of the gentry. Her theater performances sold out every single night—which sent the temperamental Edmund Kean into fits of jealousy—and swarms of young bucks surrounded her backstage afterward. Riddingham preened for having helped lead them to Caliban.

Her fame soared further when the Prince Regent gave both her and Dare public commendations. Prinny was one of Dare's intimates, but it was a high honor for a mere actress to be invited to dine at Carleton House with the likes of General Lord Wellington and Marshal Blucher and the countless other dignitaries, royalty, and aristocrats celebrating the liberation of Europe.

Solange was delighted for her. "*Enfin,* you are getting the recognition and acceptance you deserve."

Julienne couldn't help but laugh. "I shall not allow the accolades to swell my head. Next week they will no doubt forget my name."

She well knew how fickle society could be. She was sought after now because she was a novelty and because she had been decorated by the Crown. But once the luster of her temporary acclaim wore off, the nobility at least would once more turn up their noses at her.

"And what does Lord Wolverton have to say to this?" Solange asked slyly.

Julienne returned a shrug. "I have scarcely spoken to him since our return from Paris."

Except for those few occasions when they were thrown together, such as the fête at Carleton House, Julienne had seen little of Dare. And there had been no opportunity at all to be intimate with him.

He'd claimed she should be allowed to bask in her moment of glory, but it surprised her that he didn't press her to share her bed. Nor could he be found among her coterie of admirers at the theater. For the present at least, he was no longer making even the slightest pretense of trying to win their wager. His public pursuit of her appeared to be abandoned.

Perhaps he assumed that he'd already won the victory, Julienne reflected. He might be so certain she would become his mistress that he no longer needed to expend any effort to woo her.

Or perhaps he had already moved on to another challenge. Their task of searching out a deadly spy was over. Dare had no further use for her in that regard, Julienne realized.

Or he might have found another love interest altogether. She tried desperately not to dwell on that possibility. She couldn't bear the thought of Dare spending his nights indulging in some other woman's charms—even if she herself intended to sever all ties with him very soon.

Of her continuing employment as a spy, she heard nothing whatsoever. But she knew Lord Wycliff was still in the country because his wife had been delivered of a son the second week of June, while Julienne and Dare were still in France.

Her first awareness that Lord and Lady Wycliff had returned to London was during rehearsals for *Hamlet*, when Julienne was practicing her lines as Ophelia.

Midway through Act III, she found herself summoned by the manager, Samuel Arnold, to his office, where a strikingly beautiful woman with flaming red hair waited. Arnold introduced Lady Wycliff and then withdrew to allow them privacy.

"I apologize for interrupting your rehearsals, Miss Laurent," Lady Wycliff said when they were both seated. "But I wished to extend you an invitation to a small dinner party I am holding, and I first needed to ascertain your availability. I will only schedule it when your performances permit you to attend."

Julienne raised an eyebrow in surprise. "I should be free next Tuesday and Wednesday, when a comedy is on the playbill."

"Then shall we say Tuesday?"

"I would be pleased to come," Julienne said, still puzzled.

Interpreting her quizzical look, Lady Wycliff gave her a wry smile. "It will be a social coup to have you, of course, considering your current fame, but that has nothing to do with why I'm eager for your presence. Lucian and I would like you to be our guest of honor. It will be a very small gathering, with only our closest friends."

"I'm not certain I understand, my lady."

"Please, will you call me Brynn? Titles are so formal, and I hope very much that we might become friends."

"Very well . . . But whyever would you want me as your guest of honor?"

Brynn's smile this time held a wealth of warmth. "Because I should like to express my gratitude in some small measure. I owe you a great deal, Miss Laurent. This is the first time in seven months that I've been free to enjoy the slightest privacy, without numerous bodyguards hounding my heels to protect me from Caliban. And I have you to thank for freeing my brother Grayson as well. Gray was forced into hiding last year in order to escape Caliban's retribution, but he will be able to return home now that the threat is gone."

Julienne grimaced. "My small role in Caliban's demise has been much exaggerated, I fear."

"I don't think so. Dare told me everything that happened in France—how you risked your life, and how you aided his investigation before that. He could never have located Caliban's trail if not for you. You are indeed a heroine."

Julienne felt her color rise at Brynn's effusive praise. "Dare had much more to do with defeating Caliban than I."

"Well, I would like to thank you both. You can't imagine how relieved I will be to have my brother back safely. Gray has been in Scotland all this time, ever since he . . . became entangled in Caliban's gold-smuggling operation last fall. Gray was badly wounded and barely escaped with his life, and he had to feign his death to protect his family. He took refuge at Lucian's castle in the Scottish Highlands. But Philip Barton has gone there to fetch Gray, so I'm hoping to see him any day now. Perhaps in time for my dinner, where he can thank you in person."

"Truly, thanks are not necessary, Lady Wycliff."

"Brynn, please. And may I call you Julienne?"

"Yes, if you wish to."

"I do. I would very much like us to become better acquainted. Dare speaks so highly of you. And I must confess, you have been good for him."

Julienne eyed her curiously. "What do you mean?"

"He seems more settled now, more serious, as if he has finally found a purpose in life. He is a very special man. Lucian and I both care for him a great deal. I would hate to see Dare hurt—" Brynn broke off with a slight shake of her head. "It is none of my business, of course."

"I certainly have no intention of hurting him," Julienne assured her.

"But your wager?" Her warm eyes searched Julienne's face. "I understand you vowed publicly to bring the Prince of Pleasure to his knees."

"Our wager was a scheme Dare concocted so he could pursue his investigation of Caliban," Julienne lied.

"Then you do care for Dare, at least a little?"

"Yes," she said in a low voice. "I care for him."

Brynn's smile was slow and brilliant. "I despaired of him ever finding a woman who could make him happy, but I think perhaps he might have succeeded. Well," she added briskly, rising, "I have kept you from your rehearsals long enough. I will send a carriage for you next Tuesday at half past seven, if that will be convenient. Lucian knows your direction. It's his business to know those things." Brynn held out her hand to clasp Julienne's. "And if I may be of service to you in any manner whatsoever, please, you have only to let me know. I can never repay you."

When her visitor was gone, Julienne sat there for a long moment, remembering her admission that she cared for Dare.

She did care. Deeply. She was still wildly in love with him, even more than she had been seven years ago. God help her.

She'd been fooling herself for weeks now, trying to convince herself that she could walk away unscathed, unwounded. But when Caliban had aimed that pistol at Dare, intending to kill him, she knew she could no longer deny her heart. She loved Dare—so much that it hurt.

Julienne drew a sharp breath. She had delayed long enough. She had to end her relationship with him completely, or her misery would only grow worse. She couldn't bear to remain near Dare, loving him as much as she did when her love wasn't returned.

And what if he could come to love her? Would his devotion be strong enough to keep him faithful over the years?

She could picture the dismal future: Dare would buy her a house in nearby St. John's Wood, perhaps—

the prime London quarter where gentlemen often kept their mistresses. She would wait for him by the window, yearning for him to bestow his crumbs of affection. Dare would make regular visits for a time, until he grew tired of her. Until he found someone else to take her place.

Julienne thought of his countless women and cringed. Her heart would bleed if he turned to other lovers. And a rake like Dare wasn't likely to remain constant without ardent love to bind him.

And what of marriage? a small voice inside her asked. It would be an impossibility, of course. A marquess could not wed a notorious actress. But if by some remote chance Dare offered for her hand . . . ?

She knew any such proposal would only come out of guilt or pity, because he felt responsible for the suffering she had endured. She couldn't allow him to make such a sacrifice. Dare would swiftly come to resent her, and that would be even more unbearable.

No, she would have to free him of any obligation to her, before she lost the will.

Julienne shut her eyes, knowing she couldn't postpone the inevitable any longer. And yet her foolish heart already trembled at the thought of leaving Dare. She didn't want to imagine a future without the sight of him, without the exquisite feel of his touch, without the joy of his conversation or the delight of matching wits with him. . . .

The prospect set a vast emptiness yawning within her. But she had to act.

She would spend the rest of her life striving to find some sort of peace without him—if that were even possible.

An ache shuddered deep inside Julienne.

She would never forget Dare. Never. He was graven into her soul.

Dare was already present when Julienne was shown into the Wycliff drawing room on Tuesday evening. When their eyes met, she felt her heart leap at the smoldering intensity of his gaze.

He came forward to greet her, and she couldn't help noticing how his tailored charcoal coat flattered his tall, elegantly lithe form. Nor could she ignore the sizzle of sexual awareness that would forever be the cornerstone of their relationship; the moment he touched her gloved hand, the flame sparked between them.

Dare's sensual mouth curved wryly in acknowledgement of the sensation, but all he said was, "Come, I want you to meet my closest friends."

He led her into the room to introduce her to the company that had risen eagerly at her entrance.

It was indeed a small gathering. In addition to Brynn and Lucian, only one other couple was present: Vanessa, Lady Sinclair, and Damien, Baron Sinclair.

Julienne had heard tell of the strikingly handsome baron, who once had been a prime leader of the Hellfire League. His wickedness and libertine propensities had earned him the appellation Lord Sin.

His looks were quite arresting, with his raven hair, penetrating gray eyes, and chiseled features. His wife's loveliness, however, seemed a perfect foil for his harshly beautiful masculinity. The lady had lustrous dark eyes and sherry-colored hair that shimmered with gold and red highlights, but there was a kindness and serenity about her that immediately put Julienne at ease.

"I am honored to meet you, Miss Laurent," Lady Sinclair said, clasping Julienne's hand warmly. "Your stunning performances have provided us immeasurable enjoyment this season. And Dare has been regaling us with your amazing heroics."

Julienne shot Dare a quelling look even as she blushed. "I believe Lord Wolverton has a tendency to embellish the truth, my lady."

"Please, I am Vanessa, and this is my husband, Damien."

Lord Sinclair stepped forward. "It is indeed a pleasure to meet you. I'm well aware of Dare's tendencies, but in this case, I think you deserve the laurels. Castlereagh's endorsement gives significant weight to any claims this frivolous fellow"—he slapped Dare on the back—"might make."

Dare's smile was pained. "I vow I am being maligned unjustly. You forget, Sin, that I have a new medal to prove just how unfrivolous I can be."

"Indeed you do," Damien agreed with a chuckle. "It's just that I'm damned envious of your exploits. It will only add luster to your legendary halo and make you even more favored by all the ladies."

Lucian went to the sideboard to pour her a glass of sherry while Brynn led Julienne to a settee and drew her down.

"I told you we are very informal," Brynn said to her. "Regrettably our other close friends couldn't be here. Raven and Kell sailed for the Caribbean three months ago. I wish you could have met them. I know you would have loved Raven. She helped ease my way in society last year when I wed Lucian and had to face all his haughty relatives."

When Lucian returned with Julienne's wine, he proposed a toast to the guests of honor—Julienne and Dare—and was roundly endorsed. Once the applause died, Dare raised his own glass.

"I think another toast is in order," he said with a wicked smile. "To the latest addition to the League. May he have no trouble following in his father's footsteps."

Brynn shook her head fiercely. "Dare, that is a horrible thing to wish. You take that back!"

At the genial laughter, Julienne frowned quizzically.

"Our son is barely two weeks old," Brynn explained. "And already Dare is plotting for him to resume Lucian's membership in the Hellfire League." She gave Dare a mock glare. "Over my dead body."

"Dare is only jesting, sweetheart," Lucian said, amused. "He knows the League's ranks will remain thin for some time. Which reminds me . . . I would like to thank my lovely wife," he said softly, "for giving me the son I always longed for." He shared a lingering look with Brynn, one so tender and intimate, it made Julienne's heart hurt.

"At least we don't have to worry about that just yet," Vanessa murmured to Julienne, "since we have a daughter. Our difficulties will likely be of a different sort. Catherine is only three, but she has her father completely wrapped around her finger, along with every other male she sees."

"But the next one could be a son," Damien said, giving his own wife the same kind of heated, cherishing glance, his gaze burning with love.

With a secretive smile, Vanessa pressed a hand to

her abdomen. "We're fortunate to be expecting another child."

Julienne had to look away as a bittersweet yearning pierced her. She would likely never have children. Not Dare's, at any event, which was all she wanted.

Glancing at him, she found Dare regarding her intently. Julienne forced herself to smile and ask an innocuous question regarding attendance at the planned public peace celebrations, which fortunately served to change the subject.

For a time she enjoyed herself. The conversation held a amiable warmth, and Dare's friends treated her with a graciousness she never would have expected from such blue-blooded members of the British nobility. The men seemed like brothers; the teasing banter and ribbing between them showed an affection for one another that Julienne suspected was very rare.

Dinner was announced shortly, and they adjourned to what Brynn called the small dining room—which provided a more intimate setting than the formal room the Wycliffs usually used for entertaining. Over a scrumptious meal, Julienne discovered more about Dare than she had learned in the three months since meeting him again.

When one of the company addressed him as Wolverton, Vanessa momentarily looked blank before shaking her head and confiding to Julienne in an undertone, "I have difficulty sometimes recalling Dare's new title. When I met him several years ago, he was the Earl of Clune, and he had a profound impact on my life. In fact, he precipitated Damien's proposal of marriage. Dare abducted me in jest, so that Damien would be forced to acknowledge how much he cared for me."

"And did he?" Julienne asked curiously.

"Yes," Lucian interjected. "But Damien called him out for it and wound up getting shot himself."

"I wanted to shoot them both for their childish obstinacy," Vanessa admitted with wry exasperation.

"Dare managed to hit me almost by accident," Damien said. "I was fortunate his marksmanship was never very good."

Dare flashed an unruffled grin. "I've made it a point to improve my skills since then. I will never be the marksman you are, Sin, but I've become fairly adequate with a pistol and quite accomplished with a blade. You never know when you might need to duel. Or confront a ruthless spy." His grin faded. "My skills proved invaluable a few weeks ago, but I will be retiring from the spy business. No more clandestine snooping or undercover machinations from now on."

"And you, Julienne?" Lucian asked.

Dare responded for her, his tone adamant. "She is retiring as well."

"There doubtless will be factions who refuse to accept defeat and will attempt to bring Napoleon back into power."

"You will have to find someone else," Dare insisted.

Julienne might have objected, but she truly would be relieved to be out of it, and to have Dare out of it.

Damien's mouth curved in amusement. "It's hard to think of you as a spy, Dare, and harder still as a member of Parliament." When Julienne raised an eyebrow, he explained. "Dare plans to take his seat in the House of Lords."

Her startled gaze shot to Dare. He was watching her, Julienne realized, as if gauging her reaction. "I've been working on my maiden speech this past week."

Julienne felt her heart sink. Dare was planning a career in politics? She hadn't had an inkling that he meant to make such an enormous change in his life. He hadn't mentioned a word to her. But that must be how he was spending his time recently. And if a nobleman would be scorned for wedding a lowly actress, how much more so would a politician?

"What issues do you mean to take up?" Lucian asked him.

"There are countless problems facing the future of our country now that the war is finally over," Dare responded. "The most immediate are the price of staples and the plight of our returning soldiers. But I'm finding that I need significantly more study before I could propose any solutions."

"You would do best to focus on something you care deeply about."

Dare nodded. "I will have Castlereagh's support at least. He wants an ally in Parliament."

"When you give your speech, we will come watch you from the spectators' gallery," Vanessa said.

Damien was still shaking his head skeptically.

"You don't think I would be good at politics?" Dare asked him.

"I'm certain you will be outstanding. You can be as charming and persuasive as the very devil. But I've known you so long as a rogue, I wonder why you would wish to assume such serious responsibilities."

"We all must put aside our youth sometime," Dare said lightly.

He caught Julienne's gaze but couldn't read her expression. She was an actress, though. An expert at concealing her feelings.

He hoped she would be glad for him. He wished they were alone so he could probe her reaction. But he would have to wait.

Shortly afterward, the ladies repaired to the drawing room, leaving the gentlemen to their port. Dare found his two best friends eyeing him questioningly, as if he were some strange specimen of wildlife at the Royal Menagerie.

They wanted explanations, he knew: Why was this leopard so desperate to change his spots?

But it was easy to explain why he was driven to reform. Because he needed to become a better man in order to be worthy of Julienne.

He was frankly ashamed of the shallow libertine that he had been. He'd made so little of his life until now. He'd been a profligate most of his thirty-three years, intent on empty pleasures. He'd had no vision for his existence beyond the gratification of the moment. He was self-indulgent, self-centered, even selfish at times. . . .

But he was done with his rakehell days, his debauchery. From the bottom of his rake's soul, he swore to change.

He could redeem himself if he strove hard enough. He could prove to Julienne that he deserved her.

"I suppose," Damien said at last, beginning the grilling, "there is a reason for this remarkable new course you're taking? Might it have anything to do with Miss Laurent?"

"It has everything to do with her," Dare said softly. "I would go through fire for her."

"She's an exceptional woman," Lucian agreed. "I find her mettle particularly impressive."

"She has more courage than any ten men I know," Dare declared.

More courage, more fortitude, more honor, more spirit, more intelligence . . . It would be nearly impossible to become worthy of her.

"So you've finally succumbed," Damien said, a knowing gleam in his gray eyes. "I seem to recall you laughing at me when I fell in love with Vanessa."

"No, I never laughed at you." Dare met his friend's gaze with all seriousness. "I was afraid for you, Sin. I feared you would be hurt the way I was once hurt. But I am willing to admit I was wrong. You had no choice but to love Vanessa—just as I have no choice with Julienne."

"I gather you're conceding your wager, then."

"Utterly." Julienne had won their wager, Dare reflected. She had brought him to his knees—and made him supremely glad to be there.

"Who will lead the League if you resign?"

"There are several qualified candidates. But to be truthful, I don't care much what happens to it now. It has served its purpose."

Damien shook his head in bemusement. "I never thought to see the day you would give up the League."

"But I no longer need it."

All this time he'd been trying to drown his pain in pleasures of the flesh. He'd relied on carnal gratification to distract him from the emptiness of his life, filling the long hours with sophisticated games and sexual depravity. He'd used and discarded lovers the way some men did boots.

But he'd come to a profound realization since meeting Julienne again: the *true* pleasure in lovemaking was in loving.

"I've learned a critical lesson these past few months," Dare said quietly, his tone charged with conviction. "Pleasure is hollow without love."

"I could have told you that," Damien replied, his eyes dancing. "But you would never have believed me. You had to discover it for yourself."

"We're vastly pleased for you," Lucian chimed in cheerfully. "When may we wish you happy?"

"I'm not certain. I haven't proposed yet. The moment isn't right."

"You are worried that she will turn you down?"

Dare couldn't lie. It was fear that had made him delay. He was mortally afraid that his legendary skills of persuasion would fail. That Julienne wouldn't accept his offer of marriage. That she couldn't forgive him for what he had allowed to happen to her. That she didn't love him, could never love him . . .

He had felt an intense intimacy between them those few days in Paris before Julienne had seemed to draw away from him, but he knew their closeness had been driven in large part by danger.

He swallowed thickly as the familiar dread knotted his stomach. His life would be unbearable without Julienne. Only she could make him feel whole. Only she could fill that void inside him, could assuage his aching need to be complete.

Julienne had touched the innermost corners of his

soul. Without her, he would have to face the utter measure of his emptiness.

Lucian interrupted his dark thoughts. "Don't look so grim, my friend. I have devout confidence that you'll succeed in winning your lady."

Dare wished he could be as confident. For the past two weeks he had adopted a course of pursuit that ran counter to his primal instincts. Not only did he want to let Julienne enjoy the accolades she deserved without distracting from her fame, but he intended to dispense with their public mating dance altogether. To call a halt to his flagrant wooing. To end what Julienne had termed his juvenile antics.

He was through with games. He had to show her that he could be serious, that he could develop some worthwhile pursuits. He intended to court her in a way that she would see as meaningful and sincere and originating from his heart.

He could think of few ways that wouldn't be reminiscent of their infamous wager. Attending her theater performances or taking her to midnight suppers smacked too much of his recent tactics, and so would sending her expensive gifts.

Despite his raw impatience, he wanted to make this new courtship entirely different from the past few months.

And he was awaiting word from his agent in France regarding the purchase of the Folmont estates. He didn't want Julienne thinking he was trying to buy her love, although he would have stooped to even that if he'd thought it would help. But with the restoration of her birthright, she would be wealthy enough to choose her future, independent of any man, of any protector.

As for his offering marriage, he thought he would do better to re-create the romantic scene of their summer together. He intended to ask Julienne to a picnic, where he would repeat his proposal of seven years ago.

Meanwhile he had been focusing on his fledgling political career, where he could concern himself with his country's affairs and the welfare of others, so that he might actually do some good. He meant to prove to Julienne that he could change.

With that in mind, he had arranged for this dinner so that she could meet his cherished friends—and to show her that even the most notorious libertines could reform when inspired by true love.

As if able read his mind, Lucian raised his glass again. "To our new league. We've created a far better one than what we had. A league of reformed rakes." He met Dare's gaze with a brotherly smile alive with mischief and affection. "Welcome."

Dare gladly drank to that toast, praying he could join the select membership Lucian spoke of. He had never been envious of his friends until now, but he wanted what Damien and Luce had: love, warmth, children, laughter.

But most of all he desperately wanted Julienne.

For the first time in his life, though, he had no certainty that he could attain it.

Chapter
Nineteen

Determined to end her relationship with Dare irrefutably, Julienne set her plan in motion four days later.

She knew, of course, that it would take a significant event to make Dare concede defeat in the matter of their wager. Thus she intended to spurn him in front of witnesses. When she was done, her repudiation of him would be public knowledge. The entire ton would know that she had unequivocally refused his proposition to become his mistress.

And if she performed her role well, her coldhearted orchestration would prove to him how little she cared, while his overt humiliation would infuriate him enough to allow her to make a clean escape and sever their relationship forever.

She gave notice at Drury Lane, offering the manager a tale of a deathly-ill relative. Arnold promised to conceal the news of her imminent departure until the last moment, since he had no wish distress her legion of fans before absolutely necessary.

For her last performance, Julienne called on every skill she knew—and managed to make it one of her best, despite her aching despair. But when she took her bows to thunderous applause, the sea of faces blurred in her vision, and she could barely swallow her tears as she left the theater for the last time.

The following morning she vacated her lodgings with only a small valise, having arranged for her trunks to be held until she sent for them once she found new rooms in York.

The hired hackney made only one stop, so that she could say farewell to Solange.

"Are you certain there is no hope?" her friend asked sadly.

"Yes," Julienne answered in a low voice, giving Solange a fierce hug.

"I shall miss you, *mon amie*."

"I will miss you, too."

She would miss Dare even more, Julienne reflected as she returned to the carriage. The loss of him already felt like a bleeding wound inside her.

She directed the hackney to an elegant little house in St. John's Wood, which she had borrowed from another actress for the day. She had invited Dare to meet her at noon, but she intended to arrive more than two hours early. She needed the interval, not only to physically set the stage, but to prepare herself emotionally for the performance of a lifetime.

Dare bounded up the front steps to the charming little cottage, his whole being thrumming with the feverish eagerness of a young lad. Julienne's invitation had more than surprised him. He couldn't fathom why she had asked him here, unless she meant to concede the wager and wanted to use this setting to negotiate the terms of their arrangement.

If so, he would have to disabuse her of that notion quickly. He didn't want Julienne as his mistress. He wanted to have her in keeping, but permanently, forever. And he would tell her so this very afternoon. He intended to risk laying his heart on the line and ask for her hand in marriage.

He was admitted by a female servant, who bobbed a curtsy. "Miss Laurent is waiting in the boudoir," the maid informed him with a saucy giggle.

Dare followed her and was shown into a luxurious, silk-swathed bedchamber. The curtains had been drawn, providing an aura of romantic seclusion.

The stage was set for seduction, he realized, his pulse quickening further.

As the door shut behind him, Dare caught sight of Julienne. She was reclining upon a daybed, which was wider than a normal chaise longue and large enough to accommodate two lovers with ease. To his surprise, she was fully dressed in a gown of rose-colored muslin, but the small table beside her was laden with fruit and cheese and wine.

Taking a sip from her glass, Julienne studied him over the rim, her dark eyes half-closed, sensual, and compelling.

"Welcome," she said in a husky voice that stroked all his nerve endings. "I have missed you, Dare."

"I've missed you, too—like the very devil."

Her luscious lips formed a pout. "It hardly seems so. I would say rather that you have been severely neglecting me of late."

He smiled charmingly as he advanced into the room. "My apologies, my love." Reaching for her hand, he kissed her fingers tenderly. "I have been waiting for the right moment to speak to you in private."

"I have no interest in talking just now." Little flames warmed the depths of her eyes as she ran her finger down his chest to his breeches. "I think you should take off your clothes," she murmured, her voice liquid enticement.

Dare needed no second request. Obediently he shed his coat and waistcoat, then his cravat and shirt. He sat beside her on the daybed to remove his shoes and stockings, then stood again to remove his pantaloons and drawers.

When he stood naked before her, her gaze made a slow sweep of his body. Dare felt himself harden at the lust in her eyes. With a look of invitation, Julienne smiled languorously and held up her arms, bidding him to join her on the daybed. Eagerly he stretched out beside her and drew her into his embrace.

Their kiss was hard and passionate, and she seemed as breathless as he was when she broke it off. He might have protested but she gave him another slow, seductive smile and pressed him onto his back. Then she reached above his head to lift a silk scarf that was tied to a metal loop in the wood frame of the daybed.

When she attached the scarf to his left wrist, he gave her a grin that was part quizzical, part devilish. "Just what did you have in mind, *chérie*?"

"I imagine you can guess."

He could indeed guess when she secured his right wrist, then knelt to tie scarves around each of his ankles.

"You once told me had a fantasy about bondage," she murmured, bending over him. "Well, I am satisfying my own fantasy. I want you entirely at my mercy."

"I'm more than delighted to oblige, my sweet," he said hoarsely in return.

He held his breath as she pressed her lips lightly against his chest while her fingers danced over his skin, ending in a light, circling tease on his abdomen.

Dare felt desire curling, flaring, twisting inside him at the wicked sensation of her fingers.

Then he realized she had a scarf clutched in her hand. He sucked in a sharp, involuntary breath as she drew it along his body. In a moment she was stroking his rigid erection with the sensuous silk, curling the scarf around his swollen shaft, touching him with her lips.

It was one of the most erotic sensations he had ever experienced. She made him shudder, made his heart pound out of control. Dare arched his hips, his body white-hot with desire as Julienne continued her provocative ministrations, and clenched his teeth against the burning in his loins.

Then suddenly she stopped. Leaving the scarf draped over his arousal to form a tent, she rose from the bed. He thought she intended to undress, but instead she picked up his clothing that he'd left strewn on a chair and stepped back.

Her expression, which had been so ardently beguiling a moment before, was now impassive, almost blank.

"Julienne?"

Her sad smile pierced his heart. Delaying her answer, she went to the door and opened it.

"I want there to be no question that you have lost our wager, Dare, and for that we need witnesses. Your friends Riddingham and Sir Stephen Ormsby will soon be here to rescue you, along with several of your other Hellfire colleagues. I promised them a delicious spectacle."

Dare stared in shock as she turned to go.

"Good-bye, Dare," Julienne said in low, trembling whisper.

Then, with barely a fleeting backward glance, she slipped from the room, shutting the door firmly behind her.

The hackney Julienne had waiting took her to a posting inn, where she caught the afternoon stage for York. The interior was crowded with a variety of passengers, several of whom recognized her.

Acknowledging their accolades with a faint smile, Julienne squeezed farther into her corner and turned her face to the window. Yet she saw nothing of the passing countryside. The keening sense of loss was like a knife wound inside her; the sense of being cut into parts wouldn't leave her.

She missed Dare with every breath, every jostle and jolt of the swaying coach. Thinking of him was excruciating. But she would not weep. She had cried those tears out long ago.

Then she made the mistake of fishing in her reticule for a handkerchief. She found the one she had saved from Dare's clothing as a remembrance, and when she held it to her face, she discovered that the linen carried the faint scent of his cologne.

Despair rose higher, shoving at her throat, making her vision blur. It was all she could do to force back the scalding tears.

Somehow she had to forget her agonizing thoughts of Dare. Somehow she had to find the courage to continue.

* * *

He had to control the flare of panic inside him, Dare thought nearly two hours later. Julienne had disappeared, and none of the rakehells she had invited to witness his defeat knew where she had gone.

If the stakes weren't so high, if his own involvement was less personal, perhaps he could have felt a spark of admiration for her daring. It was a prank worthy of his former days—to strip him and steal his clothes and tie him to the bed while she absconded, leaving him helpless for his friends to discover. But he could find absolutely no humor in the situation.

The experience had been embarrassing in the extreme. His Hellfire colleagues thought it uproarious that after all the years of his tormenting them with practical jokes, the Prince of Pleasure had finally received justice in kind. Worse, they had all come on horseback, so that he was forced to hail a hackney with only a sheet to cover himself.

He managed to persuade the driver that he was indeed the Marquess of Wolverton and to return him to his home in Mayfair, but Dare spent the entire journey gritting his teeth and vowing severe retribution when he caught up with Julienne. Anger helped cloak his stark fear that he had lost her once more, without even telling her of his love for her.

His servants were too well-trained to show surprise when he came traipsing in, garbed like a Greek senator. And he felt better when he was dressed again in his own exquisitely tailored clothing. But as he called for his carriage, Dare couldn't rid himself of the sick feeling squeezing his heart. He had every intention of following Julienne. And he had at least two good places to begin his search—her friend Solange and the Drury Lane Theater.

What filled him with dread, however, was not knowing why Julienne had run—or what he would do about it when he found her.

Julienne arrived in York the following afternoon, her body weary from lack of sleep, her heart one huge, empty ache. Despite her fatigue, she went directly to the theater, where she was welcomed back eagerly by her former company.

To her surprise everyone had heard of her fame in routing a deadly traitor and had followed her London career avidly. Wanting to capitalize on her success, the manager gave her a role in the evening's performance of a Molière comedy and even printed a special broadsheet announcing her return.

The small playhouse was packed that night, for word of her appearance had spread rapidly. Julienne could scarcely remember a more receptive audience. Even though she went through her lines numbly, they laughed and roared at even her smallest jests, extending their goodwill to the entire company.

The play was perhaps half through when she heard a commotion offstage. Julienne roused herself from her despondency enough to wonder what was happening. Glancing toward the wings, she saw the manager wildly gesturing, apparently engaged in an argument with a tall, burly man who was dressed in a greatcoat and tricorn hat.

Moments later the burly man stepped on stage and identified himself as the sheriff of York.

His narrowed gaze latched on to Julienne. "You are

Miss Laurent?" When she acknowledged that she was, he snapped, "I am placing you under arrest."

Bewildered, Julienne stared at him. This was too strangely reminiscent of her near arrest in Paris. "On what charge?"

"Thievery."

"There must be some mistake, Sheriff."

"No mistake. You stole property belonging to the Marquess of Wolverton. You will come with me."

Her heart leapt to her throat at hearing Dare's title. She winced as the sheriff hauled her none too gently from the stage to a chorus of boos and catcalls from the disgruntled audience along with a spate of rotten tomatoes.

To her dismay, the sheriff escorted her forcibly to the green room and shoved her down onto a chaise longue beside the gentleman already seated there.

Scrambling upright, Julienne scarcely heard the sheriff take his leave and shut the door behind him. Instead she froze, stunned, to meet Dare's emerald gaze.

The raw anger in those breathtaking eyes was unmistakable, and yet she saw a hint of uncertainty as well.

"Do you seriously intend to have me arrested for theft?" she demanded, taking the offensive. "I didn't steal anything."

"You did," Dare answered, his tone clipped.

"I suppose I took your clothing—"

"That isn't all you took—but let us set that issue aside for the moment. I want to know why you left me like that. Did you think to humiliate me? Was that your way of bringing me to my knees?"

A hot-cold flush spread over her cheeks in response

to his smoldering gaze. "In part. I hoped to put a public end to our wager."

"Why?"

"Because I wanted to be done with the games. There is no point in keeping up the charade. With Caliban dead, you no longer have any need of me, except perhaps physically."

The stormy hue of his eyes softened. "You couldn't be more wrong, Julienne."

Feeling the sting of renewed tears, she averted her gaze. "I couldn't endure being your mistress, Dare."

"That suits me well, because I don't want you for my mistress. I want you for my wife."

Her breath faltered, and her gaze flew back to his.

When she remained speechless, Dare ran a hand roughly through his hair. "I should have told you sooner, I know. But I didn't know how to begin. I was terrified you would refuse my proposal. I've been trying to get up the courage to ask you since we returned from Paris."

Julienne stared. She saw vulnerability in Dare's eyes, and fear. His apprehension tore at her heart, but she shook her head gravely. "Dare, I won't allow you to sacrifice yourself for me out of guilt."

"Marrying you won't be a sacrifice. Why the devil would you think so?"

"I know you feel guilty because of what Ivers did, because of what your grandfather did."

"My feelings have nothing whatsoever to do with guilt. I want to marry you because I can't live without you. It is as simple as that."

He reached forward to take her hand. "I love you,

Julienne. Surely you realize that by now. I never stopped loving you."

At her shocked silence, his mouth curved, his smile one of misery. "What am I supposed to do without you if you leave me, tell me that? How will I go on? I've spent the last seven years longing for you. You spoiled me for any other woman, Jewel. After you, I never allowed myself to love anyone, to get close. I didn't dare risk the kind of pain I felt after losing you. I shielded myself so I wouldn't be left hurting in the end. But my case was hopeless once I found you again."

His voice, already low and ragged, took on a desolate edge. "I couldn't bear to lose you now. Do you really mean to condemn me to agony for the rest of my life?"

Longing caught in Julienne's chest, but she forced it away. "I can't possibly be your wife, Dare. I am an actress. I can never move in the same circles that you do. You will be utterly ridiculed if you wed me. Not only will society refuse to accept me, but you will be universally condemned for defying all the rules."

"Do you think I give a *damn* what society thinks?" His fingers tightened around hers, the gesture supplicating. "And I'm not so certain they'll refuse to accept you. You're a heroine at the moment. All London is singing your praises. And you have Prinny's support."

"That hardly makes me respectable. Nor will it endow me with a pristine reputation."

"But it will go a long way toward influencing opinions. Beyond that, title and wealth are all that really matter when it comes to being accepted, and you will have both when you're my wife."

"But, Dare ... I've told you, I have had other lovers. ..."

"I don't give a bloody hell how many men you've taken to your bed, as long as I am the last. As long as I'm your husband."

Julienne still couldn't let herself believe in the future Dare was envisioning. Couldn't dismiss the fear she'd always felt of earning his lifelong resentment by tying him to her.

Her heart wrenching with turmoil, she searched his face. "How can you be certain you truly love me, Dare? I think it much more likely that you've mistaken your feelings. Eventually—perhaps even a few months from now—you will come to your senses and realize that you want me only for your carnal gratification."

"No." He held her gaze, his eyes stunningly bright. "I know better than anyone what carnal gratification is, Julienne. It's basic, selfish lust of the flesh. It involves the body. It has nothing to do with the mind or heart. What I feel for you goes far, far beyond the carnal."

When she didn't reply, he leaned closer, the earnestness in his eyes growing even more intense. "I know I don't deserve your love, but I intend to change. I mean to make something of myself, to someday prove myself worthy of you."

"Worthy of me?" she asked, frowning.

"Yes, dammit." His mouth twisted in a faint smile. "Why the devil do you think I'm taking up my seat in Parliament? So I can show you I'm not the worthless fribble you've always thought me."

Julienne stared fixedly at Dare. It staggered her to

realize his sincerity, and that he considered himself unworthy of her. "Dare, I never thought you a fribble . . .
certainly not since meeting you again."

"Then you'll give me a chance?"

"Dare . . ."

When she didn't answer his question at once, he
stood abruptly and pulled her to her feet, then strode
out of the green room, drawing Julienne behind him.

"Where are you taking me?" she asked rather
breathlessly.

"The stage."

To her utter amazement, he dragged her out on
stage, interrupting the play and scattering the other
actors. Positioning her in the exact center in front of
the footlights, Dare sank to his knees before her and
took her hand, the very picture of an avid suitor. The
rumble of surprise from the audience died down so the
spectators could hear his every word.

"Several months ago in London we made a wager,
Miss Laurent. You vowed you could ensnare my heart
and bring me to my knees. Well, I'm on my knees to
you. I'm declaring you the victor. You've won, Julienne. Utterly and completely. My heart is yours. You
have the absolute power to break it, as you will."

At his public declaration, Julienne wanted to laugh
and cry at the same time. Dare was showing the world
he loved her; he was showing *her* he loved her.

He clenched her hand hard. "Julienne . . ." His
voice had gone beyond strained and sat on the cutting
edge of pain. "Tell me honestly that you don't love
me—that you can never love me—and I'll let you go. It
will probably kill me, but I want you to be happy."

She couldn't bear the desperate entreaty in his eyes.

"Oh, Dare, of course I love you. I've always loved you."

With a raw sound, he rose to his feet and hauled her into his arms. His kiss was fierce, fervent. He twisted his hand in her hair and held her still for the hungry plundering of her mouth.

Julienne could scarcely hear the wild cheers of the audience over the pounding of her heart.

When Dare finally released her, it was only to envelop her in a smothering embrace. "You drive me to madness, do you know that?" he said raggedly.

"I could say the same of you."

He held her tighter, his shoulder absorbing her sigh. He wanted to tell Julienne of his profound relief. How utterly alone he had always been without her. How he ached with the intense need to bury himself inside her. But that would keep. For now he only wanted her promise to wed him.

"You have to marry me now," he murmured against her hair. "I won't allow you any other choice. You stole my heart, Julienne, and your only hope to avoid imprisonment is to wed me."

He could feel her surprise, sense her smile. "Is *that* why you brought the sheriff here? To accuse me of theft? So you could intimidate me into accepting you? No, you don't need to answer," she said, exasperated laughter lacing her voice. "It is just the sort of outrageous scheme you would think of."

"That was the only way I could be sure you would hear me out. But now that you have . . . I'm never letting you go, Julienne. I intend to bind you to me in every way possible."

She drew back, uncertainty shadowing her beautiful features. "You may come to tire of me someday."

"No, never. *Never*." Reaching up, Dare cradled her face in his hands. He would never tire of her. Her sensuality and intelligence would keep him forever tantalized. He couldn't possibly feel this way for any other woman. Couldn't desire anyone else the way he desired her.

His thumbs stroked her cheekbones, her lips. "Will you be my wife, my precious Jewel?"

Shouts of encouragement came from the audience—"Say aye!" "Marry the bloke!"—but Julienne spoke clearly over the din.

"Yes, Dare. Yes. I will."

Elation, fierce as fire, swept through him. With a fervent prayer of thanks to the heavens, he scooped her up in his arms and carried her offstage to the thunderous sound of applause, away from prying eyes.

In the shadows of the wings, he set her down and wrapped Julienne in his arms again, his face nestled in her hair.

"I only hope," she murmured, "that you don't come to regret this."

"My sole regret is all the wasted years between us. We have a great deal of time to make up for, Julienne. I can only try to atone for all the pain you suffered. I swear I will do my damnedest. And I'll show you I can be a different man, that I can be better."

"I don't want you to be different, Dare. I love you exactly as you are."

He lifted their clasped hands to kiss her fingers ardently. "Say it again—tell me you love me."

"I love you, Dare. I always will."

"I will never tire of hearing that. And I swear on my life, I will never again give you cause to doubt how much I love you."

Shutting his eyes, he drew Julienne to him again, cradling her close against his heart. She was wrong; he wasn't mistaken about his feelings. He understood completely the meaning of true love.

True love was Julienne. She was his heart, his life, his hopes, his every dream.

She was his precious love. He would spend the rest of his life proving it to her.

And now that he had found her again, he would never, ever let her go.

Epilogue

Kent, England, July 1814

The cottage where they'd held their lovers' trysts seven years ago had changed little in the interval. The property had been carefully maintained, the garden lovingly tended and allowed to flourish. Now a profusion of sweet summer roses ran riot, perfuming the warm afternoon air as Dare carried his bride over the threshold.

Setting Julienne on her feet, he kissed her deeply, wanting to sink so completely into her that she would never be free of him.

They were married now, wed by special license because Dare had refused to wait the necessary three weeks for the banns to be read. They'd left London this morning for Kent and traveled directly to Wolverton Hall, where Dare gave his new lady only moments to change her carriage dress before he whisked her off to the cottage.

"At last," he murmured hoarsely when he allowed Julienne to catch her breath. "This has been a dream of mine for an eternity, returning here with you."

Her smile was magical and set his pulse soaring—

which naturally dictated that he claim her mouth again. Responding eagerly, Julienne reached up to tangle her fingers in his hair, while her kiss reached deep inside him to twine around his heart.

When finally Dare forced himself to draw back, his blood was so heated, it was simmering; he wanted her so badly, need was like a fire inside him.

But there was no rush, he reminded himself. They had time on their side. A lifetime together—and he wanted to savor every instant.

"I want to make love to you in the rose garden," Dare said thickly, pulling the pins from her hair.

"I thought you would never ask."

Clasping his wife's hand, he led her outside to the rear of the cottage. Late afternoon sunlight cast a golden warmth over the walled rose garden, wrapping them in a cocoon of privacy. In one corner, beneath a cherry tree, a blanket awaited them, along with the basket Dare had ordered brought here.

"You planned this, didn't you?" Julienne asked in delight as he plucked a red rose and tucked it in her hair.

"Down to every last detail. I told you I have been waiting forever for this moment."

Dare dropped to his knees on the blanket and fished in the basket. With Julienne watching, he drew out a bucket of iced champagne, a crystal goblet, a huge bowl of ripe strawberries and another of clotted cream, and finally a small vellum-wrapped packet tied with red ribbons.

When he glanced up to see her standing over him, he couldn't help but be amused. "See, you've won our damned wager, my love. I'm on my knees to you. Again."

"Are these my winnings?" she asked curiously when he handed her the packet.

"No, this is my wedding gift to you."

He drew Julienne down beside him and braced his back against the tree trunk, tucking her in the curve of his arm. "Open it."

Inside was a deed, along with several other certified documents. He saw her eyes grow moist as she read the deed. He had purchased her ancestral home, the Chateau-Folmont in Languedoc.

Her tremulous smile told him clearly that he had pleased her.

"*Thank* you, Dare," she said in a fervent whisper. "This means so much to me. And I know my mother would have been overjoyed."

"I will take you there someday. Perhaps next year."

"There is no hurry, is there?"

"No hurry at all," he answered, suspecting that the memories of their recent ordeal in France were still too raw for Julienne to wish to return just now. "But you have yet to decide where you want go on our wedding trip."

They had discussed beginning in Italy and perhaps venturing as far as Russia. Dare wanted to show Julienne the world. They had also considered taking Lucian up on his offer of his castle in the Scottish Highlands, since during the summer months the British Isles would be far cooler than the rest of Europe. Moreover, Brynn's brother Grayson seemed to have disappeared from there, and Brynn had begun to worry.

Dare might have volunteered to search for him, but he judged that he'd done his duty for the moment.

And he had more important matters to attend to just now, namely his new bride.

"I admit Italy sounds lovely," Julienne said, folding the packet and returning it to the basket for safe-keeping.

"It's almost as lovely as my wife." He nuzzled her ear. "I'll show you the all delights of Venice and Florence and Rome."

Interrupting his attentions then, Dare poured a goblet of champagne, and they took turns sipping from the same glass while he hand-fed her strawberries dipped in cream.

"We will have to return by fall," Julienne reminded him between bites and his nibbling kisses.

"By September," Dare agreed. This fall would be busy with more race meets. They had missed the Derby at Epsom Downs in early June, while they were in France, although neither of Dare's entries had won. "The St. Ledger is held in September. And Parliament reconvenes in November."

"And Arnold expects me to begin rehearsals by late October."

Julienne's contract had been renewed at Drury Lane with her promise to star in two performances a month. She hadn't wanted to quit acting altogether, and to her relief, Dare hadn't expected her to.

"I am glad," she admitted, "that you didn't insist I give up my career simply because I am a marchioness."

Humor danced in his eyes. "I value my skin too highly to risk disappointing your legion of fans. And it would be a pity to deprive the world of your tremendous talent."

"Do you truly mean that?" Julienne asked, warmed by his praise.

"Unequivocally. I have the greatest respect for your acting skills. Your genius is what brought down a traitor." Dare bit into a cream-drenched strawberry, then offered her the other half as he chewed thoughtfully. "Although . . . you may want to consider retirement once we have children."

Julienne turned to gaze at him solemnly. They had never discussed the issue. "Do you want children?"

His gaze was serious and devilish at the same time. "Not only do I want children, my darling, but I want the sublime pleasure of making them with you."

"May we begin soon?"

His slow, lazy smile was absolutely devastating. "I thought you would never ask," he replied, raking a searing look over her.

They undressed each other without haste, pausing to savor the texture and feel of each other's bodies . . . the sun-warmed skin, the heated pulses, the vital curves and hollows.

Julienne shivered when Dare's lips suckled the breast he had just bared.

"I know some inventive methods of using cream," he murmured, "but right now I only want to taste you. Come here, love."

He lay back languidly on the blanket, the image of virile strength, and reached his arms up in invitation.

Julienne, however, hesitated, wanting to treasure this moment. She could scarcely believe she wasn't dreaming. Dare was actually her husband at long last.

Breathless with wonder, she let her gaze drift over his body, drinking in his incredible masculine beauty . . .

his lithe elegance, his lean hardness, his erotic smile, his emerald eyes that smoldered now with heat.

Every part of him was dear to her. She loved him with such deep certainty that *he* was part of her.

He was her heart, her passion, her joy. He was her destiny; he had always been so. Yet this moment had been so long in coming.

Rapt desire filled her as she bent over him. She ran her hands up his body, her fingers splaying along his muscles, supple and rippling beneath his feverish skin. She heard his ragged moan as her lips met his in a lingering kiss. . . .

But Dare apparently wasn't willing to allow her control this time. Impatiently he shifted their positions, so that she lay beneath him, at his mercy.

His touch was exquisite and scorchingly sensual, his eyes bright and burning as he caressed her with his long, skillful fingers. He made love to her just as he had all those years ago, tenderly but impossibly demanding. He cherished her with his mouth and hands and body, arousing her to the burning point.

When he at last entered her, Julienne sighed with utter bliss at the sleek power and hardness of him.

Wrapping her legs around him, she moved with Dare in perfect unison, arching against him, crying his name as he claimed her, filled her, possessed her. And when the shattering explosion came, they melded together, two hearts coming home at last, forged into one by endless caresses of fire.

Afterward they lay together dreamily, breaths mingling, relishing the blissful sense of entwinement. Holding Julienne close, Dare felt a contentment so rich it vibrated deep into his soul.

This was pleasure, he thought. The kind of heartfelt pleasure that came from true love. This was joy. The kind of precious joy that made his heart sing.

Almost as if she could read his mind, Julienne nuzzled his shoulder with her lips, her voice weak when she whispered, "I can well see how you earned your nickname, the Prince of Pleasure. . . . But I confess I don't mind disappointing your legion of fans . . . all the countless damsels who will be heartbroken because you are retiring from the lists."

Summoning his strength, Dare raised himself up on one elbow so that he could see her beautiful face.

"I'm not retiring," he contradicted, offering her his bone-melting smile. "Merely concentrating all my effort on one particular damsel." Bending, he touched his lips to hers as his voice lowered to a rough whisper. "I want to pleasure you all the way down to your soul, my beloved Jewel."

Julienne reached up to bring his beguiling mouth down to hers. "You always do," she murmured, giving herself up again to his enchanting caresses.

*Please read on for a delicious taste
of the next exciting tale of love from*

NICOLE
JORDAN

London, September 1814

Partially shielded from view by a potted palm, Max Leighton leaned against a marble column and surveyed the crowded ballroom without enthusiasm. After enduring so many years of war, he had returned to England determined to lose himself in the mundane pleasures of civilian life.

But this was not what he had in mind: being pursued by countless matchmaking mamas and their nubile young daughters, eager to ensnare him in their nets. In the current craze of victory celebrations, a wealthy, decorated war veteran made an extremely eligible matrimonial prize, Max had learned to his chagrin.

His mouth curled in a wry grimace. He had little appetite for fighting on the battlefield of love, especially when he had no interest in settling down in marriage just yet. But even the more seasoned beauties of the ton were vying for his attention now. Needing a respite from his popularity, he'd escaped the ballroom floor moments ago and sought refuge behind a palm.

What had happened to him? Before his army days, he

hadn't considered balls and soirees and garden parties so trivial. But perhaps the genteel challenges of the Beau Monde simply couldn't match the satisfaction of saving Europe from the bloody machinations of a despot.

Or perhaps it was the women themselves who aroused his dissatisfaction. None of them had the honest charms of one particular woman he'd found impossible to forget.

His gaze narrowing, Max let his mind drift back as it had countless times since his mission of mercy more than a year ago.

He had never expected to discover a Mediterranean island paradise, or experience an enchanting night of passion with an innocent temptress. He hadn't been able to forget that night on Cyrene or the bewitching woman who had offered him solace.

He was inclined to return to the island and seek out Caro Evers, simply to see if the magic he'd felt with her was real or the result of the extraordinary circumstances, if, during the long months of war, he had built her up in his memory into an impossible ideal.

"Don't tell me you are in hiding!" an amused male voice broke into his reflections. "Don't you realize how many belles you are disappointing?"

Lord Christopher Thorne stood before him, surveying him with wry understanding. They had met the previous year during Max's brief visit to Cyrene, and in recent months had become friends.

"Here, perhaps this will help," Thorne said, offering him a snifter of what looked to be brandy. "I thought you would prefer this to my aunt's insipid punch."

It was Thorne who had introduced him to some of the more notorious pleasures London had to offer.

And Thorne who had coerced him into attending the ball this evening.

Max raised his glass of brandy. "This helps," he said, "but you are still bloody well indebted to me."

Thorne flashed a grin. "I am indeed." He was primarily in London for the fall Little Season because he'd reluctantly promised his aunt, Lady Hennessy, that he would squire around his young debutante cousin, who was trying to acquire some social polish in preparation for her coming-out next spring. He had asked Max to attend tonight so he didn't have to endure Lady Hennessy's ball all alone.

He gave Max a friendly cuff on the back. "It must be a severe plague, being hounded so mercilessly by so many women who love you."

"It isn't my person they love. It's the size of my income and my prospective title that draws them." As the only living male relative of an elderly uncle, Max was the heir presumptive to a viscountcy.

"Along with your charm and looks," Thorne interjected. "And the fact that you're a celebrated war hero. Have you any notion how many men would kill to be in your shoes?"

Max returned a pained smile. "I would rather be anywhere else than here. Back on your island, for example."

Thorne shook his head. "I'm not certain that would be an improvement. Cyrene has more than its share of marriage-minded debs. There are some two dozen British families who lead society there. They have their own little ton and can be quite as ruthless as London's Upper Ten Thousand."

"I would be willing to risk it just for a little peace."

Thorne gave him a scrutinizing glance. "Ah, I fancy I know what your problem is. You were infected."

"Infected?"

"By Cyrene's spell. It gets in your blood."

Taking another swallow of brandy, Max shook his head. "I heard something about a mythical spell, but I don't believe such things."

"Even so, the island affects some people strangely. It has seductive qualities that can be downright dangerous."

That much was true, Max agreed silently. He had found it enchanting, seductive, beguiling. . . .

"Is that why you settled there?" he asked his friend. "You were seduced by the island?"

To his surprise, Thorne gave an enigmatic smile. "In part. But Cyrene has other appealing traits that aren't apparent at first glance." Thorne paused. "Perhaps you should visit there after all. The tranquility might do you good."

"I certainly haven't found tranquility here," Max muttered, eying a blond-haired widow who was scanning the ballroom, doubtless in search of him.

"Then come home with me at Christmas," Thorne said. "I have obligations that will keep me in London until then, but I plan to spend the holiday on Cyrene and would be delighted to have you join me."

"I could easily be persuaded. I'm eager to see for myself that Yates has recovered." And to meet a certain ministering angel again . . .

He knew better than to bring up the subject, but the question seemed to be dragged out of him. "What do you hear about Miss Evers?"

"Caro?" Thorne's eyebrow rose with curiosity. "Ah,

I recall you met her when she nursed Yates." He smiled slowly as if recalling a fond memory. "Why, she's as singular as ever. Caro tends to set the blue-blooded denizens of Cyrene on their ears with regularity."

"She did strike me as rather unconventional."

"She is that indeed," Thorne said with a low laugh that suddenly faltered. "What in blazes . . . ?" His eyes narrowed. "Speak of the devil."

Following his gaze through the palm fronds, Max glanced past the throngs of dancers toward the main entrance to the ballroom. A woman stood there, looking starkly out of place among the begowned, bejewelled, befeathered ladies. She wore plain, dark traveling clothes, and she was searching the crowd impatiently.

Max felt every muscle in his body tense. He recognized her from his dreams. The proud carriage of her slender body. The delicate strength in the set of her jaw. The compassion in her healing touch . . .

Wondering if he was dreaming, Max blinked rapidly, just as Thorne said in a suddenly terse tone, "Excuse me. Caro may be looking for me. I need to discover what brought her here."

As his friend strode away, Max remained where he stood, feeling slightly stunned. Like Thorne, he had no idea what had brought Caro Evers here to London, specifically to Lady Hennessy's ballroom.

Yet he had no doubt whatsoever why his life had suddenly brightened.

Relief flooded Caro when she spied Thorne approaching. At least she wouldn't have to search further for him.

When he reached her, she forced herself to return

his smile of welcome, knowing that she was the object of countless curious stares. The notoriety didn't bother her—she was fully accustomed to it by now. But no one needed to suspect that she and Lord Christopher Thorne were anything more than longtime acquaintances and neighbors, or that she had come here to fetch him for an urgent mission.

"Did you just arrive in London?" he murmured as he bent gallantly over her hand.

"Yes. I called at your house but was told I could find you here. Thorne, it is Isabella. She has been taken captive."

His pleasant smile never wavered, although a spark of dark emotion flared in his eyes. "I am delighted to see you again, Miss Evers. Come, you can give me all the news from home."

Tucking her arm in his, he ushered her from the ballroom and along the elegant corridor to a large library.

Caro shivered as he closed the door behind them. A fire had been lit in the grate, but it was still far colder here than home on her beautiful island.

"So tell me what happened," Thorne said brusquely, all business now that the need for pretense was over.

"Isabella was returning home three weeks ago when her ship was overrun by pirates. Thorne, it's almost certain she has been enslaved."

"Sit down and start from the beginning," he suggested as she began to pace.

"I couldn't possibly sit. I have been doing nothing but sitting on board a schooner for two weeks now. I wish it didn't take so blasted long to reach London!"

"Well, you won't do Isabella any good by wearing

out my aunt's carpet," Thorne retorted. "Would you care for some sherry?"

His pragmatic tone had a calming effect. Taking a deep breath, Caro moved over to the hearth and held out her gloved hands while Thorne went to a table and poured her a glass of sherry.

Memories rushed through her mind as she stared at the flames. Lady Isabella Wilde was her dearest friend—a beautiful Spanish widow who frequently traveled the globe, living life as she pleased. The adventuresome Isabella had been like a mother to her, ever since Caro's own mother died when she was a girl. Isabella was also a role model of independent thinking and had encouraged her in countless ways to pursue her dreams.

Caro was fiercely determined to free her friend from captivity—and so were all the other Guardians. There was no question they would mount a rescue. Caro had come directly to London to give Thorne his orders.

He handed her a full wineglass, then settled himself on a sofa while she explained the facts they had pieced together after Isabella was taken captive by Barbary corsairs.

"The only solid information we have is that her ship was taken to Tripoli, where she disappeared. Presumably she was sold as a slave, but those are only rumors. There was another English gentleman on the same voyage, however, who was taken prisoner with her. We know he was allowed to ransom himself and return to England. And we think he might have some clues as to Isabella's whereabouts."

"And Sir Gawain wants me to track down this Englishman?"

"Yes. He is a wealthy merchant by the name of

Tarquin Jones, who hails from Manchester. Are you acquainted with him?"

"I've heard of him. He owns a dozen factories in the north."

"Which is how he could afford the exorbitant price of his ransom."

Her sherry remaining untouched, Caro set her glass on the mantle to reach into her reticule. Drawing out a thin sheaf of folded papers, she handed them to Thorne.

"All the particulars are here," she said. "Everything we know about Jones. The most likely place to begin looking for him is perhaps Manchester."

Thorne perused the details quickly. "I am to question Jones," he verified, "then proceed to Tripoli and link up with Hawk to continue the search?"

"Exactly. And I don't need to tell you how imperative it is that you proceed quickly."

He nodded. "I will leave for Manchester tomorrow morning, as soon as I amke certain Jones isn't here in London somewhere. That will also give me time to arrange a few details to put my current assignment on hold."

The light of anticipation in Thorne's eyes greatly encouraged Caro. For the first time in weeks, she felt her taught nerves relax the slightest measure. She was infinitely glad to have Lord Christopher Thorne on their side.

She had known he would be eager to participate in the rescue, since he loved the thrill of danger. And of all the Guardians besides Caro, he was closest to Isabella, so he understood perfectly her anxiety for her friend.

Thorne rose from the sofa and crossed to her, taking her gloved hands in his larger, stronger ones. "We'll find her; never doubt it."

Caro smiled faintly. She was far more troubled about this mission than any previous one, doubtless because she had such a high personal stake in the outcome. "It is just so frustrating to be this helpless. I cannot stop seeing her at the mercy of some cruel master. She is all alone, Thorne—"

"Have you considered another possibility? That Isabella may look upon her captivity as an adventure rather than a tragedy?"

He was trying to reassure her, Caro realized, yet he did have a point. Most women would be terrified to be enslaved by Barbary pirates, but the spirited Isabella was far more resourceful and enterprising than any normal woman. If anyone was a survivor, it was she.

But still it distressed Caro immeasurably that they couldn't even begin to make detailed plans until they discovered exactly where Isabella was being held, and until the other Guardians gathered on Cyrene, which could take weeks or even months.

"You are right, of course," she murmured. "But I shall go mad with nothing to do but wait."

Thorne chucked her under the chin. "Oh, no, my girl, you won't get off so easily. At the moment I have the perfect task for you. You may make my excuses to my aunt. She won't be eager to free me from my promise to squire my cousin around London."

"Why me?"

"Because Aunt Hennessy likes you. And she will be more willing to forgive me if you ask it of her."

Lady Hennessy had sponsored Caro's disastrous London season years before and held her in affection, despite the scandal she had inadvertently caused.

"Just tell her that Bella has gone missing, and that

I'm needed to rescue her." He lead Caro to the library door and opened it. "Do you mean to stay here tonight?"

"If Lady Hennessy will allow me."

"I have no doubt she will—if you promise not to cause a scene at her ball. She is still trying to live down your disastrous season."

Color rose in her cheeks at his teasing. "Of course I won't cause a scene. I intend to make myself scarce as soon as I speak to her."

"She will be grateful, I'm sure." Thorne turned to go, then glanced back over his shoulder. "Oh, and Caro? One other thing you may do for me . . . Extend my apologies to Max Leighton."

Caro felt every nerve in her body tighten. "Major Leighton is here?" she asked, her voice a bit too high and breathless.

"*Mr.* Leighton. He's a civilian now. But you should know that. He is in all the society pages."

She did know. Sir Gawain had all the newspapers shipped to Cyrene weekly so he could keep up with current events in both the world and in the Beau Monde.

"Why must you apologize to him?" Caro asked, trying to appear casual.

"Because I dragged him to this ball so he could keep me company. It was a supreme sacrifice on his part, considering how persistently the ladies are hounding him. I regret having to abandon him to their sweet mercies. Tell Max I am sorry and that my invitation to him to visit Cyrene at Christmas still stands."

Caro lowered her gaze to hide her dismay. "If I see him," she answered reluctantly, "I will give him your message."

"That isn't good enough, love. Promise me you will

seek Max out after I leave. Otherwise I will have to delay long enough to do it myself."

"Very well . . . I promise."

"No doubt he will be pleased to see you. He was just asking about you earlier tonight."

She gave Thorne a startled glance. "He was?"

"Yes. You evidently made quite an impression on him during his brief visit to the island last year. Now go find my aunt. I will return as soon as possible."

As Thorne strode away, Caro stared dazedly after him, wanting to curse. The last person she wanted to see was Maxwell Leighton, but it didn't seem now as if she would have much choice.

Caro returned to the ballroom with grave reluctance. She wasn't a coward—ordinarily. But the thought of encountering Max Leighton again was unnerving.

It astonished her that he had asked after her. *You evidently made quite an impression on him.* Heat rose to her cheeks. She could only imagine what he thought of her behavior that night. Acting like a perfect wanton. Pleading with him to make love to her. Practically seducing him. Even now her face burned at the memory. Even now the memory of his touch filled her with a sweet, aching longing.

Did he have the same remembrances of their night of passion? After all the women he had likely been with, Caro doubted it had meant anything special to him.

She certainly would never forget it, though. That magical night had shown her so clearly what she was missing in her life. And Max's wonderful lovemaking had only increased her yearnings. . . .

It had been a profound mistake to surrender to her

wanton urges, but still she cherished the memory. So much so that she didn't want them spoiled by cold reality, or the disappointment of encountering him in the light of day. She had read numerous newspaper accounts of Max Leighton over the past few months—the titillating gossip about his amorous affairs and the predictions regarding the race to secure his hand in marriage.

Lamentably, however, she saw him the moment she entered the ballroom. The crowd had parted slightly, revealing his tall, commanding form a short distance away. Rather than a uniform, he wore an exquisitely tailored blue coat that molded his muscular shoulders to perfection.

He was surrounded by a half dozen beauties, as she expected. Determinedly she tried to repress the hollowness in her chest. After the terrible conflict with Napoleon had ended, she had often wondered if Max was still the wounded warrior, or if he had somehow managed to heal. He did *not* look as if he was suffering now.

Just then he turned and met her gaze across the ballroom. Her heart seemed to stop completely. He was still the same unforgettable man she saw so frequently in her dreams. Those were the same striking features. The same compelling blue eyes fringed by dark lashes. He still possessed the same powerful, potent masculinity.

She could feel herself flushing with warmth as his glance hotly connected with hers.

For now, however, she needed to find Thorne's aunt.

Dragging her gaze away with effort, she spied Lady Hennessy along one wall, sitting with the other dowagers. Grateful for the distraction, Caro threaded her way through the crowds.

The portly, silver-haired lady looked up with surprise, her expression first breaking into a smile of delight, then fading to one of concern. "My dear girl, whatever are you doing here? Sir Gawain? Is something amiss?"

Caro bent to kiss the soft cheek that was presented to her. "Sir Gawain is well, my lady. But I fear I have some other regretful news—as well as a request regarding your nephew. May I have a private word with you?"

"You seem to be taking an extraordinary interest in Miss Evers, Mr. Leighton," a plaintive female voice murmured. "Surely you realize that she is merely trying to draw attention to herself."

Forcing his attention back to his companions, Max raised an eyebrow. "You think she is here merely to create a scene?"

A half dozen ladies responded, all eager to regale him with tales of Caro Evers, it seemed.

"My coming-out was the same year," one remarked.

"I remember her as a shy, awkward creature. No social skills to speak of."

"She could not even dance."

"But it was the scandal she caused that was the final straw."

The trills of laughter became a chorus as they all seemed to share a common memory.

"What sort of scandal?" Max asked curiously.

"Miss Evers dressed up as a man to attend medical lectures."

"She was caught studying naked bodies!"

Several of the ladies shuddered. The tall blonde

who had hunted Max earlier added with malicious glee, "And for that, she was banished from the ton in disgrace."

His brows narrowing, Max fixed the lady with a cool frown.

"Do you know her, Mr. Leighton?"

Smiling faintly, he came to Caro's defense. "I had the distinct pleasure of meeting Miss Evers last year when she saved the life of one of my lieutenants. In fact, I consider her to be one of the most remarkable women of my acquaintance."

His response put an abrupt pall over the conversation. "Now if you ladies will please excuse me," he added wickedly, "I must go pay my compliments to Miss Evers."

Ignoring the looks of dismay on their faces, as well as the blonde widow's indignation, Max turned sharply and made his way across the ballroom toward where Caro Evers was deep in conversation with Lady Hennessy.

It was obvious that some urgent business had brought her to London, and he was highly curious to know what it was. He was even more interested to see if any remnant of the fire that had once blazed between them still existed.

He kept his gaze fixed on her, and was gratified to see how she froze when she looked up and saw him.

Her gray eyes were as large and lustrous as he remembered, like silver smoke, while her features had the stamp of character and intelligence. Not stunningly beautiful perhaps, but with an inviting appeal all the same.

Max bowed to his hostess, Lady Hennessy, but it

was Caro he addressed. "Good evening, Miss Evers. I wasn't certain I would ever have the good fortune of meeting you again."

She frowned, as if searching her memory. "Do I know you, sir? Oh, yes . . . Major Leighton, is it not?"

Max feigned a wince. "You wound me, Miss Evers, if you cannot even recall my name."

She pursed his lips. "Oh, I recall it quite well, Mr. Leighton. How could I not, when the gossip columns are full of your amorous adventures?"

With deliberate gallantry he took Caro's hand and bent over it, pressing his lips against her gloved fingers, interested to see how she responded.

Not only did she give a start, but when her eyes locked with his, something warm and primitive arced between them. Her gaze flickered lower then, over his mouth, and Max knew for certain that Caro Evers had not forgotten him.

A sharp surge of male satisfaction rippled through him, even though she withdrew her hand coolly.

"Actually I was on my way to find you," she said. "Thorne asked me to convey his apologies to you. He was called away on sudden business. He regretted"— she glanced pointedly toward the gathering of ladies Max had just abandoned—"having to leave you to the tender mercies of your gaggle of admirers."

She rose then, speaking directly to Max. "I hope you won't mind if I excuse myself, Mr. Leighton. I have had a long journey, and I have another long one ahead of me tomorrow."

She bent and kissed Lady Hennessy's cheek. "Thank you, my lady. Thorne will be glad that you have released him from his promise."

The dowager shook her head with mock sternness. "You can't fool me, my girl. I can see right through him. He wasn't brave enough to face me, and so he coerced you into pleading his case."

Caro smiled. "True, but you must admit, you are quite formidable when you get in a high dudgeon."

She turned to Max, her gaze flickering over him before she nodded toward the cluster of ladies who were still watching him. "Perhaps you should return to your devotees. It is obvious they anxiously await you. Goodnight, Mr. Leighton."

Max remained where he stood, staring after her. He had just been dismissed, he realized.

It was a novel experience for him, and one that should have piqued his indignation. But it had the opposite effect—arousing the primitive male urge to chase fleeing prey.

Watching him, Lady Hennessy let out a deep chuckle. "Perhaps you have already discovered that Caro is not like any other normal young lady."

"Indeed," Max said wryly.

"She despises balls and all the other trappings of society. I doubt she will come down again this evening." Her eyes took on a calculating gleam. "But she is staying upstairs in her former bedroom. If you wish to speak to her, you will have to go after her."

Max curved his mouth in an amused, calculating line of his own. "Thank you, my lady. I have every intention of doing just that."